Gathering Shadows

Gathering Shadows

PLAGUE OF SOULS BOOK ONE

SIMON BARRON

MP
MP PUBLISHING

Gathering Shadows

First edition published in 2015 by
MP Publishing
12 Strathallan Crescent, Douglas, Isle of Man IM2 4NR British Isles
mppublishingusa.com

Jacket designed by Alison Graihagh Crellin.

Publisher's Cataloging-in-Publication data

Barron, Simon.
    Gathering shadows , plague of souls book one / Simon Barron.
    p. cm.
    ISBN 978-1-84982-282-4
    Series : Plague of souls.
1. Elves --Fiction. 2. Dwarfs --Fiction. 3. War --Fiction. 4. Fantasy fiction. I. Series.
II. Title.

PR6102.A7723 G38 2015
823/.92 --dc23

ISBN 978-1-84982-282-4
10 9 8 7 6 5 4 3 2 1
Also available in eBook

For Mum

With special thanks to the Biscuit Gang

The words of a dead man are modified in the guts of the living.
WH Auden

A human being is only breath and shadow.
Sophocles

O thou whose face hath felt the Winter's wind;
Whose eye has seen the snow-clouds hung in mist
And the Black-elm tops' 'mong the freezing Stars
To thee the Spring will be a harvest-time.
O thou, whose only book has been the light
Of supreme darkness which thou feddest on
Night after night, when Phoebus was away,
To thee the Spring shall be a triple morn.
O fret not after knowledge—I have none,
And yet my song comes native with the warmth.
O fret not after knowledge—I have none,
And yet the Evening listens. He who saddens
At thought of idleness cannot be idle,
And he's awake who thinks himself asleep.
John Keats

It is forbidden to kill; therefore all murderers
are punished unless they kill in large numbers
and to the sound of trumpets.
Voltaire

Life itself is but the shadow of death,
and souls departed but the shadows of the living.
Thomas Browne

Power, like a desolating pestilence, pollutes whatever it touches.
Percy Bysshe Shelley

Prologue

Far below the ledge of rock, a mist had begun to form from the early morning dew. The forestland could no longer be seen at the foot of the mountain known in these parts as Ironforge Loft, southernmost peak of the Claymore Range. But the forests below held no interest for Soora, wild and deadly as they were, and neither did the mountain range to the north, whose frozen conditions were among the most deadly on the continent. Soora adjusted the blades on his back to shift the weight from his weary shoulders, then crossed his arms over his powerful chest in grim contemplation.

The chilling cold chased in from Soora's back as the morning winds stirred the range. The sun had yet to crest on the eastern horizon, and might not do so for an hour, but Soora was awake and the sky was bathed in the eerie glow of an autumnal false dawn. It was no surprise for Soora to be fully awake at such an early hour, for it had been many years since he had enjoyed a restful sleep and he had never yearned for idle slumber. He had come to understand that his actions, however mediocre or inconsequential they might seem, were actually both imperative and burdensome. The importance of what he was to accomplish was as clear as the broken nose on his weather-drawn face. He had suffered fitful dreams as a child, and long since then had been plagued by wakeful visions. Something in his birthright or heritage had granted him a most terrible fate, a heinous legacy. He knew his future deeds bore dire consequences for the living and the dead, and there was nothing he could do about the weight of that burden. It was all that he could do to suffer it through grim acceptance and avoid the madness that threatened daily to consume him. The Gods had their ways and their purpose; who was Soora to argue with that?

For years he had plied a mercenary's trade in the harsh winterlands of the northern extremes. More times than he could possibly remember he had almost lost his life to the freezing temperatures. Ice blizzards and frostbite had scoured his skin and lashed at his hands and face, but he had lost neither limb nor digit to the cold. Remarkably, days after such times it was hardly possible to see any evidence of the hardship. He had seen days wherein no sunlight shone; had survived avalanches that had possessed suitable force to flog entire forests to the ground. He had battled many human foes in the mountains and valleys of the tribal north, settling age-long conflicts and arguments with the quickness and finality of his twinned short blades. Innumerable times Soora had been pressed into protecting his own life from starving packs of timber wolves or the odd roving bandit clan harried north by force of arms. And he still remained. He still stood.

Subconsciously he toyed with the leather ties that sealed the pouch at his hip as he considered his next actions. He had been a child when he left the temperate lands of the south, but he was a man now, his teeth long cut in mortal conflict.

Soora regarded the cave at his back once more and his clutter of simple belongings, collected in the stitched leather bag that sat alongside the remains of last night's fire. His woodland bow rested atop the bag. This morning he would hunt as he travelled, and with a little luck he would be amongst the northernmost farmlands by dusk tomorrow.

He turned away from the cave once more, stretching his tired limbs skyward.

Before him, beyond the mist-shrouded forests of the Claymore Fells, touching the edge of the horizon, was civilisation—the countries of Shenmadock and Ipsica. In his soul, he knew that he would come to utterly destroy them.

Chapter One
Hangover

Was there anything in the world quite as bad as a hangover brought on by cheap wine? Andi suspected not. No matter how many times she'd gone to extremes with wine, Andi never learned her lesson. It was probably her own fault for not choosing the watered wine the courtly ladies usually drank. Andi didn't have any qualms about being drunk, though. What she found most alarming were the things she did whilst drunk, and perhaps that was why she was in a cell right now instead of in her lodgings at the Ragged Boar Inn.

The thumping pain in her head had abated a little since waking some time ago, but the wild fuzziness and periodic disorientation came and went like some enraged tide upon the rocks of her skull. She dared not move for fear of encouraging a bout of nausea. There was little in the world more ignoble than seeing a woman vomit, and judging by the snores and occasional farts from nearby, Andi was aware that she was not alone in the cells.

Still lying on her side, her back toward her unknown companion, Andi risked a look around her cell, trying hard not to move too much. The cell bay was damp and smelled like mildew. The walls were a mix of sedimentary rock and hard-faced bedrock that led her to assume some of the cell bay was below ground. Light from a tiny window, more like a ship's porthole, could be seen at the far end of the cavern. The ceiling was flat and carefully constructed, with many supporting columns around the room, between which sturdy bars and gates had been erected to form the cages of the cells. Andi's own such cage had a wall of rock adjacent to the gate that opened on to the cell corridor. She could see a single solid oak door down the corridor away from her that she judged to be the only exit to freedom.

She closed her eyes again as the strain on her vision began to tell. Trying to relax, she let her mind wander to the previous evening. She remembered having toyed with the idea of donning a decent gown and travelling to the main keep for the evening, trying to bluff her way in to see the Guild Market that convened upon the keep's inner grounds every Fourthday. But she had lost the desire once the evening late-summer rain had come. She travelled alone these days and those gowns were both difficult to clean on your own and scandalously expensive to have cleaned professionally. Instead she had chosen to remain in her traveller's garb, had tied her hair up for convenience, and purchased a bottle of wine in the rudimentary but pleasant Ragged Boar Inn.

She had sat and listened as the barkeep ranted about the drop in business with the coming winter, then later as it grew busy she had purchased another bottle of the northern red. It had been bitter, but passable after the first two glasses, and she couldn't taste it at all after the third. Andi found she could drink any man under the table without much trouble. But evidently she'd lost a little concentration and let her drinking get out of hand. Because the last thing she clearly remembered was finishing the second bottle off and trying to ignore the noise of a small band of brigand mercenaries in the corner. Then it got blurry. However, the evidence seemed to suggest that Andi had found her way into the keep after all, less by bluff than misdemeanour.

She hoped it was nothing more than a breach of the peace. She had been involved in her fair share of drunkard brawls. Her soft-skinned complexion and slender figure often attracted the attentions of the boisterous and arrogant, and she had no time for such fools. If they ever pushed their luck, more often than not they discovered her to be more powerful and infinitely quicker than they might have guessed. Andi frequently dressed modestly, but she was no shrinking violet or demure lady.

But a drunken misunderstanding or aggressive reckoning had never resulted in anything more than exchanged punches or the occasional sword slash. Andi had a feeling absolutely anything could have happened last night and she might not remember it. She'd woken with this kind of feeling in her youth, when she'd kicked around for a time with a group of cutthroats and con men from Mashtok, far to the north of Shenmadock. She'd been much younger then. This had all the hallmarks of a personal setback, and Andi didn't like that one bit.

Another fart erupted in the cell next door, interrupting her thoughts. Much louder than any previous, this one almost blasted into existence. Andi heard the owner stir in reaction. *Probably flinched,* she thought. She heard mumbling—something that sounded like "Tell me that's bad!"—before the stranger convulsed with bearish coughs that seemed to be bashed from his chest like heavy thumps on a deep kettledrum. It appeared her cell buddy was awake at last. Andi had no idea what time it was, but the hazy summer sun was high enough to stream in through the tiny opening near the ceiling.

A heavily accented voice mumbled expletives and curses as the man repositioned himself on his cot following his coughing fit. "Gods be! I've got to put down that pipe before it eats me alive!"

Andi considered keeping her silence and ignoring the oaf, but thought better of it. This individual was probably her best chance of learning why she was incarcerated. "Nothing like a coughing fit to clear the head," she said.

Seeming to notice for the first time that he was not alone, her cell neighbour was startled out of his bunk. Andi rolled over to look at him, and had to stifle a laugh. Her cell partner was no man. She raised herself on one elbow to look properly. Standing before her, brushing himself down and mumbling in disgruntlement, was a dwarf. He was hardly more than four feet tall, and mostly armour and hair. Wide-set, silver eyes regarded her every so often from beneath bushy, red-brown brows, as though ensuring she wasn't sneaking up on him. A long, bulbous, and lumpy nose dominated his face, but it was the facial hair that amused Andi so much: he wore his moustache in an outrageously wide style, extending almost to the width of his shoulders. This alone would have made Andi laugh, had it not been for the huge, wide-brimmed hat that he dusted off and plonked atop his balding pate. "I'm sorry, lass. 'Scuse my manners; no call for me to be coughing all over the place." She didn't miss the fact that he wasn't apologising for the flatulence that had woken him. "I smoke entirely too much moist-weed; it's a habit I can't shake when I'm bored."

Andi smiled. "I'm not in much better condition. Suffice to say, I think us both the worse for wear following last night's antics." Andi turned on her hard straw cot, dropped her feet over the edge and rested her elbows on her knees. She was now at eye level with the dwarf even sitting down. "Any idea how we've come to be the only two to share these cells, Master Dwarf?"

"Manic."

"No doubt," Andi agreed, distractedly pulling loose straw from her hair. "I can't remember a thing after that second bottle of Ipsican Red."

"I'm no *Master Dwarf*, is what I mean. Manic is my name; Manic Frostfinder."

"That's a strange name, if you don't mind me saying."

"Aye, well, I come from the mountain cave clans," he said, as though that explained everything. "My family were deep-grown dwarves, used to conditions far deeper in the mines of the Choat Mountains than most dwarves have ventured. Diamonds and gems in those hills react different to most, you see. Something in the silt deposit affects them. That's why they're so precious; they tend to be softer 'n most. My people called the softer diamonds 'Frost Gems'. My ancestors hunted out the colder deposits deeper than most dwarves will dig, or so history says. So they called us Frostfinders." While he told his story, Manic Frostfinder busied himself with becoming more presentable, expending most attention on his extended moustache, as he twisted the ends over and over to perfect the points. Andi noted that he did not possess the voluminous beard sported by most dwarves. In fact she imagined that this was the first time she had ever seen a dwarf's chin.

"I didn't mean that name," said Andi, "although the story was fascinating. It's your given name—Manic—that's odd. Still, you seem to know a lot about gems."

Manic Frostfinder laughed once, quick and gruff. "Show me a dwarf who doesn't know a gem and I'll show you a fat, hairy halfling!" He sat back on his bunk and heaved a tired sigh. "Truth to tell, I don't know where they got Manic from. Could explain why I'm here though, eh?"

Andi immediately liked the dwarf. There was no reason to: he broke wind loudly and seemingly often, his appearance was shocking and vaguely distasteful, and he seemed unfamiliar with what not to share with people he'd just met. But that was refreshing. It occurred to Andi that all too often people were reticent to share themselves with others. It could be a lonely existence that way. Andi was willing to bet that Manic Frostfinder found coming across friends as easy as falling off a horse.

"Think we're in any serious trouble, lass?" Manic asked.

"I doubt that. I think we've just been put in here to sober up after whatever fuss did occur had been broken up. If we were going to the gallows, you wouldn't still have your armour on."

"Maybe they were scared to reach under my moustache!" He let out another hearty laugh, and a low grumbling cough followed. "So what's your name, or should I just keep calling you 'lass'?"

"Kind of depends on when you meet me, to be honest," she said to herself.

"What does that mean?"

She hadn't really intended him to hear. "Oh, nothing. Just call me Andi. Almost everybody does."

"Andi? What kind of name is that for a girl? Is it Briadranon?" Manic pressed, referring to the Free Cities of Briadranon, a country to the northeast, and coincidentally Andi's country of birth. But that was long ago when the more mighty nations of Ipsica and Shenmadock were locked in constant war.

"No," she lied, "it's short for Andrijanna." She avoided the topic of origin.

"That's posh; still sounds foreign. Shouldn't it be shortened to Andri?"

The opening of the wooden door down the cell passage saved Andi from having to continue the discussion about her name. It was a topic that discomfited her at the best of times, worse still when in a cell.

A fat human bustled through the door, dressed in a guard's outfit and wearing what Andi had learned was a sergeant's insignia. He clutched a bunch of keys. Behind him stood two other guards, each sporting ceremonial pole-arms that didn't seem too threatening. The danger posed by the short swords worn at their hips was not lost on Andi, though. It was clear that they considered the two prisoners not to be any immediate danger, but they were taking few chances.

"Where's my greatsword? And my knife?" Manic bellowed, making the guard sergeant pause momentarily. The dwarf had an impressive bark, not unlike a staff sergeant's might be. Perhaps unlike this guard sergeant, Andi was willing to bet Manic's bite was indeed one to match his bark.

After his momentary lapse, the guard sergeant gathered himself once more. "Be quiet, dwarf! Your belongings will be returned to you in due course." He unlocked the gates to each cell and stood them slightly ajar. Manic went to rise from his bunk and make for the gate, expecting to be set free. "Stay yourself, dwarf! You're going nowhere yet." A serving girl came through the doorway and placed buckets of water inside the gate to each cell, then beat a hasty retreat. The gates were closed and bolted once more. "Scrub yourselves up; you're to be granted an audience with my lord this morning. You can't go in stinking like orcs." The serving girl returned with two crude soap bars and tossed one in each bucket. The guard sergeant followed her out of the cell door, but the door did not close.

"Well, he's pleasant!" Andi grumbled as she rolled up the sleeves of her loose cotton tunic. Her dark green cloak was cast in the corner, but seemed clean enough. She fished around in the water until her fingers found the soap. She looked forlornly at the bar. She was used to more natural cleaning remedies; this caustic rubbish would burn the skin given half the chance. She used it sparingly, washing down her forearms and using just the rinsed water from the bucket on her face. She left her hair as it was, fixing a couple of errant strands using the reflection in the water for help.

Manic was not so demure. He used the soap liberally and the water sparingly. He not only seemed largely immune to the acidic properties of the soap, but actually to revel in the invigoration of it. He growled and bellowed with satisfaction as he rubbed the grainy suds from his face and beard. By the time he was finished, his bucket was empty and the front of his armour awash. He seemed very pleased with himself.

It wasn't long before he took to running the empty bucket up and down the bars of his cell in protest at their protracted wait.

"I can't abide this any longer! Must I remain the only source and means of problem-solving in this entire duchy?" Duke Reinhart stalked up and down the length of his throne dais. The audience chamber was a grand, high-ceilinged affair that ran the entire length of one short side of the inner keep. The chamber was two stories high with a wooden latticework ceiling and a balcony adorning all four walls. Andi assumed the balcony had doors to other rooms on the floor above, but couldn't see from her present position.

A large mantelpiece and fireplace dominated the left wall—an exterior wall, judging by the stonework and supports. No windows opened into the chamber and the fireplace was cold, so the only means of illumination came from many torches wedged into sconces around the walls. Despite the numerous flames the air was quite clean and Andi figured there must be louvres high in the ceiling corners, designed to allow smoke to leave the building.

Andi had figured the lord was Reinhart, Duke of Unedar, and boy was he ranting on, directing his tirade at a small number of well-dressed, ornately bejewelled advisors, none of whom seemed eager to supply an answer to their duke's seemingly rhetorical ramblings. "By the Gods, I'd give anything for a platoon of Lord Handee's Wayfarers. They'd report back with more information than your pathetic

Whisperers, cousin!"

Thin and gaunt of feature, the duke's cousin reclined in a stiff-backed wooden chair near an unlit fireplace. He seemed lost in thought, and paid his duke no heed.

Reinhart was the antithesis of his cousin in almost every respect. Tall beyond six feet, his shoulders were broad and draped by a long cape that flowed down his back. His hair had once been sable black, but was now more grey than dark. His face was clean-shaven and his jaw wide and powerful. Duke Reinhart was impressive to the eye, and his voice held volume when he was enraged. "Leave me be for this morning; I'll hear no more of your excuses!" The advisors scuttled from his sight, murmuring in deference or discontent. Andi noticed the duke's cousin went nowhere.

Two elderly advisors remained at the rear of the chamber, previously hidden from Andi. They stayed nearer the shadows and observed. One may have even been scribing events. This duke certainly seemed to have his court in order, something one would expect from a duke who shared a land border with Ipsica. It had been decades since any considerable strife had existed between Shenmadock and Ipsica, but tension over trade and land disputes was never alleviated, and Reinhart's eastern border of Unedar faced Ipsica all the way to the foothills of the Southern Range.

The guard sergeant ushered Andi and Manic forward before the fire, into the clear view of his duke. Reinhart turned an appraising eye on the pair.

"What's this, now?"

The guard sergeant said, "My lord, these are two brigands that were arrested last night, following the riots in the foulberg."

"Whoa, brigands?" Manic complained.

The guard sergeant shoved Manic in the shoulder. "Quiet, dwarf!"

"Thank you, sergeant; that won't be necessary." Reinhart

stopped pacing the dais and regarded the two 'brigands'. He seemed to contemplate something as his vision wandered across the floor. Andi got the impression that the duke was massively preoccupied. As if awakening from a dream, he brought his full attention to bear on them.

"Give me the details," the duke ordered the sergeant, still eyeing the pair.

"Last night there was a fracas in the foulberg," explained the guard sergeant, mispronouncing fracas as *frackass*. "A detachment of the keep guard was dispatched to assist the town's peacekeepers in bringing about order. From some accounts it was the kindling to riots, sir."

"Riots!" barked Reinhart. "Never have I presided over a hamlet, village or town beset by rioters, and I don't intend to start now with my duchy!"

Manic made to object: "I doubt that we…"

"Quiet, Master Dwarf!" Reinhart cut him off curtly. "What else, Sergeant?"

"During the ruckus one man lost his life and the Ragged Boar Inn was messed up something proper. The victim was a traveller; probably another brigand by his looks and his belongings."

Reinhart recommenced pacing as the sergeant spoke, returning to his own preoccupation. Finally he said, "I don't have the time for this! Cousin?" The wiry noble was likewise lost in his own inattention. "Jakrat!" shouted Reinhart, snapping the younger man from his reverie. "You're the bloody magistrate; you deal with these miscreants! I'll be in my chambers."

With that the duke stormed from the room, his cloak blowing behind him.

Jakrat rose from the chair by the fire and approached Andi and Manic. Suddenly Andi thought she sensed a change in the guard sergeant's demeanour.

The magistrate walked around the pair, appraising

them carefully. Andi was attractive, as she had come to know through grim experience, and Jakrat's baleful gaze discomfited her. However, she quickly deduced that the magistrate wasn't leering at her; he was judging the worth of them both. Even his gait was that of a jackal, his features pinched and measuring. Dark eyes peered from under a knitted brow, but his thin-lipped mouth was curled in a cruel half-smile.

"Brigands!" Jakrat rolled the word around his mouth. "What to do, what to do, what to do?"

"You could let us go," suggested Manic impertinently.

Ignoring the insolence, the magistrate seemed to consider this for a moment; the crackling sound of the torches burning in the sconces seemed to be magnified in the silence.

"No." The word came out in a drawn, thoughtful way. "Sergeant, throw them back in the cells. I need to think."

"Yes, m'lord."

With that, they were both unceremoniously bustled back toward their dungeon cells to await their fate.

They didn't have to wait long. The feeling of nausea brought on by her headache had slowly given way to a general grottiness by the time the guard sergeant returned to fetch them once more from their pit of misery.

Hours had passed since the magistrate Jakrat had dismissed them, and Andi's patience was wearing thin. Yes, in her life she was at something of a crossroads. There was nothing pressing she had to be getting on with, but that didn't mean she was happy to languish in a cell, having been accused of...

Well, just what was it they had been accused of? Manic and Andi had spent a dozen minutes chewing over the details they had heard. There had been mention of a near-riot at the inn she had been staying at, and apparently a traveller had lost his life in whatever strife had taken place. However, while Andi had killed her fair share of people for a wide variety of reasons, she couldn't rightly recall having murdered anyone last night. Unfortunately she couldn't even remember reaching the bottom of her second bottle of red, so...

Something had her panicked, though, because she had an icy feeling in her stomach that she and Manic were going to be dealt with expediently. The opening of the cell corridor door gave that icy feeling a deeper meaning when the guard sergeant walked in and ordered them to gather their wits.

This time they were manacled and led from the cells down another tributary corridor leading in a different direction. A few turns later and they emerged from the keep up a steep set of steps to find themselves in the inner bailey of the Castle of Hightower, capital of Unedar, and their current temporary home.

As they were marched to a portion of land-clearance in the shadow of the main keep, Andi got a sudden impression of just how temporary that home would be, for they were being led to a gallows. They had been joined by a row of four or five sorry-looking characters who had clearly spent a little longer in the dank cells.

"Now hold on a second!" Andi began. She received a swift bash to the side of her head from the guard sergeant's gauntleted fist for her troubles.

"We haven't even had a trial!" complained Manic, quite rightly.

"Yes you have!" declared a glib voice from behind them, and Magistrate Jakrat overtook them. "I judged the evidence and found that last night an affray was caused, and that during that affray a man lost his life. The only malcontents discovered to be the protagonists in that affray were a female human and a male dwarf. From just a glance at their confiscated belongings, it seemed sensible to deduce that the accused were thieves or even assassins." Jakrat stopped in the shadow of the keep and turned to face them, heels together and hands clasped behind his back. "In short, you two are guilty as hell and will hang."

"That sounds a little convenient," accused Andi, furious despite her impending execution.

"Getting hanged doesn't sound convenient at all," complained Manic.

"Indeed." Jakrat smiled cruelly. "In point of fact, stranger, I've got much better things to worry about than troublemakers, thieves and beggars, and so does my cousin, the duke."

With that, the magistrate nodded to the guard sergeant to lead the group up to the platform of the gallows where a pair of nooses hung above a broad trapdoor. They would be ushered off this mortal coil in pairs.

Suddenly Andi swung her manacled wrists up into the guard sergeant's face like a mace, catching him above the bridge of the nose. He ducked reflexively away from the assault as the nearest guard reacted. Andi wrapped her manacle chain over the sergeant's head and used his neck to help her roll across his back. As the second guard approached, Andi lashed out with a windmilling of her legs, kicking the guard twice in the face.

Taking his cue from Andi, Manic stooped and ran headfirst at the second guard, who had been standing by the gallows stairs. His head thumped into the guard's stomach heavily and the man almost went down.

Andi, having regained her feet, pulled the chain back around the sergeant's neck and began throttling him as two more guards approached from the keep. Someone nearby was blowing a whistle.

Unable to free himself from the winded guard, Manic was thumped on his back by the man's elbow and went down heavily. That was when Andi felt the cold steel of a halberd blade placed warningly on her shoulder.

Immediately she was forced to relax her grip on the sergeant, releasing him.

Once free, the guard sergeant snarled: "Run her through!"

"Stay that weapon!" shouted Jakrat. "She'll hang, as ordered. We'll have no bloody executions in the bailey, sergeant. Unless you want to fetch the mop?"

Clearly unhappy, the guard sergeant nodded for the bearer of the halberd to lead Andi up the stairs, closely followed by Manic. Their one attempt at escape had failed.

One of the other prisoners had begun to cry softly, her pitiful sounds of misery the only thing to be heard on the still air. High above, isolated clouds drifted slowly across the sky, promising drizzle. Nearby a few of the keep staff had emerged to view the spectacle, having been alerted by their brief but violent resistance.

In the late summer sun, Andi saw a peculiar sight: a figure dressed in a monk's black robes approached from the keep to come and stand by Jakrat, its head covered by a cowl. The figure's features were entirely shrouded in shadow and its hands were hidden in the folds of the robe. Something about the figure sent a chill down Andi's spine…or perhaps it was her impending doom that was to blame.

They reached the platform and the hangman went about setting the trapdoors as the cowled figure engaged Jakrat in a quiet conversation. Jakrat seemed unsettled by what was being said, and just when Andi had given up all hope of a saviour he suddenly held up his hand to stop the hangman dropping the noose around her head. The loop of rope hung above her like a damning halo.

Jakrat's eyes narrowed at Andi for a moment, as a thought appeared to come into his mind. He listened to something else that the cowled figure was muttering, and Andi thought she could hear a parchment-brittle voice say, "It is not enough to suspect its location; we must possess it.

Time grows short!"

Jakrat stared at Manic and Andi once more, and then dismissed the cowled figure with a wave of his hand and a supplicating expression on his pinched face.

"Sergeant, bring me those rogues!" he barked.

Andi looked down at her diminutive associate. "That doesn't sound good." The ironic timing of her statement wasn't lost on Manic, and he huffed out a laugh at her literal gallows humour. Anything would have to sound better than the clattering of an opening trapdoor and the thrum of a rope pulled rigid by a deadweight.

Once they were led from the platform, Jakrat took them around the side of the keep while the other unfortunates were taken to the gallows to face their own doom.

They followed a pathway that led to the left past spacious stables, with an iron forge for the smithy standing proudly in the entrance. The group stopped just beyond the stables, a thin drizzle starting to carry high on the breeze despite the reasonable sunshine. Autumn was round the corner.

Before them was a large iron grate at the base of the west wall of the keep, rusted through the years and with sturdy hinges on one end and a hefty lock on the other. It looked nothing less than another dungeon gate.

Andi regarded the iron fixture dubiously. "Change of lodgings, magistrate?"

"Nothing of the sort, woman. I have a task that needs completion, and now I also have the expendable yet capable resources to achieve it. I think a pair of fetid thieves may be just what I need."

As though punctuating his point, they heard the clatter of the gallows trapdoor, telling all those within earshot that two souls had been given bittersweet release from their suffering.

Manic hoisted his tool-belt and strode forward to gaze down the grate. His face didn't inspire much confidence in the future. "What's down there?"

"Down there is a gem known as the *Baerv*. It is a rare yet strangely valueless jewel that was lost, or perhaps hidden, a long time ago, along with several traps and dangerous caverns. If you survive long enough, you'll find it hidden within…" he struggled for the words, "an ornate contraption. Historically it was something of a local legend, with various visitors to the duchy attempting to find themselves a trinket and badge of honour on fête days. So far we have been unable to retrieve it. Fetch it for me and your debt is paid." Jakrat looked pointedly over his shoulder at the cowled figure, who remained by the gallows, watching the group from a distance. The magistrate seemed unconvinced and even less impressed with Andi and Manic.

"How many other people have you sent down there?" Manic asked.

"I have lost count. Plenty."

"So, there's going to be bodies down there?" Andi pressed. "Any recent?"

"Not particularly," he said pointedly.

"Why do you need it?" asked Andi. "If it's worthless, why bother?"

Jakrat looked at her closely. "I said it was without value, not worth. And you will notice that it is not me but you two who will be 'bothering'."

Andi nodded, reluctantly conceding the point. "What's in it for us?"

"If you succeed, I will consider your debt paid—time served, if you will—and you will be paroled. You will have to flee the duchy, of course, but you will be free to go."

"And if we fail?" Manic asked, glancing at the corner of the keep. They heard the release of the gallows trapdoor again, signalling the demise of two more unfortunates.

Jakrat smiled his cruellest smile yet, and said, "If you fail down there, I won't be needing the gallows."

Chapter Two
Cold Feet

"This makes no sense!" Manic grumbled. Andi figured the cold, damp atmosphere was starting to make his head ache. Surely it could never be considered fun to romp around in moss-ridden catacombs that were essentially *tombs*. That's what the place felt like: a giant crypt. When a place claims many lives down through the years, it greases up with death. Death seems to permeate the stone itself, almost as though the rivulets of moisture were signs of Death himself sweating through the rock walls. It was dark, it was damp and it was treacherous. The dwarf, although raised in caverns and mines, was clearly not having much fun either.

Andi was just happy to be out of those accursed manacles.

They had dropped down through the grate a few minutes ago, and Andi had done well not to break a leg on landing. The drop had been further than anticipated, and onto solid rock. Looking up for signs that Manic was following her, the sun glaring through the open rectangular grate, she couldn't escape the feeling she was lying in her coffin. They had then travelled only a few yards before Manic had started to grumble.

The tunnel was broad: fully five yards across. There was enough width and height in this portion to lead a wagon or two down. The floor was flat and scattered with loose rocks, and was developing a steady downhill gradient. They proceeded forward, being careful not to slip on the loose stones and slippery rocks.

The path ended in a curve to their left and a sharp drop down to the termination of what appeared to have once been a well shaft. There was no skylight seen above, however, and the shaft was apparently long in disuse. Andi dropped nimbly off the ledge and sank quietly to her haunches on landing. She moved forward a little to give Manic room to manoeuvre his larger bulk over the edge. He thumped to the floor behind her, once again cursing under his breath. The chamber before them was oval, with a fairly flat floor but an arching ceiling. Stalactites dripped with the morning moisture seeping through fissures in the bedrock and soft soil some way above.

There were piles of bones here and there; ancient, by all appearances. Some could have been human, elf or dwarf in origin, for all she could tell.

Andi heard Manic trip on a rotten piece of rope behind her. "Careful, dwarf, we can't afford for you to turn an ankle down here. We'd never get you out."

"Don't worry about me, skinny. I can balance myself fine down here."

"Be that as it may, this cavern doesn't look particularly safe to me."

"I hear you, lass. Lead on." She moved steadily forward between two thin and short stalagmites, careful to keep her footing even. She heard Manic following her.

The cavern was around nine yards in diameter with a low exit on the far side. As they approached the gap in the wall, she saw the stone was worn uniformly smooth. "Manic? What do you make of the walls?"

"Naturally formed. This was probably a section of an underground river at some point. The hands of man or dwarf don't smooth walls like that. Only rushing water, loose stone and sand can get that finish." To Andi's left, he ran a grizzled hand along the wall near her hip. "Beautiful," he said quietly. She looked back and saw him admiring the stone cavern.

Andi smiled at her new, diminutive friend. "Starting to feel at home, I see," she said. He nodded wanly. She had a thought: "Manic, if these are partially or wholly natural formations, would it make sense that a river once ran through here?"

"That might stand to reason," he said, "but those are the only signs. I can't see where the river would have run from." He shrugged in the dark.

Andi pictured the cliffs to the south of the town of Hightower. The castle itself sat proudly at the southern point of the town, overlooking the seas. "What do you think the chances are of us being able to find a way out of these caverns, maybe to the cliffs?"

Manic seemed to consider it for a moment. "Water can go places we cannot, Andi. It may well be possible that the only exit from these catacombs is in the form of tiny, narrow fissures."

"It's worth keeping an eye out, though, don't you think?"

Manic nodded. "Worth a look," he agreed.

"Well, either way," she said, "by my layman's reckoning, with this being a natural structure it's probably stable. But it also makes it more likely that natural things will have made a home here. So I'm inclined to think those noises up ahead might be critters."

Manic stopped rubbing the wall in order to listen more carefully. A couple of seconds later his face changed as he picked the sound out. "That's something moving up ahead, for sure." As he spoke he took an involuntary step back from the dark, squat passage. Andi couldn't help but crack a grin.

"Now come on, Master Dwarf, don't be trying to have me believe you're scared of things that bite in the dark."

"When you've seen the critters I've seen in caves like these, and the amount of meat they can bite at once, you'd be reticent to go leaping in there with both feet, Andi." But with that, he stepped around her and ducked into the passage, obviously spurred on by her playful chiding.

Following close behind him, Andi almost had to crawl on all fours. A couple of times she caught the back of her skull on the smooth ceiling, thanking good fortune for the effects of rushing sand and water. Any jagged edges up there and she'd be covered in her own blood by now.

Not soon enough, the hobbling figure of Manic became a silhouette in the diffused, grey light ahead of him. He slowed his approach and then seemed to have room to stand up in as he moved aside to afford Andi a full view of the cave ahead.

The eerie light came from glowing, iridescent moss that covered the rock ceiling, mainly in the numerous long cracks, forming a map of pale blue light. The floor ended in a ledge, upon which they crouched. The cavern was almost spherical, with no meaningful stalactites in sight. Their ledge was only a few yards across, and two feet deep at its broadest point. Across from them, the tunnelled cavern seemed to continue into the rockface, with a similar ledge adorning that entrance. The entrance was a good six yards away, well beyond jumping distance, even if they'd had a decent run up to it—which they didn't.

However, the real problem lay four feet beneath their ledge. The bottom of the spherical chamber was filled with dark, murky, unmoving water. Upon the surface a layer of oily silt was detectable, but nothing broke through to disturb the stillness. That stillness made Andi nervous.

"I don't like this," murmured Manic, pulling at a corner of his tunic that jutted from beneath his breastplate.

Dubious, Andi examined the ceiling sections a little closer than before, seeking a climbing aid. "What's not to like? It's just a pond." Even to her own ears she didn't sound convincing.

"No, I don't like water, woman! I can't...swim."

Andi looked at the dwarf as he shifted his own gaze around the cavern, more desperately seeking a solution. His armour was solid and substantial. It had obviously seen a battle or four. It would weigh him down fatally. His tool-belt sagged at his waist, giving Andi an idea.

"Can I borrow this?" She took a rock hammer from a loop on his belt and removed a length of thong from the side of her jerkin. She figured the exposed skin of her ribs or flank would do nothing to excite the dwarf.

"Don't lose it! Bad enough that I don't know where my weapons are, and to be stuck down here with a skinny human and no blade to protect her with."

"Who says I need protecting?" Andi bristled. Pushing the length of leather through a hole in the bottom of the hammer's handle, she tied it to form a large loop. Then she passed it over her left arm beyond the elbow, turned the loop to form a figure-of-eight and slipped her hand through the loop once more. The hammerhead fit between her fingers neatly, if uncomfortably. The blade on the hammerhead looked keen and sharp. It would do nicely.

"What are you going to do with that?" Manic asked, watching her hands work.

"Well, have you seen any bodies down here yet?"

"Well, no, but what's that got to do with things?" He looked frustrated and clueless as to how they would cross the pond.

"I figure the people who came before us must have made it across, and so somewhere ahead will be a rope or whatever—something that they used to cross this pond. I'll climb around to the other side along the wall, using this hammer as a kind of crampon, get that *something* and come back to help you across. Sound like a plan?"

"It does, although what happens if you get to where the bodies are and the thing that turned them from beings *into* bodies does the same to you?"

"I...don't know." Andi hadn't thought that through. She had no short sword, nor her bow. She was not confident about fighting off something barehanded, but there was no other way across that she could think of. "I'll think of something."

Keeping her elbow bent to secure the thong support, Andi reached and jammed the hammer into a high outcrop of rock on her right. It held securely. Slowly applying her weight, Andi set off across the circumference of the chamber. Crossing the middle point, she found it more oval than round. She looked back to see Manic watching her carefully, but keeping a sharp eye on the pool below.

"See something, Manic?"

"I don't know. Maybe. It doesn't seem as...still as it was before. And I can hear something, too. Like wind blowing."

Andi held her position, safe with footholds and the lodged hammer. "From where? The corridor ahead?"

"No, behind us. But it's not windy."

"Well, I'll keep moving and you go and check it out."

He shrugged and shuffled back down the passage at a crouch. As she adjusted and shifted her weight across, Andi heard the water erupt behind her. Through instinct she managed to pull her feet up, bearing all the weight on the hammer. She heard a snapping noise very close below her and then another splash. Looking down, all she could see was the freshly disturbed water lapping at the rock.

Her head whipped to the left. The far ledge was almost within jumping distance, but not quite. Not from a hanging start, anyway. And she'd have to drop her feet to carry on moving. She didn't know what to do. "Manic?" She could now hear an increased ruffle of wind. Or something like wind. More like...

Three or four bats flew from where Manic had gone and she could hear the dwarf thumping back up the tunnel. "Manic!" Andi screamed. "Jump at me!"

His shape burst from the dark, surrounded by dozens of bats, his moustache flowing behind him. He fixed his panicked eyes on Andi as his right foot struck the edge of the ledge.

His leap was impressive for a dwarf.

The water rushed up at his feet. Andi's chest lurched as she realised he wasn't going to make it. Steely-looking teeth snapped at Manic's legs, missing by scant inches. Andi saw the face of a fish without eyes as it disappeared below the surface.

Then Manic began to fall. Without thinking, Andi dropped her feet back to a secure ridge to bolster her grip and reached out with her right hand. The rock hammer slipped but then held firm, the leather strap straining at her left elbow.

Manic threw out a hand, his eyes wide. They clasped each other round the wrists and Andi tried to bear his weight in a swing. She thought the leather strap would sever her elbow at the joint, and her shoulder stretched agonisingly at the extra weight. She used his momentum to swing him toward the far ledge.

Something rushed toward Manic's feet.

With a surge of effort she used the hammer blade as a pivot, bringing the dwarf up in an arc, and then let go of Manic's hand.

For a terrible, absurd moment Andi watched the dwarf tumble through the darkness and thought he wouldn't make it. Then as her back swung up toward the rock wall, the hammer gave way.

Suddenly she was falling forward, the ledge only five feet from her. In a panic she turned her body and threw out the rock hammer. The head snagged between two outcrops of rock, halting her fall. Her feet dropped into the murky water and she heard the blind beast change course behind her.

Quicker than she'd moved for years, she pulled her feet up and kicked away from the wall. For a second she thought she had the ledge in reach, as her legs swung through behind her. But she slipped.

Burly hands locked round her wrist, and for an unbearable moment she was held beyond the ledge as the sightless fish rushed her way. Then Manic pulled her up and over the lip of the ledge. She swung her own legs up and laid still for a moment, breathing heavily, her heart pounding in her chest.

Somewhere below a final splash of filthy, oily water was followed by eerie silence. Only the heavy wheezing of the two new friends could be heard echoing through the cavern corridor. Even the sound of bats had drifted into silence.

"That was a little *too* close. And what the hell was that fish thing all about? See the teeth?" Andi had spent a few minutes trying to wring most of the filthy fluid from her soft boots, but they were still damp, and the discomfort was making her irritable.

"They'd have hurt," he said.

"Is understatement your forte?" Andi snapped.

Manic grumbled. He didn't seem too happy himself about the entire jungle swing incident. Evidently he'd landed on his rump, and not daintily. But Andi had never met a dainty dwarf.

They had moved a small distance down the corridor before sorting themselves out. There'd been a small amount of backslapping, but that had been short-lived as the aches and discomforts had asserted themselves. They'd moved on. The corridor had opened onto a taller passage, apparently fashioned by hand or machine. The floor was cracked tile and every so often they passed wall sconces for torches.

Without the light from the moss it was difficult to see, but Manic led the way. Even in pitch darkness Andi knew she needed no help, but she wasn't about to share that fact with Manic. She let him lead her down the corridor as though blinded, with a hand on his shoulder. Whatever the reason for her ability to see in the dark, Andi was always reticent to reveal that she was any different, even to colleagues or friends.

Along the way, Manic stopped every so often to dismantle a series of small traps, designed to wound and maim more than kill. Each contraption seemed ancient in construction and probably would not have gone off at their passing, but Andi was glad Manic saw fit to spy them out and remove them. They were moving forward carefully, but would probably be running back in a hurry if that fish had been any measure of the wildlife they might encounter, so she was glad to have these traps out of the way. Running was difficult with a pulverised ankle or ruptured kneecap.

After a dozen yards more the corridor ended in a tall doorway, from which a short series of steps descended to the floor of a wide chamber. The ceiling was relatively high, with ornate walls decorated with statues and rock sculptures. The floor-tile pattern was elaborate and appeared ancient in design. Andi had never seen such art in a floor before, and although the colours of the tiles were dulled with age, she could tell it had been quite magnificent in its day. But the smell in the room was concerning. The subtle but foul stench told her something long dead was still decomposing.

While Andi was trying in vain to extricate more fluid from her shoes, Manic had managed to light a fire in a pile of rags he'd soaked with a pungent-smelling brew. He then used the rag taper to light a long stick he'd located at the foot of the stairs, manufacturing an impromptu torch.

All across the floor was evidence of death. Many deaths, in fact. Nearest to them, not three body lengths from the foot of the stairs, was a pile of bones, most of which were crushed flat. Rags and broken armour littered the same pile.

"By the Gods, lass. This is a tomb. I should have warned you." He stepped forward onto the tiles toward the flattened bones.

"Manic, wait! I think we ought to be a little more careful about where we tread in here." The freshest body was quite some distance ahead, mouldy flesh still clinging to a skull through which a two-foot bolt protruded. The man had probably been dead before he hit the tiles. But whoever he had been, he'd been close to his goal. Just beyond his body was an elaborate and sophisticated-looking statue. The fixings seemed to catch the distant light of Manic's torch more than anything else in the hall. Andi figured she was looking at fixed gems, and not a small amount of them either. "Manic, the tiles are trapped. It must be the only way."

"That's what *he* thought," Manic said, "but look!" He knelt near the closest pile of bones and held the torch at human knee height. In the light, Andi picked out a strand of silk stretched across the room. It was a knee-high trip wire, and a similar one had caught this traveller cold. Manic looked at the ceiling, pointing once more with the torch. "A cylinder column, see?"

She could see it now, in the ceiling. Normally human eyes would find it difficult to pick the marks out from the stairs, but it was clear to Andi.

"Watch..." Manic stepped to the side and pushed lightly on the silk. There was a soft rumbling and suddenly a column of stone thundered down on top of the flat bones, shattering them even more. The boom of the stone column resonated through the chamber, making Andi's ears ring. Manic was laughing.

"By Soriana!" Andi invoked the name of the Goddess of Luck. "Was there any need for that?" She moved to Manic's side, slinking carefully beneath another silk line and moving forward silently and lightly while avoiding tiles with disturbed dust on them. She noticed something odd. "Still, look at the tiles, Manic!" She halted near another pile of bones. "Notice something strange?"

"Not really, although there's another silk line right by your head." She flinched, and made a mental note to be more careful. Strangely, she seemed unable to spot the silk lines very well.

"Thanks! But look: the dust and stones on some of the tiles moved when that thing dropped down. Some of these aren't tiles at all: they're stone."

"You're right! The dust has moved into the grooves of the stones. These here are tiles." He pounded a foot down on one. Nothing happened. "But this is stone. Step on this with enough weight and you'll set something off." He kicked lightly at another two-foot bolt in the ribs of another skeleton nearby, then looked at Andi in the orange glow of his torch. "I guess you were right about the floor, too. Reckon if we stay clear of the stones and silk we'll be fine?"

"I think we have a better chance than these poor saps, sure enough."

They moved off amongst the traps, wary that not all the bolts had been fired yet. Thankfully they reached the last and most fresh carcass without further incident. Maggots were still cleaning the bones, and a chill swept up Andi's spine. She never found the thought of carrion-feeders pleasant, although they were undoubtedly a necessary part of nature.

They were now as close to the odd statue as any being had come, for there were no bodies. *Unless someone had already been here in centuries past and made off with the gem*, she thought.

Together they made their way to the statue. Closer

inspection revealed more about its nature than had been apparent at a distance. Resembling an idol more than a simple statue, it was constructed of stonework, sculpted wood, and bronze fittings and decoration. Some of the wooden awnings were patterned using firebrands and the stonework was decorated with gems of varying clarity. There was clearly no way to remove the gems, for they were so well buried in the rock as to resemble deep-set eyes for the most part.

To the left of the statue was a simple, tall cabinet with brass latches at the top and bottom. No markings could be seen and a thick layer of dust covered the top of the doorframe.

"The cabinet will be booby-trapped," Manic told her, sounding superior. "It's too obvious. What do you make of this?" The dwarf indicated a small wooden panel set in the floor, slightly raised above the level of the stone. It was apparent that the wood continued down into the rock floor.

"Looks like another trap to me, but you're the expert." She did well to remove any sarcasm from her voice. She decided that in this place the ego of a "trap-finder" was not a bad thing to massage.

"Well, it could be a trapdoor, but I can't see any hinges. I think maybe the wooden panel might lift out, but I dread to think what's down there in the dark." Andi was sure she saw him shudder. "Anyway, this is what has my attention."

Manic was staring at what must have been the *Baerv*. It was precisely how Jakrat had described it: flawless and gleaming, yet somehow too perfect. It looked like a massive fake.

It was positioned perfectly inside a bronze plinth, set in the stone base of the idol; marks in the soft metal suggested someone had worried away at the jewel in an attempt to remove it. A brainless thief, no doubt!

Manic moved to examine the right side of the idol, on

his knees, his torch held high to save burning his precious facial hair. Andi decided it was a good idea, and dropped to her haunches to examine the left corner. It was then she spotted yet another silk link running from the crack at the bottom of the cupboard door behind the idol. "Manic!" she hissed. "Don't move! I've found something."

"What? What is it?"

Andi moved back to look at the Frostfinder. He hadn't moved since she spoke. Oh he knew traps all right; or knew them well enough to freeze stock-still when told. It was then that Andi caught the flickering flame of the torch. Flickering away from the wall. "There's a breeze near you, dwarf. Look at the flame."

"You told me not to move; now I'm to look around at the sights?"

"Sorry," Andi muttered. She wasn't used to taking someone else's well-being into account in these situations. She never usually gave a second thought to anyone else. A look over Manic's raised arm revealed a minute, featherline crack in the wall behind him. He was more or less leaning on the edge of the wooden panel. "Come out: I think you're OK to move. Just do it slowly." He did as she said with careful concentration. Once he had moved, Andi leaned in to look behind the statue. She didn't have to go far. A strand of silk came from behind the base of the idol and ran into a minute tapered hole in the stone of the floor, near the panel.

"I don't like this," grumbled the dwarf, fidgeting agitatedly at his tool-belt. "And you owe me a new rock hammer."

"We get out of this and I'll buy you a damn *war*hammer, how's that sound? Now be quiet; I'm thinking." Something didn't make sense. There was little attempt to conceal any part of the contraption; certainly nothing like the care taken in all of the traps leading up to this. "I don't think it's a trap, Manic."

"Tripe, woman! It has 'trap' written all over it!"

"That's why I don't think it's a trap. Hardly devilishly concealed, is it, a dirty great wooden slab in the floor?"

Manic frowned and tapped a finger to his chin in thought. "No, no, it isn't. But a poorly concealed trap will kill you just as quickly. You think it's connected to the cupboard door?"

Andi grinned at the dwarf. "One way to find out." Before his objections could register, Andi pulled open both doors of the cupboard. A cloud of dust mites billowed forth, but she was neither impaled nor crushed.

However, Manic had to act sharply to ensure he wasn't crushed against the idol as the wooden panel dropped into the floor and a section of the ancient wall came loose, forming a heavy, tall, stone door that rushed open. It slammed into the side of the statue with a satisfying and resounding crash that had both of them clutching their ears. Through the echoes it was possible to hear the ringing, melodic whine of the jewel spinning on stone.

Manic took the scene in quicker than Andi. The door crashing open had broken the bronze seal on the *Baerv* and released it to the floor. The new doorway to the right led to a freshly revealed passage. Andi cast her eyes over the rubbish stored in the shelved cupboard only to discover a glass cylinder inside that was slowly filling with sand. As the cylinder filled, the door began to close.

"Hurry, woman! We don't have time to gawk."

"What's to say that's the way out, Manic?" She had to shout as the rumbling from the door grew louder.

"Me! I can see daylight! Come on!" Snatching up the *Baerv*, he rushed headlong into the new corridor.

Just as Andi was set to follow, her eye caught a glint from the bottom shelf of the cupboard. Therein lay a large and oddly shaped gem of a silvery-white hue. She'd never seen such a colour. Quickly and without thought she snatched it from the shelf and hurried to squeeze through the closing gap. She grazed her shoulder blade on the closing door and pulled her arm through just in time to save her fingers.

"Took your time!" Manic quipped, as he leaned against a low wall. The height in this passage was once again restrictive, but it definitely seemed to lead toward daylight. Indeed, he had extinguished his torch.

"What do you make of this?" Andi handed over the stone she'd discovered.

The dwarf turned it over and over for a few moments, struggling to get an accurate impression of the gem's worth in the low light. "It looks a little dull, but I've never seen a gem this colour. It's pretty huge, too. I think perhaps this might be worth more than the *Baerv*, to be honest." Manic looked Andi up and down, clearly appraising her clinging clothes. "Want me to hide it?" She nodded, and Manic found a hiding place for the mysterious jewel somewhere behind his chestplate. Then he took a closer look at the *Baerv* with some dissatisfaction. "I think Jakrat's right: this thing is almost entirely without value. I think it might even be glass!"

"Hmm…he admitted it was without value, but it was certainly worth something to him."

From ahead they could hear sounds, and judged they had emerged somewhere within the same inner bailey.

"Whatever he wants it for, he can keep it!" she said.

"Just so long as he keeps his promise to set us free," said Manic, worried.

Andi couldn't help but chuckle. All of this was just so typical. Walking toward the light ahead, Andi made a mental note to remember that Manic had concealed that second gem about his person, and hoped they weren't searched when they vacated the dungeon. Jakrat had not forbidden them from helping themselves to any spoils they might stumble upon, but who in this world—other than a total fool—ever trusted a noble?

"Magistrate!" called a guard excitedly, as Manic and Andi emerged from the stand of trees in the shadow of the inner bailey wall. The corridor they had uncovered had led to a small and ancient rockslide, and they had been forced to climb from the cavern beneath. The opening of the door below had caused a second landfall, revealing a way out. Outside the air was clear and fresh, and the drizzle had dissipated.

A guard on the wall above had been first to spot them, and had called a warning. Now Jakrat and a couple of keep guards were rushing over, the magistrate's face a picture of genuine surprise that they had survived. Curiously, Andi noted that he looked more relieved than happy; profoundly relieved.

Andi determinedly clutched the *Baerv* in her fist. Her mind was awhirl regarding how to ensure their safe release before giving up the jewel, but she could think of nothing.

Jakrat reached them, his eyes alive and sparkling beneath his hooded brow. "You made it!" He declared the obvious. Andi made no move to hand the jewel over.

Over Jakrat's shoulder, emerging from the shadow of a small doorway in the keep wall, Andi spied the cowled figure watching them closely, robed arms seemingly extended.

"What's going on here?" demanded a booming voice from the other end of the bailey. The duke approached, his cape flowing as he made purposeful strides to reach them. As the duke came closer, the cowled figure folded its arms, inclined its head and seemed to melt back into the darkness of the doorway.

Not one of the duke's men, then! Andi thought. *Interesting!*

"Escapees?" asked Reinhart, his regal jaw jutting in indignation.

"No, cousin," said Jakrat. Andi had half expected his voice to betray that he had somehow been caught out at something, but instead it was confident and perhaps even cocky. "These were the brigands involved in the foulberg disturbance last night."

"I know who they are, Jakrat! What I want to know is what they are doing walking around the bailey."

"They've been completing some work for us, cousin."

"Really?" Reinhart sounded dubious. "What kind of work, exactly?"

Andi took a gamble on her instinct, and held out the *Baerv*.

There was a moment's pause, and then Reinhart said, "What's that?"

"The *Baerv*!" Jakrat answered.

Reinhart looked taken aback. "Really?" Andi nodded, and plonked the valueless gem into his hand. "It's been found, after so many centuries?"

Jakrat nodded.

"Why?" asked Reinhart of his cousin.

"We need it," Jakrat answered enigmatically. Manic and Andi exchanged glances. "This pair have proven that they are clearly thieves."

"What?" barked Manic.

"I was right to send you both to the gallows. Guards, take them away."

As the guards made to place them both back in manacles, Reinhart held his hand up, halting them. "You're going to hang them?"

Jakrat now looked a little nonplussed. "Well, yes, my duke."

"Why the hell would you do that?"

"Murder," Manic said sullenly.

"What?" Reinhart asked.

"We suspect they are responsible for the death of a man at the Ragged Boar Inn last night," said Jakrat, rapidly losing confidence.

Reinhart peered sidelong at his cousin. "When I told you to take care of the judgement on this pair, I didn't mean pin a murder charge on them and have them hanged for the crows, just because you couldn't be bothered actually working for a living!" Reinhart's scorn for his cousin was suddenly clearly evident. "And regardless, that man slipped on the spilled alcohol in the Inn and cracked his head on the bar. Folan the barkeep told me he saw it happen. Oh, this pair might have had a hand in starting the brawl, but they're not guilty of that man's murder."

Andi was furious at the magistrate's attempts to have them framed, but forced herself to remain calm, seeing as her fortunes seemed to be improving.

"Have these jumped-up charges quashed immediately!" Reinhart told him. Staring at the pair, Reinhart weighed them up. "You have proven yourselves resourceful, though," he mused. Narrowing his eyes, he seemed to have an idea, and Andi experienced another sinking feeling in her stomach.

Reinhart said to Jakrat, "Have the cleric Eidos join me here at once."

Jakrat nodded and flipped Andi and Manic a scornful look before making to depart. "And here!" Reinhart stopped him. He threw the *Baerv* to his cousin, who caught it gingerly. "You wanted this so badly; put it somewhere so I don't have to see its ugliness."

All concern regarding Andi and Manic fled Jakrat's face as he finally got his hands on the gem. He nodded to his duke and then made for the keep.

The duke indicated that the pair should fall into step with him as they proceeded to walk in the sunshine around the bailey. "My apologies for whatever misunderstanding has taken place. I want you to know that summary executions are not this duchy's usual conduct."

Andi nodded, accepting his apology, for it seemed genuine.

"Things have been unsettled along the border recently," the duke revealed. Andi knew that recent times had seen peace between Shenmadock and Ipsica, but something about the duke showed he was feeling the strain.

"There are reports of activity on the border to the east, but our own useless scouts are uncovering nothing of worth.

And with rumours of a number of abductions from the villages and farmlands to the north of here, I have my resources stretched beyond capacity. I fear this is why Jakrat was happy to string you up." Reinhart smiled apologetically at Andi. "He thinks he's helping."

Andi rolled her eyes, which made Reinhart laugh. "Listen, he's right in his assumption that I need help—independent help, that is. You seem a resourceful pair," he said. "I can pay you well."

Suddenly alert to the prospect of making a profit, rather than being concerned for his own mortality, Manic's ears seemed to prick up. "How well?" he asked.

Chapter Three
Quarantine

Rain thundered heavily from the darkening sky, turning the cobbled streets to shallow rivers and soaking Stefon to the bone. He hated the rain. It must have been the rainiest autumn for years, he mused. Certainly that he could remember.

"I hate the rain," Rish grumbled next to him. Stefon's oldest friend tried in vain to shelter beneath a roof's outcropping, but the awning was too short and the rain was driven by a northerly wind. Rish was just as wet as him.

It came as no surprise that Rish despised the rain. In almost every respect he resembled a cat, having been brought up to live on his wits and reflexes. His slender frame and athletic quickness made him a strong ally, though, and good to have at your side in a bar brawl.

Beyond Rish, Stefon could see Jewl resting his broad back against the same building, not mindful of the rain. Jewl's mighty arms were crossed before his chest and his greataxe rested against his portly belly. Jewl was the friendliest dwarf Stefon had ever met, but that said nothing. Dwarves were a pain in the backside, being surly and covetous at best, and greedy and vindictive at worst. Stefon had little time for dwarfs. *Little time*…Stefon couldn't help but chuckle at his *little* joke.

"Something amusing about this job, Stefon?" Rish asked, obviously irritated that someone could laugh in the rain. "Something funny about standing in the rain just to make a collection? I had a date tonight, you know!" Rish ran a hand through his shaggy long hair, shaking water from it.

"No you didn't," Jewl corrected. "Maybe you had an appointment at that brothel you frequent, but that's hardly a date, you shrew."

Stefon laughed.

"It's *better* than a date, you jumped-up, fat halfling. You're guaranteed to lay down with a girl when whoring, and it probably costs you less, when you take everything into account," Rish reasoned.

"Well don't forget to put some pennies aside to pay for the priest's time when he has to cure your knob-rot!" Jewl barked a laugh. "Salves aren't cheap!"

"Quiet, you two!" Stefon admonished. "It's almost time. The sooner we get this done the sooner we get back home, but that's no reason to get sloppy. I'll get the package from them and you can leave the talking to me too. Jewl, you back me up." The dwarf hoisted his axe and stepped away from the wall. "Rish, can you cover us from the back with your bow?"

Rish shook his mop of hay-coloured hair to rid himself of more rainwater before grumbling in agreement. He looked wet, bored and frustrated, and Stefon couldn't blame him. In contrast, Jewl simply endured the rain, which seemed to be struggling to soak into the brown bush of his beard. They stepped into the cobbled street from beneath the building's overhang, heading toward the warehouse complex across the way.

The night was darker than usual for this time of year. Rain had fallen upon the city of Wahib for days upon months now: unseasonable weather for this time of year, but the winter winds were not yet upon them. The great wall that encircled the city protected most folk from the windy winter seasons, but those in the foulberg outside the walls often suffered greatly.

But this was no average year and the inhabitants of the sovereign city of Wahib would sooner be anywhere else but inside the city walls.

Wahib was in quarantine. For some time now the city militia had sealed the walls of a city built to withstand decades of siege, and now Ipsica's second most prodigious populace was very slowly dying.

"I can see light," Rish murmured, suddenly seeming the seasoned professional he was, now that they were about their business. "It's coming from the side door, over on the left there." He indicated the small door at the far corner of the building that sat sheltered beneath the warehouse's outer wall. It stood ajar and Stefon could see the golden cast of light from a naked flame peeking through the crack of the opening.

"That's where our friends will be, then. Let's get out of the rain." Stefon moved at a steady jog, keeping his eyes on the doorway and the corner beyond. This was a routine job, but he was aware of the potential for an ambush that the right-hand bend represented. Being a leftie, Stefon kept his weaker right hand resting on the hilt of the sword still secure in its scabbard as his left clung tightly to his loaded and cocked hand-crossbow, his index finger on the release.

The warehouse was abandoned, Stefon was sure. Many businesses had either been left to decay or had collapsed financially during the quarantine, and this was sure to be one of them.

They approached the doorway at a slow walk, Jewl taking the lead. Without breaking stride, the dwarf stepped up to and straight through the door. Stefon paused long enough to shake his head ruefully before following his foolhardy friend.

They stood in a disused office, confirming Stefon's suspicions that the place was now out of business. Only dust lined the shelves and no signs of recent use were evident. The source of light, a burning torch, was resting under a brick on the counter with the flaming end across their path, and a simple wooden door stood open ahead of them. Diffused light could be seen inside the adjoining room.

Jewl reached for the torch.

"Leave it!" Stefon hissed. The dwarf's callused hand hovered for a moment near the torch as though not trusting Stefon's opinion, and then he pulled it back.

Suddenly the reason dawned on Jewl. "It'd make us a target in the dark, right?"

Urging him forward, Stefon thumped him softly on the shoulder. "That's right, little britches. Bad enough that we risk being a silhouette by leaving it behind us."

They pressed on through the small room and Rish stayed at the outer door, ensuring they weren't flanked from behind.

This kind of routine pick-up was usually exactly that: routine. So much so, Stefon felt insulted and worried that Ratna was sending them on this kind of task. It also made him wary that they were being employed for such a simple collection. Stefon's services were not usually cheap, even for jobs such as this. Rish was equally displeased and insulted, having a much larger lump of pride in his heart than Stefon.

So they were going by the manual, taking every precaution; if indeed there even existed a manual for mercenary groups such as theirs.

Jewl, full of confidence, pushed the next door fully open and strode through into the dull light of the next chamber. As Stefon followed him, he saw that they had entered the main warehouse section, but the place was not empty as he had predicted. Whoever had left this place had abandoned it with quite a number of containers and crates in the main hold. Stefon knew that there was not likely to be much in the way of valuables left in the crates, for the weeks following the enforcement of the quarantine had seen widespread looting before the city militia set about executing those found stealing. Oddly, looting became a less popular pastime then.

Most of the crates were stacked quite high, and it was difficult to retain a line of sight across what Stefon knew would be a long and deep area. A high series of lightweight boxes formed a wall to the right of their door into the middle of the room, and torchlight could be seen illuminating the area round the corner, casting gold pools of light on the dusty floor. The air smelled musty and old; the scent of dampening wood and growing rot in the walls made the space around Stefon seem thicker. The constant thrum of the rain on the wood-and-tile roof high above was testament to the determined downpour outside.

Jewl confidently jogged his axe onto his shoulder and strode—as much as a dwarf *can* stride—into the room, heading for the end of the box wall. Stefon easily kept pace, his hand-crossbow by his side. Rish moved away from the wall to their left, an arrow notched and the bowstring drawn taut, though not fully. Stefon could see his eyes flickering constantly across the tops of the boxes and crates, down to gaps in the warehouse floor where danger might lurk.

Voices could be heard around the corner: male voices speaking in low tones. Jewl reached the corner, and the voices stopped. Stefon followed him.

Three figures awaited them, in the glow from a torch in a brazier to the right of a small office desk. On the desk was a small leather saddlebag. It appeared to contain coins, but it was difficult to make out in the close light and with the thickness of the saddle leather. One man sat behind the desk, his hands resting in plain sight on the wood of the tabletop. No weapons were in sight. He was middle-aged for a human: perhaps late thirties. He wore a simple tunic and coat with no courtly trimmings and he only wore the simple band of a wedding ring.

Over his left shoulder was a thick-set man with deep-set eyes and a mean stare. He carried a heavy broadsword in his hands, the tip in the ground as he leaned on the hilt in a poor attempt at nonchalance. He wore a heavy leather armoured vest and simple pantaloons, with a cheap and tatty-looking burgundy sash tied at his waist. Scars on his upper arms told of battle experience, but he looked slow and cumbersome.

To his right, over the sitting man's right shoulder, stood a slender, short female elf. She wore brown woodland clothing, open at the neckline to reveal tawny skin between flat breasts. At her side hung a wicked-looking thin, curved blade. Her hands were clad in tight gloves. Her blonde hair was gathered into a functional ponytail. She held nobody's gaze, fixing her eyes to the ground and shifting her insubstantial weight every so often.

The man behind the desk spoke first, reclining away from it in a show of nonchalance, though Stefon could read tiredness and fear in his eyes.

"Well met, friends! Does the rain still fall so heavily outside?"

"Of course," replied Stefon. "It hasn't stopped for months. Do you think maybe the Gods are washing the streets clean of bodies for us?" He and Jewl stopped short of the desk, remaining out of the direct fall of the torchlight. From here he could see that more crates adorned the floor of the warehouse in all directions and that the ceiling boasted a complex and impressive series of pulleys and mechanisms designed to hoist and move heavy, sizeable crates. All was dark in the compartments of the ceiling and crane array. No other figures moved from behind any crates on the ground either.

Rish stepped over to be adjacent to the elf, flanking her slightly. She seemed unfazed by his movements. Stefon could see that Rish's eyes were drawn to the elf's svelte lines, but hoped his friend would remain alert.

The man continued to rock away from the desk on the back legs of his chair. "I know what you mean. We're in for a dark winter, for sure."

When Stefon realised the man would continue to avoid the subject at hand, he forced the issue. "With the weather being as inhospitable as it is, my companions and I would prefer not to dally. It is my understanding you have something for us to take to your associate, Master Ibn Ratna Giri?"

That short reminder of the name of the person these people were dealing with had the desired effect. There was a flicker of recognition in the man's eyes before a smile pulled his mouth wide across his face, showing gnarled and dying teeth. "Of course!" He indicated the saddlebags. "Please help yourself. You should find all to be in order."

Stefon immediately didn't like it. The distance across to the table was short, but it brought him fully into the open and into the light from the torch. But he was being paid to be brave. He was being paid to take risks. He stepped forward, dust and dirt crunching beneath his soft-heeled boots.

He kept his pace slow, and reached the desk. Nothing happened; nobody moved. He looked at the man's face for a long moment before reaching for the bag.

Normally he wouldn't check the merchandise, for it was none of Stefon's business what price these people were paying Ratna for "protection", but something didn't swing right with the bags. Something about the pendulous manner of the bags, or the increased weight compared to the size, told Stefon that they didn't hold coinage.

He stopped in a half-turn as the difference registered. He looked back at the man, returned his smile and went to open the saddlebag flap.

Rish's called warning was a fraction of a second too late. But almost without thought, Stefon was already dodging to the side by reflex alone.

He heard the arrow whistle past his face before it snapped on the stone floor to his left. The old man shoved himself hard away from the desk, falling onto his back, out of sight. Rish dropped to one knee and loosed an arrow high into the eaves above them.

Without waiting for further encouragement, Jewl jumped past Stefon and unleashed a devastating roundhouse cleave at the standing man's midriff. The bull of a man was fast, bringing his blade up quickly to deflect the blow. Jewl rode the motion and used his momentum, dropping beneath the man's clumsy riposte, and turning full circle to swing the huge blade of the axe across the man's exposed knees. The massive blade bit through the flesh of his legs easily, shattering both limbs, spraying blood and shards of bone across the floor. The man landed heavily, screaming and clutching at the stumps of his legs, all thoughts of his own weapon forgotten.

A similar scream echoed in the eaves, no doubt from the hidden archer. Rish's arrow would have found its target.

The young elf drew her wicked blade and closed in on Rish as he nocked another arrow. Stefon aimed and snapped off his crossbow bolt, the short steel shaft thumping through the side of her ribcage, dropping her mid-stride. Blood squirted up from the wound and her breath rattled and gurgled. Writhing in agony, still she held onto life.

The same could not be said for Jewl's legless enemy, whom the dwarf dispatched with a drop of his weighty axe to the neck, severing his head and spilling blood across the warehouse floor. The smell of fear mingled with blood in the still, old air of the musty, cavernous chamber, the sounds of clashing weapons and screams echoing eerily into the corners.

Seeing that the trap had failed and his armed backup had been dropped or slain, the man who had done all the talking scrambled to his feet and made to flee. "Halt!" Stefon boomed, surprised by the forcefulness of his own voice. But it was too late. The man skidded to a halt, arms out to his sides, as Rish's second arrow punched through his chest. He stood transfixed for a moment, staring at the wooden shaft jutting from his lung, his feet shifting beneath him. His body then seemed to concertina, folding him to the floor like a dropped sheet.

When Stefon scrambled to the dying man's side, he was murmuring, "I'm sorry! I'm so sorry!" as blood bubbled on his lips. His face was draining of colour and he had scant moments to live.

Stefon gripped the dying man by the arms to try to wake him, just to ask one vital question, but he had nothing to ask. He simply held the man up as his life ebbed away, and then placed the carcass on the ground.

"Nice shot, Rish. How do you plan to find out why they ambushed us from a dead body?" Stefon glanced at the elf, but she had expired quietly, a sad expression on her fine features.

Jewl stepped over, wiping blood from the blade of his axe with one of the severed trouser legs from the man he had beheaded. He tossed away the sodden rag when he was finished. "It's not his fault, really. The guy shouldn't have run."

"The guy shouldn't have tried to have us killed, more to the point," Rish said, lowering his bow and shaking his head as a cat shakes his mane.

"I know, but still." A quick search of both bodyguards' bodies revealed little in the way of coinage, no paper or information, and only a few simple gambling tokens made from wood.

"Let me see that," Rish offered. Stefon flicked a wooden token across to him and finished searching the third body with no reward. "I recognise this. It's one of the gaming chips from that place in the poortown quarter. The place your friend with the crazy hat owns."

"Quinly?" Stefon suggested.

Rish nodded.

"Captain Quinly? That pirate? Why would he want you dead?" Jewl pressed.

"He wouldn't, I don't think." Stefon mulled it over as they gathered themselves to leave. Rish retrieved his only attainable arrow, giving up the one fired into the loft for lost. They extinguished the remaining torch.

Captain Quinly Bunnelshut had known Stefon for more than half his life. In return, Stefon knew his litigious past, with whispered accusations of piracy and murder performed at his command, but Quinly had never faced a gallows-walk and had always conducted business in Wahib without danger of arrest, so Stefon trusted him that far. He had never expressed any animosity toward Stefon or his friends. In fact, Stefon considered Quinly a friend.

"Well I hardly think a piece of round wood suggests Quinly has our card marked, but it certainly gives us another place to ask questions." He looked at the dead man, then at the faces of his friends. "This collection was from the Tanner Guild, right? One of the leather places?"

"Hence the saddlebags?" Rish quipped with a wry grin.

"Yeah." Stefon kicked the useless bags across the floor, small pebbles and stones skittering out of the flap. "Full of rocks."

"Hey, just like Jewl's head!" Rish grinned as he covered his bow with a waxed shawl to protect the composite bone and wood against the rain then slung it across his back.

"Well I don't know about you chaps but I don't like the idea of going back to Ratna without an explanation for what went on here. Bad enough we don't have the payoff, but to turn up without a reason why?" Stefon shook his head as he stowed his hand-crossbow in his shoulder sling-bag. "I fancy a talk with Captain Quinly."

Jewl and Rish both nodded, Rish's grin slipping. No one found the prospect of running afoul of Guild Master Ibn Ratna Giri an appealing escapade.

Quinly's establishment rested up against the old brewery building in the rundown sector of town that had once boasted the finest freshwater fish markets and mongers in the eastern realm. But overfishing of the rivers closer to shore and the swell of population in coastal regions had caused the industry to first falter and then die. Many buildings still wore the emblems and signatures of once-proud fishermen and businesses under the eaves, but none still functioned. In actual fact, over the years the old buildings had become refuge to the poor and desperate, and those wanting to make a quick fortune from little outlay. Crime in the region had soared and only those foolish enough to know no better and those disreputable enough to have grown eyes in the back of their head ventured into poortown.

Quinly had raised himself a tiny empire within the grimy hovel of poortown, preying on the predisposition of urchins and reprobates for gambling and drinking. He ran a small concern, housing tables for numerous games of chance and skill, and a long bar for serving various nefarious beverages. Above the main room were a series of three smaller chambers with long and soft velvet and leather sofa-chairs. Members of Quinly's club were permitted up here to chew the hallucinogenic Strangemeal concoctions favoured amongst poortown traders and privateers, or just to enjoy a smoke of moist-weed and a potent drink in peace.

Stefon had always been welcome above the bar, but had never seen the attraction of altering perception with Strangemeal's effects. He never enjoyed eating regular fungus and moss, let alone the particular moss and fungus that grew in the wilds of the foothills of the Choatian Range in the north, from which Strangemeal was developed. He preferred his wits precisely where he could find them.

When Stefon, Jewl and Rish entered Quinly's place, it was more than half full, as was to be expected on a Fourthday evening. Tomorrow was the beginning of week's end and those who were short of work or commitments often began the weekend festivities a day early. All the gambling tables were in full swing and more than a few rowdy patrons were kicking up a fuss about the harshness of the Gods or the cheating house. One particularly drunk halfling was being dragged to the door by the scruff of his jerkin by one of the half-orc door staff, forcing Rish to dodge sharply to his left to avoid being trampled. The halfling was lashing out at anything moving with a vicious-looking long dirk, but the half-orc kept him at arm's length until he was forcibly ejected to the rain-washed street outside.

As the doors slammed shut, Stefon immediately recognised the pungent odour of moist-weed intermingled with the smells of too much drink and not enough air. He was tempted to cover his mouth with the front of his tunic, but didn't want to look any more the highwayman than he already did. He ran a hand forward across the top of his head, shedding water from his short hair.

They moved amongst the crowd smoothly, seeking out the bar. Softly, Rish pulled at the hem of Stefon's short archer's cloak and indicated he was going to chance his hand at one of the tables in the corner. Unfortunately gambling was one of many vices Rish possessed, but thankfully it was a vice that sometimes served him well, for luck seemed his ever-present friend.

Stefon watched him blend into the crowd before pressing on for the bar. Once at the counter, he motioned the barman over. Jewl ordered a drink and the fat sweating man set about preparing a short whiskey and water. As the pungent whiskey sloshed into the pewter beaker, Stefon asked, "Is Quinly about?"

"Captain Bunnelshut? Of course!" The barman grinned, displaying four rotting teeth and a row of bleeding gums. "He's upstairs, sir."

Stefon knew that being referred to as *sir* in this place meant he had the OK to travel upstairs. Nobody was a *sir* unless they were connected. Nobility and royalty probably wouldn't even receive such deference—should they ever be stupid enough to try and enter such a place without a very effective disguise.

At the end of the bar near the back wall, a staircase spiralled up into the ceiling. Stefon moved over to it, past another half-orc at the foot of the stairs, and ascended to the chambers above.

As he rose, the stench of swilled alcohol and tabac from downstairs gave way to the familiar sour smell of brewed or smoked Strangemeal. The stairs opened out into the first room. It was twelve yards square with a large portal in the right-hand wall that led through to another similar chamber. A low-slung and simple cast-iron chandelier held slow-burning candles, some of which were guttering. The room was poorly illuminated and at shoulder height a layer of smoke floated thick like winter fog on mountaintops.

Now Stefon did cover his mouth and nose with his tunic, holding it in place with his right hand and walking stooped beneath the smoke layer. He had no desire to feel the effects of Strangemeal even second-hand. Nobody laughed at his movements, nor indeed did they even seem to notice. Four people populated this chamber presently, one of whom he recognised immediately.

On a squat square seat that was evidently soft and had too much give, reclined Quinly. His ever-present sweeping velvet hat flopped to one side of his head as he sipped at a cup of brew, seeming to savour the flavour. He looked half-asleep, but Stefon knew better than to judge this man on appearances. Quinly was with another individual and opposite them in the corner near the second chamber were two obviously heavily inebriated men.

Stefon approached carefully, wary of Quinly's companion who looked far more alert than Quinly did himself. The second individual looked like an elf, and appeared even more ill at ease in such an establishment. But the longsword at his side and the sharpness of his eye told Stefon he was feeling no ill effects of secondhand smoke.

"Captain, mind if I sit with you a moment?" Stefon asked politely, bringing Quinly back to their world with a sway of his head and a sharpening of his eyes, like they were two glass marbles rising from a pool of muddy water. It took a moment for Stefon's face to register with him, but then a grin creased his pallid cheeks and he huffed a laugh. Stefon was no scryer or soothsayer, but he was pretty sure Quinly was pleased to see him.

"Stefon! My good friend, sit down!" Stefon did so, to Quinly's right side, across from his elven friend who remained silent but watchful. "I'd offer you a cup but I'm sure you'd decline."

"That's right; thank you, though."

"What brings you down to my neck of the woods this late of an evening, young Stefon? Trying to find Rish, no doubt? Spending money he owes you?" Quinly laughed more. His clothing was simple and tatty, despite the presence of a few faded pearls or gems that hinted at former resplendence. He wore a yellowed cravat and tall riding boots that had long since lost their lustre for want of saddlesoap or tanner's gubbin.

"Not entirely, although this *is* about money." Stefon tried to keep his voice level, but during the journey from the warehouse ambush to Quinly's place his anger at being attacked had slowly begun to rise. "I had a job go a little sour tonight. We were making a pick-up and were ambushed.

Unfortunately for them, they underestimated their target."

"Not for the first time!" Quinly said. He seemed relaxed, but Stefon could see a little recognition crossing his face. "It wasn't a collection for Ratna, was it?" he finally asked.

"From one of the Tanner Guild families," Stefon confirmed. "Don't really know which one. Needless to say, all those who attended the exchange are now dead."

Quinly's shoulders dropped visibly and he shook his head. "I know the family. Are you sure they tried to kill you?"

"Of course, Quinly! They loosed a damned arrow at my head!" Stefon's bellow was attracting attention, and he made a concerted effort to lower his voice. "I can tell when someone is trying to shuffle me off. Did you have something to do with it?"

"Kind of," he admitted. "But I didn't know you were doing the pickup!" Quinly quickly followed: "I certainly didn't tell them to kill anyone. I'll set this right." He turned to the elf beside him. "Could you do me a favour and send old man Gill up here, and tell him to bring his money?" The elf looked at Stefon distrustfully; in response, he couldn't help but raise an eyebrow. It seemed tonight was his night for picking fights. Quinly put a placating hand on the elf's shoulder. "Stefon is to be trusted. Apparently it is I that should be watched. I'm getting sloppy. Please, go."

The elf stood, casting an impressive figure in the dark, smoke-filled room. Silently he turned and headed for the stairs, leaving Quinly and Stefon alone. "What's going on, Quinly?"

"Let me explain. Purse-strings are getting tight for a lot of people on the outskirts of poortown. Families are starving, Stefon. People are becoming desperate." Stefon had heard such sob stories more and more of late. He had always believed on some level that people were using these hard times to justify behaviour that they would normally not display, but perhaps he was wrong. Perhaps he was judging them harshly. Stefon had no family of his own to concern himself with; he had been orphaned at birth. Family was a concept lost on him, and Rish too for that matter. It was something that they identified with in each other.

Quinly pressed on with his explanation. "Ratna's protection racket is possibly appearing less good value for money in a city that is under quarantine and policed by the city watch's martial law."

Stefon clucked his tongue ruefully. "You know Ratna, Quinly. He won't forget this type of betrayal from these people quickly or easily, and he'll make them pay. This quarantine won't last forever, and then these people will suffer for their shortsightedness."

"Easy for you to say, Stefon." Quinly put his cup aside and leaned forward. "You've come a long way since we first met, and by the Gods you're resourceful, but you don't know how this plague has affected the people of this city. The normal people, I mean."

Stefon held out his hands in supplication. "Don't get me wrong: I don't care if these people pay or not. As long as they don't fire arrows at me when they renege!"

As Quinly was about to reply, he stopped and looked over Stefon's right shoulder. Someone was approaching with a slow and laboured, shuffling gait. Stefon turned to see an old man with crazy white hair sprawling across his head and the haunted look of defeat in his eyes. He came and sat in the seat recently vacated by the elf. In his emaciated hands he clutched a canvas sack that looked to be holding coins.

"Master Gill, this is my friend Stefon. He is here to make the collection we tried to avoid this evening." The old man stiffened, but Stefon could see no fear in his eyes. He wasn't scared; he was resigned.

"Have no fear, old man," Stefon told him anyway. "I'm not here to run you through. I'm just here for Ratna's money. It's only business."

"This is my business," croaked the old man. "This is the best of what I have left. I won't see the end of this quarantine…"

"Come now, Gill!" Quinly interrupted.

"No, Quinly. I'm old but I'm not deluded. I'm no fool! This plague will eat this city until nothing moves. And the people will be trapped in here to rot. If this rain had ever stopped, they'd have razed this city to the ground by now. You mark my words, boy! Wahib is doomed."

"I kind of doubt that, old man," said Stefon. "True, down here in poortown people are falling ill, but that's the sanitation, or lack of it. The powers-that-be know what is going on. Once they find the cause, it will be removed. The soothsayers and spiritual leaders won't stand by and allow a plague to grow in Wahib. And they began this quarantine to ensure the safety of the rest of Ipsica."

"Oh, the ignorance of youth is blissful tolerance. You think that polytheist up the river in Otack gives a toss of a coin over your life or mine? Emperor Ibn Sa-Jiek won't budge a muscle while this plague is contained here—not until it's touching him, his wives, his concubines or his innumerable bastard children up the river in that city of bastards."

Taken aback by the bitterness of Gill's tirade, Stefon looked at Quinly.

"Gill lost his son to the plague last week."

"I'm frail, I'm weak and I'm soon for another world," Gill continued, his voice reduced in volume and ferocity. A weakness seemed to swell through him, heaving a sigh. "My son was in his twenty-sixth year and strong like an ox, but he grew sick so quickly. What we thought was a chest cold from the autumn rains turned nasty overnight. Before we knew what was happening, his chest was rattling and he could hardly raise a breath. Then his vision failed, his eyes turning milky. When he fell into the stupor and the fever came, we knew it was hopeless.

"No one came to help. Our calls for the priests fell on deaf ears. When I went up there myself, men with sticks beat me back from the steps of the Tower of Light. By the time I returned to my home, he was deep in the fever, screaming almost constantly; his eyes and ears bleeding. It lasted less than an hour and he was gone.

"Only then did priests come to take my son away. They were wearing thick cloaks and their faces were covered by wet silk. They had protective runes and symbols tied to every limb. They fear this plague as much as anyone does. Faith is no protection, boy."

Stefon sat still and listened to the man's story with sympathy, sensing Gill's pain and anguish. He knew the money in the bag on Gill's lap meant next to nothing to him now with the loss of his son. "I meant no disrespect, Master Tanner. I'm sorry for your loss. But you understand: killing me and my friends serves nothing."

Quinly held his hand aloft. "That was my fault, Stefon. I suggested I could help him out for a nominal fee. I truly had no clue Ratna would give such a standard job to a seasoned pro such as yourself. And I'm sure Bauf and the others were terrified when you and your friends turned up. Bauf never struck me as easily panicked, but evidently he was."

Stefon nodded. "It's not a mistake he'll repeat."

Taking his leave of them, Stefon took Ratna's payment from Gill and headed down to the main floor.

What Gill had said about the emperor probably rang true. Ipsica was a unique place. The southern coast of their whole continent tended more toward cliffs than coves, bays or beaches; and that included the entire coastal region of Southern Shenmadock across the border. As a result, the Inlet of Corfel served as the main conduit for seagoing trade from Boyareen, Peena and the other southern lands. The port city of Corfel Scar, dominating the estuary of the

Blue River, was therefore the busiest, most opulent and most successful trading port in the land. That monopoly on the trading lanes of the South Sea had given the nation of Ipsica centuries of valuable traffic, and the populace had grown as a result.

Shenmadock's covetous eyes had frequently turned toward the jewel of Ipsica that was Corfel Scar, and many wars had been fought over the ownership of the docklands. Corfel Scar's monopoly had lasted until the development of the floating port at the cliffs of Hightower in the Shenmadock Duchy of Unedar. Since then the trading prices and levies had been lessened in Corfel Scar in order to compete with Hightower Port.

In similar fashion to Shenmadock's behaviour, when the port at Hightower had been finished, Emperor Ibn Sa-Jiek's grandfather had turned his greedy eyes toward Unedar, and another decade of war had followed. Historically, when nations were nothing more than dozens of principalities, Unedar had been the battleground of shifting borders for decades.

Regardless of this history of constant warring, peace currently existed between the two nations, and the border remained firmly along the spine of the Southern Range.

The high level of national income brought in by Corfel Scar, both privately to the populace in commerce and directly to the emperor via port tax and levies, had swelled the population exponentially over the decades, until now there remained no public land throughout the nation. Other than the main thoroughfares and roads, every inch of Ipsican soil was owned by someone, and usually someone wealthy. Farmers, peasants and freemen alike often worked these lands and were granted their own plots, acting as vassals to the landlord.

Such a massive expansion in population, and this absence of public spaces, meant that the Ipsican military were hard pressed to police the more rural regions of their nation. The emperor therefore decreed that Ipsican landlords were to be given carte blanche to defend their own lands and vassals. If trespassers were discovered, it became fully within the landlord's power to have them killed, and there was nothing that the military or emperor could do about it. Only the royal family and members of the Ipsican military were allowed to travel throughout the nation without fear of reproach.

Due to these peculiarities of law, the roads of Ipsica became treacherous to travel without a hefty escort, for banditry was rife therein. The Ipsican military tended to patrol only the roads and the cities, and so it was no surprise to Stefon that Wahib City had the ways and means to maintain this quarantine.

Mulling this over, Stefon descended the stairs to the ground floor and found Rish wasting money at a roulette table and Jewl at the bar sipping at another whiskey, two empty glasses at his elbow. The three made their way outside into the constant rain, reticent to repeat the feat of becoming soaked to the skin. But Ratna would not wait for his payoff and another stop was inevitable before their night was over.

Chapter Four
Employment

"I don't like it!" Manic grumbled.

"I understand," Andi empathised, "but like you said before, you've got nothing better to do. Like me, you're a traveller with skills for sale. You came down to Shenmadock looking for work and that seems to be what we've both found. It might not be what we would have chosen, and being threatened with the hangman's noose is hardly a good interview, but we're sure to be paid well enough."

Manic huffed out a laugh and took a deep draught of his honeyed ale. "I never intended to get caught up in duchy business." He cast a meaningful glare across the long alehouse floor at the back of their new companion as the cleric stood at the bar awaiting service. "A court cleric? We may as well join the local guardhouse and sweep floors for a living."

Andi shook her head, sipping her watered wine. She couldn't abide the diluted flavour, but understood the need to take it a little easier on the drink following her previous drunken enterprise almost landing her on the gallows.

Obviously they had chosen a different inn from the Ragged Boar for this tipple.

Fleetingly, Andi's mind jogged back to the meeting on the bailey grounds, when she and Manic had emerged from the caverns beneath Hightower, the *Baerv* in their possession. The image of the cowled stranger, and the curious relationship between the duke and his cousin the magistrate sprang to mind. Andi didn't know, or care, what any of it might mean for Reinhart, but she knew one thing for sure: something about the younger Magistrate Jakrat told her that he wasn't to be trusted. And the importance the man had placed on the difference between value and worth regarding the clearly valueless *Baerv* was of concern too, but she didn't know why.

Regardless, escaping the catacombs with that gem in their possession had given them the opportunity to avoid being hanged for a murder they had not committed.

And then Reinhart had made his pitch: fifty gold coins upfront to head northeast into the deep woods marking the rise of the Southern Range of mountains. Just go there, look at what could be seen and report back to Reinhart, then receive another 250 coins. Apparently Reinhart had a vested interest in what the people of the neighbouring country were up to along their border.

Andi hadn't asked what made him suspicious of the Ipsicans. A period of peace over the past two decades had followed many centuries of historical conflict between Ipsica and the Shenmadock Duchy of Unedar. The conflict was focused along the disputed border, which was marked by the wooded mountain range, leading from the Choatian Mountains to the coastline east of Reinhart's town of Hightower.

And now Reinhart wanted information about that very border! This suggested to Andi that he feared movements along the geographical divide suggesting some misdemeanour or infringement of treaty, an escalation of which might preclude a resumption of hostilities. Then, only serving to convince her more, Reinhart had insisted his junior advisor accompany them "to provide local knowledge of the area they were venturing to". Reinhart had said Cleric Eidos was a navigator and court advisor, but to Andi he looked more like a soldier, which suggested a military advisor first and foremost. Either way, Cleric Eidos was not talkative.

Almost an entire head above six feet tall and with shoulders like a castle wall, the cleric struck a more impressive figure than your average court advisor. His dress armour was well looked-after and appeared highly effective too, although it bore no marks of recent significant combat. A mane of gold hair tumbled to his neck, and a well-trimmed beard and moustache framed a face of fine features.

But Eidos had hardly spoken since they left Reinhart's keep in the late afternoon, having spent the best part of three hours looking over charts and maps of the mountain range in question. Reinhart had mentioned a series of rumoured abductions from the farmlands of Unedar recently and even hinted at the possibility of slavers and bandits marauding through the area, but that didn't have Andi fooled. In fact, it made no sense: slavers this far south? There was no market for slaves down here, so who would they be sold to? And it was a fool who would travel across the northeast pass beyond Choat with a train of slaves in tow without an army of mercenaries afoot. That would be pretty hard to disguise.

No, something else was going on, and being unable to figure it out irritated Andi.

Manic pushed his empty tankard away and glanced impatiently at Eidos's back. He had been gone for a while, waiting for a serving girl to notice his need for attention. "What do you think the rooms are like here?" Manic asked, exasperated.

"I'm sure he's not actually going to take all night at the bar," Andi assured him.

"Regardless, I need a night of sleep in an honest bed before we set off on some foolhardy wilderness trek. My build isn't made for sleeping in mud or under trees. If this place is as good as any then we might as well stay here." His thick, gnarled hand slammed palm down on the tabletop. "Service!" he bellowed. Almost immediately a serving girl appeared at his elbow. Manic indicated Eidos standing at the bar and the smudge-faced girl scampered off to see to him. Manic grinned at Andi.

"You're a bully," she told him.

"I am not; I'm a motivational speaker."

Eidos returned to the table and sat in a chair with his back to the rest of the room; something Andi had never been comfortable doing. She could tell this man was used to having his back watched for him. The drinks arrived shortly after.

"What say you, Eidos, to staying here for the night before we set out in the morning?" Andi enquired. "We can breakfast early and prepare for a long day in the saddle, and head out after the farming wagons have cleared the ford uptown."

The cleric stared at Andi for a moment; she was unable to tell if he was even mulling the proposition, so blank were his eyes. "Seems to make sense to me," he said finally, then took a polite swallow of ale and replaced his tankard, wiping the excess froth from his neatly trimmed beard. "I can pay for the rooms, if that's where this is going."

Manic shrugged. "Well, as you're offering..."

It hadn't actually crossed Andi's mind to get the cleric to pay for the rooms, but it made sense. So far, they had been well fed at the keep before they left, been given a decent package of dried provisions, and had even been loaned two horses and a pony, although Andi was dubious about the dwarf's ability to ride despite his boasting. Their horses were hobbled outside, and showing he'd learned something from Manic, Eidos called the innkeeper's son over and instructed him to stable the horses for the night, care for the tack and bridle, and give them a decent groom while he was at it.

Andi sipped at her watered wine and looked at her two most recent companions: one a strange-looking dwarf with a broad moustache and even broader wide-brim hat; the other a giant of a man who said little and seemed to think even less. But both were dangerous beings to come up against on a battlefield—she could tell that much immediately—and she was happy to do all the thinking instead of the fighting. At least while it served her purposes to do so.

Master Ibn Ratna Giri was not a happy man. Stefon and Rish knew his fury was not directed at them, but that didn't make them any more comfortable about remaining in a room with Ratna while he was in full flow.

"Who do these people think they are? How dare they! How dare they believe they can renege on me?" His mug was once again snatched from his ample desk and he shaped up to smash it against the wall. Once more he regained self-control, and plonked the mug back where it belonged.

It seemed like five minutes since Rish had explained about the ambush and the ensuing skirmish. Stefon had placed the money on the desk as soon as they entered Ratna's chambers, but that didn't seem to placate him. It would appear that Master Gill was not the first trader or Guild member to withhold payment for Ratna's local "protection". Stefon thought it best not to tell Ratna that Gill was still alive. It was information that would only lead to Gill being killed to make an example of him.

As though reading Stefon's mind, Ratna fumed, "Perhaps I need to make an example out of someone!" He stalked the room impatiently.

Standing easily four inches beyond six feet, Ratna struck a remarkable first impression. His attire was always of the finest material, bedecked with the most expensive and rare fixings, toggles and jewels. His thinning black hair was lacquered to his spherical pate using oils and waxes laced with fruit extracts. He still had his own teeth—quite an accomplishment in his thirty-seventh year—and despite being overweight was still quick and powerful.

Only on closer inspection could one see the burst blood vessels across his nose that told of his weakness for drinking spirits in large quantities. The bulbous eyes and horrid breath were testament to an unhealthy diet, and his knees were weak beneath him in cold weather.

Ibn Ratna Giri was Wahib's most prodigious businessman, having ties to government and trade throughout the city, but in reality he was nothing short of a bully, a cutthroat, a thief and a gangster. He had a hand in every racket going within Wahib, and sometimes beyond. Rumours suggested he was almost as powerful as any blood-born noble of the East, and others still hinted that his wealth even surpassed most of those. And a man became so rich and powerful by concentrating on the little things, and by not letting someone like Gill escape his wrath following such an affront as occurred that night.

"Do you have any idea how much money I've lost on people not coughing up?" The two shook their heads as Ratna retook his seat. "Me neither! But I bet it's a tidy sum!" He slammed his fist on the desk and went to grab his mug again, but stopped. The anger seemed to seep from him and he rested forward on braced elbows, staring at Stefon and Rish. "Truth is, this quarantine is eating into almost everyone. I was never prepared for it, and it can't be allowed to last."

"I hear no word of a cure yet," Rish offered. "Or even a pattern to those who are susceptible to the effects of the illness. It seems so random."

"But these things always have a pattern," Ratna mused. "It's time I got more proactive." Stefon's stomach sank. He could sense something coming that he wasn't going to like. "How would you two like to get rich?"

Stefon stiffened, trying frantically to think of a way out of what was coming next. However, nothing came to him before Rish said, "Always, Ratna. How rich?"

"Fairly reeking, Rish. I'll hand over 20,000 gold coins to you if you can get this quarantine lifted. I don't care what you have to do, but do it."

There it was: an impossible job. And Rish had just accepted it for them both.

The two friends took their leave of Ratna and made their way down to the busy tavern that marked the east section of his ground floor. The tavern consisted of a massive, sprawling room with numerous support columns and crossbeams to guard against a collapse from the floor above. A dozen wide wagon wheels were hung from the ceiling by dull chains, with numerous candles adhered to illuminate the room during the evening. Some of the biggest real-glass windows ever installed in a building not associated with a religion lined the north-facing exterior wall, and a large, expansive serving bar dominated the south wall. Portions of the bar were reserved for sitting to eat, but for the most part serving girls of varying descriptions rushed back and forth collecting and delivering tankards of ale, bottled spirits, decanters of wine or platters of exotic foods to the many tables strewn randomly across the floor. Some alcoves were placed against the east wall, secluded and dark, but the rest of the room was open and spacious.

A rumbling noise undulated through the room from the assembled mix of traders, nobles, rogues and wealthy commoners—or at least commoners with some semblance of influence or importance among their peers. Status alone was not the entrance ticket to dine or drink at Ratna's place: you had to have influence; to be a player in the games of politics, money or trade in Wahib. If you had no stake in one enterprise or another then Ratna's place held no interest for you.

At this time of night, the mix of people in Ratna's was at the most diverse. Enough wine would have been imbibed to engender even the most arrogant of nobles to consider a commoner worthy of greeting, and the decorum amongst Ratna's patrons was always strongly policed. Three large half-orcs stood near the entrance that they stepped through, giving Rish and Stefon the once-over before recognising them and paying them no more heed.

A quick scan of the faces at the tables nearest Stefon located Jewl reclining with another whiskey in hand, munching hungrily on a chicken leg. At the large, round table with the dwarf was a tall, rangy human with closely cropped hair, a plain but cleanly shaven face and sharp eyes. Stefon recognised Rebrof immediately.

Stefon had first met Rebrof just over a year ago at the end of the summer festivals. The man had fallen in with an associate of Rish's by the name of Pryn, having left service with the City Guard that summer. As a young man, Rebrof had joined the City Guard as the son of a local squire, and had subsequently risen through the ranks quickly, befitting a man of some station. But he had quickly tired of service and mustered out as soon as his commission permitted.

For reasons he often struggled to put his finger on, Stefon found he disliked the man. Something about Rebrof's mentality, outlook or demeanour irked him, although Rish never seemed to have a problem with him. In truth, Rish didn't have a problem with anyone he felt he could effectively bully or boss. Despite Rebrof's military background, status as the son of a noble and experience in a position of command, he was surprisingly weak-willed and seemed keen enough to take direction sooner than assert his own authority. He followed Rish's orders and accepted his commands with humility and grace, but he was slow on the uptake and lacked the initiative or creativity to make the grade in Stefon's eyes. Rebrof's blade was just as useful in his scabbard as it was when being deployed.

But Rish saw fit to keep the lanky human around, and while Stefon felt he could not rely on Rebrof's sword arm, he had never had reason to doubt Rish's judgement on such things. Either by luck or judgement, Rish usually got it right in the long run.

"Evening, chaps!" Rish greeted them as he and Stefon approached their table. A serving girl asked them their pleasure as they sat, immediately hurrying away to fetch the ordered drinks and a platter of bread and cheese. "We've got more work," Rish told Jewl and Rebrof. Stefon remained silent, the close heat of the place making him uncomfortable. He was ready for his drink when it arrived.

"What is it this time?" Jewl grumbled. "Tell me it's nothing boring again. I really can't demean myself any longer by doing more of Ratna's running around. He can afford to employ lackeys to get ambushed collecting his ill-gotten gold. We're better than that."

"Too true," Rish grinned. "You'll be pleased to hear it's far more exciting, and should put us on the road to being rich."

That got Jewl's attention immediately, and even managed to pique Rebrof's interest in proceedings. His weasel eyes fixed on Rish instead of his drink, and he licked his thin lips. It appeared he had some ambition after all.

"It's a foolish task and will get us killed," threw in Stefon.

"Ignore him," Rish said. "He's never liked the idea of doing something just to get rich." He looked at Stefon accusingly. "You've an awful streak of moral righteousness running through your scoundrel spine, my friend."

Stefon could only shrug, for it was true. "All I'm saying is," he pressed, "we're going to need more numbers. This task is bigger than even us four."

"Not necessarily," Rish argued. "A smaller number asking

difficult questions is actually far more likely to go unnoticed."

Jewl leaned forward, moving his whiskey beaker aside with the back of his hairy hand. "If one of you doesn't tell me what we're talking about, I'm going to start knocking heads together."

"It's nothing we can talk about here." Stefon jumped in before Rish could say a word. "We'll talk about it en route."

"En route where, exactly?" Rebrof asked. Rish also looked at him expectantly.

"Well, I got the impression that our friend Captain Bunnelshut..."

"You mean *your* friend Captain Bunnelshut," Rish amended.

Stefon shrugged. "Whichever it may be, I got the impression he knows more than the average man on the street does about the goings-on in the seedier portions of this city. He's as good a place to start as I can think of.

"And also, regardless of what you might think, I believe we'll need more help on this one. We need to speak with Pryn and that other short girl who works for Ratna."

"That girl Brooss?" Jewl asked. "The engineer? She's odd."

Brooss was indeed an engineer, and by all accounts a good student. She had researched most siege and war engines devised during the last three decades and was one of Ratna's brightest sparks regarding his wagon fleet. It was said that Brooss had redesigned most of the wagon bays and carriages to make them more defensible on long journeys. If pirates and thieves were foolish enough to try and scupper one of Master Ibn Ratna Giri's teamsters on the roads outside Wahib they were sure to face an almost insurmountable task. The only way to stop one of Brooss's wagons would be to smash the wheels off or tear them entirely in half using pit traps or falling trees. Of course, such conduct would almost certainly render the wagons entirely unusable, and make the contents difficult to shift— if they survived the attack at all.

In summary, Brooss's wagons could carry slightly less, but were never attacked.

Ratna kept her around to help with anything tricky, but mainly to retain her expertise for the time it might be needed for something more serious. Ratna was nothing if not prepared for every outcome.

Rish beckoned over one of Ratna's "go-for" boys, who were tasked to loiter around the bar in preparation for any instruction from the businessmen or racketeers alike. He instructed the young, freckled boy to find Brooss and tell her to locate Rish's associate Pryn and meet them both at Stefon's home first thing in the morning. The lad scurried off among the patrons and was lost from sight.

"I don't quite understand what you hope to learn from Quinly other than what he's already told you," Rish said as they huddled inside the small carriage they had borrowed from Ratna's stable for the trip to Bunnelshut's establishment. The rain continued to fall heavily outside, although the wind from earlier in the afternoon had abated somewhat. Stefon braced himself as the carriage passed over another series of badly arranged cobbles and stones in the road, the steel-wrapped wooden wheels protesting loudly as the two horses dragged them up a small incline out of the commercial district toward poortown.

Next to him Jewl sat quietly, almost pensive, as he stared at the nighttime city streets through the open window, ignoring the licks of rain that intermittently lashed in through the gap. Somewhere above them at the front of the carriage roof, Rebrof was steering the team of two through the rain. Of the four, he was easily the most experienced at the head of a carriage.

"He seemed to know a little more about it than one would expect, that is all," Stefon explained. "And I respect his opinion of such things. I expect to learn nothing more than where to look next. Quinly has always had his fingers in numerous pies. He's bound to know if something strange is going on with this quarantine." Stefon rubbed excess rainwater from his short, black hair with the palm of his left hand, flicking drips out of the carriage window. "At least that's the impression he gave me earlier."

Rish nodded his understanding and Jewl remained stoic, saying nothing.

Jewl was unlike any dwarf Stefon had ever met. As a species they were often short-tempered and aggressive, but certainly impatient and abrasive. Jewl was sometimes that way, but his moods were varied and often fluctuated from introspective—as he was now; possibly a dwarf's least characteristic temperament—to outright giddiness. Those who knew him only a little found the lottery of his moods discomforting. Stefon found it refreshing. He liked that Jewl was unpredictable.

"Look at the state of you two!" Rish commented from across the carriage. "If you don't cheer up, people are going to think your faces are to blame for the weather. You'd think I'd sold us into slavery or something. All we need to do is use our special approach to this type of situation to…glean what afflicts these people. We can encourage the imperial chirurgeons and the priests to improve their efforts. Maybe we can even sneak into the hospital building uptown and take a look at the notes ourselves.

"Heck, Pryn has a little skill in anatomy. Post-mortem, he calls it." Rish looked out the window for a second, while no-one replied. "Saw him do it once. Damn gruesome stuff. It's brutal, you know? I know more than one priest who'd consider it sacrilegious."

The carriage lurched to a sudden stop, the horses loudly protesting at the treatment. A glance through the rain to his left told Stefon they were at Bunnelshut's for the second time that night. It was nearing midnight and the establishment had more people leaving than waiting to enter. It would be a good time to catch Quinly.

Moving quickly, Stefon pushed open the low carriage door and jumped into the rain that had gathered in the guttering, dirty water splashing up the sides of his leather boots. Without stopping he rushed in under the cover of the building front, followed quickly by Rish and Jewl. Rebrof called a stable hand over and ordered him to keep the carriage dry but handy, for they would be leaving soon. Intimidated by the tall human, the boy rushed to do his bidding, leaving Rebrof to follow his companions into the darkness of Quinly's bar.

Once inside it took them only moments to find the rakish Captain Bunnelshut sitting in a dark alcove at the back, going over the night's gambling account books. Beside him sat one of his team of underhand accountants, employed more for their creativity than their diligence.

As Stefon and Rish sat on the bench opposite the two men, Jewl and Rebrof retreated to a watchful but discreet distance; Jewl loitered nearby against a thick pillar whilst Rebrof waited at the bar that was now being cleaned up. Service had clearly ceased a few minutes before.

"Two visits in the space of one sundown. I'm flattered," Quinly said, resting back from his work and rubbing his eyes. He had dropped his wide hat onto the bench next to him and looked much the worse for wear at this time of night. With a motion of his hand, he ushered the accountant away, leaving the three of them alone.

"I regret this isn't a social visit either," nodded Stefon. "I need to twist your ear over something you mentioned earlier."

"The plague again?"

"Not so much. This quarantine."

"Ah! Thought so." Quinly shook his head. "Well, I don't know what I can tell you of interest, to be honest, but ask away."

"We appreciate that, but we know you'll be able to tell us who we should talk to," said Rish. "How about that?"

Something in Quinly's manner gave Stefon the impression he was hiding something. He looked tired and would probably have covered it up more effectively had he not been on the verge of dropping off to sleep right then and there. But he *was* tired, and Stefon found himself able to read the man better than he had in the past. He seemed uncomfortable with the topic, glancing round to see if they were being overheard before he answered.

"I don't know why you're asking, but I'll tell you this for free: some things don't ring true with this quarantine and a person who starts sticking his nose in might not live too long to regret it, if you take my meaning."

"It's not subtle," Stefon said drily.

"Well, the first odd thing I came across when people started coming to me for help was that some tradesmen favoured by the royal court in Wahib seemed privy to the quarantine ahead of time." He looked from Rish to Stefon. "Before it came into force they were prepared for the difficulties and had brought in stores for the winter ahead. Those men and their families are not suffering the same as our friend Gill."

"So?" Rish asked.

"Well, they should be. Even those who have saved previously and were suitably thrifty immediately after the quarantine came into effect are suffering. I'd wager that those who were able to import enough to tide them through to winter were given foreknowledge of the quarantine."

Stefon sat back slowly, letting the ramifications of that information wash over him. Rish looked from him to Quinly and back, obviously confused. "So?"

"Rish, think about it," said Stefon. "When the authorities discovered how bad this illness was it had only been around for little more than a day; two at an absolute maximum. People started being reported fatally ill on..."

"It was a Fifthday, before week's end," Quinly offered.

"Right. And that crazy church brought it to attention at their Sun Day ceremony that they have every week, when most are recovering from Sixthday drinking binges."

"Religion? You mean The Light?" Quinly again provided.

"That's them. Those fanatics spoke of the coming of the End of Days, and then the authorities sealed the gates Firstday morning of the next week. Literally hours were involved. Two days for the spread of the news at most before the quarantine came down. So how did those merchants and importers know so early to prepare for a lengthy cessation of trade like this?" Stefon turned back to Quinly. "They were tipped off. They were informed."

"I think so," he agreed. "And they were informed with enough notice to get increased stores bought and imported before the gates were shut. That kind of thing doesn't happen quickly."

"So someone knew there'd be a quarantine before the illness was fully discovered?" Rish asked. "How's that possible?"

"Maybe they knew about the quarantine because they knew about the illness that much earlier?" Quinly offered.

"That makes no sense," said Stefon. "This plague is deadly, and very quickly so. If you know anything about this illness then you know the nature of it. You know how deadly it is. If those traders, and more importantly the people who tipped them off, knew about the nature of the plague before the quarantine, they'd have hightailed it out of Wahib. There's no way they'd have stayed around. It's not like they're benefiting from staying; they're just not suffering as much as they should be yet."

"That's right too." Rish rubbed his forehead. "This is giving me a headache."

"There must be something more to be gained by the

people involved in order for them to hang around in this mess. We need to speak with these merchants, or maybe the person who tipped them off," Stefon said impatiently.

"OK then," Rish agreed, happy something was settled upon.

"But we can't! If we go straight for the jugular then whoever tipped the merchants off is sure to find out sooner than we can act. We have to be more…" he searched for the word, "circumspect."

"Just a second," Rish interjected. "What happens if the quarantine had nothing to do with the illness?" Stefon and Quinly looked back blankly. "You know, what if it was a coincidence? Poor timing, whatever?"

After a moment, Stefon agreed. "That would make a strange kind of logic. It would explain how quickly they seemed to react to the plague before the true extent was really known. But if that's true, it makes our current situation worse. And consider this: what if we have the cart before the horse? What if the quarantine wasn't a reaction to the plague, but the plague was simply necessary to get away with a city-wide shutdown?"

"Who the hell would benefit from that?" Quinly asked incredulously.

Stefon was silent for a long time, mulling the situation over. "No one," he agreed. Just as it seemed Quinly was about to nod off, Stefon made a decision. "There's nothing else for it. We simply have to speak to one of those merchants. One of the well-to-do ones. If we speak to one then we won't expose ourselves too much and we just might learn something. And if it does arouse suspicion maybe that will actually help flush out who we *really* need to talk to."

Chapter Five
A Watching Brief

Shen Utah slumbered. A canopy of dark clouds traversed the sky above the ancient, walled capital of Shenmadock, but no rain would fall tonight. Reaching toward the clouds like slender, yearning fingers stretched the spires of the Royal Palace, a reminder of ages past when the nation was ruled by a monarchy. Nestling beneath the shadows of the palace, the melting pot of cultural modernity that was the Temple Link area crawled to the walls, resplendent with just as many theatres and music halls as churches or temples. On the rise to the east sat the wealthy regions known imaginatively as the East End, with the High Wall District beyond. All the money and the power of this mighty city resided in these areas, but the heart of Shen Utah beat within the western ventricle known as The Lows.

The narrow streets, no more than lanes and paths, were testament to the centuries that The Lows had stood against progress, and the architecture of those stone buildings tended toward an authenticity far beyond anything one could stumble across within the grander thoroughfares of Temple Link or beyond—much to the learned aristocracy's chagrin.

The Lows crept across the western portion of the city from beneath the ancient walls all the way to the fisheries and docks, and were both the beating heart and churning guts of Shen Utah. For all the noise the aristocracy might make about their fledgling democracy and growing culture of change, they could never escape from the reality that it was The Lows that fed the city of Shen Utah and kept her breathing, from the mire of the gutters to the shanties of the outer city beyond the walls. The Lows and their inhabitants, that was.

One such inhabitant shifted his weight slightly to relieve the pins-and-needles in his right calf, and settled once more in the shadow of a gabled dormer overlooking a small square in the depths of The Lows. Night shrouded the city, and the shadow of the gabling was darker still. No one could see or hear the skulking form of the young thief Acaelian as he sat his watching vigil over the square below.

Two hours or more had gone by during his wait, but this had passed like a swallow on the wing, as time spent watching over Claudia always did. And as always there were things Acaelian really needed to be about, but he felt powerless to draw himself away.

In the earlier hours after sundown, the working women of The Lows known as Wheels frequented the streets, alleys and lanes in an attempt to draw patrons into their brothels. The later hours saw no real need to drum up business.

Despite it being the evening of a Fourthday, the night Acaelian always thought of as the gateway to the weekend, business on the street seemed slow, and Claudia stayed out on the thoroughfares talking with her Wheel friends as they smoked their tobacco or chewed their Strangemeal concoctions, trying to dull their senses for the indignations some nights' work might bring. Flying in the face of a stereotypical whore, Claudia never partook in the same habits as her friends, and she also shied away from the use of the term "whore" itself. Acaelian was always careful to refer to her as a Wheel, if he had to refer to that part of her life at all.

A series of lamplights helped illuminate her face as she nodded seriously at some comment made by her friend. The cold of the night had drawn rouge on her soft cheeks and her breath plumed on the chill night air. Suddenly she broke into laughter, her eyes shining with mirth and her nose wrinkling as her laugh petered out. The noise of her delight climbed the walls of the city and passed Acaelian in his hiding place, and it was music to his soul.

Looping arms with her friends, they turned inside the brothel, Grig's Wheelhouse, as a group of sailors rounded the corner onto the square. The remaining Wheels began hollering the off-duty seamen over, offering all sorts of lewd things that soured Acaelian's moment of yearning.

His elvish features darkened with his mood, black eyes becoming jets in the night. He turned from his vigil and climbed soundlessly up the tiles of the merchant's building. In spite of the advancing hours, Acaelian had a job to do. Using his weight carefully, the elf Glimmer—as the thieves of Shen Utah were known—moved to the far edge of the roof and dropped effortlessly over the guttering. His featherlike weight caused no strain on the roof. He dropped to the windowsill below, and then the lower awning. Finally he plunged the ten feet to the stone street beneath. The basement window nearby was his entry to the merchant's house, and the promise of gold coins within, but as he moved toward the flat window a shadow passed across him from above and a huge weight thundered down, smashing him against the far lane wall and collapsing him unceremoniously to his rump.

Standing over him was the sneering, slender form of Grimlaw, a weighty-looking bag in his clutches. "Too late again!" Grimlaw chided. He hefted the bag to emphasise his point. Once again Grimlaw had snaffled a steal from under Acaelian's nose, and only his procrastination upon the roof was to blame.

Grimlaw's cruel grin spoke of the satisfaction he gleaned from outdoing his fellow Glimmer. He stowed the score in his backpack, keeping a close eye on Acaelian as the elf regained his feet and tried in vain to brush away the filth from his fall. He could feel a damp patch on his skull where he had collided with the wall, and a quick investigation with his fingers produced bloody fingertips from within his matted black hair.

"Looks a nasty gash, my friend," Grimlaw gloated. "This merchant certainly has been doing his work. I'll have a good weekend on this score, for sure."

Acaelian held his tongue. Grimlaw didn't even deserve his derision.

"See you back at the Guild, loser!" With that, Grimlaw looked up and down the street and then took to his heels with a laugh.

Acaelian let him go. If he had been more hotheaded, he would have broken his fellow Glimmer's nose, retrieved his score and damned the consequences. Strictly speaking, Grimlaw had broken a Guild law by muscling in on Acaelian's score, for the Guild controlled the regions afforded to each working Glimmer, in order to avoid precisely this type of overlapping of activity. It wasn't the first time Grimlaw had pressed upon Acaelian's territory, for the teenage human was an ambitious, hateful and ruthless thief.

But Acaelian had seen his type before. Despite being within his moral rights to exact revenge on Grimlaw for pinching his score, Acaelian knew it was one of the most important rules of the Guild that Glimmers never mugged, pickpocketed or burgled each other. If Grimlaw wanted to flout the rules, that was his prerogative and he would fall foul of it in time. There was no need for Acaelian to compromise his own skewed morals. Finer Glimmers than Grimlaw had crossed Acaelian in the decade he had been an adolescent elf thief in Shen Utah, and each one had received his just desserts; the same would be true for Grimlaw. The city of Shen Utah was ruthless, but she was just, too.

Nonetheless cursing his bad luck, Acaelian gathered himself and turned down the street somewhat dejectedly.

It was some hours later that he found himself on the dock wall of the fisheries as the morning boats set sail for the estuary of the River Jow, seeking their daily catch. The slow movement of the waves against the bows of the ships as they cut free of the docklands settled his mind. The docks were full of morning activity, but would soon calm down, awaiting the fishing vessels' return.

Acaelian still looked a boy, but had the experience and cunning afforded to him by more than twenty years in this world—which still made him an adolescent by elf standards. His dark hair was kept cropped short, and the bleeding on his scalp had abated after a short while. The lump would take longer to go away.

A half-smile crept across his face. Despite an impressively silent approach, the elf knew that an apprentice spy was creeping along the wall of the harbour at his back. As his stalker neared, Acaelian said, "You're improving."

A frustrated growl from behind him confirmed that his friend Click had sought him out. The young boy sat heavily on the wall next to him, looking unimpressed. "I hate that. I imagine you can probably hear me no matter which street of this city I move along."

"I don't know; we'll have to try someday. But seriously, that was good. You're improving, which is the important thing. I imagine an unsuspecting quarry of yours would not be so lucky as to smell last night's garlic on your breath as you approached from upwind."

Click's eyes closed briefly at the schoolboy error he had made. "Yes, 'It's not always the sound of your approach that will give you away'. I was so careful to make sure to come at you from the west, thus not revealing my shadow. I didn't even think about the wind!"

"The smell isn't strong," comforted Acaelian. "But try to avoid putting the green vein at the heart of the garlic clove in your food, if you've the chance, for this carries the greatest smell on your breath."

"Thank you," Click nodded. He was a quick student. Startlingly bright for a human, Click was a product of The Lows as much as anyone Acaelian had ever seen. He remembered the morning the child had broken into the Guild of Spies. Click's father had been an assassin of some repute, but Acaelian could see from an early age that the boy had no appetite for murder. One had to have a particular set of inbuilt moral neutralities to be a Black Cat, as the assassins of the Guild were known.

Click never showed an aptitude for the dark arts of murder for money, and so his father had taken him as far as he could, imparted as much of his knowledge as he was able to benefit him in the branches of the Guilds, and then cut him adrift. That was the way of things in the Guilds. Once members were old enough to have a chance of fending for themselves, they were pressed into service as messengers and gutter runners for The Lows. This taught them the narrow byways, alleyways and cul-de-sacs of the city, hidden from the average Shen Utah citizen. By the time a child of the Guilds neared ten he or she would know the city by heart, and be able to disappear after two corners in any portion of The Lows. Whether assassin, thief or spy, this was vital.

By the age of ten it was deemed time to select a Guild House to follow. Click had immediately shown enough poise, subtlety and discretion to draw him toward the Guild of Spies, or the Whispers.

It was widely considered that one would never become rich living life as a Whisper, but it was a vital part of the

Guilds. Without the Whispers there would be no flow of information to aid the assassins or the thieves alike. Without the Whispers they would be unable to control any threat to the Guilds. Information was power, and power was vital; and so The Whispers were vital. This meant that the members of the Whisper Guild paid the lowest tithe for membership, and benefitted from the highest protection.

Click was fifteen now, and nearing full membership of the Guild. His ability to stumble across information was impressive. He worked hard to seek it out, but secrets never hid from Click. He would go far, so long as he learned his lessons quickly and avoided the fatal pitfalls a second mistake could lead to.

"So what eats away at you this morning?" Click asked the elven Glimmer.

Acaelian shrugged and forlornly tossed a stone into the harbour. "That shit Grimlaw did it again."

"I knew it!" Click was clearly not surprised. "Well, how can he get away with it? I can't believe…hold on a second. Did you leave it too late again?"

"Of course," Acaelian pined.

"Oh no, Acaelian! What's happening to you? I swear you're the best Glimmer I know. Gareth the night-watchman says you're possibly the most gifted thief ever to run the rooftops of Shen Utah. He says you've the potential to be legendary."

Acaelian turned a dark smile on his friend. "Glimmers who become legendary soon become dead. Assassins benefit from being legendary, for the fear created by the knowledge that such a threat is stalking a victim can result in deadly mistakes. A thief needs to remain incorporeal; nothing more than shadows and glances. I hope I never become legendary."

Click ruffled his blond hair. It was a habit he had. "You know what I mean," he said. "A legend in the Guild."

"Maybe that's why Grimlaw hates me so. He's trying to make a name for himself at my expense. When you become elevated by others, you become a target."

"You really are in a foul mood this morning."

"I know. So anyway, what brings The Lows' best apprentice Whisper to the docks this fine morning?"

"I was looking for you, of course."

Acaelian raised his eyebrows in surprise.

Click shrugged. "Grimlaw rolled into one of the Guild Houses earlier this morning bragging about turning over that fat merchant, and I remembered you were working the mercantile sector this week. I judged from his supercilious grin that something untoward had occurred, so I came here. I remembered that you like to sit by the water when your mind is all a-storm." Click flourished his arms to complete the tale of his arrival.

"Bloody spies," muttered Acaelian, producing another shrug from Click.

"Anyway, the *reason* I sought you out: the Shredder has definitely struck again."

Acaelian's heart jumped in his chest, and for the fleetest of moments his elvish composure faltered. His reaction clearly belied his concern.

"I thought you would want to know sooner rather than later. You missed your merchant score last night because you were watching over Claudia, right?" Acaelian simply nodded. "Well, the news isn't on the street yet, but the last victim they scraped off the cobbles of Temple Link last weekend has been identified: she was a Wheel, one from the northern brothels."

A murderer stalked the city of Shen Utah. More than half a dozen Wheels had been found murdered on the streets of Temple Link, normally a secure and safe environment for any Shen Utah citizen. But now the city trembled with fear at the threat of this brutal and faceless menace, and scandal followed in its shadow. Scandal, for the victims were all women of unfortunate morals, according to the acolytes and priests who uttered sermon after sermon on the topic, in order to assuage the populace's burgeoning fears that they might be next.

The churches and temples considered the unfortunates to be punished for their weaknesses, but Acaelian thought it poignant that the patrons of those victims were spared the temples' wrath. The assumption was that the murderer was picking out those Wheels foolish enough still to be working the richer quarters. Common opinion held that the killer was of higher birth, and resented the presence of "that type of woman" in the beds of the aristocracy.

Acaelian thought it odd that they should openly consider making such a judgement. Had people not considered the dangerous possibility that such an implication might bring the generally pious population of Temple Link into disrepute? The aristocracy carrying on with lowly whores? It would be scandalous!

The murderer himself was brutal and efficient. Dubbed "the Temple Shredder" by the locals, the nature of the murderer's crimes was heinous beyond description. Speculation was rife as to the details, and the City Watch were not being forthcoming in order to confirm the speculation or to quell it.

That the victims were raped was clear. Whether this sexual assault might take place after death was unconfirmed. The bodies were never recognisable, for the victims' faces and chests were hacked into pulp by an axe of some description. But adding to the concern of the populace was the efficiency of the attacks. The sheer amount of damage the killer was able to inflict on the victims spoke of both a frenzied and prolonged attack, but the scene of each crime was in such an area that at most the killer had ten minutes to complete his gruesome task before someone would stumble across him or hear the screams. Yet not once had the attack been witnessed by eye or ear. No, it had always been the case that only the body was found, with blood and entrails frequently painting a grim testimony to the brutal crime.

The entire episode was coloured by wickedness; the Temple Shredder was pure evil.

"I've already told Claudia not to work the Uptown," Acaelian told Click.

"I thought you might. It's just that I've learned something that might throw into question a few things we've taken for granted in this whole mess."

"Go on," encouraged Acaelian, turning on the wall to concentrate properly.

"One of the younger Whispers stumbled across something alarming last weekend, but hadn't thought to sell the information. As such, it didn't take more than a measure of whiskey for him to start regaling his weekend's adventures. He'd headed east into Temple Link late in the evening of Fifthday, trying to pick up a titbit of information here or there. I think he ended up in some old woman's bed, trying to glean some morsel of scandal, but left empty-handed some time before dawn.

"It was as he was skulking from some alley or other in the Temple Link, trying to avoid any unwanted attention from the old woman's husband, that he heard the rattle of a horse and carriage being driven as though bursting from the gates of hell. He chanced a glance from the shadows, and saw the back of a black carriage disappearing into the morning mists.

"He was just about to leave when he saw the mess on the ground. He crept along the side of the street to get a closer look, and was the first to find the victim. The body was hacked to a pulp, with deep cleaves in the face and chest. The clothing was torn and drenched in blood. The cobbles of the lane and the wall were splattered similarly.

"Before he was discovered having found the body, my colleague scrambled away, struggling with what he saw."

Acaelian's eyes shone as his brain worked on the information. "Oh no," the Glimmer muttered. "This doesn't bode well."

"I know," agreed Click. "It's clear that they dumped the body there from that racing carriage. That explains why the killer seems so quick! He murders them elsewhere and somehow dumps both the body and the blood on the street. Maybe even kills them in his little carriage!"

Acaelian stood from the wall and took a few steps away, his hand across his narrowed-lipped mouth in thought, before he said, "I fear it's worse than that, Click."

Chapter Six
Interference

The sun rose over the range of trees far to the east of Hightower on a crisp autumnal morning clear of cloud cover. Despite the bright sunshine, Andi could immediately feel the cold through her riding cloak and knew the wind would start to pick up early. She, Manic and Eidos had broken fast early, saddling up soon after dawn and preparing for the long ride ahead of them.

To the north of the foulberg surrounding Hightower, a road ran through fields tended by farmers and hands from the houses outside the town. According to Eidos, a few miles beyond those fields the road dropped to meet a small hamlet that had grown up centuries before around a ford at the river. The cleric had explained that the ancient descendants of that hamlet had moved south to form the keep that protected them to this day, which was now called Hightower.

A few hundred yards beyond the last of the homes in Hightower's expansive foulberg, the three companions could see a column of wagons and carriages with cavalry escort moving in toward the tower along the main road from the west. The convoy consisted of two heavy carriages and a large baggage wagon at the rear. The cavalry escort was made up of a dozen proud stallions ridden by uniformed soldiers bearing the crest of the royal court of Shenmadock.

These were the royal military guard; loyal protectors of the Shenmadock Lords. A standard-bearer riding at the front of the cavalcade carried the ducal crest of Shen Utah, central eastern duchy of Shenmadock, seat of power for the western realm.

Behind the standard-bearer came a creature Andi had never seen before other than in paintings of legend. The lower torso, covered in downy beige fur, walked proudly on four thick legs. Rising from the shoulders of the quadruped section stood a powerful human torso, muscles glinting in the autumnal morning sun. A broad, flat face adorned a large cranium, topped by a gleaming golden crown. The creature carried a sceptre in the right hand and looked around at the local area as he led the column toward Hightower Keep.

The three companions slowed to get a better look before spurring their mounts on. "Was that a Wemik?" Andi asked nobody in particular.

"Yes, it was the Wemik," replied Eidos. "That was Lord Handee of Shen Utah, Senior Lord of Shenmadock and Principal Lord of the Council of Lords, to give him his full title. He's come for his annual congress with Duke Reinhart."

"So that's Lord Handee?" Andi mused. Everyone had heard of the influential noble, but few of little import ever caught sight of the Wemik in person. He was rumoured to be well over a century old, and the main point of speculation regarding Handee was, more often than not, about exactly how long a Wemik lived. They were a rare breed and no-one but a Wemik truly knew the answer for sure.

"I've never seen a Wemik," said Manic. "Kind of funny-looking."

Andi glanced at Manic, with his broad hat flopping in the breeze and his ridiculous moustache that was pulled into much wider points using beeswax. She laughed to herself as she agreed. "They're certainly individual. Does he walk everywhere he goes?" she asked Eidos.

"Of course not."

"I was going to say, it's surely hundreds of miles to Shen Utah."

"That's probably correct," Eidos agreed. "And it's not a comfortable journey skirting that region of the Choat Range. No, he would normally ride in comfort, probably in the first carriage. The second will contain his advisors and consorts, with the latter wagon carrying his supplies and baggage. Somewhere there shall be a further wagon or two with camp and mess supplies for the escort. They will have no need to enter Hightower and so will remain at camp."

They rode on in silence for a few yards before Andi continued. "What do they talk about—Handee and Reinhart, I mean?"

Eidos pointedly regarded Andi over his shoulder, searching her features for a second before replying. "They have a great deal to discuss at all times, and these meetings are a rare occasion to discuss politics, the law and suchlike in person, rather than through dispatch riders.

"In the hierarchy of Shenmadock, Senior Lord Handee is most influential of all beings. My lord, Duke Reinhart of Unedar, is not without influence, though, for he sits upon the Council of Lords. Each of the five dukes of this land are powerful, and enjoy heavy influence in the Council of Lords at Shen Utah Palace, but the Senior Lord always holds power of veto. For them to meet regularly is important, especially considering the distance from here to Shen Utah. Hightower is the most removed of all duchy capitals. It makes sense for Lord Handee to journey so."

"Right," Andi said. She was silent again, but could not resist asking another question: "So it has nothing to do with us, then?"

Again Eidos regarded her. "I don't follow your meaning: you're just a criminal fulfilling your duty for discharge and penance."

Before Manic could shout his innocence, Andi pressed her point. "That's not...quite accurate, but I'll let it go. My point is that we're not the only people to have been sent this way to scout around, right? I overheard Reinhart and his cousin yearning for Wayfarer Scouts from Shen Utah, and the like. I don't mean to suggest Lord Handee is here to oversee our punishment, but rather that he is here in connection with the reason we are being sent to scout the eastern region."

Eidos hummed in thoughtful agreement. "It's true that rumours of unrest along our eastern borders could not be more poorly timed, but the fact remains that they are simply that: rumours. And until we have something more concrete to report then Handee and Reinhart have nothing concrete to discuss." Again he looked into Andi's eyes to impress his point. "Nobles, and lords in particular, do not waste their time discussing hearsay and conjecture, miss. They deal in facts and facts only."

Andi shrugged to show that the distinction meant little to her. "Whatever you say, Eidos. You know your duke better than I."

Eidos didn't answer, and the subject appeared to be closed to further discussion.

Later they approached a short rise in the land and saw the road fork in two at the crest. The three riders followed the main path over the incline and down a descent steep enough that it might threaten to injure a galloping horse. To their left they saw the other path lead to a series of wide switchbacks that had been dug and furrowed into the drop to make the ascent more manageable to horse and cart teams.

At the base of the drop, a settlement was gathered around a wide but shallow river that flowed steadily from the northeast. The women of the hamlet could be seen going about various tasks that the break of every day brought, and children strove to keep from underfoot for fear of a thick ear. The able-bodied men of the village would be working the fields in close vicinity to the hamlet, and indeed Andi could make out small figures in the distance as she, Manic and Eidos rode down the path and into the settlement, between the simple, modest homes.

Travellers to and from Hightower were frequent upon the road through these parts and so the villagers largely paid the group no heed. Keeping to the clearly marked thoroughfare, they carefully skirted the central portion of the hamlet: a small town square with a heavy-looking stone ornament placed in the middle. Some of the younger children played around the base of the ornament while those slightly older watched the tradesmen in the village, trying to learn what they could.

This provincial lifestyle was something alien to Andi. She had been born to nobility, something akin to royalty in the eyes of the courtiers of Briadranon. Her father, Marquis Edwin de Krasital, had been someone of importance in the city of Krasital on the southern border of Briadranon, many decades ago. She had grown up in courtly fashion, with all the associated trimmings. As a youngster, she was rarely left wanting. Until her father unleashed the fury of his ill-kept temper, that is.

Drawing her attention away from the children at play, Andi shook herself from her reverie, clicking her mount forward. Having obviously noticed her reaction, she heard Manic laugh behind her. "Getting clucky, lass? Maternal instincts kicking in?"

"Not on your life, dwarf!" Andi snapped back playfully, but she felt no joy from the banter. Although she had left that life behind many decades before—her youthful appearance belying her true age—the memories were still fresh of that homelier time. And were she not vigilant, the things she had seen and done since then would cause bitterness and anger to grow in her about the twists of fate that had befallen her path in life. Instead she used those experiences. Everything contributed to make her the person she was today. Andi was, without arrogance or exaggeration, possibly one of the most dangerous people one could meet.

The ford of the hamlet was easily crossed, the water splashing pleasantly across the hooves of their horses as they traversed the wide and shallow stream. More simple dwellings thinned out as they neared the edge of the hamlet. When Eidos led them out of the village heading north, Andi spied a young girl kneeling by the milestone at the roadside some twenty yards outside the village boundaries. She appeared upset about something or other. Normally Andi would have ridden on by, considering it to be none of her business. However, the child saw them coming and obviously recognised the insignia on Eidos's white tabard, for she got to her feet and wiped at the tears that were on her dirty cheeks before rushing forward.

"Sire! Please help me, sire!" When Eidos neared the girl, she slowed and surprised Andi by reaching for the reins of his horse. The proud mare shied at the motion and Eidos did well to control her in order to save trampling the child. The girl snatched her hand back and stood coyly, her hands clasped together before her mouth as she suppressed further tears. Her lower lip trembled terribly.

Eidos settled his mare and dismounted. Signalling for Andi and Manic to wait for him, he knelt by the girl at an unthreatening distance and said, "What can I do for you, girl?"

Her straw-blond hair was dirty with dust from walking along the dry path and her simple clothes looked slept-in. "Sire, are you from the Castle Guard?" she asked.

"Not exactly," Eidos told her. "But I'm probably better than a guard. What can I do to help? Take your time. What's the matter?" He spoke to the child with the practised manner of those comfortable around children.

"My mum was taken away," the child blubbered. "We were in the northern pastures and she was turning the root vegetables. Daddy's been really ill recently. I went with her to help." Tears were streaming down her face again, cleaning fresh tracks in the dust. "I saw all these men leading wagons. Two men on horses left the wagons and rode over to my mother while I played in the long grass nearby. Before she could even shout hello the first man rode at her, knocking her down. They threw her on the back of the other horse and rode back to the wagons. I didn't know what to do!"

"OK. It's all right," Eidos soothed. "Try to stay calm. Was your mother still moving when they threw her on the horse?" The girl shook her head, huffing out shaky breaths as she steadied her crying.

"These men on horseback," Andi interjected. "Were all of their friends on horseback?"

"The wagon people?" Andi nodded. "No. Mostly they were walking. I think there were about eight men on horses. And there were horses pulling the wagons too."

"Did any of the men see you?" Andi asked. The girl shook her head. "Did they have weapons?" This time she shrugged her shoulders.

"Little girl," Manic said. "Tell us about the wagons."

"Erm, there were two of them. Really big. It took four horses each to pull them. And they were them big horses."

"Listen." Eidos put a heavy hand on her frail shoulder and her big eyes, moist with tears, locked onto his face. "What were the wagons carrying?"

The tears tumbled as the girl squeezed her eyes shut. "People," she whispered.

Eidos gripped her firmly by both arms to ensure she was listening. "We'll find your mother, OK? Rest assured, we'll find her and return her. But you need to tell us when this wagon train took your mother and which direction were they going in. Think carefully: it's important."

"It was last night, just before sundown," the child told him. "And they were going north, I think. But I don't really know. They were definitely not coming this way. That's why I knew to run home. But I'm scared of what Daddy will say."

Eidos stood and grabbed some food from the stores in his saddle-packs. He handed an apple and some bread to her and told her to race home to her father. She was to stay there or with her neighbours, and to await their return. Her father would not be mad, for she had done the right thing. She scurried back down the path the way they had come.

"Slavers!" Manic grumbled. "I can't stand them."

Andi knew that the slave trade was unheard of in this region for at least the last ten years, but it was possible, however remote the likelihood, that slavers were foraging this far south to find their bounty. The practice made Andi sick to her stomach.

As Eidos remounted, Andi resisted the urge to ask why he wasn't involving the keep guards, but she figured it was a jurisdiction issue. The guards would not be allowed to leave the grounds of Hightower or the foulberg nearby, even to come to a hamlet so near, and a detachment of soldiers from the keep would take many hours to assemble and send forth. So it seemed the responsibility rested with the three of them alone.

Eidos reined in and headed up the trail but was overtaken quickly by Manic who put heels to the flanks of his young short-horse and shot forward with reckless abandon. All that could be seen was the squat form of the rotund dwarf being jarred and shaken by the bumpy ride, and his large-brimmed hat bending back in the wind.

Andi couldn't help but chuckle. Then she put heels to her own mount and chased after the others, heading north apace.

The merchant's quarters were on the plush side of mediocre. His chambers were in an area of Wahib that skirted poortown, just down from the commercial district and a ten-minute brisk walk from Ratna's place. Although far more plush than anything seen in poortown, this was not quite where Stefon had expected to find him.

Stefon and Rish sat quietly, listening to the merchant rattle on about the difficulties he'd been facing since the quarantine and how terrible it was for the city as a whole. It had taken only a small amount of encouragement and a subtle degree of flattery from Rish for the plump merchant to display his grand ego. In haughty tones, and with a wry smile, he had explained how good fortune had led to him being well prepared to last a while without imports.

Stefon wanted to press him further, but sensed something in the merchant. While the trader was bragging to strangers, he was also very aware of something he needed to be careful about. Not for the first time, Stefon regretted not having this conversation in the evening, over a glass of port. There was nothing like flattery to deceive the intoxicated. But a man with his wits about him and half a brain in his skull sooner or later worked out what was going on. There was only so long that his and Rish's story was going to last. They were masquerading as local traders looking to make ties with more successful merchants during these troubled times. But after a while, to the trained eye, they were going to stop looking like traders and show themselves to be the scoundrels they were.

As things were going, they were not about to hear the merchant readily admit he had been tipped off. However, upon their arrival the man had eagerly boasted of his connections, as was the fashion in the lower order of Wahiban society circles. When you had little or no actual influence or power, but a certain wedge of fiscal holdings, then it was very much *who* you knew. Those people in power with whom you had successfully become affiliated directly improved your lot. Just being seen alongside them at a society gathering or gala was deemed enough to enhance your profile. Stefon had immediately picked up on the mention of Governor Meena Saqir's name in almost the first sentence upon being welcomed into the merchant's modest chambers.

After finishing the bitter fruit drinks they had been offered, Rish made their excuses and the two friends bade good day to the merchant and departed the premises. Stefon watched Rish like a hawk as they left, keeping a close eye on his fingers. It would not be unlike him to pilfer a modest trinket from a side table on the way out; not for financial gain but more for the thrill. But he behaved himself and kept his sticky fingers laced behind his back until they reached the damp street outside.

The two slowly made their way back to the safe house, taking several unnecessary turns to ensure they were not being tailed. When they felt secure, they turned down their narrow road and entered the simple town dwelling that served as their meagre mustering point.

The building itself, just like those alongside it, leaned over the narrow lane like a drunken sailor. The greyness of the stonework was testament to the filth of the weather and the windows were shuttered from inside, as though the inhabitants sought to retain all possible heat. In truth, the shutters served to protect the residents' privacy.

Inside they found Pryn, Jewl and Rebrof waiting for their return. Rebrof was brewing coffee in a large kettle on the giant stove in the corner and the others were reclining on two of the numerous cowskin-bound, grain-filled bags that served as chairs in the communal area.

Pryn nodded once to them as they entered and began doffing their outer clothing. He stood easily eight feet tall; most rooms and buildings were not built to accommodate him. A mane of jet-black dreadlocks was tied back and fell down his broad frame. His shoulders were twice as wide as Rish's and his mighty chest seemed cut from living oak. A strange occurrence when young had served to alter the pigmentation of Pryn's dark skin, giving it a vivid imperial blue lustre. His hands were always hidden inside leather-and-plate gauntlets that he cared for constantly and oiled well. His eyes were large and black like jet stones.

Constantly quick to temper, he also had a sharp wit and generous laugh. However, Stefon had seen the mighty Pryn become so enraged that he successfully pulled an orc's arm clean off at the shoulder because he suspected him of cheating at cards. The orc hadn't even been playing in the game. Stefon decided not to hold any information back. Pryn was unpredictable, but clearly a better ally than foe. And regardless, he had always liked the giant.

Stefon recalled the first time they had met, during an operation outside of the walls of Wahib City. He and Rish had been commissioned to escort a train of caravans destined for one of Ratna Giri's warehouses. The caravans carried contraband goods, including twelve barrels of Strangemeal from the northeastern farms of Ipsica, at the foothills of Choat, where a few of the remaining farms producing the drug were still operating.

Stefon had met the caravan train outside a small farm owned by an interested party and had inspected the wagons and their crew for hidden weapons. As Rish had signalled the move out, Stefon had stopped them, for something about the rearward wagon had alerted him to a problem.

The back two wagons carried six barrels each of the Strangemeal crop, but the last wagon sat incredibly low on the axle. As he had mentioned this to the shrugging teamster, the wagon doors had burst open and a huge stowaway had sprung from within. He was massively built, with corded veins jutting from bulging muscles as he heaved a greatsword cleanly through the nearest guard's chest.

The rest of the caravan guards were slow to react, but Rish had immediately recognised the danger Pryn posed... and had promptly run away.

Ever the diplomat, Stefon had started shouting for everyone to calm down, which had had about as much effect as one might assume. Pryn had killed three guards by the time Stefon had unsheathed his own sword.

It was as Pryn had borne down upon him that Stefon had seen the fear in his eyes, and had suddenly understood. In order to squirrel the caravan train through the gates of Wahib City, Stefon's team were dressed as City Guards. As he had raised his sword to try to deflect Pryn's strike, a rock had struck the huge man square on the bridge of the nose.

Almost immediately, blood had exploded from it, cascading down his chin. His eyes had instantly watered and he had dropped his sword. He had clapped hands like drain-lids to his face in agony.

Stefon had looked to see Rish standing proudly near a squat building, another rock in his hand.

Resisting the urge to slay Pryn where he stood, Stefon had acted on a hunch and discovered that Pryn was simply terrified of discovery, and imagined he was at the gates of Wahib already, having stowed away on the wagon days before. The lads they had lost to Pryn's bad reaction had been costly, but they were just hired thugs; no one "skilled".

However, the lost mercenaries had meant that they were short for the required escort back to Wahib, and would undoubtedly be stopped at the gate. Being the type to take advantage of any opportunity presented to him, Stefon had pressed Pryn into employment in exchange for getting him into the city. The mighty warrior had agreed after some thought. The tricky thing had been finding a selection of uniform pieces that they could cobble together for the huge character. But they'd managed, as they always did.

Once inside the city, Pryn had left them to their devices, disappearing into the grime of the Wahiban underworld and operating as a freebooter for some time. Needless to say, Pryn and Stefon's group had often crossed paths, and now Stefon considered Pryn to be more of a strategic partner than anything else.

Bringing himself back to the present, Stefon shook the cold of the city from his bones and savoured the bitter smell of brewing coffee beans.

"You're back sooner than I thought you'd be," Rebrof commented. "Coffee?"

Stefon could rarely resist the offer. Coffee was one luxury that he found it difficult to deny himself, even though his personal stockpile of ground beans was running perilously low due to the quarantine. The beans were imported from lands across the sea in the south, to which Stefon had always wanted to travel. He had longed to see that strangely verdant and arid part of the world that gave them the finest coffee and sharpest fortified wines he'd ever known.

Right now, his second home fairly hummed with the bittersweet aroma of ground coffee forming a rich brew, and he nodded eagerly. Rebrof added two cups to the four already arranged on the work surface.

"Who's the fourth mug for?" Rish asked.

"Me," came a melodic voice from behind them. Stefon turned to allow the diminutive figure of Brooss to pass between himself and Rish as she dusted off her gloved hands. Brooss was less than five and a half feet tall, with jet-black hair that was gathered at the back of her head and allowed to cascade down. Her shoulders were slender and her form was athletic, if a little thin. She was pale as the moon but her eyes were constantly dark, hinting at a mordant sense of humour.

Stefon wasn't sure about Brooss yet. More precisely, he

wasn't convinced he liked her. He knew he could trust her, for she was a member of Ratna Giri's organisation—like Stefon and Rish—and had conducted herself consistently and professionally on every occasion they had worked together. Rarely offering much without being asked, Brooss was nevertheless eager to follow orders and carry out tasks. He just wasn't sure he liked her. It was that simple and prejudiced.

"Morning, Brooss!" Rish greeted her. "Been busy this morning?" He was staring at the way she moved in her dusty grey work trews. Rish had always been drawn to Brooss. In a certain light, Stefon supposed he could see why, for she had a somewhat plain prettiness. But she was nothing like the type of female with whom Rish would normally associate: she wore no make-up and was never seen in a dress. Her pallid features were even and fine, but there was nothing about her that stood out. She was neither buxom nor comely, but Rish always seemed to dote upon the young engineer, and hang from her every word, an effect Stefon had seen no female have on the rogue before.

"I've been working on one of Ratna's carriage wagons. I've got it outside now," she answered. "It's not got as much in the way of room for goods and cargo as his standard wagons, but I've managed to increase the wheel speed on it and even made the ride smoother." She turned to face them and took a seat in the corner, her hands behind her head. "I'm working on faster wagons that can carry armed men to travel in convoys with cargo wagons. That way you can put more goods in your cargo wagons and have defence from these other wagons. Like escort wagons." She looked pleased with herself. "And these new ones will be able to travel almost as fast as a chariot, but still carry soldiers over track terrain, like roads or whatever, without pitching the crew aside. It's a considerable achievement."

Rebrof handed her a cup of hot coffee and then proceeded to pass out the rest. He always deferred to the ladies. Rebrof was a gentleman, at least.

There was a pause as those in the room thought of something to say in reply to Brooss's uncharacteristic diatribe. Finally, she dropped her gaze to her coffee. "I was just saying, is all."

Rish and Stefon found seats and were handed their coffee in due course before anyone broached the subject of their morning excursion. Finally it was Pryn that pressed them.

"So are you going to spill what it is you pair discovered this morning in your little meeting or am I going to have to pound it out of you?" Pryn's threat was not idly spoken or received.

"Really the only scrap I was able to pick up was a feeling I got when he mentioned a particular official's name: Governor Meena. It was nothing noticeable, really; not like he got shifty-eyed or anything. Just a feeling."

"He was bragging at the time," offered Rish. "But yeah, he mentioned this Meena like he was all set to start some elegant monologue about him, but then cut himself short."

"That's right," said Stefon. "It wasn't the name; it was how he stopped himself. It's nothing really, but at least it's a name we can look into, and it would probably make some perverted sense too. He might have a hand in what's going on. I don't know. Even if he *is* the governor, he might not have the influence or power to be in control of what's happening, but he'll know more names than we do right now."

"Well, he might not be someone as important as the governor, but I know a guy. He works on the city militia, posted to the postern gate this time of year. He has his finger closer to the pulse of this city than most of his colleagues. He's been passing around some interesting information, once the liquor starts flowing, so it might be a little safer to speak with him first, before you go knocking down the door to the governor's mansion!"

"And I'll tell you something else for free," Pryn went on.

"Whoever it is you've got yourselves involved with, boys, they don't waste time. Questions have been asked. Some big movers I don't know much about have been asking the wrong questions about you three." He indicated Jewl, Rish and Stefon.

"Already?" exclaimed Rish.

Stefon was stunned. "How? I mean…how?"

"My guess would be that there are agents all over the city, looking out for people being prepared to ask certain questions." He looked from face to face. "What we don't know is what they're willing to do to those who are asking."

"Well we've done nothing untoward yet," Stefon said, in order to convince himself as much as the others. "But it's obviously best we keep an eye on each other's backs." He sat back thoughtfully, his coffee resting on his hip. "But how could they be alerted to us already?"

"By the Gods, Stefon! That could be by any number of routes," Rebrof told him. "For instance, if one of the agents Pryn spoke of was in Ratna's place when you guys discussed what to do, it's easily possible someone overheard. Or maybe someone overheard and sold the information to an agent. Maybe someone…"

"I get the message. The fact remains, someone is sitting up and taking notice."

"Still, look on the bright side," offered Rish. "You're still alive."

"You call that a bright side?"

"Think about it. If they considered you or me to be a real danger, we'd be dead by now. So if we're careful and sensible about this, then we're still fine."

Rish had a point. Unfortunately so did Rebrof when he replied, "Since when were you guys careful or sensible about anything?"

Whatever that sound was, Andi definitely had a bad feeling about it.

They had worked the horses to a lathered sweat after leaving the village at a gallop earlier that morning. It was nearing noon, the sun high to the south in the autumn sky, when they reined in to a slow walk to rest the animals. Manic had been a dwarf possessed, leading the group of three forward on such a charge, but Andi sympathised with the dwarf's feelings regarding slavers. They were hateful beings.

As they had walked the horses, the three companions had eaten dried fruit and hardcake rations in the saddle. This was to save time, but Andi got the impression that Eidos was worried that they had lost their way. The longer they went without finding signs of a large caravan, the more likely they were to miss the slavers' train altogether. Autumn was not the season to go tracking, for the changeable weather patterns made it almost impossible.

Ironically, at the moment these doubts had tumbled through Andi's mind Eidos had spotted the tracks. Two sets at first: shod horses at a gallop through relatively long grass at the roadside. This was strange in itself, but inconclusive until they had come across the fork in the road ahead. After dismounting and conducting a closer examination, Eidos and Andi agreed they had found the tracks they were looking for, and the child had been correct: they led northeast, toward the range of wooded hills and mountains beyond that could be seen decorating the horizon. The Southern Range: the mountains that marked the border to Ipsica.

Just as Eidos and Andi were reaching agreement on these facts, Manic also dismounted, his eyes fixed firmly on a bank of trees a short distance away to the north*west* of the junction. He sniffed keenly at the northerly breeze that had been blowing softly all morning. Then, without a word, his eyes glazed over and he slid his mighty greatsword from its scabbard. With surprising speed and agility the dwarf rushed forward, sword gripped overhead in both hands, toward a stand of trees a short distance away.

Eidos looked at Andi for a moment. "Does he do that often?"

Standing near him, Andi merely shrugged and gripped the reins of her horse, which had become skittish at the sudden activity. She took a moment to consider her options, then held out the reins to Eidos and called for him to bring the horses to the trees and tether them; she would follow Manic on foot.

Freeing her bow from the saddlebags, she chased after the receding form of the dwarf, almost catching him as he disappeared into the treeline. Andi could hear Eidos bringing the horses up from the rear as she jumped over an upturned root and made her pursuit of Manic between the narrow trunks. As they joined a woodland path through the trees, Andi overtook Manic and tripped him from behind, sending his bulk thumping to the pine-needle-strewn ground. His wind had blasted out and his fury seemed to dissipate slightly.

And that was when she heard *the sound*. Unlike any animal cry she had ever witnessed, it rose through the trees from ahead of them: a sound like cast iron pressed to a grinding wheel. It was certainly not of human origin.

Up ahead, along the path, Andi saw a horse lift its head in answer to the shriek. She hadn't noticed the mare before, but now she saw it was not alone. Near her on the path was a dead horse, blood seeping from a large gash across the throat.

Eidos caught up, his armour making intrusive noises in the relative quiet of the woods. "I've hobbled the horses outside of the trees. I see you found him, then?" He sounded unimpressed.

"Manic, what's the matter with you? Have you lost your mind?"

Now that Manic had regained his breath, a certain

amount of his composure had also returned. But his face
was still set in grim determination and his fist held firmly to
the grip of his sword. Through gritted teeth, he uttered one
word, and it turned Andi's blood cold.

"What did he say?" Eidos asked.

Andi drew an arrow from the soft leather quiver on her
back and nocked it ready, as she looked hard down the path
for signs of movement. The trees were evergreen pines and
the canopy served well to keep the sunlight out. The place
smelled of sap and moist fungus, but there was another
smell too, and it was coming from up ahead. Manic must
have a bloodhound's nose to have picked up the scent from
back on the trail.

"He said 'goblins'," Andi told Eidos. Manic had returned
to his feet and moved forward along the track, toward the
origin of that terrible shriek. Andi followed close behind,
her bow ready to loose at the merest sign of the green-black
hide of any goblin marauders. They were almost unheard
of in these parts; but then again, so were slavers.

"Eidos, make sure that horse doesn't interfere, will you?"
She indicated the untethered animal grazing nearby.

"Of course." As they passed near the dead horse,
Eidos took the bridle of the roaming mare and looked for
somewhere to tie it. Opting for the quick and easy solution,
he tied the reins to the bridle of the dead horse, ensuring
it wouldn't spook and trample them as they made their way
forward. Not ideal, but it would have to do for now.

Ahead, the path led up an incline and then seemed to
drop away. There were signs of a makeshift bridge, but it
had long since crumbled. Crawling forward on their bellies,
the three made for the rise and stopped just short. Sounds
of conflict could be heard over the brow. Slowly Andi crept
forward and peered over the edge.

They were at the bank of an old stream that had run
dry long ago. Nearby they could see another horse standing

patiently at the creek, adorned with strange barding: a metallic armouring of deep red and green.

In a glade beyond the creek, a fight was in progress. In her first glance she could make out the bodies of two men, vicious wounds peppering their faces and necks and long sword or axe slashes in evidence across their torsos. One man remained standing, sword and buckler in hand, frantically defending himself from attack by an odd bipedal creature.

Standing just over five feet tall, the being had green, oily skin that glistened in what little sunlight made it through the tree canopy. It had an elongated snout and a mouth of needle teeth. A yellow fin ran along the top of the head and a forked tongue slithered from its maw as it concentrated on raining blows upon the defender's shield with a slender, long-handled axe.

The beast had a lengthy, muscular tail that ran from under a simple brown garment held in place by a thick leather belt. A bronze chestplate was secured by leather straps to form armour, and two sturdy legs pumped and strained to keep the green monster out of the reach of the human's desperate lunges.

Andi looked back down the trail and saw that Eidos had caught them up. He crouched a short distance behind Manic. She told them, "It's no goblin."

"It's not?" Manic asked with obvious surprise. He shuffled forward to gain a view for himself. "Oh, yes. You're right. Kind of smells like one, though."

"I'll trust your judgement on that score, my friend," Andi told him, looking closer as the second man tired, retreating under a barrage of blows.

"Well what are we waiting for? Let's get in there and help the man! He's no match for that thing alone!" Manic went to rush over the lip behind which they were hiding, but Andi placed a restraining hand on his shoulder.

"Wait a second," she said, spotting something of interest. She waited another critical moment, then let the dwarf go. "I think you're right—come on!" They rushed over the rise, weapons drawn.

As Manic and Eidos hurtled over the brow, Andi pulled her bowstring tight, drawing a bead on the green monster as it completed a ferocious assault, driving the remaining human back toward a fallen trunk. The hopeless man had no energy left with which to react and his heels caught fully on the fallen wood. Manic was only halfway to the mêlée when the monster swung the axe in a crippling overhead blow that crashed down on the man's face as he fell. His skull was heard to crack open and his limbs proceeded to twitch and jerk as his life ebbed away.

Despite the defeat of the man he meant to save, Manic didn't stop his charge, raising his sword overhead and bellowing a battle cry. The green monster twisted, suddenly ready for the unexpected assault. Instead of engaging the dwarf fully, he deflected Manic's lunge and stepped to the side, the dwarf tumbling forward heavily on the grassy underbrush at the foot of a thick pine.

Andi had a clean shot, but had a strong feeling she didn't need it. Nonetheless, she kept her bead on the target as Eidos stepped before the beast, his mighty axe glinting in a shaft of noon sun that slanted through the trees.

That was when the beast spoke. It remained tense and alert should Eidos attack, but held the long axe in a defensive grip, its posture supplicating. From this distance, all Andi could make out was a sibilant, lilting tone, but no words. But she had a mind for what was being said.

Andi took a chance to look again at the bodies. The last man to die had worn a long whip at his side, one not used for combat. Another of the bodies nearer their hiding point possessed half a dozen sets of manacles secured to a thick travelling belt. These were not soldiers or travellers, traders or mercenaries. These were slavers, and hopefully part of the train they were following.

And if this beast had been fighting them then, Andi was more than ready to consider it a potential ally rather than a foe. The creature was almost certain to possess information they required, and was evidently more than capable of handling itself. Things in life were rarely so black and white, but in this instance Andi was inclined to consider the situation to be just that clear cut.

Chapter Seven
Brothels and Wagons

Somewhere out over the city walls of Wahib, the effects of the sun could be seen. In some distant land the sun was shining, but in Wahib only the rain came, relentless and despairing. Pryn, Stefon and Rish wended their way through ancient, narrow streets toward the city walls of the southwest quarter. The rain had tapered to a steady, misting drizzle and Stefon was struck by a nostalgic moment as he saw a rainbow arc over the domed rooftops to the south.

It was after lunch and the streets were as busy as they were at any other time of day during this quarantine. Traders were struggling to offload what goods they had left, and had been able to beg, steal and borrow against. Inner city farming communities were struggling to supply enough goods to those citizens brave or desperate enough to be seeking foodstuffs in the depths of an apparent plague. Many residents survived on the siege grain stores that the Wahib City militia distributed every Sixthday, but the sustenance that grain provided simply didn't carry the vitamins and minerals one needed to repel infection and illness, let alone a plague. For that, one needed fruit, and fruit needed farming.

Stefon knew that once the populace came to the knowledge that they were becoming a melting pot of disease, and surely vermin, there would be a riot of cataclysmic proportions and the city of Wahib would unquestionably fall from within.

It gave him impetus to press on more fervently with the task given them by Master Ratna Giri, and accepted by Rish. Stefon had no desire to die in Wahib.

And so he and Rish were following Pryn down to the postern gates in the southwestern wall to meet an old acquaintance of Pryn's: a City Guard he had apparently served with some years before. As far as Stefon knew, Pryn had never served in the City Guard of Wahib since he had lived there, but he had no information about his life before that, so he could only trust that Pryn knew the man well enough to ensure they were not compromised.

Since discovering they had attracted some attention, Rish had taken to paying particular interest in those who might be following them. He was no source for conversation as they moved from muddy alley to cobbled street, his eyes trained on every corner or turn they passed that might reveal a tail.

Conversely, Stefon had taken to watching every turn they *approached*. He was nervous about the level of desperation that a city in such turmoil could engender in a group or an individual with an agenda. If these people were protecting something, they might act rashly, and the next corner Stefon followed might lead him into a trap.

Nonetheless, the three arrived at the postern gate safely and on time. The walls of Wahib stood high over them, providing a little respite from the drizzle. The postern gate, named for its infrequent use, was a broad but short gate in the southern walls that allowed for overflow traffic in the summer months of high commerce and trade. The gate itself was constructed of heavy, ancient oak and was barred by innumerable metal seals across the lock—a grim testament to the finality of the quarantine.

The noon guard were changing out and a guardsman was passing handover notes to his relief officer. He spotted Pryn from the corner of his eye, nodded once and finished his transition with his subordinate before hoisting a small leather bag onto his shoulder and walking calmly over. He fell into stride next to Pryn and Stefon, with Rish following behind as they moved off away from the wall. Such a well-guarded structure was no place for a delicate conversation.

"How fares thee, Pryn?" asked the weather-faced ex-soldier as he held a hand across his brow against the steadily increasing rain. "Do you never age?"

"I try not to, old friend. These are my colleagues, Stefon and Rish." The three exchanged polite greetings before Pryn pressed the reason for the meeting. "You remember we spoke last week in passing about something odd you'd noticed?"

The guard nodded, recognising that Pryn was being deliberately vague.

"Well, we need to know anything you can tell us about it."

"I'll tell you what I know, although nothing can really be proven. I've been instructed to increase vigilance on the postern gate after rumours of a way out of the city under here. I don't know how I'm supposed to guard *under* here, but that's the gist of my instructions this week. Another guard told me it has something to do with the storm drains that lead to the river outside the walls, but I don't know if that's true. The strongest rumour we have is that it may lie beneath Anya's Brothel in poortown—but we're not daft enough to go poking around there, if you'll 'scuse the pun." The guard wiped rainwater from his face and jogged his bag higher on his back, the strap rubbing against the leather shoulder armour. His simple helm held off most of the rain, but his face was exposed to the elements. Looking at the man's eyes, Stefon thought he looked tired.

"Anyway," he continued, "that's something of note for this week. But what we were talking about last week: that's even more speculative. Someone broke the quarantine."

"Really?" Stefon asked. The idea that the plague had already breached the walls was terrifying. Could what was happening to Wahib also be occurring throughout Ipsica?

"It's a rumour, but one that is doing the rounds well enough. I reckon it's the truth. A small group of people made it through the rumoured tunnels of the postern gate and beyond the river. They had enough provisions to get them to safety, but they didn't make it even to the outer farming community."

"Did they fall ill? Were they already ill?" asked Stefon.

The group turned down a narrow alley where they had cover from the relentless rain for a few moments, and they stood to talk undisturbed. Rish kept a close look on the alley entrance as they spoke.

"No, they were perfectly healthy. It was only just after the quarantine was set up. The story goes that a team from the city followed them from the walls and descended upon them. But they weren't killed. Despite putting up a serious fight, they were brought back into the city alive and were never seen again."

"Nothing strange in that," Stefon commented. "They'll be stretching rope somewhere in the palace grounds to serve as an example."

"Well don't get me started on *that*," the guard said with a knowing look. "But no, you're right: I suppose they were never expected to resurface. However, no one expected the team that went after them to disappear too."

Stefon shook his head. "Well, if they were a detachment of the palace guard then they wouldn't be spotted just milling around, right? They'd be in the palace."

"They weren't palace guards; they were dressed as local city militia. Moreover, a man I knew quite well led that team.

As far as I knew, I thought he had actually mustered out of the city militia some time ago."

"Retired?" Stefon asked.

"Of sorts. He's a capable guy, so he was never fully without something to do. He's a resourceful chap." Pryn's friend looked up and down the alley before continuing. "So much so that I've heard he isn't missing any longer. In fact, I've heard he's on the run inside the city somewhere."

"Really? What's his name?" Pryn asked in his rumbling tones.

"Simeon. That's all I've got for you, Pryn, honestly. It's only rumours, but what else is there these days?"

"No problem; thanks for the time." Pryn slapped him on the arm as his friend went to leave. "You keep safe."

Stefon reached out and caught the man's arm. "Wait! One more thing. You mentioned the palace hangings and the bodies before. What's so strange about that?"

"Go to the palace and take a look yourself. Considering the high level of incidental crime these days, with petty theft, looting and the like, lots of people are being arrested, and more being sentenced to death to set Wahib's much-fabled example for the rest of us. But there's not one body hanging from the walls of the old palace. Not one. They get carted off to the cemeteries or the morgue in the hospital, not left on the walls like usual."

Stefon still held on to the guard's arm. "But surely that's because of the threat of disease? They can't leave the bodies lying around or hanging. They'll cart them off to the place they keep the plague victims, won't they? Burn them up?"

"You mean the hospital furnaces?" The guard pulled his arm free in growing irritation. "That'd be the hospital and church grounds in the east of the city. I wouldn't know about any of that; I'm just a guard. But you feel free to go poking around down there if you're so keen to go and contract something permanent and nasty." He looked at each of them as he left and then muttered, "Good luck!" before stepping into the rain.

"Stefon, I think you made him nervous with all those questions." Pryn was leaning against a low wall under a heavy tarpaulin that had been erected over a small marketplace some weeks ago and which still withstood the weight of the daily downpour. Midafternoon had seen the clouds thin and a moment of sunshine had poured across the Wahib sky, bathing everything in an eerily clean light. Now the drizzle had returned and soon it would be pouring again.

"Who cares?" grumbled Stefon rhetorically, struggling to hide his displeasure.

Pryn, Stefon and Rebrof stood together beneath the tarpaulin for shelter to discuss what they were to accomplish by their next move. Stefon wasn't convinced that entering the hospital grounds during daylight hours was a sensible idea, but that was exactly what they had planned.

Rish had taken Jewl with him to a seedier, southern portion of the city, specifically to a brothel well known to the rogue. It just so happened to be the very brothel that Pryn's guard friend had indicated to be the location of a rumoured subterranean escape from Wahib City. Hopefully Rish would be able to use his months of loyal patronage to hold enough sway in order to reveal anything of interest. It was worth a try.

However, Stefon wasn't convinced of the other half of their plan. As far as he was concerned, the only thing to be gained by exploring the hospital was to risk greater exposure to the contagion, putting them all in harm's way. He had no idea what reason Pryn had for not believing there to be high risk involved. Surely traipsing into the morgue and hospital was a bad idea! There had to be a better, safer way of finding what they needed. Unfortunately, he couldn't think of what that might be, and Pryn had proved himself correct so many times on things like this that Stefon was willing to follow him—for the time being.

"Are we ready?" Pryn asked.

"As we'll ever be," muttered Stefon.

They set out across the broad, cobbled street to the gates of the infirmary grounds. The hospital grew from the flatlands in the deepest basin of Wahib City, the buildings on the raised ground to the north and east casting shadows across the courtyard and walls of the infirmary below. The ancient architecture reeked of gothic symbolism and menacing sculpture, creating a mean visage incongruous with good health, holiness, cleanliness and the sanctity of life, making the hospital seem larger than it actually was. Always an imposing building, the recent rain and thunderous skies only served to increase the foreboding nature of the structure.

Stefon pressed himself forward, ignoring the voice in his head that said to stay away. Rebrof took the lead and Pryn angled away to the right. He would act as rear point, should anything untoward occur.

Pryn stopped by the small guardhouse attached to the tall gate. It was empty, and so he took advantage of what little shelter it provided, hunkering under the slanted wooden roof. There he would remain in order to protect the other two, should they need to beat a hasty retreat.

Rebrof and Stefon proceeded to enter the grounds though the gates that stood unlocked. The courtyard had several emergency carts and carriages strewn about with uncomfortable but quick-functioning bridles and tack. These were most often used to rush to and from emergency situations that were alerted by the city watch through the use of shrill whistles. It was a system only ever employed in Wahib, to the best extent of Stefon's knowledge. The city was proud of its determination to protect and care for the citizens within. Ironic, really, considering the current situation!

In late afternoon, there were a few orderlies and preachers moving to and from the main building and some of the surrounding prefabricated housing that had been erected on the grounds between the hospital itself and the exterior wall. No one paid the group much notice. They were dressed as innocuously as possible, with no weapons in plain sight, although Stefon hadn't been able to resist bringing his hand-crossbow with him in a leather satchel slung over his shoulder.

They moved with quiet purpose to the main entrance, climbing a set of five steps and passing through large oak doors. Inside the reception, people clamoured for attention from the woefully undermanned administration staff behind a long counter. Some people were frantically enquiring after relatives or loved ones; others were complaining of their symptoms and demanding immediate aid, while others still rested quietly and patiently in chairs and on benches nearby—they were clearly very ill.

Wasting no time and trying not to breathe too deeply, Stefon proceeded with all the authority he could muster beyond the counter and through a set of wooden swing-doors that creaked loudly. Inside the corridors of the establishment, the walls were daubed alabaster and the floor was polished stone. No grouted seams were visible on the floor and no paintings or decoration adorned the walls. Lanterns were arranged at regularly spaced intervals to illuminate those areas without access to natural light. The place looked functional and unpleasantly sterile.

Ahead, the corridor met a crossroads, with a flight of stairs leading up from the right corner and a long passageway continuing to the left. Beyond that, the passage ended in a doorway with a fitted glass panel. In hand-painted Ipsican scrawl, a label indicated the room to be *Records*.

"That has to be our best bet," said Rebrof, without breaking stride.

Despite the austere décor of the building, the corridor was littered and filthy. Chirurgeons, preachers, nurses and orderlies moved from room to room along the corridors with eyes downcast and their apparel in dishevelment. Again, nobody paid them heed as Rebrof and Stefon pushed open the unlocked door to the Record Room.

The large room was dark, with only a small amount of natural light filtering through the two windows in the right-hand wall. The sky was dull and so the room was grey and smelled damp. Stefon resisted the temptation to retain a lamp from out in the corridor, for without it they would remain undisturbed longer.

Without preamble, Rebrof set about filtering through the records for anything that might be of use, but after a short period it was clear they wouldn't find what they sought. With the dramatic increase in the effects of the plague, it was obvious that the administrative upkeep of the facility had fallen foul.

"We need to see the morgue," Rebrof said ominously. "There's nothing here, but these chirurgeons and soothsayers alike are meticulous note-keepers. We're sure to find at least *something* in the vicinity of the bodies themselves."

Rebrof stepped towards the door and Stefon placed a restraining hand on his upper arm. "I don't like that idea very much," he said. "Seems like we're getting a little too close and personal with these plagued bodies."

"I've thought about that," said Rebrof. "The way I figure it is that if this was a contagion then they'd have identified it already and would be taking steps to curtail whatever was causing it. But there's no mention of an actual disease, and it's the populace that's called it a plague. People are stupid. They're scaremongers sooner than deep thinkers." He indicated the cloudy glass in the Record Room door.

"Do you think you'd have as many chirurgeons and orderlies milling around working hard, if all hope was lost, or if there was even the slightest chance of death? You think they'd stick around here if the contagion was highly communicable?" He fluttered his hands like a bird. "Viruses flying in the air, mouth to nostril? I think not. That's not how it is transmitted, if it's even being transmitted at all."

"You mean you think it might not be infectious?"

"Of course. That all these people aren't all dropping dead coupled with the simple fact that the pattern of disease seems purely random leads me to be pretty confident about the safety of being around a plagued body." He took Stefon's hand off his arm and turned to face him, looking down from his three inches over six feet. "Be honest. Something is going to kill you sooner or later, Stefon. At least if we try and find a way out of Wahib, we won't die inside these city walls. And we might just save the city."

Stefon gave Rebrof's words some consideration.

Not for the first time, he wondered about the nature of Rebrof's work before he mustered out of the armed forces. For a trainee officer of little success or repute, he seemed to be fairly well-educated about a great many things. Understandably, these topics were not necessarily those that would benefit an officer in the army, but they seemed to suggest an intellect beyond that of a failed soldier.

"Very well," Stefon relented, "but let's be quick about it. You may make reasonable logic, but it still doesn't make it sit any easier with me. Let's get moving."

He followed Rebrof back out of the door into the corridor as a particularly chubby orderly waddled past, his jowl slick with sweat. Again they were passed by without being marked as out of place.

Moving quickly, they followed the passage right, away from the flight of stairs, and again turned right at the end of the corridor. A short walk between nurses carrying trays of various vicious-looking implements of torture—apparently designed to aid recovery somehow—and they arrived at a pair of push-doors made of thick, heavy material fixed in place by slanted metal return hinges. The doors were designed to be pushed open by wheeled gurneys or carried stretchers and to swing back into place. Down here not many people could be seen. One nurse passed them as they entered the morgue, but she paid them little attention. It was unnerving Stefon that they were so easily passed and ignored.

Once inside, they again moved swiftly, sensing that neither had any great desire to remain in the morgue, despite Rebrof's logic. The room had a low ceiling with many lamp fittings and high-strung candelabras of simple, functional design. Most were constructed with polished metal crowns to reflect as much light as possible. At least a dozen rectangular tables were arranged throughout the room with four central pillars running across the length of the chamber, separating the tables six by six. The floor was of slate tile with rustic grouting between, and every seven or eight yards the ground slanted in a particular direction. Each slant edged to a drain, of which several were visible. Stefon could clearly see that the nearest drain still carried the familiar dark red stain of old blood.

"This will be the examination room, then," muttered Stefon, his voice unnaturally loud in the odd chamber. "Kind of glad it's empty."

"Odd though, don't you think?" replied Rebrof. "Should there not be carcasses for examination still here? Work-in-progress, so to speak?"

Stefon thought on that for a quick moment before coming to the same conclusion. An empty examination room during a pandemic was strange. Trying to avoid looking at the instruments fixed to the walls, he moved swiftly to a set of similar swing doors at the far end. Rebrof had picked up a series of well-turned parchments from a bench nearby.

"Post-mortem exam reports," he said, and started reading. "'No clear sign of contagion evident. No organ damage prior to secondary symptoms. Rapid stomach decay in final stages of illness...'" Rebrof tapped the page. "He's removed the word 'infection' here, and replaced it with 'illness'. Obviously he doesn't believe this is a plague either."

"Interesting," Stefon said, as he neared the far doors.

Rebrof continued reading. "'Upon further consideration, this looks more the work of a virulent poison rather than a biological infection. But with the late reaction in the alimentary canal, ingested poison is impossible. An airborne poison would be too difficult to control and would have long since been cleared by recent storms. The only external sign of evidence that something might have been introduced to each victim might be the eyes.'

"But that's where he stops on that report and starts another. The report is curtailed and signed by a reverend of some description, but I don't recognise the seal. Apparently the examination was over when this church person decided it was."

Rebrof threw down the parchments and made to catch up with Stefon as he pushed gently on the left-hand door. "Odd that a member of some clergy was signing things off in a mortuary."

"Kind of makes you wonder who was directing the autopsy," agreed Stefon. "And more importantly, why." Rebrof joined him at the doorway and then followed him through.

They stood in the mortuary chamber itself. The room reeked of embalming fluid and poorly masked death. The chamber was easily twice the size of the examination room and there was shelf upon shelf constructed from reinforced metal. These shelves were partitioned to allow the storage of bodies before disposal, but most were empty. Only those sections in the rear, nearest the external doors, were populated by well-wrapped bodies.

"Check the doors," ordered Stefon. "See where they

lead. I don't like the fact that we're so alone back here; it makes no sense."

Wasting no time, Rebrof moved swiftly to the wooden external doors and checked the handles while Stefon walked carefully along the shelves of bodies. A click indicated that Rebrof had no trouble opening the locks. He glanced at Stefon over his shoulder. "I'll be back in two seconds." Then he was gone, the door thumping-to quietly behind him. With the thick, wooden doors standing slightly ajar it was possible to hear the rain again outside. Though normally depressing, the sound gave Stefon a familiar feeling; something known and comfortable as he stood alone in a room of bodies.

Impatient for Rebrof to return from his search, Stefon thought it best to appear interested or professional should someone who actually belonged in the mortuary interrupt him. He stepped closer to the nearest wall of shelves bearing bodies. They were each wrapped in embalming rags and cloth, so as to appear only vaguely humanoid, like some strange chrysalis. It was impossible to tell if this victim had been human, elf, dwarf or even orc. In actual fact, it had long since been proven that this affliction was indiscriminate regarding race. The nearest body at eye-level was smaller than those nearby. But clearly it was not orcish or dwarven in origin. It more strongly resembled the size and shape of a female human or maybe a male elf. Or a child.

A child. An innocent child.

Stefon gingerly prodded the shoulder wrappings, his fingertip pushing into soft flesh, and then immediately pulled his hand back. Something in the room wasn't right. Suddenly he felt watched. Glancing around, he saw he was still alone, although he could hear the sounds of the hospital in distant, muffled tones, as though heard through water.

The movement of air brushed across his cheek and echoes of the empty chamber reflected back each minute sound his every movement produced. Invisible insects crawled across his skin; the hairs on his arms and neck stood up and his forearms pimpled with gooseflesh.

Reluctantly, he reached out once more to confirm what he had felt. He pushed his finger into the shoulder and pulled his hand away again. The flesh beneath certainly had natural give. It possessed the same suppleness as that of living flesh.

Stefon had been around enough bodies to know the effects that rigor mortis had on a corpse, and this shoulder was not rigid or…he reached once more and forced himself to allow his finger to linger longer.

Was it…warm?

Once again he removed his hand from the body. Perhaps it was the surprise of feeling the unexpected warmth from the carcass, or perhaps it was simply a draught from the open doorway, but Stefon felt a chill scurry up his spine.

He glanced around at the other wrapped bodies, then at the doors.

He was still alone. But still he felt watched.

With a mental snapshot, he recalled a trick from his youth, during a time he had spent as a kitchen hand in one of the inns downtown. When he was caught pretending to be asleep or unconscious in order to avoid work, the innkeeper would place a stubby thumb against the inner portion of one of his eyebrows and gently press against the bone. After scant seconds the pain would surge to such immense proportions that he couldn't help but pull away.

Reticent to investigate further, but curious beyond mere morbidity, Stefon reached out again and placed his thumb carefully against where he judged the brow-line of this child victim to be, and let the weight of his hand push his thumb down upon the cloth shroud.

Sweat beaded on his brow despite the chill that swept around him. Moments passed. He was aware of an ache growing in his arm from holding his hand steady.

The door nearby abruptly swung open and Rebrof appeared.

With a startled yelp, Stefon snatched his hand away from the carcass and stumbled back onto the hard slate floor. He scrambled away from the shelf, refusing to remove his gaze from the chrysalis-shaped child corpse above him.

Rebrof quietly closed the door and rushed over to Stefon's side. "What are you doing on the floor?" he asked, concern on his face.

Stefon could not speak. He was catatonic. Only one thought lanced through his mind: *The head had moved.*

"It moved!" Stefon insisted. "I'm sure of it. Only a little, but the head moved! I swear on my mother's life!"

"Aren't you an orphan?" Jewl asked from his corner of the safehouse. Rish and Rebrof bleated with laughter, the latter brewing another coffee on the stove.

In the hospital, Rebrof had scooped Stefon up from the floor and rushed him from the morgue. He had checked him over for injury and, when he'd decided all was as it should be, had frog-marched him to the main entrance, ignoring any questions that came their way. They had left the building without incident; it had taken only a moment, although the nurses and orderlies had begun to notice them as they hurried past. Stefon's face had been ashen. Pryn had fallen into step with them as they hit the street, and all three had returned to the safehouse.

On returning, they had found Rish and Jewl preparing a bulgur wheat and root vegetable meal. Immediately Rish had sensed the danger and rushed to assist. Stefon had gathered his wits, but he was still wired and the adrenaline surge had left his hands shaking and his face pallid.

"I don't care about the sensitive nature of the security in the city. Something is afoot and I want none of us moving around the streets without being properly armed," he insisted. "That goes for you too, Brooss."

A feminine voice muttered agreement from out of sight beyond the stove in the kitchen area. She returned and sat across from Stefon, a bowl of broth in her lap. "So are you actually sure it moved? Did you see it move?"

Stefon was becoming exasperated. "Look! I didn't see it move, no. But I didn't need to. The thing was under my hand. I looked up at Rebrof when he came in through the back door, and the head moved from beneath my thumb. I didn't have to see it. I'm sure it moved." The others in the room were silent, and a couple looked openly sceptical. "Look, I know it sounds odd, but there was something else. The body didn't feel...cold."

Pryn put down his cup and leaned forward, elbows on his knees; his famous gauntlets were draped across his lap. "Look, something spooked you, I can see that, but just what are you suggesting? That they were asleep? If they were awake enough to move from under your thumb, do you not think they'd have been awake enough to get up and go home?"

"Something's not right. That's all I'm saying!"

"I agree," Rebrof conceded finally.

"Thank you!"

"I went to check out the incinerator units in the grounds while I left Stefon alone with the bodies. The kilns of the incinerators were clean. The chimneys and kilns are well-maintained, so rain wasn't pooling inside, but there was a small amount of moss growing in the corner *inside* the nearest kilns. I don't think they've been fired for some time."

There was a long silence. At last Rish broke the stillness with the question that must have been on every mind in the room. "Then...where are the bodies?"

No one had an answer.

Andi, Manic and Eidos rode along in silence as their new reptilian companion spoke at length about himself.

He was a Finhead; a species Andi had never encountered before in all her travels. Thankfully he spoke fluent Shen, though it was obviously not his first language. His sibilant lilt lent hisses and lisps to the words that made his accent sound almost Ipsican, although not so plummy. The actual name of his particular species was unpronounceable, so they called him a Finhead. His name was equally unpronounceable, and so they called him Finhead by name also.

Once the situation in the wooded glade had calmed somewhat, they had managed to speak with Finhead without Manic trying to carve him in half. The three dead humans had indeed been slavers; apparently from the column Andi's group was tracking. The slavers had been catching up to the rear of their column when they had spied Finhead walking south toward Hightower, and had attacked.

Immediately Finhead had assumed it was a mistake and had fled toward the woods in an attempt to avoid confrontation, but they had given hot pursuit and crashed into the wooded area with little regard for their mounts, quickly overtaking him. It was when they had faced each other off that Finhead had realised they were slavers. One had unhooked some manacles and the other possessed a net he was ready to use.

Not willing to be enslaved, Finhead had unslung his axe and quickly dispatched the first two slavers before they had realised their opponent's strength and skill. From Finhead's reckoning, the last slaver had put up a mighty struggle, almost heroic, lasting beyond ten minutes in the glade, evading the mighty axe and threatening to strike with his own blade. But it had been a mismatch and it was only a matter of time before Andi and the others had seen the slaver sent to his grave.

Once it had been established that Andi and her companions posed no threat, Finhead had started speaking urgently in his deep, guttural, heavily accented Shen, urging them not to attack.

He was a traveller looking for employment, and it took little effort for Andi to convince Eidos that it was a good idea to employ the warrior until this band of slavers was dealt with. A token amount of gold had changed hands and a promise made of more upon completion of their foray east. This band of slavers seemed more heavily armed than might have been suspected, and they certainly had more guards and men-at-arms in the band. So much so that Andi had a curious feeling that more was afoot than first appeared.

Finhead was more than eager to accept the commission as this opportunity to cut up slavers was simply too good to miss.

They had ridden steadily throughout the morning, not putting the mounts under much pressure other than a canter along the more level, beaten paths. For the most part they rode across empty fields and rolling grasslands towards the very large expanse of trees that dominated the eastern horizon, shadowing the tracks of the column as closely as they needed. The column's tracks showed no signs of trying to hide their passage or their numbers; neither did Andi's group encounter any rearguard elements.

Andi judged they would reach the first thickets of browning, deciduous trees by late afternoon, even at such a pedestrian pace. Beyond that, the time they made today would be down to how dense and difficult to traverse those woods proved to be. She held little hope, for the skies to the east looked dark and foreboding.

"So tell me something, Finhead," she said. "Where exactly does your species originate? I've never met one of your kind before, or even heard of them."

"That's kind of rude, Andi," Manic said.

"Not a problem, Master Manic; I am not offended." He turned in his saddle on his barded mount, with Manic between them. "We are mostly found beyond the volcanic twin spires in the far southern lands beyond the seas outside Ipsica." Finhead spoke a long, growling word that Andi assumed was the name of the place, but she had no chance of remembering or discerning the sound from any other that he had used in his native language. "I've travelled farther from my land than any of my kind, to my knowledge. I am proud of my travels and the things I have seen."

"Why do your people not travel widely?" Eidos asked.

"Tradition, friend Eidos. We are mainly tribal and clan-based. Although we are as developed as most civilisations, with arts, scripture, knowledge and culture to match that of any Ipsican or Shenmadock town, our own society has long held to a system of family honour, strength in numbers and a reliance on unity."

"Why, then, did you leave?" Eidos pressed.

Andi sensed reluctance in the foreigner to answer the question. After the shortest of pauses, he said, "It was a misunderstanding. Following an altercation and a death—for which I was not responsible!—I felt compelled to explore farther than our village valley. I just never stopped. I left one morning and never returned. I did not intend to be gone so long, but if you had seen some of the things I have encountered on my travels up the far coast, you'd have carried on too."

There was a lull in the conversation. Andi looked at Finhead's face and found it unreadable. The alien features gave nothing away, and she was disquieted by her inability to gauge the emotions of the newcomer. She usually liked to keep on top of her companions' feelings, no matter how innocuous things might seem at the time. It always gave her the edge on anticipating what they might do when situations got contentious or dangerous. And having the edge even on your companions was all too often the difference between life and death—one's own or someone else's.

Fifthday night approached in the city of Shen Utah, and Acaelian the Glimmer sat impatiently at a table on the edge of the Temple Square, an ancient and regal portion of the city in the centre of Temple Link and something of a tourist attraction as it afforded the most impressive views of Shen Utah Palace. An empty coffee cup stood before him and there was a wild look in his eye. Claudia was late.

After speaking with Click on the docks that morning he had left his friend on the harbour wall and headed into the city, searching for Claudia. He had left messages at her usual Wheelhouse—or brothel—and another at the hostelry she sometimes frequented when she needed space. That done, he had forced himself to seek out shelter for a few hours, for the morning hours were not the time for a thief and a whore to find spare time together, when they should both be resting.

Finally Acaelian spied her shapely figure approaching from across the square.

Claudia fascinated Acaelian. Elves and humans had a historically chequered past, and rarely made good friendship material, but he was something different from elves of traditional bent—and Claudia was certainly a unique human, if you pressed Acaelian for his opinion on *that*.

Short, and with long brown hair, there was nothing traditionally beautiful about Claudia's countenance or demeanour; for more often than not she forced herself to carry the sleazy air of the streetwalker. But to Acaelian, in those hours when she was herself he saw the golden heart and quick smile, the imperfect wrinkle of her nose when she laughed and the self-conscious gait when she walked in the daytime. He hated that she had to do what she did in order to survive life in The Lows, but he was less than perfect too.

Claudia greeted him warmly with a long hug and he

savoured the hint of jasmine in her hair before the friendly embrace ended all too quickly. She sat, and a serving girl took her drink order as the sun began to set over the grand rooftops around the square to the west.

Acaelian endured the small talk that women seemed to thrive upon for a short while before interrupting her next question. "Claudia, I need you to do me a favour," he said.

"Anything. You've done so much for me over the years."

Acaelian allowed himself a crooked, self-deprecating smile—something very much against his nature. "You might not like it. Don't work tonight."

Her shoulders slumped: Acaelian was repeating a plea he had made a number of times over the years. He had even encouraged her to quit the business and allow him to support them both from his ill-gotten gains, but she had refused. In hindsight she had been right, for presently he was frequently dangerously short of making his tithe payments to the Glimmers' Guild every month.

"Aci!" She used her pet name for him and then paused as the serving girl delivered her green tea. When she had gone, she continued: "I've told you before—I must work."

"This is different, Claudia. It's becoming too dangerous."

"It has always been dangerous, Aci; this is the world you and I live in. At least until we find buried treasure or something." It was a flippant remark she always made to take the weight out of a difficult conversation.

"I'm speaking about the Shredder."

Claudia was silent for a long moment, for the threat posed by the murderer terrorising the city of Shen Utah was at the forefront of many people's minds.

Acaelian pressed his point. "I've learned some things. It may no longer be of use to avoid travelling outside of The Lows. Although the bodies are all found in Temple Link, I have information that they're being dumped there. That means the murders could be taking place anywhere! It also means that the victims could be snatched from anywhere. Working the streets in The Lows is just as much a lottery of death as anywhere else in the city. Please, reconsider working this weekend. I have a terrible feeling."

Claudia stared into Acaelian's dark, beseeching eyes; her own flickered from left to right as she considered his earnest plea. "I can't," she said desperately. "I must meet my responsibilities to the Wheelhouse; I am short for the month already, now the autumn season has turned so. Working the streets has always been dangerous."

"Nothing like this!" Acaelian snapped. "Please heed me."

"If I don't make my tithe payment to my own Guild then Grig has to toss me out on the street, and then I'll run a whole list of deadly risks, from death from exposure to the elements to death at the hands of any number of nefarious characters, not just that one sick creature.

"No, the risk posed by not working far outweighs the threat posed to us girls as we stand outside Grig's place, trying to get the patrons in."

Acaelian went to push his point further, but knew it was no use. Claudia's argument held an inordinate amount of rationality and intelligence, and she was absolutely right. It didn't mean he had to like it, though.

"Keep someone with you at all times when outside," he told her, as she finished her drink and gathered herself to leave. "Approach only groups of males—no fewer than three. We think that in order to dump the bodies, the killer needs an accomplice. A pair of people, even a couple, may pose a deadly threat."

"Aci, my brave thief, you always watch over me. I am grateful." For a moment Acaelian feared that he had been viewed spying on her, but then realised she meant it metaphorically.

She leaned over the table and kissed him delicately on his cheek. Were he anything but elven he would have blushed at the view her plunging top gave him and at the thrill of the blissfully moist touch of her lips. But instead he retained his famous elvish stoic composure, dropping his gaze as she stood straight again. Regardless, he was sure she must have known he had stolen a glance, for she afforded him a lopsided smile as she bade him farewell and then turned away and strode across the Temple Square.

Some hours later, as the sun fell beyond the horizon, Acaelian found himself brushing up against the more dangerous portions of The Lows, while he wandered as aimlessly as his thoughts.

A chill swept through the cobbled streets, the buildings on either side of every thoroughfare leaning over the inhabitants like a bully. Despite this, Acaelian trusted the city. He felt an affinity with it. It spoke to him; and it spoke of a fear. The Temple Shredder had inflicted a deep and dangerous wound on the populace, and suddenly the city feared to tread upon the cobbles at night. But the city spoke to Acaelian of a balancing of things, for it had never been the case that those of the Temple Link knew such fear that they were loath to set foot beyond the safe thresholds of their opulent homes. Inhabitants of The Lows lived with that fear always.

The elf rounded a corner and spied a familiar tavern, populated with just a few sad figures at this time of day. Later the tavern would be packed, and fights would undoubtedly ensue, but for now Acaelian felt the need of a short ale.

He drifted in through the door; no one paid him any interest.

He purchased a cheap half-pint of ale and rested his elbows on the bar, cradling his chin in his hands dejectedly. His mind flashed with problems and quandaries, and more than once with the image of Claudia's face in the early evening honeyed light.

Suddenly he was not alone. A laugh sounded at his side and he turned sharply to see a toothless grin beaming at him from within a haggard old face of worn, leathery skin.

Acaelian relaxed as he recognised Jon, an aged member of the Guild of Assassins. As one of the most successful and respected Black Cats in Shen Utah, Jon had done very nicely for himself and reached an age whereupon he would benefit from retirement—an impressive feat for a man whose very business was dealing in death.

Jon was a likeable old rogue, quick with a joke and even quicker with a drink. Despite his rapier wit and rapid grin, something about Jon spoke of a hollow sadness. The elf believed that living such a life may have removed something from the human, and that made him sad too.

Regardless, Jon was a wise individual, and always a source of sage advice.

"Where did you appear from?" Acaelian asked, laughing at Jon's expression.

Jon's brow furrowed with amusement. "I've been here literally the entire time you have."

Acaelian shook his head. "I didn't see you."

"You saw what I wanted you to see, and that was 'nothing worth registering'. I taught you that a long time ago, boy. And, as I recall, you learned it very quickly. I imagine that were we both to leave this place right now and a member of our illustrious city watch come and question these patrons…" Jon indicated the rest of the customers in the drab tavern, "not one of them would be able to describe either of us."

Acaelian remembered being taught a great deal by the Black Cat—and he appreciated every nugget. Most apprentice thieves are given their training by an individual mentor, as Acaelian had been. The problem comes with professional pride, for no mentor truly wants to be superseded by his own apprentice. Jon had no such misgivings, and had taught Acaelian things no member of any other Guild would learn. It had made him the thief he was today.

"So, judging by how away with the fairies you seem to be, is there anything I can help with? Can't have a protégé of mine wandering around without one eye on his surroundings."

"It's silly, really."

Jon blinked and clucked his tongue. "That's how most things seem until you speak about them."

"I'm worried…about a girl."

"Oh Lord!" huffed the old man.

"No, nothing like that! It's this Temple Shredder business."

"This girl; she's not a Wheel, is she?"

Acaelian hesitated, steeling himself for the obvious response, and then nodded.

Jon laughed once, like an old dog barking. "For goodness' sake, boy, surely you're brought up better than that, even on the streets. *Especially* on the streets!"

"It's not like that," protested Acaelian.

"I didn't bloody ask!" Jon cut him short. "Just be careful wherein one dips one's wick!" He laughed again and then shook his head. "We of the Guilds lead dangerous lives, Acaelian. The Thugs in the Guild of Pillars face the most physical danger, but they're prepared for it. In fact, by and large they go looking for it! The rest court danger on a daily basis, be they Whispers, Black Cats or Glimmers; and we're prepared to face it. But Wheels, they prepare themselves for all manner of sordid affairs, without a thought for their own protection—within or without.

"Most will not live to be lonely spinsters, Acaelian, let alone happily married women. They either contract something nasty, dying with bubbling coughs and itchy parts, or they come a cropper on the job at the hands of some overzealous client or even a vengeful wife. I'll tell you this much: when I worked the dark corridors of this city there was many a time I took commission from a wealthy woman, tired of her husband's non-chivalrous ways. Most of the time it was to arrange *his* death, but more than once jealousy drove them to call for the Wheel's head too.

"Such doings can screw with your mind, boy. Look at how this is making you feel already. This could cost your head. If you go on a job like this, without checking your corners and being one hundred per cent vigilant, some wary merchant will have your head from your shoulders."

Jon shook his head at Acaelian's clearly deflated expression.

"Acaelian, in our lines of work we can't afford such ties, for they make us weak. For your own sake, I think it best that you do what you can to forget this woman. Cut her from your mind, and from your heart if necessary. Or I fear it will be the death of you."

Acaelian sipped at his ale thoughtfully, his chest hollow. The thought that Claudia could never feel anything for him had always plagued his friendship with the girl. However, was he capable of turning his feelings for her away, snuffing them out as easily as a candle flame? For while his feelings for her were merely unrequited, there was always a lover's hope. Once he turned away from her, destroyed his feelings for her, then that hope was gone.

Jon turned from the tavern counter, the candles turning the walls the colour of bruised flesh as the sun dropped lower in the sky. The old man hesitated before placing a hand on the elf's shoulder comfortingly. "I'm sorry I don't have more pleasant advice, but I certainly don't have better..." The hand gave him an encouraging squeeze, the strength of which surprised Acaelian, and then Jon left him alone with his thoughts.

"I'm telling you, my coins are on cannibals," Jewl said, his short, stocky legs extended before him. "It's bound to be cannibals. You know, I heard a story that a city in the south fell under the power of a cannibal conclave and the populace just started decreasing. No one worked out why until it was too late. Almost everyone had been eaten up."

The rest of the safehouse living room was in confusion as the group gathered a few belongings and their weapons. "That makes no sense," replied Rish. "Who was doing the cooking? Unless the cooks were cannibals too, wouldn't there be a point where the cook thought it odd that the kitchen boy was criticising the quality of a joint of meat by asking how well hung 'Old Uncle Harry' was?"

"I'd *heard* that about Old Uncle Harry," said Rebrof, slinging his pack onto his shoulder and settling a longsword in the scabbard on his hip. His tunic was bright white and he'd obviously made an attempt to have it freshly pressed. He wore a long cloak over the strap of his pack as protection against the elements. He looked every part the soldier-captain he once was.

"I can't see it being cannibals," said Stefon without mirth. "That'd be too easy. Now get your gear together: we're going to see what we can find out."

Jewl was obviously reticent to leave the relative warmth of the cosy safehouse and venture out into the rainy grimness of the early evening city.

"Where are we going, exactly?" Rish asked. He had dressed economically: several layers of cotton wrapped by supple leather armour. No tassels or corners of garments were left to dangle freely, and the colours were dark, mottled grey and unremarkable. Unless placed under direct study, the feral Rish would be easily forgettable, and that was how he liked it. In a belt scabbard he wore a short sword and tied into his pack was a lovingly wrapped shortbow. Once strung, the bow was deadly in his hands.

"I want to take a look at a couple of things. First we need to check out the connections to Governor Meena Saqir. I think the best way to do that is to look at his accounts. Those fat money merchants around Wahib love to keep records and parchments of all sorts. Hopefully we can make that work against the governor." Stefon fixed his belt buckle securely and grabbed his hand-crossbow as Jewl hefted his mighty greataxe to be cradled in his arms.

"Sounds like a load of wasted time to me," the dwarf rumbled. "Why don't I just go to the man's mansion and smack him with my axe?"

"Dead men don't do too much talking, Jewl," Brooss told him.

Stefon looked around the room. Jewl, Rish, Rebrof and Brooss were all ready. And they looked a mean group to cross. Add to that number the large and imposing frame of Pryn, who was just returning from the garderobe out back, and Stefon had a dangerous, versatile group at his command.

"OK, I've thought this through and spoken with Rish and Rebrof. I want to check out this chap's place of work. At this time of day we should find his actual holdings empty." The sun had long started to set and the lane outside was already draped in the insubstantial light of dusk. "Brooss was able to provide the address of his registered offices, which apparently Governors aren't actually supposed to have. So listen, Brooss." She looked up from adjusting the string of her bow. "I don't want to know where you got that information." She smiled and nodded. "I want Rebrof and Pryn to come with me to see what we can find in that place, if anything. Rish, you take Jewl and Brooss back down to the area between the southern postern gate and that brothel you were at this morning. I want you to see if you can find anything to indicate a subterranean entrance or passage into the areas underneath Wahib itself—something that might lead south or west under the city, toward the postern gate.

From all accounts it should be an entrance large enough to allow the passage of at least a handcart."

Rish let out an unconvinced hiss of breath, but stopped short of openly protesting the assignment.

Stefon put out a placating hand. "I don't expect you to stumble right across it. If you can't find anything of interest then stake out the brothel itself. I have a bad feeling about that place, and the fact you learned nothing at all of interest earlier today actually alarms me."

"Oh, she was lying!" Rish nodded. "Trust me on that."

"I don't doubt it. If we can't find you here when we return then we'll continue down to the southern streets and seek you out down there. Try to avoid trouble, and certainly don't court any confrontation." He looked from face to face. "Remember we're probably being watched."

Rish shrugged, obviously unimpressed by the potential threat Stefon perceived.

With that they were ready and Rebrof lead the way, opening the door to create an increase in the din of the rain tattooing off tiled rooftops up and down the long lane. The precipitation had returned with a vengeance since late morning's mild respite and the lane was awash. Brooss's modified wagon was at rest in the middle of the narrow cobbled passage, potentially barring the way for other drawn vehicles attempting to traverse the lane. The team of two horses was well covered and carefully prepared for the poor weather, but they still nickered impatiently. The sky overhead was darker than this time in the afternoon would normally suggest, and it almost felt like dusk.

Rebrof stepped out under the awning of the entrance to Stefon's safehouse. Leaning forward and peering up at the sky, he put out a hand, palm up, to test the force of the rain.

It was as Stefon was going to say something about the futility of such a test that he sensed something was wrong. The hairs on the nape of his neck bristled, his palms became clammy and his heart suddenly raced.

But it was all too late. Rebrof grunted and leaned over fully. Stefon saw the arrowhead protruding from the back of Rebrof's hamstring, having punched through the front of his quad muscle. Rebrof's sword hand, which had been testing the rain, was impaled by the same arrow, pinned to his thigh. Rebrof began to scream.

Stefon tried to push past him or to drag him back inside but it was to no avail; Rish was too close behind Stefon to allow him room. "Archer!" Stefon warned, straining to get a decent hold on Rebrof.

And then the second arrow struck. Rebrof's scream was immediately cut off. A wooden shaft was suddenly jutting from the crown of his skull, a great gush of crimson fluid arcing into the rain. His body slumped forward.

Stefon was exposed.

Giving Rebrof up for dead, Stefon vaulted over the falling body and made for cover behind the large wheel of the armoured wagon in the street. Hurling himself forward and twisting, his rump skidded on the rainwater and he thumped against the wood of the wheel. "Archer high!" he called again, struggling to unsheathe his sword. Brooss had already taken up position in the doorway and was nocking an arrow to draw a bead on their unseen assailant.

Blood from Rebrof's body sluiced down the centre gully of the lane past Stefon's back. The carcass of his comrade lay motionless.

Snapping out of his reverie, Stefon finally brought his weapon from the scabbard and hefted it, getting up to his haunches. Coming down the lane from the north, he could make out an indistinct, shimmering figure. In the dull light no details could be seen, but it moved quickly and carried a blade in the right hand.

"Ambush!" he shouted. Looking back down the street to

the south Stefon could make out another two figures coming up on either side of the thoroughfare. No commonfolk could be seen and no help would be quick in coming.

Brooss fired an arrow from the doorway. There was no answering cry and Stefon could see her frantically nocking another arrow. "Infantry! One north, two south!" he cried as he scrambled to his feet. In seconds the first elements would be upon him, and it wouldn't do to still be prone.

He quickly guessed his own best chance was to take on the single assailant, yet instead he rushed south, trying to intercept the two attackers coming up the lane. For his personal safety, it was a bad idea, but he'd have the slightly higher ground and needed to buy some time for the others.

Rushing the first black-clad swordsman with his shoulder, he slammed into his chest and drove him back against the wall. Swinging his blade up, he caught the second man's attack high over his head, deflecting the black blade and thrusting forward with his own backhand swipe, again driving the man back.

From high to Stefon's right side, he heard an anguished cry quickly followed by Brooss's call: "Archer clear! Move!"

Trusting that someone would back him up, Stefon ignored the first man, who was trying to regain his balance, and instead forced the issue with the black-clad figure before him, driving on with a flurry of blows that his foe managed to deflect and parry without reply.

Stefon felt, more than saw, the approach of the first assailant almost before it was too late. But the figure's overhand cleave—aimed squarely at the nape of his neck—was smashed aside by Jewl's mighty greataxe. Jewl then bellowed in fury as he pursued his opponent, who defended skilfully.

Stefon's challenger took a short hop back, earning room to prepare another assault, and Stefon steadied the blade in his left hand, taking a good look at him.

He stood no more than five and a half feet tall, and was clad all in black. The material of his clothes was somehow difficult to gauge with the eye, as though it was actually incorporeal; almost insubstantial. Perhaps not even like material at all, as though a grasp at the blackness would return only dark, misty air. A single eye-slit in the darkness of the face revealed two narrowed eyes, full of the determination to kill.

In his right hand, the man hefted a narrow, curved blade that was blackened to be unreflective. But there was no mistaking the keenness of the blade or the eagerness of the bearer to test the same.

The man lunged. Stefon parried the blow easily across his body but was forced to jump up and away as the narrow blade ricocheted off his sword and whipped back around, under his unguarded side. The black blade slashed through the air where his guts had just been with a deadly whistle. Stefon staggered back, preparing for another assault.

Jewl swept past in his peripheral vision, using the length of his greataxe to good effect, prodding and then swiping at the other enemy, who had no answer for the heavier weapon that was being wielded with such expertise.

Behind Stefon, up the lane, shouts could be heard; then footfalls on cobbles in the rain. One of Brooss's arrows whistled over Stefon's shoulder toward the opponent near Jewl. Amazingly the black blade swept through the shaft of the arrow, cleanly snapping it in twain.

But it was clear these black figures wanted no part in an outnumbered scuffle. The farthest took to his heels and was quickly followed by the man standing before Stefon. He let him go, instead checking if Jewl was OK. He was.

"Let's get going!" Jewl followed him to the wagon.

Brooss jumped down from the driver's section of the carriage, having already prepared the reins. She unslung her bow and started taking aim up the lane. Rish had dealt a vicious wound to the northernmost foe, but another black figure had spirited his injured comrade away into a nearby alley. There was no sign of the archer on the rooftops opposite.

Rish knelt near Rebrof's still form, checking for vital signs. With an arrow in his head, there was obviously little hope.

Pryn was opening the top sections of the wagon and waving for Stefon and Jewl to climb aboard. Stefon saw the reason for concern. Independent of the black-clad foes, two local militia were racing down the street toward them, one with bow in hand. But behind them came a tall figure in a long, black cloak. The hood was pulled up, but Stefon recognised a cleric of The Light when he saw one. And they were not to be trifled with.

Rish looked up and shook his head. Rebrof was dead.

Pryn yanked Jewl up into the cab and held out a hand for Stefon. "Rish, come on!" Stefon yelled. But it was obvious that Rish and Brooss would have no chance of boarding before the soldiers caught them. "Go!" Stefon yelled at Pryn before evading his outstretched hand and running for Rish. "Go south, lose any tails and find that entrance! We'll come to you." He then rushed to Rish's side.

Brooss let fly another arrow that took the nearest guard in the bow-arm, spinning him round and forcing him to lose his grip on his weapon. She was an accurate shot; that was for certain. She hadn't intended a mortal wound. They had no quarrel with the city militia.

"Leave him, Rish!" Stefon said. "Rebrof's gone, and we've no more time." The two fled across the lane, taking Brooss with them. The only avenue for escape seemed to be the building across from the safehouse.

It was an old, abandoned apothecary's workshop with a steep, wooden stairway that ran up to a door in the first floor exterior wall. They took the steps two at a time: Stefon first, Brooss between them and Rish bringing up the rear.

Below them in the lane, they could see the last city guard

giving chase to the wagon, but it was futile. There was no possibility that a man on foot would catch the wagon now it was in motion.

As Brooss covered them with her bow, Rish pushed past to get at the lock of the door at the top of the stairway. "It's not locked," he told them after a quick look, "just stuck." He pushed his shoulder into the jamb and the wood creaked in protest.

Stefon looked up the street for the cleric and found the tall figure standing in the centre of the lane, his cloak pushed around his legs by the light breeze. He seemed untouched by the rain, and he was staring at the rear of the receding wagon. As Rish forced the jamb once more, the cleric looked around the lane for a moment, as if seeking a sound, before turning to look up over his right shoulder at Stefon.

Even in the small amount of light afforded by the dull, rain-swept afternoon, Stefon could make out no features. But as he was fixed with that glare, he could swear he saw red eyes flash with mysterious fire somewhere in the cowl. The cleric raised an arm and pointed with sinister poise before Stefon heard the muttered accusation, "Seer…"

Stefon spat an oath. He had no idea what a seer was, but he had no interest in finding out what the cleric had in mind. "Rish, open that!" The cleric threw open his cloak and reached inside with his right hand, producing a massive bastardsword. The blade was easily beyond four feet in length, and thicker than Stefon's arm. The steel appeared to reflect an iridescence that wasn't there, as though it radiated a light or power of its own generation. It fairly sang with unnatural power.

Stefon panicked and rushed up to the door, throwing his weight into the panel nearest the lock-plate as Rish applied his own force. With a splintering crash, the door gave and the two friends tumbled through into a wide first floor foyer.

Without preamble, Stefon jumped back to his feet and

rushed forward toward an open doorway in the far wall. Rish seemed to sense the panic and took after his friend as Brooss rushed in behind them, trying to replace her bow on her back.

"The cleric?" Rish asked.

"He's right behind us," Stefon said, "and he looks really mad." Inside the corridor beyond the foyer, the passage ran left to right; at the far end there intercepted a stairwell forming a T-junction. Stefon ran for the junction, Rish close behind and Brooss following on. He was sure he could hear the pounding of the cleric's boots on the stairwell outside, but it may have been his thumping heart.

At the junction, the stairs ran up to the right and down to the left. The steps were of old, rotten wood but seemed fairly sturdy for their age. Stefon stepped out of the way and onto the first step up, giving room for Rish and Brooss to pass beyond him. The stairway above was clear.

Rish rushed past him, a look of calm determination on his face that Stefon knew well. This was business, and Rish was a pro. He took the stairs down carefully and deliberately, short sword in his right hand, his left extended for balance.

Brooss reached Stefon and looked at him for instruction. "Just keep going," he told her. She nodded and rushed down the stairs after Rish, who had reached the hall at the foot of the stairs and was waiting for her, keeping the route covered.

From the stairs Stefon couldn't see whether the exit was open or what type of door might be barring their escape down there, but all such thoughts fled his mind when the cleric stepped around the doorframe from the first floor foyer.

The cleric threw off his cloak as he passed through the door, dropping it to the floor. He stood at over seven feet tall, perhaps a match for Pryn, but his chest was broader than Stefon's by half. He wore black cotton garb of simple design, being made up of lengths of material wrapped around the torso. Tight black leggings and black animal-skin boots couldn't hide the strength of the cleric's legs. His sword was held effortlessly in his right hand, despite the fact that it must have weighed near forty pounds. Following what he thought he had seen in the rain outside, Stefon had expected to see burning pits of fire where the cleric's eyes should have been, but instead he saw a plain, unremarkable face with almost docile eyes. Sandy hair was cut close about his ears and brushed up away from his tan face. He had no expression, even when he opened his mouth to once again utter the word, "Seer."

The idea occurred to stand his ground and fight this foe. Stefon had known that one day he was likely to run foul of the clerics, being a professional consort of less-than-righteous morals. But he had never looked forward to the time. And now he understood why: he'd never felt such palpable fear. He ran.

And the cleric came after him.

As Stefon took the downward stairs two at a time, he felt the boards creak beneath his feet, the wood warping under the pressure. And he heard the thunderous footfalls of the cleric rushing to catch him.

The hall below was empty. As the chamber came fully into view, he saw the doorway onto the street was wide open and could see Brooss running down a short path to the road beyond. The small hallway also had exits to either side.

The cleric could be heard booming down the stairs behind him.

Stefon took the last four steps in one leap, reaching out with his right foot, hoping to land on the run.

But he didn't land at all.

Instead he was seized around the back of the neck and seemed to stop stock still in midair, his feet flailing forward through momentum. And then he was dangling, struggling for breath, a vast hand encircling his neck.

Being turned in midair, he came face to face with the

cleric, now standing in the hall regarding his prize with detachment. His face still betrayed no emotion as he hissed, "Seer!" in Stefon's face. With both hands, Stefon was scratching and clawing at the fist around his neck, kicking to try and find release, but it was to no avail. No breath came and his vision was swimming. Blood pounded in his head as the pressure built, and his consciousness began to fail.

Suddenly the crushing hand was gone and he tumbled for an age before his rump slammed on the stone floor of the hall. Pain flashed through his back, jarring him back into more lucid consciousness.

Rish moved like a blur, thrusting the blade of his short sword into the torso of the cleric again and again. Blood sprayed across the dusty floor and walls as the mighty cleric struggled to smash Rish with either fist. But the scoundrel was too quick, too evasive. He easily dodged the hefty blows thrown his way, again slamming the blade into the man's back-back-ribs-ribs-thigh-chest-stomach, drawing strangled bellows of rage and sapping his strength.

Although he must have been in colossal pain, the cleric wasn't slowing, no matter how many times Rish plunged the blade home, and it was merely a matter of time before he was crushed by a lucky swipe of the cleric's fist.

On the floor at Stefon's feet lay the awesome bastard-sword the cleric had dropped, probably when Rish had assaulted him from one of the side doors to the hall. The blade still seemed to ring eerily with undisclosed energy, faintly radiating dull red light.

Despite his reluctance to touch the weapon, Stefon snatched it up and scrambled to his feet. Although he expected to be borne down by the weight of the blade, it fairly leapt into his grasp, gliding like warm syrup as he sliced it through the air in a wide swipe from left to right.

The motion of the blade was unlike any weapon he'd ever handled. It took no effort to slice the blade into the cleric's midriff. Likewise it seemed an equally effortless task to complete the stroke and to carve through the cleric's guts and spine, cutting him cleanly in two. With a torrent of blood from the sundered torso, the two halves of the cleric tumbled to the floor and the hall was in silence.

The blade rang in his hands, thrumming from the impact with a power and energy he couldn't describe, and for a moment he stared at the weapon with clear awe as the ringing of the strike faded.

"Stefon," Rish said, shaking his friend by the arm. "We've got to get out of here. We're safe now, but it won't be long before those militiamen find this mess." The hall was bathed in blood, as was most of Rish's leather armour. But that would wash out in the rain. "You planning on taking that?"

When Stefon looked back at the sword it seemed to have narrowed, and maybe even shortened in length. He put that down to the effects the huge cleric had had on his original perception and shrugged it off. "I'm taking it for sure." He looked at the scabbard on the cleric's ruined waist and plucked it from the carcass. Slipping the blade into the matte black scabbard he found it a perfect fit. The weapon's pommel showed no evidence of the resonating power he witnessed when wielding the sword.

It all seemed impossibly smaller than before.

Trying not to let his discomfort show, Stefon hefted the new find in his right hand and set off after Brooss, who waited for them at the end of a short path. Rish followed and all three proceeded north at a brusque walk, keen to be away from the scene but wary of attracting attention. No one followed them into the darkening night.

Chapter Eight
Hating Horses

Andi's group had come across the tracks a half hour into the forested hills en route to Shenmadock's eastern border with Ipsica. The sun had set behind them in the western sky, bathing most of the barley-coloured fields at their backs in an eerie peach-and-amber light, followed by moonlit blues. The current dusk would soon pass into night.

As the gradient had grown on the incline of the hills, the group had dismounted and were leading their horses by hand, ensuring not to make too much noise. Trusting Andi to follow the tracks at their feet easily enough, the others kept a rigid vigil on the woods around them and the path ahead. With the early evening light, this was often the hardest time of day to see detail at a distance, and they were wary of ambush.

Just because the slaver column was showing no signs of hiding either their numbers or any evidence of their passing didn't mean they weren't prepared to deal harshly with any foolhardy crusaders that might be in silent pursuit. A trap was not only possible, but in Andi's opinion highly likely.

And yet for more than ten miles they followed the tracks into the mountains without encountering any protective rear elements of the column.

But what was certain was that the cavalcade was close. Their path had turned north a short distance into the tree-line and then a few hundred yards later had momentarily formed a switchback; the steep incline of the hills often forced travellers traversing them to protect their animals by treading a safer, more gentle route over the pass. The current stretch of path went north-northeasterly for quite some distance, but Andi sensed they were making good progress east nonetheless, and she had a growing feeling that the slavers were indeed making for the border and beyond to neighbouring Ipsica.

They were fortunate that this had been a comparatively mild autumn by recent standards, and the South Range was still easily passable. Once winter struck, the ice and snow would descend within a week of the cold snap, and then traversing the mountain border would be highly treacherous, if not fatal.

The forest around them was quieter than expected for an evening. Only a few birds chanced a song as Andi passed, leading her mount behind her on a loose rein. The cold of the night could be felt growing on the air, for the skies above and behind them were clear and cloudless.

On each side of her walked Manic, to her right, and Finhead, to her left. The tall reptilian carried an odd-looking ornate bow of light-stained wood. The bowstring was pale and the quiver on his back carried arrows fletched with orange and pink feathers. His was the only long-range weapon among their number aside from Andi's own composite shortbow.

Andi halted their progress for a brief rest and some water. Earlier in the afternoon, she and Finhead had dropped a couple of pheasants that had been spooked by their passage, and both would be stripped and prepared for dinner. But they would need a fire, and Andi was reticent to light one knowing that the enemy column was surely near enough to spy firelight through the trees.

"This can't go on much longer!" Eidos commented, as they distributed some cured meat from Manic's pack.

"It's OK," said Manic, misunderstanding his human comrade. "We've the meat from those pheasants and enough fresh water. There was more water on those horses you left in the forest glade back there." Apparently he needed a little more water on average than the others, and became crabby without it. "What did you do with that horse, anyway? We might have been able to use an extra mount."

Eidos chewed his dried meat ration for a moment before speaking around the clump in his mouth. "Nothing; just tied it up and left it where it was."

Andi called up a mental image of the forest path they had travelled before meeting Finhead. "Just a second; what did you tie the horse *to*?"

He chewed a couple more times while he stared at Andi, sensing her tone. "The other horse," he replied matter-of-factly.

"The dead one?"

He nodded.

"You tied a living horse to a dead horse and left it there indefinitely?"

Again Eidos nodded.

Manic laughed, shaking his head. "You crazy bastard. The horse is going to go totally bonkers being tied to his decomposing friend forever!"

Eidos stopped chewing, obviously just thinking about this."I didn't consider that," he confessed with a huffed laugh. And even though it wasn't very funny—actually quite tragic—Andi found herself laughing too.

The soft laughter petered out into the dark forest around them.

And then Andi's inhuman hearing detected sounds reverberating round the trees that were not indigenous to the woodlands. They were faint and indistinct, but it sounded like the familiar din that usually originated from a gathering of people.

Andi held her finger to her lips and removed her bow from her saddle-pack behind her. She dropped what provisions and equipment she still carried and snatched up her quiver of flight arrows. "I can hear them!" she told the others, referring to their quarry of slavers.

Having seen her reaction, the group were keenly scanning the trees around them. Despite the relatively recent sunset the woods were rapidly becoming dark and soon Eidos would be unable to see clearly without firelight.

Having spent his years of development underground, and being of dwarven birth, Manic would be able to see well enough in even the darkest night, so long as the moon lent some of its glow. Only pitch blackness would rob him of sight.

From earlier discussion Andi recalled that Finhead viewed the world in a black-and-white, greyscale way that, while it made it difficult for him to distinguish colours, also made seeing in darkness almost second nature.

And as for herself, her unusual heritage meant seeing in conditions of low light was not a challenge or a strain and was as taxing as seeing in clear noon sunlight.

Moving quickly, with catlike agility, Andi rushed to the nearest tree and pressed her shoulder to the trunk, bow in one hand and black quiver in the other. A quick moment of concentration was all that she needed to locate the direction of the noises. They originated up the track in the direction they had been heading.

Eidos lumbered up next to her, his axe gripped tensely in his hands, armour glinting in what shafts of moonlight managed to make it through the tree canopy. Unfortunately it would be a cold night, for the moon was high and the sky was clear of cloud. Eidos had no chance of passing unnoticed through the dark woods with such polished armour.

"Where are we going?" he asked her.

Realising he probably hadn't detected the noises from such a distance, she pointed in the direction of the enemy with her bow and replied, "They're that way. Maybe a hundred yards or more."

"How can you hear that? I can't hear a thing even if I strain."

"It's luck, although I've never decided good or bad."

Eidos had a look on his face that showed he plainly didn't follow that last comment, but to his credit he let it pass without inquisition. "What do we do?"

Manic and Finhead crouched near them, questioning expressions on each face. They were all armed and prepared, unnecessary items piled by the horses.

Glancing again at Eidos's armour, Andi thought it best to get more information about their targets without being seen, and Eidos wasn't dressed for that. And of course Manic had proven himself clumsy enough to be of little help either. The world was Manic's China Shop.

"I'm going to go and have a look; nice and quiet-like." Andi made to move away and Finhead followed her. She stopped and turned to face him in the dark. "I probably move swifter and quieter alone, my friend."

"I understand that, but you'll find I'm no hindrance." In the dark she saw his alien grin and was oddly disquieted by the expression. It might have been the forest of needle teeth contained within. Glancing back at the others, she saw Manic slumped against the tree, his arms folded across his chest and his sword nearby, while Eidos still crouched, watching.

Andi nodded once to Finhead before positioning her cloth quiver on her back and rushing off at pace through the low undergrowth, endeavouring to keep close to the trees she passed. She didn't intend to make a target of herself for any keen-eyed sentries the slavers may have set up. The fact that the column had travelled throughout the day with such disdain for would-be attackers, coupled with the noise they were presently making in the growing gloom of the woods, concerned her. It was as though they simply didn't consider the prospect of being attacked a possibility.

Her opinion changed as she and Finhead travelled farther ahead. Through the thick tree trunks before them, light from fire could be seen on the bark and Andi motioned for Finhead to stop near her.

To his credit he had made excellent time keeping up with her, and had created no more noise than she had. He wasn't even out of breath.

"Well done," she whispered, trying not to sound too condescending. "I think it's best if we use the trees to get a view of things. We're not lucky enough for them *not* to have posted sentries."

He nodded in the dark. "I'm too heavy to climb a tree without breaking it. I will stay here and guard your descent should you need to do it in a hurry. If trouble approaches I shall thump the trunk with the hilt of my axe twice in order to alert you."

Andi wasn't sure she felt comfortable relying on the stranger, but it made perfectly good sense, so she resisted arguing. Instead she moved forward further, careful not to make much sound, and then ascended the nearest tree. It was easy going and Finhead stayed close to the roots, his odd-looking bow in hand. After a few moments of moving from branch to branch she reached a decent height and straddled a firm branch, keeping her torso close to the trunk of the tree.

She was almost forty feet off the ground, higher than she had anticipated, and had a good vantage point. Looking down through the thinning foliage of the tree, she could see a glade thirty yards beyond.

The slavers had indeed set up camp, and efficiently too. There were two slave-carrying wagons, with lockable cages, arranged to form the side of an improvised corral. The cavalry horses were staked out here and were being tended to by two of the slavers. The slaves themselves had been allowed out of the cages to exercise and were now tied to the wheels of the wagons.

A third wagon, apparently for support infantry, was positioned at the far left portion of the camp, with two soldiers already asleep in the bay.

In the centre of the camp a fire was being nurtured, with two stew-pots positioned using a prefab spit and cradle. Andi could see the broth was coming to boil already. Idly she thought the fire-and-spit arrangement was potentially perfect for her pheasant haul.

Sentries could be seen walking the perimeter as the slaves were being tied up, and a couple more were evident in the trees beyond the firelight, invisible to human eyes in the shadows of the trees and the dark of the night.

The majority of the slavers were gathered about the fire. After a quick scan she took their number to be a couple of dozen armed men. Mostly they carried longswords, but a few had poor standard bows or crossbows near them. Those already around the fire were passing a bottle of something undoubtedly potent between them.

She was unable to discern a likely leader, although it was easy to spot the more organised slavers as those bullying and restraining the slaves, despite the captives appearing defeated and docile.

Andi descended the tree and motioned for Finhead to follow her away from the camp, back toward Eidos and Manic. They intercepted the wide deer trail that the train had been following and made it back to the others without incident.

Andi repeated to the group what it was that she had seen from her high perch.

"The sentries were alert and awake," Finhead informed them, "but they were less than vigilant. They were going through the motions. I believe they are not expecting an attack, or even a roaming beast worthy of a scuffle."

"So what do we do?" asked Manic, still slumped against a tree.

"We must report what we have discovered to Reinhart back at Hightower," Eidos said, his axe lying near him. His arms were across his chest and one foot was against the tree at his back. He looked less than impressed at being left behind on the reconnaissance trip.

"What would we be reporting back with?" Andi asked. "What would you say?"

"I would inform his Lordship that slaver crews were operating in the eastern provinces of this duchy, and that they are removing tenants of the farmlands in and around Hightower."

"But what else? He'll ask who these slavers were. He'll ask for a description of them: where they hailed from and what weapons they used. He might ask about the slaves and where they were from. But I'll guarantee you this much: he'll ask you where the slaves were bound for and why the hell you didn't set them free."

Eidos looked at his feet.

"Now I don't know where they're going, but I'll tell you this much: I'm not leaving without doing something about that caravan. Even if it's just staying tight to them until they get where they're going."

"I never took you for a hero," said Manic.

"I'm not," she confessed. "But the more we accomplish on our own, the more Reinhart is likely to pay out. Getting to smack up a bunch of slavers is a perk, but money is the only motivation I understand."

"I'm not sure…" Eidos grumbled.

Finhead hissed his disapproval, which earned him a sour look from Eidos.

"Oh, I've had enough of this messing about!" barked

Manic. "I say we take them while they sleep!"

"It's a fool's errand, Master Dwarf!" complained Eidos. "They number twenty-plus in a dugout emplacement, and we're simply four, who don't know each other very well. Those odds are folly, even with surprise on our side. They would have us defeated before we reached the fires!"

Andi pondered the idea in the deepening twilight as the bugs of night took to flight around them and the furtive sounds of nocturnal crawlers filled the undergrowth nearby. She stared at what they had to work with: their weapons and armour, their provisions and equipment, their mounts and their bedding packs. It wasn't much.

But then something crossed her mind. She grinned at the others.

Manic looked back and could only mutter, "Uh-oh."

As night wrapped the streets of Wahib, water flowed through the gutters in streams, carrying filth and germs past every home. Children, driven mad by the lack of freedom, still splashed happily in the mire, grey water lapping up beyond their knees. Their parents were nowhere to be seen.

Probably dead, Stefon thought.

He hunkered lower in the overhang of the closed bakery as the downpour continued like a giant veil of water two feet from his face. Overhead the intermittent rumble of thunder rolled across the sky, closely followed by a slash of lightning that cut the clouds open above them.

To the north, above the adjacent rooftops, Stefon could make out the twinkling firelights of the richer portions of Wahib, where the mansions of the important citizens dappled the hills of the northern quarter. The mansions overlooked the rest of the city, and overlooking them in turn stood the old spires of Wahib Palace, which now served as a governmental hub, administrative centre, city garrison and pointless echo of a forgotten time.

Dwarfing the once-magnificent spires stood the Tower of Light, whose illuminating brilliance painted the night sky with startling white throughout each night, and managed to pick out the dance of the raindrops even at this distance.

Another flash of lightning was followed by a peal of thunder that boomed through the heavens. Brooss flinched at the staccato blue flash. Approaching deep autumn, this weather was more than unseasonable; it was unnatural. Even during the most humid early summer evenings Wahib rarely saw thunder and lightning, and never with such heavy rain.

"Are you sure those are Meena's offices?" Stefon asked Brooss with incredulity.

"That's what my information tells me, and it's pretty reliable."

"They don't look like a governor's holdings," Rish offered.

He was right. The address was on a long, drab terrace of squat, two-storey buildings that weren't particularly wide. The exterior was stone and masonry that was suffering the worst the weather had thrown at it for the past months. Giant slabs of clay-work masonry were missing and stone bricks and mortar were exposed to the elements. Stefon surmised that these buildings wouldn't survive much more of this rain. The front door was wooden and the windows were boarded up.

"Well I guess all we can do is take a look." Stefon scanned the street once more, only to discover that the children had moved on down the road and no other onlookers were present. "Come on."

He led Brooss and Rish across the wet-cobbled street to the far side, the new weapon fastened to his belt giving no sense of weight whatsoever. The blade didn't seem to be on his belt at all, other than the feeling of movement from the hasp as he ran for the wooden door.

Without waiting, he threw his shoulder into the door panel just above the main lock and the wood exploded inwards with a dull crash, splinters showering across the inner hall as he skidded to a halt, caught off-guard by the weakness of the door.

Rish moved past him, proceeding down the hall to investigate the kitchen. "That was subtle!" he muttered as he went. "Never think to just knock?" Stefon shrugged as he secured the door behind Brooss, who entered last.

There was no illumination inside the building. The left-hand wall was the separating section for next door. A flight of stairs proceeded up from the hall to the first floor landing along this separating wall. The hall itself led through to a kitchen area in general disrepair. The partition wall to the right had signs that a doorway was once in evidence there, but it had long since been sealed.

Nothing moved inside the building and a thin layer of dust covered everything. Nonetheless Stefon had to resist the urge to draw his new weapon, for something in the place had him on edge.

Brooss pointed at the blocked-up doorway. "That's odd," she commented. She had drawn a thin blade, two feet or more from guard to tip. She moved cautiously down the hall and stopped at the foot of the stairs, waiting for Stefon.

The doorjamb was too damaged for him to close the door properly, so he picked up some loose stones from the hall and crammed them into the base of the broken door, wedging it shut.

Reaching the foot of the stairs, he saw another door in the right-hand partition wall that led to a room cluttered with cases and file boxes. They were all empty. The rear windows were also boarded up, but enough light filtered through gaps in the boards to reveal the room was in disused disarray.

"This place looks abandoned," Stefon muttered, nudging an empty box with his foot. "Long abandoned."

"Well you say that," replied Rish, returning from the kitchen, "but there's a teapot in there with leaves that smell fairly fresh. Not recent, but not ancient either."

"What do you make of this missing room?" Stefon indicated the boarded-up doorway as he rejoined the others in the hall.

"It's not uncommon for older buildings like this to be reformed inside," Brooss said. "Property owners in such a sector will purchase portions of neighbouring buildings when they need to expand but can't afford to buy out another holding. This kind of thing is really not unusual. I think on the other side of this sealed door you'll find a room from next door."

Stefon led them upstairs to finish the search and found the first floor room at the back in worse condition than the one below it. Although all exterior walls were secure, the ceiling section at the join with the back wall had long ago collapsed. The attic space above was visible and a ledge had formed where the attic floor had subsided. Someone had removed the larger lumps of debris that would have formed from such a collapse, although the floor was hardly swept clean.

"What do you make of that?" Rish asked.

"Hungry woodworm." Stefon looked at the floor upon which they all stood. "Nobody go dancing a jig!" he smirked. "I'll check the other rooms."

He left Brooss and Rish in the collapsed room and moved through the three remaining chambers. One was a bathroom that still contained a running pump system, although he didn't trust the stagnant water. The other two were largely empty, other than the odd piece of broken furniture. The windows were again sealed.

He returned to the damaged room, ignoring the stench of

mould seeping from the bathroom. "What the hell are you doing?" he asked. Rish was busy over by the far wall trying to propel himself up to reach the broken ledge of the open attic space. Brooss was looking round for something to help.

"I want to go up there!" He lunged again, fingers scrabbling at the wooden outcrop without gaining hold before he tumbled to the floor in a heap. He jumped up and brushed the dust from his tunic, the look of a petulant but determined child about him.

"Why?" Stefon asked.

Rish looked at him like he'd just asked the most ridiculous question ever conceived, before walking over to the wall to try again. Brooss stopped him.

"There's nothing to launch up from," she told him, "but I think I can reach it from beneath if you give me a boost with your hands."

"Good idea—then you can secure a rope or something and drop it down for us," Rish said with glee. Stefon almost expected him to clap his hands. Rish was so odd.

"For goodness' sake," muttered Stefon, as his excitable friend laced his fingers together and crouched to allow Brooss to mount the improvised foothold. She put one foot onto his hands and bounced, counting to three, as Rish matched her movements. On three Rish heaved upward and Brooss kicked up, reaching out for the ragged ledge.

Although the distance from floor to ceiling didn't seem that far, Brooss appeared to travel in the air for some time, her feet together and her hands reaching beseechingly for a handhold.

Her head and shoulders disappeared from sight and her arms snagged on the rim, pulling her legs under the ledge. For a moment Stefon thought she might not gain a hold and he expected to watch her slip from the ceiling, but she managed to secure some grip and her legs kicked forward, curling up as she struggled into the attic above.

Finally her feet hooked up and around, out of sight. Rish looked back at Stefon with an impressed look on his catlike features. "I really didn't think she'd make it."

"What's she supposed to achieve when she's..." Stefon's question was cut short by the familiar sound of a crossbow release-catch some distance above. It was followed by a sickening squeal from Brooss.

Rish started frantically searching for a way up to her.

Without thinking clearly, Stefon just rushed forward, bursting into a sprint toward the far wall. As he passed the panicking form of Rish, the world seemed to take on a strange aspect; suddenly everything seemed a little more vivid. Sounds were keener: he could hear every crunch of dusty footfalls, every heartbeat of those in the room, every whimper of pain from Brooss. The smell of the room surged like a torrent of mustiness and damp. The colours of the drab building flushed with a vibrant quality, like he'd been seeing all his life in black and white.

Abruptly he jumped towards the far wall, as though his actions—whilst still at his command—were not quite his own. He jumped high up, seeking to plant his feet on the masonry and kick back toward the attic. Both feet landed securely on the wall, first right then left, and he seemed to hang suspended in the air as his perspective turned and he was propelled up and across to the attic landing.

As he careened toward the prone form of Brooss he reached for his duffel bag, in which was concealed his handheld crossbow.

He took in the attic scene quickly. Brooss lay wounded by a crossbow bolt in her left shoulder. The attic was empty, with a passage leading from the back wall, toward the front of the building. In the middle of that wall was an ornate contraption: a large crossbow was set up with a cascading quiver of bolts leading to the stock. As he landed, he saw that the bow had already reloaded and the bowstring was automatically being drawn back by a complex series of cogs and weights. He took aim with the handheld crossbow that he pulled from his bag.

As he focused on the target, searching for a way to stop the mechanism, the colours in his vision grew brighter still and his sight seemed to focus on the contraption. His vision narrowed in on the bowstring, as though he were looking upon it close-up. He pulled the trigger, sending his own small bolt across the attic and through the string, snapping it cleanly and rendering the contraption nothing more than a ridiculous array of cogs, weights, pulleys and a now-useless crossbow.

Stefon's heart was thundering in his chest. He scrambled to Brooss's side and started examining the wound. Thankfully the bolt had passed in and out of the shoulder muscle. It would be painful and bleed heavily, but it would mend.

His hands were shaking violently as he worked diligently at preparing the wound, cutting away the material of her blouse and daubing the blood. His vision seemed slowly to return to normal as his hands settled down. When he finally heard Rish calling from below, his entire perception was back to normal.

Brooss was stable and able to walk fine, having recovered suitably before shock set in, so Stefon retrieved a length of rope from his bag and tied it to the crossbow machine, dropping the other end to Rish. He climbed up it nimbly and used Stefon's offered hand to climb over the edge.

For the first time in a long while Stefon saw Rish show open concern. He moved over to Brooss and looked at the wound himself. He was fussing over it more than usual and Stefon smirked as he moved away to investigate the passage the crossbow had been guarding.

"The crossbow was set up on a trip mechanism," Brooss said. "It was just over the ledge by about two feet. I couldn't duck in time. Didn't even see the damned contraption until it was too late."

Leaving them to it, Stefon stepped to the open passage and stared down a long shaft that dropped to what he judged to be the ground floor. A rope ladder was fixed beyond the lip of the passage.

Stefon called to the others that he was dropping down to check it out. Rish waved him on, concentrating on Brooss. Shrugging, Stefon descended the rope ladder, finding it to be of good condition and secured safely.

An exit at the bottom of the shaft opened into the room that was boarded up on the ground floor. Apparently the room wasn't sold off to the neighbours; it was sealed off from the public. Stefon set about finding out why.

The slaver camp was slowly coming to a quiet rest. The guards on first duty had retired and those detailed for second watch had taken up the vigil. With the change of watch, it seemed generally held that the noise in the camp was to be kept to a minimum. Those of the first watch who had not bedded down shared a few quiet canteens of some alcohol or other, probably fortified wine. The forest had grown eerily quiet with the deepening of night and only the most furtive of nocturnal urchins were stirring in the dark woods.

It all made for an awkward task to prepare Andi's plan. The others had seemed reluctant to accept the idea, but had been forced to follow suit when Andi had simply tired of the conversation and set about preparing what they needed.

That had been almost an hour ago and everything was now in place. Near Andi's flank, Eidos's horse nickered nervously. Andi couldn't blame it. Once again she checked the impromptu harness fixings and found them secure enough. With a few kicks the horse might shuck loose of the harness and load, but it should be adequate. Actually, that might even be advantageous.

Andi looked over her shoulder at Manic, seeing the dwarf nod once. His mighty sword was free of the scabbard and jammed into the soft turf at his feet. He would await a signal arrow from Andi, which she would fire from her vantage point high in the trees, closer to the camp than she had been before.

But first she had to achieve something more...morbid. She drew her black-bladed short sword and moved off through the low bushes and tree trunks, stepping carefully on soft undergrowth using the balls of her feet. She made almost no sound; perhaps as much as the passing of a fox.

She had wrapped black and dull brown lengths of cloth around her leather armour, stopping the thicker material from creaking and ensuring nothing hung loose to give her away. The cloth continued up her neck, over her chin and mouth, and covered her face beyond her nose. Mud and dirt had been smeared all over her face and her hands, ensuring only the whites of her eyes were not shrouded in darkness.

The blackened blade of her sword was disguised with matt charcoal waxy residue imbued in the folded steel of the blade. As a metal, it had been rumoured to break more easily than normal folded steel, but she rarely found herself in the situation where she was defending herself blade to blade. More often than not her victims had no idea an attack was coming until it was too late and they were already dead. The effect of the charcoal residue was that the blade reflected very little light, even when sharpened over the years. And it was just as keen and reliable as the day it had been made for her.

Some time ago Finhead had moved off on his own to circle the camp and come in a third of the way around, silently disposing of the sentries he encountered and then setting up a low trajectory position for his savage bow. The reptilian was easier to spot than Andi, having no clothes to disguise his shape, but he moved almost as silently and would not prove a clumsy problem.

Unlike Eidos. He was behind Andi, near Manic, standing by for the same signal. He was strangely worried about his horse, but Andi knew it would be fine. The impromptu harness wasn't so rigid as to stay attached forever, but Andi was confident it would survive a couple of bucks from the animal, and that would be enough.

Andi stopped stock-still, hunkering low near a stand of thick bushes around the base of a giant tree. She could hear breathing ahead. Then she could see the condensed exhalations hanging in clouds of vapour that quickly rose and dissipated in the night air that was growing colder by the hour. The sentry was close by. Within yards.

Then he stepped from behind the tree she was crouched near. He had been relieving himself against the trunk and was now retying his britches. He was facing her. He could have been looking right through her, but he didn't react to her presence.

She knew she should wait for him to turn away from her, but if he worked out what he was looking at, then…

She struck. With two quick, light, silent steps she was in front of him. Suddenly he found himself looking at a pair of eyes seemingly suspended in the forest air. Then the blade of her sword slammed up under his chin, through his mouth and into the base of his brain, killing him instantly. There was only the sound of the sword thumping home: a muffled sound like a stone being dropped onto thick, sodden moss.

Andi gripped the dead man by his tunic with her free hand, holding him up on the blade of her sword and by his clothes as his limbs twitched away. She was worried someone might be able to see his shape from the camp and didn't want him just slumping to the ground. Carefully she walked him away from the camp and around the tree, where she lowered him to a gap between two roots. She put her foot on his upper teeth to pull out her sword, wiping it quickly on mulch from the forest floor as a gurgling spray of blood jetted from the gash under his chin. The sight did not repel her. She'd seen it before.

Moving faster now, she glided amongst the trees, moving to the right and seeking the second forest sentry. The smell of the stew that had been cooked in camp was drifting to her on the cold night breeze and she was glad. Luck was with her. With the breeze blowing through the camp toward her, she was confident that the smell of blood from her victim would not carry to the sensitive noses of the horses pitched in the impromptu corral. There was no danger of the smell making them jittery and alerting the horsemen that had settled nearby.

Hopping over a fallen trunk and rounding another mass of low shrubs, Andi came upon the second sentry. She approached from the side, so low that she was almost on all fours. Jumping through the night, her blade slashed backhanded across the guard's larynx. He had time to utter a quiet, inquisitive hum before his throat was split, propelling blood from his artery high into the tree canopy above. His head fell back and he collapsed like a concertina. Andi was gone from sight by the time his body quietly thumped to the ground, blood still rushing in jets through the undergrowth.

She reached one of the tall trees she'd spotted before, which provided a good view of the camp, and slid her blade into the scabbard. In a fluid motion she began ascending the trunk, using low branches to hoist herself up higher and higher, until she found a series of wide, high branches on which to position herself. Some wildlife scuttled out of her way on her journey up, but nothing reacted in great alarm and no one in the camp below bellowed a warning, so she assumed she had achieved her position without compromise.

Unfortunately it was a little difficult to see back to where

Manic stood with Eidos's horse. However, the camp was arrayed below, clearly illuminated by the few fires the slavers had kindled, which were now sending up high flames against the gathering cold. Many slavers had retired and were trying to gain sleep beneath thin, inadequate blankets, gathered close to fires. The slaves were now back in the carriages, huddling together against the cold, some crying quietly. From the corner of her eye, moving silently amongst the trees, Andi saw Finhead. He was hunkered behind a tree. From Andi's high vantage point she could make out the body of yet another sentry at his feet. His bow was in his hand and he was looking up at her.

It was good that he was awaiting her signal, but it disquieted her to know that he could so easily spot her. She prided herself on being almost incorporeal, and it sat uncomfortably with her for the reptilian to be able to locate her with such little effort. Perhaps there was something in his unfamiliar physiology that aided him. Either way, she planned to learn more about his species before her lack of knowledge had a chance to count against her.

She made a small, one-handed gesture to Finhead, and he ducked back further into cover, awaiting the signal.

She unslung her bow and, aiming as carefully as she could, loosed an arrow behind her through the trees. She was sure she could make out the bulky figure of Manic far behind, but it was difficult to be sure. In any case, there was no sound of Manic or Eidos crying out in pain, so she figured she hadn't hit them by accident.

However, she had to assume the arrow had arrived close enough to give them the signal they needed. She turned back to the camp and prepared herself. Placing the quiver higher on her back allowed the arrows to clear the soft leather more easily. She took the first five arrows and jammed them one by one into the soft flesh of a branch in front of her, between her knee and her foot. Those would be her backups: arrows more readily available if things went awry and she needed to fire quickly. Then she took another arrow from her quiver and settled it against the bow, drawing the string semi-taut.

She scanned the camp, looking for a likely first target. The encampment still had guards and mercenaries up and about, some still eating and others still drinking. She was not short of targets. Not one slaver was far from a sword or bow. All the mercenaries were human, but a couple of the guards were maybe half-orc in descent. They had mean faces, protruding teeth, pig noses and monstrous shoulders, although their features were still disturbingly human.

Settling her eye on a selection of three mean-looking humans farthest from the fire, nearest to the improvised corral, Andi waited.

She didn't have to wait for long.

The forest beneath rolled with the growing thunder of pounding hooves. In the near silence surrounding the camp it sounded like a battalion of cavalry was descending upon their position.

It was plain that many of the slavers were unsure what the sound was or where it was coming from. But when Eidos's horse burst from the treeline and hurtled toward the centre of the camp, it was plain where the threat was coming from. Being pulled along behind the horse was a mass of furiously burning foliage and branches that Manic had managed to kindle in record time. Obviously the conflagration gave the horse impetus to stampede, mindless of the danger to the slavers under hoof. By the time the horse reached the fire near the centre of camp, three slavers had been trampled.

Andi noticed that, in the disarray of the flaming charge, no slaver had wondered why a call hadn't come from the sentries. Most were in panic, not even reaching for weapons but instead striving to avoid the mad horse that bucked high over the fire, releasing the improvised harness and sending the burning mass crashing into a group of three half-orcs. As Manic and Eidos burst into the camp, weapons slashing and battle cries bellowing, Andi loosed her first volley of arrows.

The first slammed through the lower portion of the target's head, impaling his neck. He clutched desperately at his throat as it filled with blood. Her second split the air behind another man's head as he rushed for his sword, then thumped into the wheel of a wagon. He grabbed his sword and freed it from the scabbard as he searched for her in the trees. Andi snatched another arrow as he grabbed the jerkin of a passing comrade and pointed with his sword in her general direction.

If her position was given away, she was in trouble.

As she fumbled to nock the arrow to her bow, the man screamed in pain. A thick arrow shaft protruded from his wrist, his sword tumbling to the floor. As both men turned away from her, another arrow slammed through the second man's face, the arrowhead punching from his skull and jabbing the first man in the eye. He doubled over and Andi's third arrow thumped into the ribs on his right side. He dropped.

Andi was glad to see that Finhead appeared to be covering his part of the bargain with some accurate shooting.

The camp was in uproar. Eidos's horse had cleared the central fire and had raced full speed for the treeline opposite. The flaming foliage it had now shed was burning atop two half-orcs that struggled and screamed, but were quickly succumbing to the fire and smoke.

Manic had arrived in the central camp area, engaging three mercenaries armed with longswords. He parried and struck about with worrying speed for a dwarf, and the men were kept at bay easily. Eidos was bringing up the rear, challenging guard upon guard, crashing through their flimsy leather armour with his heavy axe like an oar through water.

Blood sprayed around him in great, angry gouts but none seemed to touch his white tabard. He was pushing towards Manic in the middle.

The glade was filled with the sound of clashing weapons and dying men. A large mercenary with a burgundy sash was barking orders now, the slavers snatching up weapons and trying to rush towards him. Andi immediately recognised the danger of allowing the camp to gain order and unleashed two arrows in quick succession. As the sergeant in the sash screamed for men to come to him the first arrow dropped through his open mouth and drove deep into his right shoulder, pinning his mouth open. He grabbed at it but was unable to remove it or break its shaft. The second arrow thumped into his left leg. He dropped to a knee, screaming.

But the damage was done. The mercenaries were coming to order, falling back to the edge of the corral where the sergeant had gone down. There were maybe a dozen slaver-guards left. Manic's blade made it eleven as Eidos entered the fire surround, brandishing his axe with grim determination, his sandy hair wild and his features set firm. Blood dripped from Eidos's axe-head, but still his tabard and armour remained untouched.

Five or six guards were scrambling to form up near the dying sergeant, but they had no shields and Andi knew they would quickly fall if they stayed there. However, a group of three slavers were racing for the wagon full of slaves at the far end of the glade, unseen by the furiously battling Manic and Eidos.

Andi loosed an arrow at their backs, catching one in the hamstring, dropping him in immediate agony. As Andi had hoped, the screams got Manic's attention and he quickly instructed Eidos to deal with the formed-up guards as he chased down the remaining two who were making to flee.

But he probably wouldn't make it in time, and Eidos was going to struggle against six opponents.

Their attack hung in the balance.

Andi grabbed up two of the backup arrows and nocked them at the same time, holding her bow horizontally. She released both arrows into the gathering group of six, hoping to strike down more than one foe. But she didn't wait for confirmation. Instead she rose and slung her bow across her back. She took two quick strides and jumped from the high branch of the tree, reaching for a set of thick branches in the next tree forward.

For a sickening moment she thought she'd miscalculated, but then the thick arm of a branch stopped her fall and caught her under the shoulders. She used the momentum to swing under the branch and scurry along it to the trunk. A couple of quick hops and she was round the front of that branch. She was now halfway to the forest floor and on the edge of the glade clearing. A lot easier for her to be seen, but she was now in a prime position.

The arrows had only felled one of the group, both in his chest.

Manic was now at the wagon, but it was pulling away, the two fleeing guards behind the team of two horses still tethered to the slave-wagon. They were driving the horses hard to escape to the east.

Andi took aim at the back of one of the guards' heads and snapped off a shot. In horror she looked on as Manic clambered up the rear of the wagon and began crawling across the roof.

Her arrow thumped down into his left shoulder. Nevertheless he drew his sword and, angered further, assaulted the two guards.

Feeling guilty, Andi concentrated on the five remaining in the glade. Another thick arrow from Finhead sailed over the corral and punched through one man's head from behind. Andi fired twice from her position and then dropped the twelve or so feet to the forest floor, rolling forward to absorb

GATHERING SHADOWS

the impact on her knees. Her arrows had fortunately felled another two and only two remained. They were pulling at each other, either to defend or to flee.

She nocked an arrow and took aim threateningly, hoping to take the two alive. But they were desperate men and rushed Eidos as he advanced. Andi could do nothing but watch as Eidos dealt out death with three deftly executed strikes of his axe, the last severing the head of the final man standing, sending it toppling into the fire.

The camp fell silent, the smell of blood and burning flesh thick in the smoky air. The fleeing wagon had halted and Manic stood atop it looking back in their direction, a triumphant grin on his oval face and the arrow still protruding from his left shoulder.

Chapter Nine
Borders and Walls

S tefon sat surrounded by ledgers and tomes, journals and logbooks. Some were covered in a steady film of dust but others were clear and crisp with recently dated entries for credit and debit transactions, debt reconciliations and credit arrangements.

The majority of it made little sense to him, but Rish had made quick work of the information. Although Rish was reticent to leave Brooss up at the top of the shaft, he understood that it served a purpose. It would be near impossible to move her down the shaft safely without risking further injury, let alone try to get her back up afterwards. But they required the information they came for, and at present Brooss was content to rest up in the disused attic space as guard, should anyone approach.

Just what she was supposed to do about it if anyone *did* show up was left unsaid. She had her bow, but not the strength to use it with accuracy. Her sword was even less use than that. They had disassembled the crossbow contraption, and she was currently trying to repair it enough to be of use, but perhaps her shouted warning would suffice.

So he had dropped down to help Stefon with the find and was proving to be a more than competent auditor.

"We've got some pretty regular, boring stuff here,"

Rish mused. He placed his hand atop a tall pile of ledgers. "That is, if you class general embezzlement as 'regular' for a governor. Some cynics would think so, but not I. This guy has remained in a place of some distinction for years."

"Almost a decade," Stefon confirmed.

"Right, and he's lorded it up with the emperor's representatives from up the river and he's lined himself up for some potentially lucrative courtships too—especially considering he's such a fat bloater. And despite all that, he's totally lined his pockets using funds lifted from the taxation of the river routes and the favourable conduct of several local debt controllers."

"None of that really means much to me, Rish. Is he bent?"

"As a fifty-ounce feather."

"I don't know what that means," Stefon confessed.

"It's not really important; I'd have expected all these entries." Rish slapped his hand on the pile for emphasis. "But this little lot here!" He picked up a small pile of ledgers on the desk at the far wall. "They have some interesting entries recently. All high figures, always the same high figures and never with a named debtor."

"Maybe he forgot?" suggested Stefon, playing devil's advocate. "The link you're making is a little tenuous, Rish."

"You're right: it is!" admitted Rish excitedly. "That is, until you see that he has entered debtor and creditor details for every single transaction for the past eighteen *seasons!* This guy, or whoever does his books, is too meticulous to forget to enter the details of such a generous debtor. It's omitted on purpose."

Stefon rubbed his head in thought. "OK, then suppose he's left the name of the entry out to protect himself from prosecution."

Rish rubbed his chin pensively. "That would obviously make sense," he muttered. "But in that case, why that entry alone? If someone more pious than you or I had stumbled across these financial journals they'd have enough evidence of petty larceny to throw the book at our esteemed Governor. So if he was hiding this entry because he was scared of prosecution, and yet his history indicates that it's obvious he's *not* actually scared of prosecution..." He left the thought unfinished, allowing it to hang between the two friends as an unspoken concern.

"He's scared of *them*," Stefon realised, seemingly at length. "He's not scared of the courts; he's scared of the people who are paying him off. But why? He's one of the most powerful officials in Ipsica, let alone just this city."

"I have a feeling there are elements at work here that are more fearsome than any individual I can identify, and clearly more concerning than the law of the land. And if we *are* to identify the missing element, these tomes are surely the best chance we have of doing so." Rish held up the journals in question. "I'm willing to bet that this missing element is heavily involved with the quarantine conspiracy. Should we take them?"

Stefon stood and shook the scuttle of pins-and-needles from his sleeping legs. "I'd like to say no. If we take them it'll be obvious that someone has stolen from him. These are the most recent journals. He'd be bound to miss them." A smile crept across his face as Rish went to replace the ledgers and journals on the table. "On the other hand, this governor is hardly the toughened criminal we're looking for. If he finds that these are missing then he might panic and lead us directly to the nameless paymaster."

With a smirk Rish snatched the ledgers back up and secreted them about his body. Once the tomes were organised, the two began their ascent back to the loft space above, where Brooss awaited them.

It took Rish and Stefon more than thirty minutes half-carrying Brooss to wend their way back through the narrow Wahib streets as they struggled to avoid any nightwatchmen who might be equipped with their description. They were reasonably certain no guards had seen them long enough to commit their faces to memory but you could never be too sure.

And so they shuffled down narrow alleyways and lanes, some no wider than Stefon's shoulders. Occasionally they were forced to step over the dead or dying, clasping their hands over their noses and mouths to avoid breathing in anything toxic. The rain tapered to rivulets in the hostile lanes, sluicing unspeakable filth along with their passing.

The night had grown dark and cold, the rain falling noisily on rooftops above them like a terrible, despairing military tattoo.

With their steady progress, they found themselves in the slums of the southern portions of the city, Rish supporting Brooss as she tired from her wound. Stefon carried her gear on his back without complaint.

This area of the city was amongst the oldest. The ageing buildings that had not been replaced already were hunkering down beneath the barrage of rain that the inclement weather was hurling their way. They were dark constructions with gothic façades, leaning over the three friends as they passed silently.

At this late hour no sane Wahib inhabitants were around, and Stefon was tensed to the possibility of coming across someone nefarious. It would be just his luck.

Without incident, they approached the wider lane they were looking for. Their narrow road terminated in a dead end at the entrance to an abandoned sawmill. Near the end of the road on the right-hand side was the entrance to Anya's Brothel, where Jewl and Pryn had travelled to await their arrival.

Anya's place was indistinguishable from the rest of the squalor that identified this region of the city. The unwashed walls were black and rough-hewn. All windows were boarded up and no light could be seen from crack or crevice.

The door itself consisted of two old, heavy slabs of ancient oak bound with iron and shot through with rivets. No handle or lock was in evidence from the outside.

Across from the entrance and up the street was a patch of common ground where a disused warehouse had collapsed long ago. Secured near a wall under cover of darkness was Brooss's wagon, the horses lapping at rainwater that had formed a small reservoir in an upturned barrel.

Concealed beneath a broken wagon bed a dozen yards from their wagon, Stefon made out two figures hunkered down out of the rain. It was Jewl and Pryn.

The three rushed across the street, using the darkness as cover. Stefon and Rish helped Brooss into the covered section of their wagon and ensured she rested comfortably, although she was insisting that she felt fine but tired. Nonetheless, Stefon encouraged her to remain until they returned, making a cushion for her head from her gear. Rish pushed the stolen ledgers underneath her arm and Stefon didn't miss the concerned squeeze he gave her hand.

Rish and Stefon moved to the broken wagon near the edge of the thoroughfare and crawled into the space near Jewl and Pryn. The pair had seen them coming.

"What's wrong with Brooss?" Pryn asked.

"Nothing," Rish replied. "She's fine."

Stefon glanced at Rish. His face was grimly set. "She fell afoul of a crossbow trap," Stefon explained, "She'll be OK. It just took her in the arm. What have you guys found?"

"Nothing at all," Jewl told him matter-of-factly.

Pryn tutted. "What he means is, we covered every building, room, shed, outhouse and garderobe in the surrounding area and there's nothing that would constitute an underground entrance. Even the dry well near the postern gate has been smashed in. It's inaccessible."

"Well, your guard friend told us it was down here somewhere. If things get tight for us then an underground getaway might be just the thing we need to save our skins. I think we need to find it and maybe even look to see if it leads out of the city to somewhere safe."

"Agreed, but there's nowhere else to look."

"That's not strictly true, is it?" Rish mused. His slender finger pointed across the lane at the double doors to Anya's Brothel. "It could be *in* the grounds, or even in the building somewhere."

Pryn shook his head. "It's going to be pretty difficult to search without being noticed, Rish."

"Look, Anya's a scoundrel and a cheat, and they all have their price."

"OK, then let's take a look." Pryn crawled backward from under the broken wagon and stood to stretch out the kinks he'd developed from lying on the cold cobbles. The others followed him out into the steadily drizzling rain.

"Has it been busy while you've been watching?" Rish asked.

"Not really. A few guys arrived earlier, while we were sweeping the buildings this side of the street, but nothing since."

They all crossed the street and proceeded directly to the door of Anya's Brothel. As Pryn arrived at the heavy oak doors he pounded a firm fist three times against the solid wood.

After a few moments, the door was opened by a large half-orc. He wore a simple tunic and pantaloons that looked freakish on his massive bulk, his light-green skin clashing badly with the pale yellow of the tunic.

The beady eyes glanced past Pryn's large frame and brightened on seeing Rish. "Good evening, Master Rish. Come in out of the rain!" Despite the half-orc's pleasant words he snarled his greeting, his mouth turning up menacingly at one corner, causing one nostril the size of Stefon's hip socket to flare.

The four companions entered together, shuffling past the bulk of the doorman and shaking rainwater loose from their hair and clothing.

The inside of the brothel was dry and warm. Kerosene lamps with colour covers cast each room in warming tones and a roaring fire in the main chamber made a welcome change to the cold and wet outside. Scented oils in burners and smouldering incense sticks created a sweet aroma that verged on cloying. Various items of ornate furniture adorned each room, from myriad eras and with no discernible pattern or plan. Where a chair might be required, and where it would fit, it was placed—no matter what the design. It seemed simple enough, except that the wallpaper had a busy pattern and there were rugs and carpets of excitable fashion throughout, confounding the attempt to create a relaxing atmosphere in a decadent setting. Instead Anya had achieved a unique seediness and bawdy character to the surroundings that slid across Stefon's skin like warm grease.

Anya herself greeted them at the door of the main chamber. She was carrying a tray of beverages to a table in the corner near the blazing fire. Seeing Rish, she quickly distributed the drinks to the four men slumped in the deep cushioned chairs and shuffled over with short steps, a grin splitting a face that was painted with too much make-up.

"Rish, my dearest Rish, how are you?" Her voice was heavily accented from the southern countries and her skin, beneath the powder and paint, belied her origin. She was little more than five feet tall and had an unpleasantly oval face, with eyes dark as olives and lips like a spider's mandibles. Stefon knew she originated from the barren southern lands beyond the seas, where the terrain was dry and unyielding, just like the people. "Please, bring your companions to the fire; warm yourselves."

Reclining on a chaise longue was a particularly lithe elven female, most of her flesh exposed. Stefon had never found the Eldar race of elves especially attractive, although the general consensus of opinion seemed to be they were the most beautiful creatures in creation. To Stefon they tended to be skinny, unhealthy and arrogant. And they lived too long and remembered too much. What's more, they were morbid, morose, introspective and overly thoughtful. Not to mention their funny, pointy ears. Elves were definitely not Stefon's favourite people. Of course, it didn't help that most elves tended to look down on humans, and probably with some justification.

Stefon and his companions gathered by the hearth, trying to look inconspicuous.

"Can I fetch drinks for you?" Anya asked.

They ordered a selection of drinks and set about drying themselves before the searing heat of the mountainous fire. The fireplace and surround were chiselled from ornate slabs of marble and a cast-iron poker was oddly chained to a rivet driven into the base of the hearth. Stefon figure that it was secured there to dissuade people from using it as a weapon. Obviously they didn't have the best clientele all of the time.

They bided their time, settling on a set of soft chairs to the side of the fire and watching the room unobtrusively. The place wasn't busy. Only the group of men in the corner seemed to be customers, and they appeared more interested in drinking and relaxing than in anything else. But there was something about them that put Stefon ill at ease. For a start, just as he and Rish were, these men were drinking virgin concoctions from the bar rather than alcohol. And although they were doing an effective job of appearing dazed and uninterested, Stefon felt the men were watching him. It might have been paranoia, but he doubted it.

Either way, paranoid or not, there was something suspect about patrons appearing to be drunk but not drinking. Had they followed his group into the place he would have left immediately. As it was, they had been here upon their arrival, and so were worthy of a little more surveillance.

After a short time, Rish attracted Anya's attention and called her over. She sidled across and rested demurely on her haunches at Rish's elbow so he could speak quietly with her.

"Listen, you know the problems in the city," he whispered earnestly. "And you know a chap like me can't get caught short, should things get tight here."

"I'm not sure what you mean," she admitted.

"What I mean is, I've heard talk that there's an underground entrance somewhere down in this godforsaken part of Wahib. An entrance to the lower levels. A way down into the sewers and pathways that has long been forgotten. I know you know where it is." Rish knew no such thing, of course: he was bluffing, and bluffing with a fairly stacked deck. Paranoia was a loosening tool for the tongue, especially when possessed by people who realised they knew too much.

Anya betrayed only the merest flicker of recognition at the accusation, and something in Rish's face told her not to try lying. "OK, so what if I did know of something like that? How would that help you? You'd be trapped underground."

Now he had the location of the entrance, Rish pressed his luck. "Anya, I'm not a fool. We both know that it's possible to get out of the city through the sewers. What's the point in sewers if not for the purpose of shedding filth?"

As they spoke, Stefon was confident that the group across the room couldn't hear them or discern that anything untoward was occurring. But regardless of this confidence, he leaned forward with his elbow on the table and his chin in his hand, shielding the exchange from clear view by the group. One could never tell who could read lips.

Anya's face dropped in resignation. She pulled over another chair and sat with them. "Look, I may as well tell you, because it's hardly a secret. There *is* a way out of the sewer system. I was planning on using it for smuggling food and clothing through during the quarantine, but it's just not worth the risk. Especially after what happened…" She shrugged and changed tack. Rish didn't press it, knowing he'd get to that information sooner or later. The running tongue of a brothel madame was like a broken keg seal. Eventually the whole barrel would flow. "Let's just say the city militia don't seem too concerned about who they cut down and for what these days. So I delayed plans to smuggle goods in.

"But one of my smuggler teamsters took it out of my hands. Apparently he fell for one of my girls in a big way. He reckoned the longer they stayed in the city, the more likely it was that one or both of them would fall ill." Anya shook her head like a mother ruefully admonishing her child for burning itself on the fireguard. *Here it comes,* Stefon thought.

"He was always an impetuous fool," she continued. "He got it in his head to run from the city and take the girl with him. Through her love for the man, or her fear of the plague, she went with him and they entered the catacombs under the streets through a collapsed grating in our basement."

"They got out of the city?" Jewl asked.

"No…well, yes." She looked suddenly crestfallen. "They were shot a few dozen yards outside the gate from positions on top of the wall. I would never have known but for the fact that a scavenger team paid me good money to come through here. They knew that there was an entrance to the sewers here. They went out to retrieve the bodies and they paid well; I had no reason to refuse them access. It was when they came back through with the bodies that I worked out what had happened to them."

"The bodies?" Stefon pressed. "I assume this pair of fools left with all their worldly possessions. But you're telling us the scavenger team only brought back their bodies?"

"Yes."

Pryn looked at Stefon. "The only way that makes sense is if they went out specifically for the bodies in the first place." He turned to Anya. "Was there any indication that either was infected, before they left or after they were brought back?" She shook her head. Pryn turned back to Stefon. "So it's a good bet that the scavenger team *was* sent there specifically to retrieve the bodies."

"This all fairly reeks of a cover-up," Jewl grumbled. "Especially if the scavenger team knew the entrance to the sewer was here in the first place. Wouldn't take a genius in the militia hierarchy to work it out."

"But it can't be the militia. They'd use their own scavenger teams and would leave through the gates, not via the sewers. This is strange. The people who are trying to hide stuff like this seem to have nothing to do with the city militia or even the government."

"Who leads this scavenger team?" Rish asked Anya.

"Well, I didn't recognise him at the time, but I've heard his name before: Simeon."

Simeon again! Simeon, the scavenger, whom Pryn's city guard had spoken of earlier that day. Simeon: the team leader who had disappeared soon after re-entering the city and had since been rumoured to be on the run. Until now it had all been a little sketchy as to why he had disappeared and why he was now a fugitive. And more importantly, who was he a fugitive *from*?

Regardless of any of those unanswered questions, it now seemed clear that Simeon's team had been commissioned to retrieve only the bodies, and that would point to them working for those involved with this plague. And more importantly, once their job was done it looked likely that

Simeon was betrayed and had fled into the underworld of Wahib City.

With half of his team dead and fearing for his own life, the scavenger would be more than willing to spill his information to whomever helped him escape his pursuers.

Rish thanked Anya for her help and told her they'd take her up on her offer to see this subterranean entrance at some point. When they were left alone, the four friends leaned in closer to talk the revelations through; Jewl with his bearded face resting sulkily on the back of his hands.

"Of course I didn't mean to shoot you, Manic," Andi insisted. "Why would I shoot you on purpose?" The wound had been washed, cleaned and cauterised to seal it against infection, and now the dwarf was fairly drunk. He grumbled again, and then started laughing quietly to himself as his eyes closed.

They had discovered a stash of whiskey in one of the mercenaries' saddlebags and had put it to good use, sterilising both Manic's wound and senses. Now Eidos and Finhead rolled him in a couple of blankets, taking good care with his wound so as not to open it with the movement. The dwarf was asleep.

"Do you think it was a good idea?" Eidos asked from across the small fire they had controlled following the battle in the camp.

Andi eyed him quizzically. "Shooting Manic? Always."

"No, setting the slaves free."

Finhead murmured thoughfully and poked the fire without comment.

"Of course!" she told him with conviction. "We had to do it that way; it was our only viable option."

Once the fires had been extinguished, they had regrouped and scouted the camp to ensure no sappers lurked, playing dead and waiting for an opportunity. Some individuals were seriously wounded, breathing shallowly and suffering greatly. They were dispatched without ceremony or apology. No sentiment was wasted on the slavers.

It took them a few moments to pile the corpses and set them for firing, although they were not to be lit until the team was underway at first light, if at all. Carrion feeders might do as good a job.

Regarding the freed slaves, opinion was divided. Finhead and Manic had been concerned for the safety of the freed slaves, stating emphatically that the four should escort them to the nearest village before continuing on their quest.

"It's simply not viable!" Andi had pressed at the time, with a small amount of support from Eidos. "I share your concern for these people, but pressing facts remain that are unavoidable: whilst there are obviously slaver trains working the area, this was the only one we encountered. We have enough discarded weaponry here to arm these people, and with a good night's sleep and some food they'll be more than a match should they be called to defend themselves. But more concerning is our need to push on. These freed people will find their way home with or without our help, but it's more important to look at the big picture. Where were they being taken to?"

The others had stared back blankly. "Erm…Ipsica?" Eidos had asked, mentioning the neighbouring nation as though stating the obvious—which indeed he was.

"See what little provisions these slaver people had?" Andi had indicated, trying to control her frustration. "They weren't travelling far enough to reach any of the strongholds deep behind the border in Ipsica. Any settlement along the border close enough for them to reach in this direction would be the size of outposts.

"The way Ipsican rural society works is that the farming communities are held by the landlords, and cities are few and far between. Wahib, Corfel Scar and the capital Otack are massive, sprawling cities, but other than that there are few significant individual settlements. Certainly none near the border.

"Now, I might accept that they could use one of these outposts to resupply and continue, but that would be a stretch of the imagination. I think it's more important to follow their path. We need to see where these people were being taken. I have a bad feeling it is fairly close by."

And that had largely been the end of the discussion. They had advised the freed people to rest and return in the morning, but they had been understandably keen to flee the scene, obviously concerned that the likelihood of encountering more slaver parties would be increased both by remaining still and by dallying in the forest. They wanted away as soon as possible.

While Finhead had tended Manic's wound, Eidos and Andi had equipped the freed villagers with provisions and weapons and prepared the wagon for them. With exhausted but profuse thanks, the group had trailed into the woodlands heading west toward their homesteads and farmlands, from whence they had been taken.

The camp was eerily quiet in the early hours as Manic dozed. Andi was able to achieve a few hours of rest, but not much. They had let the fires burn low and wrapped up hard against the coming autumnal chill.

It was as Andi came round at predawn that she thought she heard the first sounds carried on the chilled air. Lying on the cold ground, with the campfire burned out and the last wisps of smoke from the dying flames drifting from the blackened logs and branches, Andi became aware of the forest around her: the tall tree canopy, the gently swaying branches and the verdant lichen and plant life on the forest floor.

But as awareness came to her fully, a flash of intuition revealed that something was missing. Although the soft breeze was keeping the forest foliage in a perpetual state of subtle motion, the woodlands were dead.

Andi remained very still; her eyes alert but her body unmoving.

She kept her respiration shallow.

Despite the coming of dawn and the brightening of the pale blue sky there was an absence of indigenous sounds. The forest should have been coming to life, but no animals stirred and no morning birds sang.

Straining to isolate the sounds that had woken her, Andi listened for the rhythmic, almost mechanical tattoo that had thrummed on the morning breeze: tantalisingly audible but ultimately indistinguishable.

And then there it was, caught on the morning air; rhythmic but not musical. Seemingly at random, but with a frustratingly discernible form and pattern. It was the sound of distant tools working in unison.

Lifting her head slowly, Andi looked around the camp. They were still alone. Eidos sat the last shift on guard, his back against a single dead tree stump just off from the camp circle. He hadn't seen her lift her head.

Once she was sure the camp wasn't being watched, Andi jumped to her feet and set about gathering her gear together. Eidos started at the sudden movement.

"What's going on?" he hissed, a throwing axe suddenly in his hand.

"We're breaking camp," Andi answered, raising her voice slightly in order to wake the others. It worked.

Within half an hour they were over two miles from camp, moving quickly amongst the trees with the morning dew soaking their boots and autumnal sun slanting through gaps in the thinning canopy above.

They were heading east, seeking the source of the sounds Andi had heard. It had been a while before the others had recognised the echoes in the air, but now they were all focused on the subtle sounds and were silent as they moved, ten yards spread from each other.

Occasionally, through the odd gap in the redwoods, Andi was able to spy a towering hill that rose above those around it that formed the spine of the border between Shenmadock and Ipsica. She aimed the group toward the left side of the peak, judging the sounds to be coming from the footlands to the north face. The going was arduous, for the narrow mountain paths were made treacherous by recent rain and dew. They must have been near the highest point of the Southern Range.

Despite the absence of immediate danger, the group remained silent and vigilant. No banter between the travellers filled the air and no witticisms seemed appropriate. Nor did anyone speculate as to the origin of the sounds they were pursuing.

It was noon when they stopped to rest. The morning had grown into a warm autumn day; the tree canopy and thicker foliage at the foot of the tall hill increased the humidity, and Andi felt uncomfortable beneath her dark travelling tunic and hood.

Stopping at the base of a rocky outcropping, she pulled back her hood and drank from a furrowed waterfall. She patted some of the chilly water onto her forehead and the back of her neck, savouring the coolness.

As the others took similar refreshment, she checked their position using the noon sun. Manic stepped to her side, offering some dried fruit in a leaf wrap. She undid the tie and nibbled on an apricot.

"What do you make of all this?" Andi asked.

"Well, judging by the sun's position and the time of year, I'd say we're probably further east than we thought. We've travelled some distance and may even be inside Ipsican territory by now. Certainly I think by the time we circle that hill we'll be in dangerous places for Shenmadockians to wander." He looked at her. "We'll have to be very careful. It doesn't sound like a trifling number of people are working over yonder. We'll need to be sneaky."

"Lucky that's my forte then, isn't it?" she replied with a smirk.

"More important than that, I think we need to consider another tactic for Eidos," Manic cautioned. "He's not the most nimble of warriors...particularly in that armour of his."

"I'm sure we'll be fine. We just might do well to use the height of that hill a little more. I think he has a sailor's eyepiece in those saddlebags of his—one of those long-range things. And Finhead is no mean shot with his bow." Andi glanced over her shoulder. "Judging just from the thickness of his bow, the range is more than double our horn or antler composite bows. I wouldn't like to take a hit from one of his shots. See the arrow shafts?"

Manic shook his head.

"I might be wrong, but they look to be shoots from the black locust plant, wound tight and probably laminated with an amber sap. Even the arrowhead looks barbed. Not your average construction, to say the least. I think we have a marksman in our midst."

Manic nodded sagely, although it was clear he understood little of Andi's explanation regarding the bowyer or fletch-work. Manic was a mountain and cave dwarf by upbringing and had little use for the niceties of forest lore or woodsmanship. But the meaning was obviously not lost on him. Hefting his belongings, Manic set off wide of her while Eidos and Finhead strode over, refreshed.

They moved on, keeping wide formation but moving slower, now they were nearing their destination. The last thing they wanted to do was blunder into a clearing and make targets of themselves.

Things were worse than they had assumed. Wahib City was dying beneath the boot heel of the quarantine. It was near noon and Stefon stood with Rish at the edge of the old Town Square that thronged with citizens marching in protest on the old palace.

The crowd was too malnourished, too downtrodden, to pose a serious threat to the guards at the keep gates, but their chanting and catcalls carried high on the cold afternoon breeze, and such a press of people always posed a degree of danger—to themselves and others. A short respite from the relentless rain refreshed the crowd and their anger was slowly growing.

Still no answer came from the citadel.

Beyond the walls of the keep, in the distance, the tall and sturdy, windowless Tower of Light reached regally into the air, dominating the city skyline.

As Rish and Stefon had been watching, the crowd had become increasingly hostile, some people beseechingly holding aloft the dying figures of their loved ones. People near them seemed beyond fear of direct contamination. The plague appeared so rife and indiscriminate that the populace had given up attempting to second-guess the contagion. "The Fear would find you if the fates decreed it," one stooped doomsayer had bellowed from atop a small wall at the eastern edge of the square as they had passed by, and Stefon didn't doubt it.

What he *did* now doubt was the random nature of the plague's inception. He believed, more so than ever, that the plague was somehow in existence for a reason; created for a purpose. And that purpose could only have been malevolent.

Judging by the inept and inadequate nature of the government's ability to handle the thronging crowd's angry reaction—which was surely only a matter of course following the decimation of their city—Stefon surmised that they were as much a victim of this plot as anyone else.

The ledgers and tomes from the governor's residence suggested strongly that high-ranking and quite powerful or influential individuals in the government were being manipulated by stronger, higher powers. And there was no stronger or higher power behind the mask of Wahib City than the mysterious clerics of The Light.

The more Stefon learned of this strange illness, the more he could only conclude that The Light was the missing link.

The power and influence to arrange an early quarantine, the strange behaviour of the city militia and the clerics throughout the city, the hunt for Simeon the scavenger, and the terrifying happenings behind the walls of the city morgue could only point to one organisation.

No, Stefon corrected himself, *not an organisation. A sect… a cult.*

Increasingly he was convinced that they knew the whom. However, part of the how and all of the why still eluded him. And something itched at Stefon's concern like ants in his stomach, telling him that Simeon the scavenger might hold the key to that revelation.

"This is dangerous," Rish murmured.

Stefon hummed noncommittally. "This number of people as upset as they are… it has *riot* written all over it."

"Well yes, there's that, but I've got a bad feeling. I feel… out in the open, for want of a better way of explaining myself." Stefon looked as Rish glanced around them. "And I'm sure I just saw a face I recognised. It might just be a coincidence, but I'm sure it was one of those guys who was in Anya's place last night." Rish looked at Stefon, his eyes serious. "The people who were making an effort not to listen to our business?"

"It's no surprise people are following us," Stefon told him calmly. "I know they didn't follow us this morning, but I wouldn't be surprised to find them here. They must be wondering what we're up to."

"But who *are* they?" Rish mused.

It was rhetorical, but Stefon answered anyway. "Take your pick. Maybe Pryn's incessant questioning of the city guard has drawn their attention. Maybe the Governor put two and two together and the palace guard are keeping tabs on us. Or maybe it's more spies from the The Light, sniffing around trying to find out who made a corpse out of one of their weirdoes. Or maybe Master Ibn Ratna Giri wants to know how his investment is coming along. We've not reported in all week and he may be getting twitchy."

Rish absentmindedly kicked a stone across the cobbles. "By my grave, how have we managed to anger so many people in such a short time?"

"By asking questions; it's the easiest way. But to be honest, I think this may be something different. If they meant us any real harm, they'd have made their move by now, I think. Come on!"

Stefon led them away from the madding crowd and onto a wide street leading south, away from the town square. Across the cobbled thoroughfare, Pryn and Jewl took their cue from him and fell into a parallel course beneath the building overhangs from the upper rows. They kept pace with Stefon and Rish as the group continued south.

Crossing an intersection of two streets, Rish took the opportunity to glance over his shoulder as Stefon avoided being run down by a passing cart and horse. He took two quick steps to catch up with him and whispered, "I don't think we're being followed, but we've certainly got a shadow."

"How can we have a shadow and not be followed, Rish?"

"Well, look for yourself!" Rish hissed, stopping abruptly and crouching to feign adjusting his leather boots, as though a stone were caught beneath his heel.

Stefon stopped next to his friend and looked around the street, seemingly bored. Approaching them from the rear was a lithe, athletic male human. At first glance he seemed unremarkable, being fair-haired and simple-featured, yet he moved with steady purpose and strength. Stefon avoided staring, but he indeed recognised the man from the previous night in Anya's place.

Subconsciously Stefon's hand twitched to the blade at his side, but he didn't draw his weapon. Something about the man made him hold his draw. He seemed to have little interest in Stefon, and what interest there was appeared to be mainly frustration at having to step around him and Rish as he continued on his way.

Pryn and Jewl had not stopped when Rish had feigned his discomfort, but instead had slowed almost to a crawl.

Stefon allowed the individual to pass him without indication, instead stooping to help Rish. But he watched his back closely. Something about the individual's manner had Stefon on edge. His movement was athletic but tense; his steps controlled but short and frequent. And he seemed to be…listening to something. Not listening *for* something, but *to* something. Or someone.

Before the man reached the far corner of the street, which turned down a wide lane, Stefon was in pursuit, Rish striding to keep up. Stefon's stomach sank as the man reached for a short sword beneath his left arm before rounding the corner.

Stefon took off at a sprint, desperate to reach the corner, but unsure why. He had a gut feeling something awful was afoot, but felt in no danger himself.

Skidding in the gutter sludge at his feet, Stefon rounded the corner. His eyes immediately identified a mugging. But he was wrong.

A short figure covered in a hood and thick shawl had been confronted by the individual that he and Rish were pursuing. He was drawing a long dirk from his cloak, but it would be no resistance against the broad short sword in the assailant's grip.

Over the man's shoulder Stefon spied another man, dressed the same as the attacker and carrying a similar sword.

Stefon made his judgement quickly, immediately unsheathing his new mysterious sword and leaping to the hooded man's defence. He shoved the first attacker to the side and made to defend from the far side. The hooded man lunged against the lane wall for cover as Stefon stepped forward. Rish quickly joined arms against the first attacker, short swords clashing noisily.

The second assailant approached at a run, sword overhead. As Stefon went to take the blow on his sword the man adjusted his position and swept low, aiming for Stefon's hip. A short hop backwards brought Stefon out of range. The attacker followed through, aiming a stab at the hooded man's stomach. Only Stefon's swift backhand parry stopped the strike.

The loud sounds of clashing steel filled the alley and echoed into the steel-grey sky. People would be attracted to the sounds of skirmish.

Again the stranger unleashed a flurry of blows at Stefon's midriff, pushing him onto the back foot. And yet again, when there was room he aimed an opportunist's strike at the cowering hooded figure.

This time Stefon wasn't fast enough and the blow struck the figure on the inside of his thigh, causing him to cry out and clutch the side of his groin. He fell back to his rump in agony.

Stefon attacked the assailant's flank, looking to take advantage of the overreach. He jabbed forward at his ribs, but his strike was parried. Fearing for the hooded man's life, but not knowing why, Stefon swept desperately back and forth with his thrumming sword, forcing the man to parry and dodge with frantic haste. As a mist of rage descended over Stefon's eyes, he smashed the defending short sword aside and whirled his blade around in a brutal, two-handed upward cleave.

The sound of the man's teeth smashing together was sickening as the steel punched through his chin and cleanly up through the front of his skull, splitting his startled face in twain. Blood sprayed in a fine mist into the air and sluiced down the stranger's chest as the body dropped to the lane floor.

Stefon turned to help Rish, who was still engaged with the other stranger.

Seeing himself outnumbered by Stefon and Rish, and recognising the threat of Pryn and Jewl, who were rushing across the street, the final assailant made one last lunge to buy some room before fleeing the scene at a sprint.

Rish made to give chase, but gave up after a few steps. "Does anyone have a bow?" he shouted, glancing around the group. He received only resigned shrugs in reply. His frustration was evident on his feral features. "He's getting away!"

"Let him!" Stefon muttered. "It won't be the last we see of him, I'm sure."

He turned to attend to the wounded man, pulling a length of cloth from his pack to tie the wounded limb. The jagged paving was awash with crimson blood, murky with the mud and rainwater on the lane floor.

Stefon frantically uncovered the wound, pulling at the layers of wool and hemp to get at the leg. The sword attack had severed the inside of the man's thigh, high up near the groin, and blood still pumped from the gash. A main artery had been struck.

A mortal wound.

A precise strike.

A blow meant to kill, and quickly.

Rish pulled back the hood and unravelled the scarves that covered the stranger's head. The man's face was painted with a thin film of perspiration; his skin was the colour of blown ash. "Simeon!" Rish hissed through a sharply taken breath. "The scavenger leader!"

Stefon used the length of cotton he had retrieved to wipe Simeon's brow while he applied pressure to the wound. The pain caused Simeon's eyes to flash open. They were wild with fright and hollow with malnutrition.

"Simeon, we're friends," Stefon told him. "We're trying to help you, but you've been struck. There's nothing we can do."

Simeon shook his head from side to side, delirium sweeping over him. "Please, end it!"

"We can get you help: a priest or acolyte."

His eyes fixed on Stefon's with focus and clarity. "No! Never! It must be clean. You must end it *now!*"

"We need your help. Who did this? Who sent those men?"

"The fear! The illness! The plague! It's…something else! Get out of the city if you can, but if you stay then end it cleanly. Cut your head from your body! Cut your own throats!"

Jewl stamped a foot on the ground, clearly in distress. "He's suffering, Stefon! He's delirious. End it for him!"

"City militia are coming," Pryn called from the position he had taken up at the corner. "Four bearing polearms and more behind. No more than two hundred yards and closing."

"Please, Simeon, help us!" Stefon clasped his hands around Simeon's clammy face, focusing his attention. "What did you find outside the walls? What are you running from?"

Simeon's eyes were wide with hysteria. "*The bodies…they moved…*" A spider of ice ran down the length of Stefon's spine.

The bodies…they moved…

Simeon's eyes rolled in his head, his muscles going into spasm as he entered his death throes.

"Simeon! Who were those men?" Stefon put his ear close to Simeon's mouth. His head was as heavy as a boulder in Stefon's hands as the dying scavenger exhaled one last garlic-soured breath. Stefon heard each word that marked Simeon's departure from the mortal world.

Pryn's meaty hands, clad in his glittering gauntlets, thumped together in urgency. "Stefon! We must go. *Now!*" Pryn took to his heals, pulling Jewl with him.

Slowly Stefon lowered Simeon's lifeless head to the floor and stood. The rain was falling heavier now, pattering on his shoulders in that same disjointed military tattoo. Stefon and Rish concealed their weapons and followed Pryn and Jewl down the lane at a brusque walk. Through the drumming rain he heard Simeon's last warning rushing around the canals of his mind, sewing patches of information together.

Fear The Light!

Chapter Ten
Risk

Midmorning on Sixthday in the affluent area of Shen Utah, Acaelian walked confidently among the well-dressed inhabitants, and cared not a jot for looking out of place. The sun hung low to the south as it traversed the sky, but the day was oddly mild for late autumn.

Stepping through a low oak gate, he flipped a gold coin from last night's haul to the young man on duty. Following his drink with Jon the retired Black Cat, the night had produced a little cash from some light-fingered, opportunistic pilfering outside the docklands, where some merchants were often lax with their day's take. It was nowhere near enough to make his tithe for the month, but it had been sufficient to keep him in food and pay for his entry to the rich's most popular haunt in Shen Utah: the Temple Spas.

Many decades before, the weight of buildings being thrown up on the land had resulted in a shifting of the rock and soil, and had opened a fissure releasing giant gouts of steam. Hundreds had died as the buildings had collapsed and steam had scorched the skin from many residents, but since then the city had turned the natural event to an advantage, using the steam vents to heat running water and form steam rooms and outdoor spa pools, where those wealthy enough to pay for the privilege could sit and wallow in their own crapulence.

The idea held no appeal at all for Acaelian, and he considered the concept of sitting stewing like so much meat, alongside other naked people, barbaric and distasteful.

What did interest him was one particular patron: Constable Foord of the city watch, the man placed in charge of investigating the murders in Temple Link. Being a constable, Foord was not officially a member of the soldiery but still commanded authority over those members of the city watch tasked with policing the safety of Shen Utah within its walls. It had taken largely the remainder of last night's haul for him to purchase Foord's name and influence from a Whisper, and to learn of his presence here today. This was expensive information, for a man of such influence and with such responsibilities could easily find himself the target of unsavoury types...like Acaelian.

But the elf Glimmer had no interest in causing Foord harm; he only wished to talk with the constable.

Acaelian was forced to strip to his briefs, as was standard at the spa, and was then free to wander around the large rocky expanse of pools and wooden steam-rooms open to the morning air. A burly-looking set of thugs were tasked with caring for the patrons' belongings, and Acaelian didn't feel he had much reason to fear theft.

It took him only a short while to find Constable Foord sitting in a pool that bubbled with steam. A few other men sat nearby, but other than that the constable was alone, whiling away the morning hours in comfort while the city trembled under the baleful shadow of the Temple Shredder.

Acaelian slipped into the water beside Foord. It was shockingly hot at first, but the sensation quickly became almost pleasant with continued exposure. Still, it was nothing Acaelian would ever want to get used to. The pink-jowled constable turned a pair of pickled-egg eyes on the young elf.

Judging by his thin, purple lips, bulbous build, bloodshot eyes and the myriad burst blood vessels in his nose, Constable Foord was no stranger to whiskey. He closed his eyes again and rested his head back against the rock siding. "What?" he asked, unimpressed at the interruption to his spa session.

"Good morning, Constable Foord. I wish a moment of your time."

"You've twenty seconds, you little turd."

Acaelian's endless elven patience would allow for such rudeness.

"I have some information for you, and it might take a little longer than twenty seconds, I'm afraid. I have a Whispering," the Glimmer said, hinting at the information sold by the Guild of Spies. This caused Foord to open his eyes and look sidelong at the thief.

Acaelian could see the appraising look that entered Foord's countenance as he reassessed the scamp. Lifting his head again, he peered around to gauge any threat.

"I'm alone," Acaelian told him, although he knew it would not assuage the constable's fears. "Listen carefully, for I don't wish to tarry any longer than necessary. It has come to my attention that there is a curious fashion to the Shredder's murderous tactics, and the way you're looking for him might not lead to his early arrest. In short, you need to change tack."

"What interest is this of yours, you Guild scum? I won't pay a penny for hearsay and rumour; now get out of here before I slap you in chains."

Acaelian glanced around. "You're not wearing a stitch, Constable. I dread to think where those manacles might be hidden." The city watch constable's eyes narrowed, but the elf continued before the corpulent man could interrupt: "I don't ask for money, Constable. I want the murderer off the streets, and quickly. I think the information I have might facilitate this."

Foord grinned, revealing brown teeth. "You're protecting that Guild of Whores? Ever thought that they might be getting everything they deserve?"

"No, and neither do you. You're no templeton, Foord: you hardly even believe in the one God, let alone any of the hundred other beliefs we have in this city. No, I want the murderer caught because the victims are people. You're sworn to protect people, constable."

"Don't assume to tell me my duties, boy."

"I'm not: I'm reminding you in order to cut through this layer of bravado you're hiding behind. You are hurting at being no closer to catching the Shredder, and I know it. I want to help. I don't want the next victim to be someone I know."

The constable seemed to regard Acaelian with a little more respect, his face losing the hard edge of cynicism that had haunted it. "Go on, then."

"A horse and carriage was seen dumping the last body in Temple Link, where it was found. The body was dumped along with all the blood. We've assumed some leather-work covering was used to protect the inside of the carriage and to ensure all the blood was left at the scene, to further throw you from the scent, but we don't know."

"So that accounts for how quickly the murders take place."

"More than that, Constable. It means that the area being prowled by the Shredder is not contained to Temple Link, but is more likely to be The Lows. And it probably means there is an accomplice." Acaelian began extricate himself from the warmth of the spa, grabbing a nearby towel. "Think on it, Foord. The next strike is due any day. Widen your net. Forget Temple Link; it's a herring."

"And you listen to me, scamp; this business is no place for a young…whatever you are. Don't interfere any more. The last thing we need in Shen Utah right now is the confusion of vigilantism. The logical step from that is to lynch-gangs and pandemonium. The city is in a precarious balance already; it would only take a nudge to throw it into chaos."

Acaelian simply offered his enigmatic smile and left the fat man to stew.

Once Acaelian had left the spa, Foord was joined by a slender man in his twenties, with a shock of blond hair atop a handsome face. The arrival turned watchful eyes on the constable. "What was all that about?" he asked, with a hint of humour in his voice.

"You were watching; you tell me, Captain."

Captain Carpion was the overseer of the city watch, amongst other duties in the palace. One of those other duties happened to be captain of the palace scouts: the Wayfarers. There were no finer scouts in the land that were not elven born.

"I was watching," admitted Carpion. "But the elf boy was a cautious one. Almost every other word he spoke, he managed to turn his head this way or that, or to cover his mouth as he spoke without really appearing to do so. You would not have noticed."

"You're right; I didn't care to notice. He was just a Guild rat trying to throw confusion on our investigation."

Carpion regarded Foord for a moment. "I found it almost impossible to read his lips, Foord, but I read enough of your replies to know the topic. Tell me."

The constable detailed the account the stranger had given him about the carriage, not bothering to leave out any detail. It would not serve to lie to the captain. Foord wanted this murderer caught as much as the next man.

"We've never found a way into the Guild in more than a decade, since the last betrayal. Now this boy comes to us with this information and doesn't even request payment?"

"What's your point? A lot of what he had to say made sense, but how reliable could it be? He's a Guild rat."

"So you keep saying, Foord, and that's the bloody point. You don't have any real idea how the Guilds work, do you?" Foord shrugged his big shoulders. "That boy came to us with this information. And he came directly to you in a place where the exchange would not be easily witnessed."

"You saw," pointed out Foord.

"Indeed. I don't think he was hiding the exchange from us." Carpion looked around at the patrons in the spa. "Do you think this place has many Guild eyes?"

"He's cautious of crossing the Guilds?"

"I think that elf boy just *did* cross the Guilds, Foord. He came to you with that information instead of taking it to his Guild Master. That boy has risked much— possibly everything—in order to bring you that snippet of information, Constable. That should indicate at least that he feels strongly enough about the veracity of the information that you should probably consider heeding his warning and looking into it."

Carpion's dark eyes narrowed at Foord. "But who am I to tell you your job, Constable? I know you're doing everything you can."

"Yes, Captain," Foord said reflexively.

"Good." The lithe Carpion rose from the pool and left.

Unseen by Constable Foord, Captain Carpion or Acaelian, a dark figure shifted in the shadows of an adjacent building overlooking the spa from a distance. The figure lowered a spyglass from his eye and replaced it carefully in his pack. At this distance, the figure had not heard a word spoken within the pool of the spa, but he hadn't needed to. The people at the meeting were enough.

Grinning to himself, Grimlaw began his descent from his vantage point.

"Son of a bitch!" Manic pulled himself forward in the undergrowth, bugs crawling into his moustache and sweat beading in a line on his brow. Andi had to smile. *Was there no environment this dwarf was happy in?* Taverns mostly, she imagined.

They had hiked to the foot of the hill soon after lunch and had been careful to remain undetected. The sounds of labour were close now and Andi had been able to make out a large clearing of trees to the north of the hill from their raised position on the incline.

Arrangements had been made for a rally point: secret markings made on trees near a fork in a small river running down from the hill. Then the group had split up. Eidos had led Finhead into the woods up the incline, seeking a vantage point high over the clearing below. It was unlikely that Finhead would have adequate accuracy at that range, but Eidos would be able to use his navigator's spyglass effectively. And a bow out of range was better than no bow at all.

Andi and Manic had scampered into the lower trees, heading for ground that was soft underfoot. Ground cut by fallen trees and boggy ditches had proved perfect. Stopping under a wide, fallen trunk, Andi had smeared muck from a bog and broken some sour-smelling lichen into the mix before spreading it on any exposed skin. She did the same for Manic. The concoction would hide their white skin as the autumn sun fell beyond the trees, and the lichen would keep bugs from bothering them. They had moved a little closer before finding a hollow to hide in while they waited for nightfall.

Andi knew dusk was the hardest period of the day to make out detail, and so she waited until then to move Manic forward among the trees to the edge of the clearing. They travelled thirty to forty yards, crawling through bogs and hollows beneath fallen trunks and thick undergrowth. It had been arduous, but had worked. They had reached the edge of the clearing just after the rays of the sun had left the sky and the clouds above were painted apricot. More importantly, they had done so undetected: an achievement for the dwarf. "Son of a bitch!" he complained again. He seemed to be in no mood to celebrate his success.

"Manic, please be quiet. We could be surrounded and not know it, with the noise of your complaining."

At first glance, the clearing held nothing of particular interest. A crumbling ruin knelt at the centre of naturally cleared woodland. A small river ran from the foot of the hill at their backs, but it petered out and ran away into the trees to the far side. If anything, the land was strangely flat, without the natural undulations you might expect from such a clearing. Perhaps two hundred yards in diameter, the cleared land formed a neat oval.

Toiling busily into the early evening were teams of slaves, cutting down trees to the north, on the far side of the clearing. These trees were carried to temporarily erected sawmills. Sections of timber were already being produced in large quantities. To the south of this mill, evidence of the use of the timber was present in the form of two large buildings; one only partially complete. They seemed to be single-storey, long buildings with an exit at both ends and not one window along any side. Nearby, there was enough room for at least another two buildings. As the sun was setting, the teams of slaves had been removed from constructing the second building and were now currently assisting in unloading carts that had arrived as they lay in the mud. Andi could not discern the contents of the carts, only that whatever was being transported was carried in sacks. Those sacks were being shifted, with some effort, to the ruins at the centre. The entire site was possessed of an indiscernible purpose.

Andi had expected to find more of the slaver crews driving the slaves, similar to those they had encountered and defeated on the journey into the wooded hills yesterday.

But it was not the case. Using long whips and billy clubs to motivate the work crews, tall and burly humans in unfamiliar uniforms patrolled the clearing. They looked more like soldiers than slavers. At a push, Andi might have bought the suggestion that this was a particularly organised mercenary gathering, but it just didn't make sense to her. These men had the steely gaze and concentration of trained soldiers, used to following orders blindly. Most of the time mercenaries were at least aware of the purpose of their tasks. She could tell they didn't get any enjoyment out of beating the slaves, but it was equally clear that they had no qualms about doing so. Apparently they had a deadline, and their own suitable motivation.

The entire setup gave Andi a sour feeling.

"What do you think is in those sacks?" she asked Manic.

"Food? I mean, if you look over there..." The dwarf pointed a chubby finger to the northwest section of the clearing. "I think those are tents set up for the slaves to sleep in. I'd say they were full of sleeping slaves right now. When they wake up then those who are working now will probably bed down. This is a day-and-night operation. The guards all have torches and there are various sconces erected around the mill and the ruins."

The dwarf was right. He had a keen eye.

Andi nodded. "So if we assume the guards are sleeping in the first erected building, what's the second for? There's no more than fifty guards, but that first building alone could house a hundred of them. And I would suggest they aren't finished there. More buildings may be due."

The dwarf shrugged against her side by way of an answer; he had no clue.

"I want a closer look at those ruins," she decided. "The amount of food they're stocking up in there will give us an idea of what's going on here."

Manic was staring hard at the sacks being unloaded from

the cart. He mumbled something noncommittal, then said: "You go ahead and do that, skinny-britches. I'll stay here. If I see you get into trouble I'll come running. Just don't do anything stupid, and don't get caught!"

"Getting caught would constitute something stupid, so no worries on that count, Manic." She shuffled forward, keeping low to the ground. "Don't go anywhere; I'll not be long."

Her rotund companion huffed a laugh while he adjusted the greatsword at his side, ensuring that the metal was concealed from sight. She had no confidence in his ability to remain hidden for long, and so she vowed to be quick.

The guards themselves were primarily set up to drive the slaves and ensure they were under control. Little attention was afforded to the woodlands surrounding the area. Apparently they seemed confident of not being stumbled upon. This suggested that Manic was correct in his estimation that they were in Ipsican territory now. That was worrying. But if this was some developing staging area for guards then that would suggest this was a spear-point for Ipsican attempts to reclaim territory from Shenmadock lands. And that was something Reinhart would need to hear about, especially if they were using Shenmadockian farmers and families as slaves to facilitate it. All of this was just damned cheeky. Worse, this Ipsican staging area was far closer to the border than any in history.

Keeping low to the ground, Andi crossed swiftly toward the ruins at the centre of the clearing. The majority of activity was to the far side and she wasted no time in being overly cautious. She knew the conditions were to her advantage, and she was confident in her own ability to remain undetected. Her footfalls made no sound as she darted low through untended grasslands toward the small, ruined tower.

It resembled a diminutive inner bailey, but the land

surrounding it suggested no curtain wall had ever been erected to protect it. The construction style of the crenellations hinted at a structure that had been built many decades ago and possibly forgotten about. Either way, the building had been large enough to house plenty within, had it survived the passing years better.

The entrance was on the far side, as befitted Andi's luck. However, that meant no guards were patrolling this side of the keep. She made it to the postern wall without raising the alarm, and stopped to catch her breath.

The sun had passed beyond the horizon now, and she was in her element. It would take an unearthly eye to spy her now. *Unless she really messed up.*

The evening air was filled with the sounds from the sawmill round the keep to her left—northeast of her position, she guessed. The occasional cry from slaves who allowed their standard to drop acted in counterpoint to the repetitive scratch and hiss of saw-teeth on timber. And beneath it all was the sound that had so effectively carried on the morning air more than eight hours ago. She still couldn't quite identify it, but it was close. It certainly wasn't the sound of joinery.

Wasting little time, Andi sought the first footholds in the ancient wall at her back. The stonework was pitted and uneven—perfect for scaling. Quickly she turned her back to the hill to the south, somewhere upon which sat Eidos and Finhead. At first, the sinews and tendons in her hands and wrists protested at having to climb without the assistance of ropes and clamps, but she had no time for that. Gritting her teeth, she pushed past the pain and ascended with increasing grace and confidence.

Once at the top, her fingers looped over the battlements to the side of the central merlon, she stopped for a moment to listen. Her own breathing made it a little difficult to hear all the sounds of the clearing, but she gleaned enough to know that no guards patrolled the top of the walls.

With one swift motion, Andi pulled herself up and through the crenellation and dropped to the short balcony inside, immediately melding with the wall. The stonework seemed even more questionable beneath her feet, but it held. Keeping low to the stone she crawled slowly forward, careful to disperse her weight evenly.

The sound that had tantalised her all day was finally revealed. She had expected to discover stores of food: perhaps grain and root vegetables; something that substantiated the claims of a staging area for guards and slaves alike. But what was revealed in the central courtyard of the ancient bailey rushed through her like an icy wave.

The leftmost, western wall was dominated by a smithy, the forge at full fire and being fed by a team of four. Almost a dozen smiths were working tirelessly at the anvils and forge, hammering out the metal-on-metal music that had danced on the brow of Andi's recognition all day. Arms and armour of all descriptions swamped the rest of the ruined grounds, gathered in organised piles. Everything from thick and powerful spears to broad-headed halberds, mighty swords, short gladius swords, morning stars, maces and warhammers were laced together, dominating the rest of the west wall and most of the south wall beneath her.

Chestplates, beaten-leather riding chaps, helmets, shoulder guards, chainmail shirts, scalemail vests, small buckler shields for light infantry, round shields for mounted cavalry, and Tower Shields for frontline chargers stood to the east.

And in the far north corner the produce of a bowyer and fletch-works stood gathered in bundles. Simple longbows and shortbows were bound in bundles of ten or twelve, unstrung but prepared for stringing. And alongside these stood thousands upon thousands of arrows, gathered in flimsy quivers.

The sacks being tipped from the cart revealed mined

ore for the construction of far more weapons atop those already gathered. No food was in sight; not a grain. This was a mighty arsenal, and it was only fractionally complete.

Andi was held mesmerised by the sight before her. Never had such an operation been seen. There was enough equipment already present to arm a battalion of many thousands, and they weren't slowing down.

She broke her stare and rushed back over the wall, concentrating to control her descent in order to avoid a fatal drop. Once on the ground, it was all she could do to hold her nerve. Her body screamed for her to break into a sprint, but she would be easily visible even at this late hour. Instead, she kept as close to the ground as she could, pushing on as fast as she dared.

For a panicked moment, she lost the position of her companion dwarf. But then a minute movement to her left brought him into focus and she scuttled over the last few dozen yards, skidding into the undergrowth beside him. He immediately picked up on her unsettled demeanour.

He knew not to ask, simply assuming she was being pursued. They both got to their hands and knees and rushed out of the undergrowth, beyond the fallen trees and then took to their heels in silence, desperate to reach the rallying point as soon as possible.

Chapter Eleven
A Leap of Faith

Stefon was dreaming. It was the only explanation. He felt the detached sensation of the dream-world all around him, as though every object was steeped in ethereal syrup. Time was passing rapidly but everything moved with a laborious grace.

He stood atop a gentle rise, short grass swaying in the breeze around his bare feet. Out across the land he saw familiar places, either seen or read about. The ports of the southern coast ran for miles; the serrated peaks of the Choat Hills tore the sky to the west. The wilderness lands of the north ran to the verdant pastures of Ipsica. He could even see as far as the Frozen North.

The sky around him darkened and the living things browned, wilted and died. The land seemed ravaged by pestilence and the air was thick with sulphur. Suddenly, from out of the ground sprang armies numbering tens of thousands. Each soldier's eyes were hidden behind corpses' pennies, but their limbs moved and each face was wracked with hatred. The sound of tormented souls reverberated across the sky. Beneath the marching feet of the risen soldiers, Stefon could see the faces of the innocent, crashed and stamped into mud that ran burgundy with spilt blood.

The armies of the dead were on all sides and the known lands were utterly destroyed. Abruptly all sound ceased and all figures turned to stare blankly at Stefon. And he suddenly understood...

They know...he thought. *They know I can see...this is real...*

"Stefon, wake up!" Pryn shook him awake. It took a moment for the effects of the dream to fall from his body like a silk scarf. "You were dreaming," Pryn hissed. "And not quietly."

"I'm sorry; I'm fine now." He gathered himself together and looked around the abandoned basement they had chosen as their temporary residence. "How long have I slept?"

"A little over two hours," Pryn confirmed. "It's pretty late."

They had needed time to rest and take stock before they could work out their next move, but now it seemed simple. "Get the others together; we have a lot to do."

"What do you have in mind?" Pryn asked.

"We're getting the hell out of Wahib; tonight, if possible."

It took no time to gather the others, and Stefon was still stretching the weariness from his limbs as they assembled. He looked carefully from one to the other. Pryn was alert and looked strong, but recent events had taken its toll on the others. Brooss had done well to recover from her wound, but she was not at a hundred percent. Jewl and Rish's faces were drawn and pale. If he had believed fortune was truly against him, he might have feared the plague. But more than anything, they just looked defeated.

"We're leaving," he told them. "Getting out of the city tonight. It's time we put this place behind us. There's nothing in this city for us now."

A couple of them mumbled. Pryn nodded his agreement. Rish looked pensive. "It's not going to be that easy," he told the group, although the fact of his message was hardly news to those gathered. But he was going somewhere with his thought pattern. "We need to accomplish a few things before we go."

"Like with Ratna?" Jewl asked, incredulous. "I don't want my money from him. I don't think we should risk even telling him what we found out!"

"Hell, what *did* we find out?" Pryn asked. "Nothing factual. Nothing we could actually tell the man and still expect to be paid."

"We're never getting paid," Stefon admitted. "Our payment for success on this mission has gone from a prince's ransom to our lives. If we survive, we've been successful. It's that simple."

Rish shook his head. "No, we need to have closure. We mustn't leave with nothing. This city is going to implode, and when it does people will want answers. People will come looking for us. We need to know who was responsible, for our own safety, or we'll be running for the rest of our lives...from everyone."

"I agree," Stefon reluctantly admitted. "That's why I've made the decision that I have." The others stared back expectantly. They knew what was coming. "We need to go into the Tower of Light. We need to enter that tower and find out what they know."

Stefon could tell by the tableau of despair before him that no one present thought that was a particularly good idea. "Why?" asked Jewl simply.

Stefon rubbed an eye with his fingers whilst ordering his thoughts. "Here's what we know: this city was quarantined ahead of time, before the plague took a full grip and became an epidemic. In order to achieve that, the quarantine was designed and instigated outside local government and paid for directly into the local governor's pocket. That set of bribes motivated the governor to pass the quarantine and probably to install acolytes and priests from The Light to oversee the post-mortem examinations, as Rebrof found. These entries, which we assume are bribes, in the governor's journals were the only entries without a name attached. We need to find out if these entries tally with anything in the archives of the financial records in The Light. They're just as regulated as any other religious organisation. Those entries might not carry the governor's name, but the dates and values will match. The figures are high enough that they won't just have paid the bribe without registering the movement of the funds. They couldn't. People would ask too many questions.

"Further, we need to find out if Simeon had any contact with The Light, and those kids from Anya's brothel too. At some point in the last month I'm willing to bet that one, two or maybe all three people visited the building for some meeting or other." Stefon omitted the fact that it was effectively their lives he was betting with in this instance. "The Tower of Light has a public limited records library, which records the names of all individuals who visit the religious order. It's something we'll have to do, and it's something these three people will have done. We'll be using fake names, as they may have done. It's a long shot, but they may have entered their own names. That's what we're looking for, and specifically Simeon's name—for he had nothing to hide."

Rish looked dubious.

"They weren't likely to be suspicious back then. So they might not have been being too careful." Stefon shrugged. "Finally, these clerics worry me. I want to know what they're doing with the bodies that we should have found in the morgues and churchyards. The medical furnaces hadn't been used for months and there are no piles of bodies littering the place. Those bodies must be used for something; stands to reason that The Light has something to do with it."

"It's always a religious order that would be involved with doing seedy things with dead bodies," Jewl agreed.

"Quite. We're going to be splitting into three groups. The financial records and the public records are both on the ground floor. I've got my own reasons for checking the place out, but I'll be looking upstairs. I also know what I'm looking for to do with the bodies. I'll go on my own; I don't mind. You get the info then get out of that place and make it back here."

He looked carefully from face to face. "No matter what happens in that tower tonight, whoever has made it back here before sunrise should leave before the sun comes up. Get to Anya's using the dark for cover and leave by the sewers. She's been paid already." Stefon had used the remainder of his personal fortune to achieve that. "Get out and head for Choat. Get out of Ipsica altogether. There's a strong chance we might not all make it out, and we can't all wait around for fear we *all* get snared."

Rish was staring hard-faced at Stefon. He could tell Stefon felt he might not make it out in time. But it was something he had to do. Something was happening to him. The strange dreams; the odd physical changes; the things he was able to do...and then there was the way that cleric had chased him. He'd known something about Stefon— something strange. *Seer*, he'd hissed.

Seer...

The Light knew something, and Stefon wouldn't rest if he left without knowing at least part of what that was.

The dark sky was awash with churning clouds, intermittently torn by slanting, jagged lightning. Every booming clap of thunder shook more rain from the sky; rain that fell in torrents, driven by the maddening wind that pulled at

Stefon's hair and clothing. Illuminated in stark relief with every slash of lightning, the immense Tower of Light loomed: a windowless giant of dark stone revealed in intermittent strobe. Stefon had never witnessed a more foreboding static object.

This was as bad as the weather had been during these troubled times and Stefon felt it was somewhere between ironic and symbolic that they were infiltrating the Tower of Light in such conditions.

Stefon glanced around himself. He stood in the shelter of a torn shop-awning with Rish in close attendance, much as he had been no more than two days previously. This time it wasn't a simple pickup job—which had gone completely wrong, leading to regrettable deaths. This was an incursion into the most powerful non-political entity in Southern Ipsica. This was risking everything. Religion or not, these Clerics of the Light were zealots and would deal with individuals appearing to be acting in contradiction of their aims as enemies of the faith. Retribution would be swift and uncompromising. This was beyond anything Stefon had undertaken in the past—and all they were after was information, just a little bit of the right kind of knowledge, to give them a chance of surviving in the future.

The plan was simple beyond belief. They had split into four and left the basement safehouse separately, all heading for the Tower of Light. Pryn was to proceed to the public records library in the massive converted ballroom on the ground floor and check the signature details for the dates they were interested in. Brooss was designated to examine the accounting records, under the guise of a disability claim investigation (thanks to the obvious wound she still carried). These were also on the ground floor.

Stefon and Rish were to ascend the mighty central staircase and make their way as high as they could without being challenged, then try to find out what they could about what was going on in the city. Jewl was being sensible and doing a single circumference of the outer grounds. Once finished, he would wait at the door in case help was needed by anyone leaving the building—maybe in a hurry. He had brought what remained of his naphtha sacks in anticipation of such an event. He was an expert with the explosive fluid, and could work miracles with it.

Rish had insisted on accompanying Stefon, despite the mercenary captain's assertion that there were more risky missions being undertaken, particularly by Brooss. Rish had entertained no excuses: he wasn't leaving Stefon's side. Although one would normally assume that this was an example of some impressive notion of camaraderie, Stefon was more inclined to believe it was motivated by a stranger recipe of factors: namely one part curiosity and two parts the desire to be present as insurance against his propensity for "doing something stupid".

Stefon didn't care. He had his own motivations for entering the building. Since the inception of this quarantine, and possibly a little before, he had been experiencing changes. At first he had been able to brush away any effects as mere imaginings, but in the past week the differences had become impossible to ignore. With the increased vividness of his dreams and his increasingly impressive physical feats, it seemed clear he needed to find out what was going on in his own body—and his mind. And The Light seemed to be the keepers of all information of a mysterious nature. The guardians of such information were typically secretive, and in equal measure both guarded and coveted such information.

And that cleric had called him a *seer*. He wanted to know what that could possibly mean.

Stefon's intention was clear: seek elucidation or suffer madness.

Jewl was in sight now, up the wide thoroughfare ahead of them, walking slowly toward the tall Tower of Light. Brooss had already made her way to the building and Pryn would also be somewhere near the place. The plan was already in action—but Stefon was suddenly filled with a feeling of dread. He glanced at Rish. "I think this might be a mistake," he admitted.

"You're only just realising that?" Rish asked, a smirk on his face. Seeming to realise that Stefon was being serious, his lopsided grin disappeared. "Listen, this isn't the first time you've put people in harm's way in the process of achieving your goal. It's the kind of decision that leaders are built for. That's why you lead and we follow."

Stefon shook his head. He had never thought of himself as an actual leader. Perhaps he'd imagined people followed because he was just doing things the right way, but the realisation that this was not necessarily the case was disconcerting. Mostly his friends did the things he suggested because it was he who was suggesting them. The responsibility of that hit home with sudden force. It was entirely possible, even likely, that he had made the wrong decision tonight, and it might just cost lives—and this time lives that meant something to him.

He shook his head, trying to rid himself of those thoughts buzzing around like angry wasps in a jar. What was done was done, and there was no changing that now. He had to see it through and do his best to come out of that building with as many of his crew as possible. If some of them were...

Just what was it that he was afraid of? Where had this abject fear come from? Just what did he imagine The Light to be capable of? They were a religious order—*the* religious order in this region. Did he think they would attack and kill people for just looking up information in a public records library? That was an absurd suggestion. The Tower of Light was a church; a place of worship; a spiritual home!

But even as he led Rish out into the hammering downpour and across toward the Tower grounds, that foreboding sense of impending danger still permeated his very bones, and his thigh muscles jumped and twitched with tension as he walked.

Jewl wasn't too happy. He had never liked the rain. Frost and snow never really bothered him, and ironically sunshine and warm weather rankled him more than anything else. But the rain was infuriating. It slid through gaps in your clothing and seeped through layers of every material. And it made Jewl smell like a wet dog. It wasn't his fault; that was just the way it was with dwarves...they smelled like wet dogs in the rain.

The grounds were empty, save a few miserable homeless believers, too drunk or wound up on Strangemeal to be allowed entrance to the Tower despite the horrid conditions.

Grumbling, he hoisted his bag of naphtha casings higher on his shoulder, ignoring the distinct danger they represented should one crack, and set off at a slow trudge around the rain-soaked stone and rock garden grounds surrounding the base of the Tower of Light.

Inside the Tower, Brooss had been well received. Upon arrival a tall gent of middling years had proffered a linen towel to dry her hair and had offered her a warm drink. She had declined. "It is only a short visit, I'm afraid," she had said coyly, cradling her shoulder, although there was really no need: the wound was tender, but required no further treatment. The man had nodded sagely and bade her a pleasant evening.

Even at this late hour, the Tower was busy. Academics and clerical staff mustered from office to front desk, from bookshelf to office. The activity made Brooss feel slightly uncomfortable, but she knew it would aid her attempts to remain both inconsequential and inconspicuous.

She walked with quick, light steps through the under-lit library and into the public statements and accounts section. Several steel stands helped to illuminate the room. Atop each was a wide plate on which burned chemically treated coals and fossil rocks, producing a low-burning clean white flame. As a result, the low-ceilinged room was bathed in a stark, pale light and smelled vaguely of vanilla. An officious man met her at the entrance and asked, in brusque tones, "Your business, ma'am?"

For a moment Brooss felt it was a challenge, and that she had entered a restricted or official area in error. Her mouth open, she could think of no response. After an uncomfortable pause, the man cracked what could only have been a brown-toothed attempt at a smile, and Brooss realised he was just an idiot. "Public records, please."

He indicated a row of ledgers and files in various states of disarray along the far right wall. Several desks were arranged in uniform rows to accommodate easy viewing of records. Brooss strode confidently over to a desk, placed her coat carefully on the back of one of the many free benches, and began searching for the ledgers she required.

The main Library of the Light was immense. Pryn was truly impressed. The ornate panels and columns that stretched to the ceiling high over his head were creatively worked and varnished and uniquely sculpted respectively. The deep rosewood lent the entire facility a regal tone that provoked a sense that one was in a place steeped in learning: a room to which great minds might come to...think.

It was as good a description as Pryn could muster. Clever people came to a place like this to think. Pryn's was not a great mind—and certainly not one that inclined towards thought. He was a man of action, and more often than not violent and decisive action. He was smart enough to know that the place should have intimidated him, but he had a job to do and he was nothing if not professional.

Affecting an air of confidence and a sense of belonging, Pryn strode over to the public counter and waited for one of the few clerical types behind to notice him. He was patient; he could wait.

A few moments passed before a shrewish woman of lengthening years looked up from a wide, onionskin book she was sifting through. Her beady eyes appeared massive through a pair of excessive spectacles. She scuttled over to him using short, economic steps. A knitted shawl was gathered around her shoulders and her white hair was pulled up in a vicious bun atop her head. She reminded Pryn of any stereotypical grandmother he'd ever read about, and he hated her for it. This kind of woman was always trouble.

"How can I help you?" Her voice was pleasant enough, but her smile wrinkled her nose and pushed the glasses higher on her face, making her gigantic eyes zoom in and out comically.

"I've just signed in on the guestbook at the door and was just wondering if there was any way I could see the previous registers?"

The wizened old crow's brow concertinaed in confusion as she appeared ready to ask something.

Probably wants to ask why, Pryn thought. He wouldn't give her the satisfaction. He tried thinking on his feet for a change. "I want to see if I've been here before."

Now, Pryn knew what he meant. And he was pretty sure the poisoned prune on the other side of the counter knew what he meant. But it hadn't *sounded* how he had intended, and he suddenly felt foolish and out of place.

"Well, the registers for the past week are over on the far wall, sir. It is an impressive collection of individuals who have felt compelled by the teachings of The Light. Felt themselves drawn to The Light, just like your good self."

More like moths, Pryn thought: *like mindless moths drawn to a flame.* Something in that image worried him.

Pryn nodded, attempting to dispel the feeling of unease, and tried his best to produce a pious smile. He was pretty sure he succeeded only in looking smug, but decided the journey from smug to pious was but a short one.

Rueing his ridiculous mistake, Pryn took his leave and made his way over to the register section, eager to be done with this work. It was all he could do not to cut his losses and leave right then and there, but he was nothing if not professional.

What Pryn *didn't* see was Ala May, the old librarian who had served him, turn from the counter after showing him the correct shelves. Nor did he see her leave the library by a door in the back of the office area and go looking for a cleric.

While Pryn was making a fool of himself in the Library, Stefon and Rish were striding confidently across the main central hall of The Light. They had met with no heavy resistance at the huge, ornate main doors and had proceeded through security easily enough. Rish had checked in his bow and short sword, as was the done thing at a temple or church in Wahib. The entire process had almost been welcoming, in direct contrast to the testimony of Gill, the old man Stefon had spoken with at the beginning of this whole mess. The old man had spoken of being ushered away from the premises by men armed with billy clubs and sticks. There had been no sign of any such presence today.

The building itself was an impressive structure. No windows adorned the outside wall to allow light in or out. The central column of the building, at the very heart of the structure, was a hollow shaft. All floors that extended upwards were punctuated by circular balconies; each one slightly wider than the floor above, so as to reduce the circumference of the shaft as it rose.

At the top of this shaft a brilliant white light shone down on those below, bathing everything with a diffused alabaster glow. It was a startling effect, and one that drew admirers from afar. Many visitors reportedly felt compelled or inclined to believe in something mystical when they stood beneath the stare of the impressive Shaft of Light, and most confessed to feeling a strange sense of fulfilment.

Stefon felt neither. He felt watched.

Without missing a step, he and Rish proceeded across the ground floor to a spiral staircase up to the next.

Jewl didn't know how it was that it was always him who ended up traipsing around outside while the rest of the group got to remain nice and warm inside a building. It just always seemed to work out that way.

He was near the back of the structure by now, he assumed, as there was a series of industrial entrances for waste removal or various deliveries. One sunken area was filled with containers of rubbish and waste, with small flies gathering around the crates in the teeming rain.

As he skirted the depression, something caught Jewl's eye. Something familiar and out of place down in the crates had snatched his attention, and he scanned the bags and cartons in search of what it might have been.

His gaze alighted on a long, black bulk in a far container, tied together with twine. It resembled a rug or carpet in a bag, but something in the undulations screamed something else to him.

Immediately he padded over to the edge of the depression; the stonework was treacherous from the downpour. It made absolutely no sense that The Light would dispose of a body in the waste bins—certainly not in plain sight. But he had to make sure.

Sure enough, the closer Jewl got, the more the bag resembled a humanoid body. He knelt at the edge and reached down. His fingers grabbed at the sodden bag and pulled at a knot of twine near one end.

Risking slipping into the rubbish container with the body, Jewl fought his revulsion as he struggled to keep his balance.

One more tug will do it, he thought. *Come on!*

The knot came loose and a corner of the sacking was within reach. His fingers snagged it and pulled.

Jewl snatched his gnarled hand away as though burned.

That face! Familiar...so familiar...

Recognition thundered through his mind as he jumped to his feet. He had to tell someone. He had to tell *Stefon*.

Suddenly he could hear voices approaching. They were coming from one of the rear entrances nearby.

Startled, Jewl frantically looked for an escape route. The entrance was at his back. The voices were at his back. He'd have to run right by them to escape the way he was going. He didn't have time to run around the garbage depression and back the way he had come. Looking forlornly at the refuse depression at his feet, Jewl placed a panicked hand on the wall of the building at his side.

Grabbing at the equipment in his satchel, he knew there was only one option.

"All I know is, we're supposed to burn the waste and rubbish today," came one of the voices. "This afternoon, in fact."

"We're pretty late," was the reply. "Why didn't you tell me sooner?"

"I was waiting for the rain to stop. How was I supposed to know it would get heavier?"

Two figures emerged into the rain from one of the rear entrances. They brought with them three canisters of some kind of fluid. From his hiding place, Jewl could hear the liquid sloshing around as they stopped near the edge of the rubbish depression.

Wasting no time, the two figures used a hand pump to spray the contents of the canisters over the rubbish. The last container had its lid removed and was tipped in whole, the contents sloshing out. One of the men used a flintlock device to strike sparks into a wad of rags in his hand that caught first time.

Without delay, the rag was thrown into the rubbish and the pungent liquid was ignited. Flames lashed the night sky as the rubbish was consumed. Even the driving rain could not fight the fire.

Filthy smoke billowed from the sinkhole as the two men stood for a moment to ensure that the flames took. The rising clouds of smoke served only to conceal Jewl more effectively as he continued his ascent up the side of the Tower of Light. Below him, the men seemed happy, and departed.

Jewl had to find a way into the Tower. Perhaps there was a window higher up that wasn't visible from the ground. Using the climbing clamps, Jewl forced his protesting muscles to struggle upward.

He had to find Stefon and Rish to tell them what he had found. The Light was disposing of a body. And, unless Jewl was very much mistaken, the body was that of Meena Saqir, the corrupt governor of Wahib City.

Rish led Stefon up the stairwell and out onto the first floor. The area was dominated by the central balcony that overlooked the ground floor, which they had just crossed. They took a moment to look down and admire the stonework design of the ornate floor. Various-coloured slabs of measured stone and mineral had been interwoven to create a sweeping, impressive collage of hue and form. Again, this view was famous throughout Ipsican society.

A few members of the public were present here, on their knees in quiet prayer by the side of the balcony. The surroundings were quiet, lacking the resonant sound of activity the ground floor possessed. Instead, academics and staff moved economically from room to room without fuss. The only real sounds echoed up from the ground floor itself.

Rish indicated a diagram on a nearby wall. They scanned it quickly, looking for something that might give them a clue as to where to start. It was when Rish saw Stefon staring at the top strata of the diagram that he understood. Floor twelve clearly read *Clerical*.

"Clerics," Rish mused. "You want to find the clerics themselves?"

Stefon only nodded a reply.

"Do you not remember the last time we ran into a cleric?" Rish hissed. "We had to kill him, remember? What happens if they know that?"

Stefon frowned and turned back to the spiral staircase. "How could they?"

Rish didn't have an answer.

"You can stay here if you want, or go back," Stefon offered. "I'll meet you in the basement when I'm done."

Rish could tell immediately that Stefon fully intended to continue alone if he let him, and that he wouldn't hold it against him if he left. For that reason alone, he followed.

After three more floors the current spiral staircase came to an end and they exited onto a much smaller balcony area.

The central shaft was noticeably narrower too. Various small, glass-fronted libraries encircled the circumference of the floor. A few individuals stood, reading from manuscripts or tomes of some description or other. None marked their entrance to the floor.

With a jut of his chin, Stefon indicated another spiral staircase across from them before making his way over. Rish followed, keeping his attention fixed on the individuals in the libraries. None turned their attention from their reading material.

Rish was just thinking that this was pretty strange when Stefon halted suddenly, just short of the stairwell. Someone had emerged from the passage, a bound volume gathered up in his robed arms. The man had a pinched, pallid face and slick black hair. His mouth was small and pouting and his eyes were mean and officious.

For a moment it looked as though the man was going to challenge Stefon, but his mean little eyes glanced meaningfully at Stefon's waist and he immediately backed off, vacating the stairwell. "With peace, brother." With that he hurried away to one of the glass-front libraries to deliver his volume.

Stefon ascended the stairs once more.

"What was that about?" Rish pressed, once they had left earshot.

"I don't know." Stefon stopped between floors. "He glanced at this." Stefon pulled back a corner of his tunic to reveal the polished-silver pommel of the sword he had taken from the fallen cleric earlier that week.

"How the hell did you manage to bring that into a church? I had to drop...*most* of my weapons at the door. I still have a knife behind my back, but the rest are in one of those lockers downstairs." Rish eyed Stefon suspiciously. "Come to think of it, they didn't even question you. You just walked straight through."

"I know. It wasn't until we were inside that my hand brushed against the hilt and I realised I still carried it." Stefon drew the weapon from the scabbard slightly, revealing the mercurial, pristine blade. It still shone with a colourful, unnatural power; this time a pale lime shade. "Did you notice that they didn't ask for *any* of my weapons? I don't think they even stopped *you*. You just volunteered your weapons."

Rish went to argue the point, before realising Stefon was right. He had expected to be challenged and had simply surrendered his weapons without being asked. In fact, the sentries on the doors had behaved in a slightly surprised manner.

"Is this sword some kind of emblem or insignia?" Rish mused. "Do they think you're a cleric?"

"It would explain why we've gone as far as we have without being challenged."

Rish stood for a moment, taking that in. "Come on, let's get on with it. At least this is something we can use to our advantage. That would make a welcome change, considering how badly this week has gone so far!"

Brooss laughed quietly to herself. There it was. Clear and simple, in exactly the place Rish had suggested the entries would be. For every transaction that had been detailed in Governor Meena's ledgers there was a corresponding transaction in the public records at The Light. In comparison to the majority of charity payments and such, the figures were small, but to an individual like Governor Meena it was a small fortune.

The entries themselves were similarly unmarked, indicated as taxed contributions, but the tally of amounts was unavoidable. The sums that had been paid to Governor Meena had indeed come from the treasury of The Light.

The Light had paid the governor bribes to enforce the quarantine on their orders, before the plague had taken hold. The Light had quarantined the city.

Why?

Brooss gathered the records together and replaced them in the relevant sections, careful to take her time and to leave them in presentable order. She gathered her cloak and pulled it around her shoulders as she headed to the library, with a short nod to the officious idiot sitting near the door.

It was up to the others to answer the question of why these things had occurred. Brooss had done her job: she had confirmed they were right, and now she had to leave.

Lengthening her stride, she glanced around the library looking for Pryn. At first she struggled to locate him, but as she neared the entrance to the main hall her eyes alighted on his hulking form at a wide desk. His dark dreadlocks still glistened with rainfall and his mysteriously blue skin shone with moisture.

Standing at his desk was a tall individual in a long, dark robe. They seemed to be talking, although Brooss didn't recognise Pryn's visitor.

Her step faltered as she neared the door, concern knotting her brow.

The stranger unfurled his cloak to reveal the silver hilt of a sword as another tall, robed figure approached from the counter area. Pryn sat back, showing empty hands to the strangers.

Brooss left the library. Pryn was being intercepted. Somehow they knew he was up to something. Walking sharply between people, her head held low, Brooss made for the exit.

Pryn had been just about to lose his temper. He had spent more than ten minutes without finding a single name that he was looking for. He had just begun to consider looking through the dates in question for entries in similar handwriting when a long shadow had crept across his desk.

"Good day, sir." A thick, deep voice greeted him. "I trust all is well?"

Pryn looked up to see a tall, thickset man in a long brown robe standing at his side. His hands were clasped at the front of his waist and his expression seemed kind enough. "Actually, I can't really find what I'm looking for. I think I'll give up."

"Sir, perhaps it's something I can help with? I understand you're looking for a visitor to our illustrious mission?"

Pryn looked up at the man's face. Although his smile seemed genuine enough, his eyes were hard. Discomfited by the man's knowledge, and figuring the old cow had given him up for one reason or another, Pryn picked up on the mention of a single individual.

He sat back in his chair and spread his hands in supplication. "I'm actually looking for *three* friends of mine, not just one." The man looked tripped-up by that. "But if they're not here, they're not here." Pryn shut the register. "And they're not here."

"Perhaps if you give me their names, I might be able to help?"

Pryn knew he shouldn't actually ask. He knew he should lie, and make a few names up. But something in the man's eyes burrowed deep into his own. Something in his demeanour exuded power over him. Before he could think of precisely what to do, he spoke the names, one after another, in measured quiet tones. He gave the information up as easily as if the names had no meaning to anyone. First, the couple who had escaped from the city; and then Simeon the scavenger, who had died just that day in Stefon's hands.

"Perhaps you would be so kind as to accompany us, sir? I have someone who wishes to speak with you. They might be able to help."

It was then that Pryn saw the second cleric by the counter, and the withered old hag nearby. Somehow he had allowed himself to be caught, and he didn't even know what for.

Stefon flinched. After exiting the latest of a series of spiral staircases, he and Rish were confronted by a startling sight. They stood in a small foyer, with two stone benches on either side and traditional murals adorning both walls. A set of three steps led up to an arched entrance, through which a number of prayer pulpits and simple wooden benches could be seen.

The hole in the centre of the floor had now diminished in diameter to a mere fifteen yards across. The corresponding hole in the ceiling was smaller still. From this ceiling portal, the shaft of light was bright and powerful, producing a sub-aural thrum. More felt than heard, it was like a low-frequency oscillation that echoed through Stefon's feet and along his bones.

The sight that made him flinch was the number of clerics in the room ahead. It must have been in the high dozens; most kneeling in prayer or quiet contemplation, facing the column of white light.

There was nothing for it, though: they had to proceed. A couple of the clerics had already looked their way, and to turn and leave now would be a dead giveaway that they didn't belong. After all, this was where Stefon had wanted to be. This was where the answers were most likely to be. But now that he was here, he had no idea what to do. Had he expected to find a section in one of the libraries labelled "Seers—A Succinct History of Strange Accusations"?

Suddenly he was angry with himself. He had no real reason for being here other than bull-headed stubbornness. Harnessing his irritation, he strode confidently up the three stairs, ensuring the hilt of his sword was clearly visible to all those he passed. He then walked calmly along a track that ran the length of the outer wall. At intervals there were paintings and murals, depicting various parables and religious events that were largely alien to him.

A couple of clerics watched them a little too closely, obviously not quite buying the charade, probably because he and Rish were entirely unrecognisable here. He was just becoming concerned about this when something in the nearest mural caught his eye.

He stopped before the mural and stared hard at the image: a single figure presiding over a barren landscape, surrounded by pestilence and plague. The earth seemed scorched and dead. On all sides of the lone figure were armed shapes, slender like stickmen and equally featureless. The sky above was dominated by storm clouds.

It was his dream! The dream he had experienced only recently was clearly depicted before him, but he had no recollection of having ever seen such a mural.

"It shows the coming of the darkest hours," a voice said from behind him. For the second time that day he flinched, almost jumping from his skin.

Feigning calm, Stefon looked over his shoulder into the tanned face of a cleric. The religious zealot was not looking at him; he was too busy admiring the artwork. "It is allegorical, you understand," he continued. "It depicts the singular consciousness witnessing the growing threat at our darkest hour. Notice the complete absence of light in the vision. Terrifying, no?"

Stefon shrugged as he returned his gaze to the painting. "Who is the singular consciousness?"

The cleric huffed, as though Stefon were providing him with an obvious test. "Why, it is you."

Stefon struggled to control his panic, refusing to turn to face the cleric once more. However, Rish couldn't resist:

"Him? How?"

"You are unenlightened," the cleric told Rish. "Not *just* him. The singular consciousness is also *allegorical*— it represents those who stand alone at the time of reckoning. Those who stand surrounded by the unholy and shrouded by darkness in a land brought low by pestilence—a world without enlightenment and devoid of hope. The singular consciousness stands against that which would crush this world."

Stefon glanced at Rish. He looked unimpressed.

"So when did all that happen?" Rish pressed.

"It has not yet come to pass," the cleric replied. "As my brother here would surely have explained to you, the mission of The Light is the preparation of the world—and those who would accept these beliefs—for the darkest hour of existence."

Stefon nodded, although he had no idea what the crackpot was talking about.

"But this is not my favourite." The cleric stepped to the right to indicate the next mural. Stefon and Rish followed reluctantly. As they stopped at the cleric's side, Stefon noticed a flight of wall stairs nearby leading to the next floor. The shaft of strange illumination had obscured them until now.

The painting they now stood before was more ornate and colourful than the last. At the leftmost edge of the painting cowered a host of people, gathered in terror. Dominating the centre were warriors clad in white armour, brandishing weapons of fire above the necks of the cowering figures. The right-hand edge of the painting was pure white, with strange shafts of light lancing out across the sky at the warriors' backs. It looked less than pious.

The most startling aspect of the painting came from the cringing subjects to the left: each one amorphous in aspect, melding one to another in a dark mass of familiar shapes.

Only their eyes, burning silver, were clear and distinct. "This is your favourite?" Stefon asked with obvious surprise.

"I think I can read this one," said Rish. "It's allegorical, showing the army of The Light, signifying the might of the mission's message, propelled by the immense nature of The Light itself to drive the heretics and non-believers from the land? Because heretics are stupid, and no one likes them." Rish's overexaggeration of the word *heretics* clearly mocked the cleric.

"No, actually," replied the cleric matter-of-factly. "This depicts an event that has already occurred. It is mythology in part, but entirely factual."

"How can something be mythological in part but entirely factual?" asked Stefon. "That makes no sense."

"Mythology is a symptom of the passage of time, brother. Events and achievements that were momentous at the time become 'great' after a century and thereby pass through 'legendary' and into mythology, with more years that pass. Sentient beings' propensity for embellishment may serve to aggrandise the details, but the achievement remains precise."

Stefon looked at the cowering figures. The absoluteness of the coming destruction they would suffer was disconcerting. The look of zeal on the warriors' faces was equally disquieting. "What 'achievement' does it depict?"

"Centuries ago there existed a race of humans capable of great feats—remarkable people. But they were tainted by the devil, cursed with foresight and vision. Many would be driven mad by hallucinations, but those strong enough to survive became dangerous. Their madness led them and others away from their faith. The first Clerics of The Light, the Goyl Clergy, crushed them at the battle of Bria, on the banks of the River Dranon, where the modern city Krasital now stands— Krasital, the seat of power for the nation of Briadranon. All were cleansed."

"You mean slaughtered," Stefon countered, not caring

that it was now clear that he was no cleric. The disgust was obvious in his voice.

"The world became a more peaceful place. Their darkness was purged from these lands in order that those who remained might get closer to The Light." He gazed admiringly at the painting, before turning his eyes meaningfully on Stefon. "The artist called his work *The Rout of the Dranon Seers*."

Jewl's mind reeled under the impact of something immense and unidentifiable. It was all that he could do to remain fixed to the side of the building. His brain was in turmoil. Immediately he was aware of the pure and simple knowledge that Stefon and Rish were in trouble.

He had no explanation for it. There was no simple reasoning for how a dwarf, attached to the side of a tower all on his own, could spontaneously acquire the knowledge he had. But it was compelling. It was definite. He had to do something.

But he *was* a dwarf attached to the side of a tower. A windowless tower, at that. He had ascended almost half the height of the structure and it was plain to see that there wasn't a single damned window on the exterior of this wretched monolith.

The storm-swept darkness of the city looked up at him, twinkling firelights in a tar-like sea, offering no help or inspiration.

He had to get to the top. He had to do something, or his friends would die.

Hoisting his bag higher on his shoulder, feeling the weight of the contents against his back, he removed the nearest clamp and struggled higher as fast as his short limbs would take him.

The word *seer* rushed through Stefon's ears like a tidal wave. Suddenly he was the focus of attention for almost every set of eyes in the room.

His mind returned to the street outside his safehouse earlier that week, when Rebrof had died. The cleric that had pursued them through the apothecary building had pointed directly at Stefon and hissed that word.

He had been hunted, encircled and trapped as easily as a dumb animal. Every action he had taken leading to this point had been made with no clear reason in mind. Now he felt sure that his actions had somehow been guided by outside influences, and that he had been led to this place, at this time, for this very moment.

Strangely, his only regret was that he had brought Rish with him. He had brought Rish to his death, and that was something he had expressly wished not to do. He had fought with the notion, but Rish had been adamant.

"Please, Captain Stefon, follow me," the cleric said, motioning to the flight of stairs up to the next floor. "And you too, Master Rish, of course."

They had no choice. They were led up the stairs beyond rooms reserved for strange training regimes and exercises that Stefon couldn't fathom or recognise; all conducted and performed by disrobed clerics.

Finally the stairs opened into a brilliantly lit office of grand design. The ceiling was the source of light that illuminated the entire building. Strangely, Stefon was not blinded by the brilliance. He didn't even feel the need to shade his eyes.

Their guide-cleric walked calmly across the room to the regal chair behind a grandiose desk on the other side of a banister-ringed well, which undoubtedly opened onto the central shaft of the building. Four other clerics stood to attention at evenly spread positions throughout the room.

Stefon and Rish were bidden to stand on the opposite side of the central well from their host. The shaft did indeed drop away at their feet. The feeling of vertigo was nauseating. Rish put out a hand to steady himself.

Their host settled in his chair and regarded them for a moment. His features were clean and chiselled, his brown hair secured in place by some waxy substance. His narrow eyes were dark and piercing. Neither tall nor short, not overweight or slender, this man was the personification of average.

"My name is Lesjac, Druidan Cleric and Emboldened Prophet of Light."

Stefon and Rish looked on, vacant and bemused.

"It's a religious title," Lesjac stated, losing his haughty tone. "It means I'm the boss, and God says you should do what I say." He broke into a genuine grin awash with mirth and glee.

The two friends remained silent. They knew when they were in trouble.

"Now then, seer, what should we do with you?"

"Why do you people keep calling me that?" Stefon asked.

"It is what you are, Stefon. Let me *enlighten* you; it's kind of my job. It transpired that, at their height, the race we know as seers were considerably racist as a species. It was assumed that they were an abomination; a mutation of some type. It has been well documented that they were considered their own race, but this is actually not the case.

"The seer strain is actually a gift. The abilities and traits that mark a seer as differing from others are no more or less attributable to a human than they are to an elf or an orc. Any species was capable of developing the seer strain."

"You keep calling it a strain," Rish interrupted him. "Do you mean it's a disease? Something that can be caught?" Stefon could tell that Rish was referring to the plague ravaging Wahib.

Lesjac barked a laugh. "No, my intuitive friend, it is no disease. In fact, it was the personal mission of one of my predecessors to try to isolate and harness the seer strain, but that was folly. The Goyl Clergy tried in vain to harness the power of the seers to their own ends, but failed miserably. There is no such thing as an actual strain or identifiable element that differs Stefon here from you, my friend. The Goyl Clergy were misled and poorly guided in their mission, but they did what was required in the end and routed the seers from existence."

"Being misguided seems a running theme," Stefon muttered.

"Not so, Stefon. We are supremely confident in our diagnosis that the seer strain is nothing more than a malformation; a disfigurement of the physical and psychological norm. It can befall a member of any species, and all are equally cursed. It appears that races such as the elves saw the strain for what it was: unnatural. Seers within elven clans were eliminated for the greater good, despite the fact that elves are so seldom born; such was their loathing of the seer malformation. It appears dwarves treated them in the same manner, although the impact was less upon the dwarven clans, for they are not so long-lived as the elves.

"Lesser races like halflings and orcs didn't have the social sophistication to realise that something was amiss in the seers' behaviour. But then again, halflings and orcs are retarded races, and those possessed of the seer malformation would most probably not realise.

"But humans are ambitious by nature. Therefore the human seers thrived and developed, growing as an elitist sect, believing themselves to be touched by God. Some even believed they were Gods themselves." Lesjac steepled his fingers. "They were wrong, and they were destroyed for this misconception."

"You're talking about genocide," Stefon accused.

"Strictly speaking, you're probably right. But that is mythology." He smiled enigmatically. "You haven't asked what symptoms indicate the seer strain. I'm sure you're curious."

Rish glanced from Lesjac to Stefon and back.

"I'm sure you've noticed yourself becoming...stronger...quicker...able to achieve feats beyond normal capabilities. According to our records, it tended to be the mental seer traits that would manifest first: the ability to predict coming events or actions; the ability to *see* myriad possible distant futures; the ability to react at superhuman speeds, alongside a godlike prescience; the power of the mind over people; the ability to affect their thoughts...to lead them by mental suggestion...to draw them to their banner...to *inspire* them."

As Lesjac spoke, memories ran through Stefon's mind. During the ambush at the warehouse a week ago, he had dodged a crossbow bolt that he could not have known was coming. During the visit to the hospital with Rebrof, they had wandered through without being challenged, purely because he had been so focused on being ignored. And of course, there were his friends Pryn, Rebrof, Brooss, Jewl and Rish, who would all walk into certain danger at his behest, because they trusted his judgement. Or so he thought. Perhaps it was just the case that he was conning them. *Controlling* them.

He felt sick to his stomach. Had that "control" led to Rebrof's death?

"It gets better," Lesjac continued, seeming to enjoy Stefon's guilt. "Soon you'll find you grow faster in movement, so much so that you will be a mere blur to simple mortals. You'll be able to jump great heights... carry weight beyond your own in your very hands. And that is just the beginning. The potential is staggering. I can't begin to tell you." Lesjac's awe was palpable. "*And that is why you must die.*"

"I knew I had a bad feeling about this," muttered Rish, while Stefon tried to balance his curiosity that someone seemed to know what was happening to him with his frustration that the same individual was determined to have him killed. He wanted to know more, but obviously not at the cost of his or Rish's life.

"We all know you are experiencing the first symptoms. It is but a matter of time before the physical manifestations begin to materialise. By then you will be too dangerous for other beings."

Rish held up a finger and made to speak, but Stefon cut him short. "I don't understand. Why are you trying to kill me? Am I really such a threat to your bloody church?"

"No, you're just impure. This is an act of kindness on our part. You are largely inconsequential in the great scheme of things."

"I don't feel too inconsequential, Lesjac. You've had cloaked men trying to kill me all week."

Lesjac's brow knotted. "Not so. Those men were commissioned by that idiot Governor Meena Saqir to find and eliminate Simeon. We had no idea who they were until they found and killed Simeon this afternoon. Saqir should have left it to us. Those men were bothersome, for sure, stumbling upon our ambushes and instigating the death of one of my finest brothers. No, I'd have had you killed a while ago had it not been for their interference."

Now Stefon saw that the ambush that had killed Rebrof had been set up to eliminate Simeon and his team, not himself. They had been swept up by accident, purely because they had asked difficult questions. They were in a tangled web.

"Ah, your friend is here." Lesjac stood politely to welcome two more clerics who emerged from the flight of stairs at Stefon's back. He looked over his shoulder to see Pryn being led toward them, looking downcast.

"I'm sorry, Stefon," said Pryn. "I don't know how they knew I was up to something."

Lesjac clicked his tongue smugly. "It's pretty elementary, my friend. You were looking in a register no one else is ever interested in, and you were looking for names of interest to me. With the arrival of our friend Stefon in the building tonight, it was no great leap of faith to assume you were up to something."

The clerics accompanying Pryn confirmed to Lesjac the names for which he had been searching before returning below. Stefon leaned to the side and whispered, "You told them who you were searching for?"

Pryn shrugged. He had no excuse.

"Well, that is interesting," mused Lesjac. "Those two kids that escaped the city were also of little importance. However, had they been allowed to escape, the ramifications could have been far-reaching indeed. We cannot allow what is occurring in Wahib City to permeate the rest of Ipsica or the continent beyond. That would be unacceptable. As for Simeon and his team, they were unfortunate, but Governor Meena Saqir was right to have them executed. Wahib City must remain contained."

"We were there when they killed him!" Stefon interrupted. "There was nothing we could do. He died in my arms."

"How touching!" Lesjac quipped.

"He had no plague!" The ferocity of Stefon's outburst made Rish and Pryn jump. One of Lesjac's eyebrows arched quizzically. "He was scared, but he wasn't sick. Why kill him once he's back in the city? He's no threat to the rest of Ipsica then! He must have known something! I think the governor killed him because he knew that The Light had the quarantine set up before the Plague. With his last breath he told me to 'Fear The Light'. What do you suppose he meant by that?"

Lesjac shrugged before motioning with a finger to the clerical guards standing to attention around the room. "Kill them."

Stefon braced himself, stepping away from the balcony and reaching for the sword still at his hip. Rish moved in a similar direction, ready to try and defend himself. The four clerics drew their weapons: the same thrumming blades Stefon found so familiar now.

Stefon and his friends were in big trouble.

Stefon and his friends were in big trouble.

Jewl frantically climbed higher, the fuse-wire gripped in his teeth leading to the naphtha charges he had just affixed so carefully. The thought thumped through his mind again, word for word:

Stefon and his friends were in big trouble.

The dwarf was high in the sky, whipped by wind and rain as he fought to retain his grip on the clamps attached to the side of the building. The entire city was laid out hundreds of feet below him. One slip and he was history.

With his head to the wall, he held the end of the fuse near his right hand and began striking flint against the masonry. One spark…another…

The fuse smouldered and then caught in a phosphorous conflagration that rushed toward his lips. He dropped the fuse from his mouth, allowing it to drop away beneath him.

Then he prepared himself.

Stefon prepared himself. The sword in his hands felt light once more, and the blade seemed longer than it had ever been in his grasp. The two nearest clerics advanced, their blades levelled at Stefon and Pryn.

"Can't we just talk about this?" Rish ventured. There

was no answer. Lesjac remained behind his desk, his fingers steepled thoughtfully and a dark look of malice staining his features. He no longer appeared amused.

Stefon took a tentative step toward the rightmost foe.

The room exploded with sound. The floor beneath his feet pitched as though sundered by an earthquake. Blasts of heat and dust blew in from all sides and lumps of stone and rock rattled across the floor.

They were all stunned and blinded.

Suddenly, through the destruction Stefon saw Jewl emerge, swinging on the end of a rope coming in through one of many new holes in the surrounding wall. As he reached the zenith of his arc, he detached the rope and landed heavily on his feet.

A fizzing sword lashed out above Jewl's head, but he ignored it. Instead, he sprinted straight for Rish, Stefon and Pryn.

Stefon returned his sword to its scabbard. He had a sinking feeling that he knew what the dwarf had in mind. Jewl had blown a number of holes in the wall around the full circumference of the building. Now the dwarf rushed at them with short, stamping steps, a heavy bag in his hand.

He produced a grappling iron and started swinging it at his side as he ran past his three friends…and jumped clean over the balcony.

Without thought, Rish followed him, hurtling down the shaft to certain doom.

Stefon spared a glance at Lesjac and saw his face set in pure fury as Pryn leapt over the railing, closely followed by himself.

The drop was immense. He couldn't see the floor.

All that was visible was rubble and dust descending in the shaft of light, and his three friends tumbling likewise.

Jewl's grappling iron had landed and wrapped around the far railings of the floor below. A rope was unfurling from the heavy bag he had already dropped.

The wind whistled past Stefon's ears as he picked up speed, plummeting to his death.

The dwarf was descending the rope at speed, using a clamp-wheel to secure himself. Pryn had a grip on the same rope, his ever-present gauntlets guarding his hands from burns.

But Stefon was freefalling. As was Rish, his arms whirling in panic.

They had gone past two floors...then three! He was still gaining speed.

They were going to die.

Abruptly, Stefon's vision snapped to focus on Rish's tumbling form.

Involuntarily, he pressed his arms to his sides and accelerated downward...

Jewl's wheel-clamp was secure. He controlled his decent as Pryn grasped the same rope in his gauntlet-clad hands. The huge man struggled to control his fall, but he had righted himself, at least. Pryn's flailing legs grappled for the unfurling rope.

But Rish and Stefon were in trouble.

The slim form of Rish zipped past them, his face set grimly. His fingers grasped vainly for the rope. It was far beyond his reach.

As Jewl span around the unravelling rope, Stefon plummeted past, streamlined.

They were halfway to the floor.

Rish was falling backwards, shoulders first. The wind blasted in his ears. His heart thundered in his chest. He held his breath.

No matter how hard he stretched, the rope was no-where near.

His leap had been too short.

Suddenly, emerging above him and surrounded by a halo of light, Stefon rushed toward him... coming ever closer.

The belt round Jewl's waist cinched tighter as the clamp slowed his descent. Six feet below him, the large frame of Pryn had wrapped his long legs around the rope, and he was slowing too.

They were beyond halfway to the floor and still dropp-ing calmly.

Rish was falling faster.

Jewl could see people, tiny at this distance, scattering for cover.

Stefon was like a crossbow bolt, surging ever faster.

He snaked his right arm out, his clothes flapping mercilessly in the rushing wind of their descent. His hand reached for Rish, fingers stretching imploringly.

Rish's anguished face was white, his eyes huge with terror, as he reached out for Stefon—his only hope.

They were six floors from death.

Stefon's world had dissolved.

All that existed was Rish's hand and the rope. He surged through the air, his eyes stinging with the wind. On his right was his best friend; on his left, the rope.

Their fingers collided, and suddenly their hands locked around each other's wrists in a desperate grip.

Stefon's left arm shot out, reaching for the rope. The broadness of his chest slowed his fall as the wind resistance told. Through sheer will alone, he *pulled* the rope toward them. He *willed* it to be.

Suddenly the rope whipped out to his palm, his fingers clamping round the braided strands.

His hand erupted in pain, but he gripped harder.

He smelled acrid, burning flesh, felt the skin being ripped from his palms.

Still he held tight, his legs dropping beneath him.

As though from a far-off land, he heard a chilling wail on the rushing wind.

As they controlled their fall, secured to the rope, Jewl and Pryn watched, dumbstruck.

What they had seen flew in the face of everything they knew about the way the world worked. Stefon had caught Rish, gripped his wrist and then reached out for the rope—a rope that had been so far away from his grasp that Jewl knew instantly they were both dead men.

But the rope had *gone* to Stefon. Without reason, the rope had *moved* to his hand. And without any protection for his hands, Stefon had grasped the rope travelling at seemingly inexorable speed.

Jewl's rope shredded small chunks of skin and flesh from Stefon's palm.

As the descending dwarf looked on, Stefon took Rish's weight and slowed their fall. They were two floors from death, and Stefon slowed their descent with the nakedness of his burning palm, enough that Rish simply thumped the quartz-and-marble floor without so much as a loud slap. His breath exploded from his lungs and he looked stunned, but he was alive.

Stefon tumbled onto the rope bag that lay on the floor and rolled onto his side.

Pryn landed next, booming to the ground on his mighty legs and rushing over to check on Rish. Pryn's gauntlets were glowing with heat from the friction.

Jewl carefully applied the brake on his clamp and landed the softest of them all, immediately detaching the rope and running over to Stefon.

He lay deathly still, curled on his side.

Frantically Jewl pulled at his friend's shoulder to check the pulse at his neck. He was alive. His heart was thundering, but he was alive. He had lost consciousness.

His right hand was curled like a claw, and Jewl could glimpse exposed bone. The stench of seared skin and flesh was rank.

Pryn was helping the winded Rish to his feet, a look of bewilderment on his face that must have mirrored Jewl's own.

They had witnessed something immense. They just weren't sure what.

The people that had scattered from the main floor were now braving a glance or two at the impromptu stuntmen. The guards on the main doors were likewise taking an interest. And they were armed.

Without delay, Jewl called Pryn over to carry the unconscious Stefon. Helping Rish keep his feet, the stout dwarf proceeded toward the main doors as fast as his stumpy legs would propel him. Whilst supporting Rish, there was no way he would be able to wield his greataxe, but he would have to think of something.

"What the hell do you think you're doing?" enquired one of the two door-guards loudly, drawing his short sword.

As Jewl was contemplating dropping Rish's dazed form and drawing his axe, the main door burst open. A dark-clad figure whirled into the main hall, a long, slender sword flashing from side to side, hamstringing the two guards.

As they dropped, screaming in agony and gripping their legs, Brooss replaced her sword in her scabbard and beckoned her friends after her as she left at a sprint.

Outside, in the hammering rain, Brooss jumped aboard one of her armoured carts and snatched up the reins. The side door stood open and Pryn rushed ahead, unceremoniously bundling the unconscious form of Stefon into the empty bay and then helping Rish aboard after.

Once Pryn and Jewl hauled themselves in and secured the door, the wagon lurched ahead, throwing the occupants to their rumps.

Brooss wasted no thought for the comfort of her passengers as she set a breakneck pace through the narrow streets, making good their dramatic escape.

Chapter Twelve
Trawling Through the Mire

Claudia had been true to her word. Acaelian watched from another dormer shadow on the rooftop of another inn as Claudia and the other Wheels conducted their business on the cold streets and lanes outside the Wheelhouse in pairs or more. Claudia seemed to be taking a lead with the girls, despite only being twenty years old at most. It settled Acaelian's troubled mind to know she was at least taking some of his advice: remaining in groups to ensure safety in numbers.

With a satisfied smile, Acaelian left his hiding place and traversed the rooftops for some distance before dropping to the streets and seeking out the larger groups of revellers that would be out on the streets of The Lows at this time of the week's end. Picking pockets and cutting purses was much easier with the inebriated, even though the drunken reaction could often be deadly if the theft was discovered. A drunken victim of pickpocketing didn't call for the city watch; he drew his weapon.

Acaelian turned down a narrow lane in the misty gloom of the frosty evening and stopped short. A shadow blocked the end of the lane. It was a figure leaning against the right wall. When the man saw Acaelian, he stepped away from the wall and strode slowly forward, a grin on his face.

Toothless Bill, Grimlaw's brother, stepped confidently toward him. Standing well over six feet tall and built like a privy, Toothless Bill got his name from the sheer number of teeth he had missing following innumerable brawls.

Toothless Bill was a Pillar: a member of the Guild of Thugs. Pillars were mostly used as enforcers for racketeering in The Lows. Businesses would always need protection. A business needed to pay its protection money or learn a harsh lesson from a Pillar or two. And sometimes the other Guild Masters pressed Pillars into more diverse tasks.

Acaelian sprang nimbly from the balls of his feet just as a billy club whistled through the air where he had been standing. He landed on a low windowsill and gripped onto a drainpipe.

Someone had come at him from behind. He was surrounded.

"Get down before I have you shot!" uttered a familiar voice from the darkness. Stepping from a doorway in the left wall, Guild Master Faragwin, leader of the Glimmers, afforded Acaelian a knowing smile.

Gaunt and tall, Faragwin was in his late forties now, and life had not treated him well. He resembled a man more than ten years his senior: grey hair and sallow skin wrapped a lumpy skull and his eyes were mean. Like him or not, this wiry man was the power in the Glimmers, and he was an effective leader.

"You've an audience this evening, my elven friend."

Acaelian dropped to the street once more and stepped forward. "Really any need for all this, Master Faragwin?"

"You tell me." A hood was thrown over Acaelian's head, hurling him into darkness.

He was unceremoniously bundled from the street and in through Faragwin's doorway. He was squirrelled through a series of rooms, and then suddenly the many hands pushing him through the darkness gave him a heavy shove.

The ground disappeared from beneath him. For a moment he thought he might have been hurled down a well, but then a set of wooden steps struck his legs and pitched him forward. His shoulder and head crashed down heavily and his mind swam. A flat floor halted his fall.

The tumble down the flight of stairs produced more than a few bruises before Acaelian was hoisted to his feet once more and dragged through a basement. He began to lose his bearings when they entered another steep stairwell of stone and this time was led deeper underground.

He was being frogmarched through the sewers, but to where he had no clue. For nearly half an hour they trudged through miles of filth and detritus, the stench easily permeating the cloth sack around his head.

"What is this all about, Faragwin? Where are you taking me?" It was clear that they were going further than any of the Glimmer Guild Houses or underground hides. In fact, Acaelian thought they were probably outside of The Lows by now.

"Shut it, boy!" was his reply. "It seems you've got plenty to worry about, but your first loyalty is to the Glimmers. You've only got a day left to make your tithe payment, and you're hundreds short. I can't overlook this anymore, Acaelian. You're constantly shirking your responsibilities to your Guild. Make this payment or you're going to find yourself freebooting outside the Guilds, and you know how long you'll last like that. You'll be dead in a week."

The reminder of his outstanding tithe payment was a dagger in Acaelian's heart. He didn't need telling twice about the constant threat of being cut from the Glimmers. It would be nothing short of a death sentence to any thief, regardless of his skill. Grimlaw, for one, would take advantage of Acaelian's fall from the Guild to press any advantage. He'd be easy prey without protection.

Faragwin held his tongue for the remainder of the

shrouded trip through the sewers of Shen Utah until finally Acaelian was shoved up a steep staircase and through a series of echoing chambers. The last chamber was illuminated, warm golden light suffusing the mesh of the cloth shroud around his head.

Suddenly this shroud was removed and Acaelian found himself in a subterranean sacristy that appeared to still be in use. The secret door behind him was thumped shut and he was left with Faragwin at his back.

The room was illuminated by several church candles, burning brightly in sconces. Behind a small desk sat a tall man with sharp, twinkling eyes bright with intelligence and flanked by crow's feet. He was broad, and sat erect as the newcomers settled on their feet before him. To Acaelian it was clear this man radiated power and confidence, and when he spoke his voice was rich with both education and authority.

"Well done, Faragwin: you managed to get the young elf here whilst only inflicting a few hundred bruises, welts and cuts. Such a small foe must have terrified your Pillars. I trust Acaelian only managed to slay half a dozen of your men?"

Acaelian stayed silent, but Faragwin took the bait. "He didn't have a chance to put up much of a resistance, sir. We were efficient and the trap was well-planned." The response was a boast, but Acaelian saw the point this stranger was trying to make.

"So it was after the trap was sprung that you had him beaten?"

Faragwin opened his mouth to respond, but shut it just as quickly. He wasn't a stupid man. He knew he had made a mistake.

"Sir," Acaelian spoke up. "I fell down some stairs."

"Admirably spoken, young Glimmer. It speaks well of you to show loyalty to your Guild, even though I would surmise that you had a little assistance in that fall.

"My name is Swindle," the man introduced himself, and suddenly Acaelian's stomach plummeted. He was possibly in a bit of trouble here.

The five Guilds of Shen Utah operated under their own governance and independence, but never against another Guild. The Pillars were the Guild of Thugs; the Wheels, the Guild of Whores; and the Black Cats were the Guild of Assassins. Acaelian belonged to the Glimmers, the Guild of Thieves; and his friend Click was an apprentice Whisper of the Guild of Spies. All five Guilds co-existed because each Guild Master sat upon a Guild Council called the Sinecure. The sixth member, and leader of the Sinecure, was a figure of legend in the underworld: a man called Swindle. *This* man.

More of a title than a name, Swindle presided over the Sinecure and was the single most powerful individual in the Shen Utah underworld. In recent decades, Swindle had made impressive changes to the Guilds. It was now rote that every member of a Guild be given an education. Even the Thugs of the Pillar Guild were afforded enough learning to work with numbers and have the ability to read. Swindle was an influential, powerful man. For Acaelian to be in his presence was a bad tiding indeed.

"Acaelian, I'm afraid I have received some disturbing news. As I mentioned, your first loyalty should be to your Guild. It is a simple premise, but one upon which this Sinecure is built. It is the first law that keeps each of us safe. I am told that one of the Glimmers has broken this trust."

Acaelian's heart was thundering in his chest, though his elven coolness kept his reaction unseen.

"You went to the city watch. You were seen sharing a spa bath and murmurings with a constable of the city watch, Acaelian. I think some words are required here, before I have to have your body shortened by a head's length."

"This city has more eyes than a potato," mused Acaelian, ordering his thoughts. He had two choices, but feared that either answer would lead him to lose his head. He bit his lip and then decided—perhaps rashly—to tell the truth. "A piece of information fell into my lap—information about the Temple Shredder murders." Acaelian regaled his tale for Swindle, leaving only the identities of those involved out of his account.

"That sounds like a puddle of shit!" barked Faragwin. "You were selling names, weren't you? You're falling short on your tithe, and can't meet it! How much did they pay you to sell out your friends?"

Acaelian heard the hiss of a blade being drawn behind him and closed his eyes. He waited for the push of the blade on his neck, remaining very still.

"Faragwin, stay that blade!" ordered Swindle, his voice suddenly booming in the ancient sacristy. The hour was early in the morning, and no one in the church above would hear them.

Swindle seemed to look right through Acaelian as he mulled the testimony over. Finally he said, "Faragwin, wait outside in the stairwell. Close the door behind you."

When they were alone, Swindle regarded the thief closely. "I don't know how you came across that information, but I have heard the same. I need you to tell me the name of the person in the city watch to whom you took this information. I commend you on omitting the names of your Whisper friends, and that is fine, but you need to tell me where this information has now gone."

"I spoke to Constable Foord," Acaelian admitted.

"It is apparent that he then spoke to his captain, Carpion. This is not such a depressing development. Carpion is a capable fellow. More importantly, he knows a thing or two." Swindle nodded, although Acaelian didn't really know what those last words meant. "You did wrong for the right reasons, Acaelian. It's a difficult situation to find oneself in. You don't know the full of it, though. I have an understanding with Captain Carpion—a fruitful one. There is a plan, and your interfering might jeopardise that. Therefore I am instructing you to steer clear of this situation. I don't want to see you trying to influence any more Wheels, or—God forbid—trying to capture the killer yourself. Do you understand?"

Acaelian nodded.

"We are now aware that the snatching might indeed take place in The Lows, and so we can alter our net accordingly. As soon as the killer moves to strike again, we and the city watch shall be ready." Acaelian's heart began to dance with hope. "This next victim shall surely be the Temple Shredder's last," Swindle declared.

It took a moment for that statement to hit home with Acaelian. When he worked it out he stammered, "No! Your trap requires a bait! You're going to allow another Wheel to fall to his murderous axe!"

"There is no other way to ensure we capture the killer and his accomplices. It's been considered long and hard – this is the only way."

"It can't be! If all the Guilds and the city watch work in unison, we can capture the killer without another dying."

Swindle stood, and Acaelian was surprised by his height, for he was an imposing figure once upon his feet. "Son, hear this and secret it away somewhere safe in that old-boy's head of yours: no one in the Sinecure or Guilds knows of this trap. That is why I had to bring you here and make the threats I have. You and I are the only members of the Sinecure and Guilds that I can rely on in this. The rest are criminals, after all!" he said with a wry grin. "It is entirely possible—nay, likely—that the killer is a Guild Member."

The idea shocked Acaelian, but slowly made inevitable sense. "That's worrying," he said, with considerable understatement.

"Of course," agreed Swindle. "So now you see why you must not interfere? My arrangement with Carpion merely allows some city watch to access areas of The Lows they dare not enter without my leave. It will take all of my energies and attentions to ensure this goes to plan, and I can't be worrying about an over-exuberant elf who thinks he can make a difference."

"I understand," Acaelian told him, although he chafed to admit so.

"In spite of all that we have just discussed, following your recent transgression it is still dangerous for me not to make an example of you, especially when it comes to your dealings with the Guild, and Guild Master Faragwin in particular. But I am aware that there is something important about you, Acaelian. Make your tithe payment, or there is no way I can intercede on your behalf. This is imperative for you, and it should be this, and only this, to which you turn your attentions. There would be nothing to stop Faragwin throwing you out as a freebooter should you fail.

"To this end, I might have some information that can help you. Open the door and bring Faragwin back in here."

Acaelian did as he was told, and the wraith like form of Faragwin shambled back into the room. He didn't seem too annoyed at having been sent outside. Evidently this was how Swindle liked to conduct his business. The significance of their location in a church sacristy was not lost on Acaelian either. Even within Temple Link, there was nowhere Swindle could not conduct his business unmolested.

"Master Faragwin, give Acaelian here the docklands job." Acaelian watched Faragwin's face register a little shock at the assignment. "Boy, there is a vessel in port for two more nights, carrying supplies and commerce bound for the city of Jow upriver. I have reason to believe therein lies a wealthy stock of gems and gold, by way of a bribe of some sort. I have powerful friends who would benefit from the haul never reaching its destination. Faragwin here can give you the details."

Swindle moved regally toward the door from the sacristy

and nodded his assent for Acaelian and Faragwin to leave.

When they were upon the sewer steps once more, the shroud was again produced. Acaelian just tipped his head cooperatively and was once more plunged into darkness for the return journey. Through the cloth hood and rushing sewage, Acaelian could hear the Glimmer Guild Master muttering, "Lucky bastard."

Chapter Thirteen
Jakrat

"Ashedload of weapons does not an army make, young Andi." Eidos kicked a rock from their path as they laboriously ascended a long rise in the thickness of the forest. Throughout the afternoon of the previous day and all through the night they had been following deer trails and shallow creeks, resting for an hour just before dawn, when the body is at its coldest. They sought to leave the mountain forests by noon, having made excellent time overnight. "I fear you may be overreacting," the Hightower advisor continued.

"In my experience, it's far better to overreact and be thought cautious than underreact and be proven incompetent!" Andi snapped, in no mood to argue the point. "The fact remains that there was a little *more* than just 'a shedload of weapons'. I saw thousands, and they weren't even slowing production."

"But you saw no soldiers. Guards, yes, but no soldiers."

The tall cleric was proving frustratingly difficult to convince regarding the enemy at his border. It seemed starkly obvious to Andi, and to Manic, that these developments should have been of concern to Eidos, but he seemed immovable, flatly refusing to believe that an army might be massing at his border in weeks. It was almost as though to acknowledge or admit such a fact would crack his façade of bravery and give way to abject terror.

The forest was now fully awake; the sound and movement of nature all around them. It was comforting.

Andi was pleased they had made it from the Ipsican border in good time and without incident. They had set off directly west, making for the plains as swiftly as possible. They had long since taken the decision to abandon the horses in favour of swift and untraceable steps through tight woodland, but Andi knew that decision would return to haunt them when they desired the overland speed of mounts. Once clear of the woodlands, she wanted to be at Hightower as fast as possible. She had information to sell to Reinhart.

"Listen here, you bowl-headed monkey-lover!" barked Manic, displaying his formidable diplomatic skills. "Such a cache of weapons isn't just going to sit there! What the hell do you think they're going to do with them? A weapon is made for one thing: killing!"

"All I'm saying is that we need a little more concrete proof before we march into my lord's court screaming 'invasion!' These Ipsican people have been our peaceful neighbours for a long time now. Yes, historically speaking there have been tensions between our nations, which are well documented. But these are decades old. Now the divide is spanned by family ties. For many decades, Ipsica and Shenmadock have shared a border peacefully—beneficially, even. Marriage between nations is common. Why would the populace advocate such an invasion?"

"By God's grace, Eidos," Finhead exclaimed in his sibilant tongue, "how did a court advisor survive so long while being so naïve?" Eidos's expression darkened at the insult. "Everyone knows that such decisions aren't *voted* on. There is no ballot to declare invasion. Such decisions are the work of ambitious individuals, made for personal reasons, often against the wishes of the populace and largely conducted without their knowledge, let alone their consent!"

"I agree!" Manic grumbled. "The Ipsican people won't know that an army shall be massing at their borders, any more than the Shenmadock populace are aware of the same threat. It is simply another reason to conceal their work in the woodlands. I'm willing to bet that idiot Emperor Ibn Sa-Jiek has moved a few counters on a few maps, high up in a tower of that citadel of his, and the people on the ground are the ones to see the real consequences of his decisions." The dwarf spat on the ground in disgust. He obviously had little love for so-called nobility.

"But we know there are slaving teams around here," persisted Eidos, although it was clear he knew he was losing the argument. "They're pulling slaves in for whatever tasks they are being pressed to over there, whether that's erecting buildings or hammering out weapons. The slave trade is a profitable venture. As is weapon-running."

"Oh that's absurd! Who would they sell that many weapons to?" Andi said, exasperated. "You don't see many armies waltzing round the planes in their thousands, empty-handed and looking for a *massive* smithy!"

Eidos mostly pouted from that moment on, his expression not dissimilar to a child robbed of a bone rattle. Normally such a petulant reaction would have irked Andi, but she was beyond that. The silence was welcome.

It was less than an hour later that they stumbled across the hunting lodge. So well camouflaged was the structure that Manic damn near walked straight into the rear wall, mistaking it for a large collection of ferns. The lodge had been there for many decades, probably used by generations of the same families since its construction.

A single-storey, single-room building that stood no more than seven feet tall, the walls and roof were a tangle of heavy wattle-and-daub topped by twisted branches and loose fern leaves. Ageing slats of wood, raggedly sawn and arranged, protected the structure from the elements, the wood treated with a staining sap of some description. The floor was raised from the ground on short stilts and slats to help shield the inhabitants from damp and cold. Vermin scurried within the shadows beneath.

Andi kept her hand on the haft of her sword as they circled the building, two on either side. All seemed quiet; the lodge deserted.

However, a quick search of the hut revealed a grisly tableau. Inside the simple, single room were six small, wooden beds topped by ordinary palliasse mattresses. On each of these beds lay an eviscerated corpse. All six cadavers were male. All were simply adorned in flannel loincloths.

Andi left the lodge to reach the midday air and take deep breaths, controlling her emotions. She had little liking for the presence of Death, nor the proximity of the produce of his handiwork. She sat near the remains of the lodge fire-circle while Eidos and Finhead entered the lodge to survey the remains.

After too long had passed, the two exited; Eidos descended the two steps and approached Andi and Manic, who had remained nearby.

"I can't discern any cause of death. At first glance they look old enough to have simply expired. However, all six dying in their sleep of natural causes on the same night?"

"Unlikely," agreed Manic.

Eidos continued, "I think it might be food poisoning— an accident—but our green friend thinks something more sinister."

"The bodies are obviously wasted away," Finhead took over, "but they're not *old*. I mean to say they are not long dead. I'd say no more than a fortnight, maybe a little more. And another thing: although they *look* old, these bodies are of men who died at no more than thirty years of age. The degree of wasting is not in keeping with their age at death, the period of decomposition, or any disease I know of. It makes little sense."

"For goodness' sake!" Manic bellowed. "Is nothing straightforward in this godforsaken forest?"

No one had an answer, and all sat or stood in silence—a short vigil for the dead.

Then they gathered their belongings and continued into the forest, starting the descent toward the planes of Shenmadock, north of Hightower.

As the morning mists lifted from the flats below, the forest was quickly swamped in a pea-green shroud. Soon enough it became difficult to see more than five yards ahead, and the going became treacherous underfoot. Their progress slowed dramatically.

Something eerie and disconcerting settled over the group. They were clearly disquieted by the discovery of the bodies in the lodge, and this gathering mist only served to exaggerate the feeling. Stopping to adjust her boot heel, Andi tried to reassure her colleagues. "This mist is rising off the flats ahead and from the valley to the north. It won't be long until..."

Her voice trailed off.

Another voice reverberated in the stillness—a forlorn wail that swirled in the forest around them, calling over and over. The voice was broken, desperate and lost. "Baillion!" the voice pleaded. "Baillion!"

A chill scurried up Andi's spine. Without conscious thought, her sword was in her hand, her eyes scanning the woods around them. The other three had heard the voice too, and were equally skittish.

"What is *that?*" Manic hissed.

"These forests are haunted!" exclaimed Eidos. "We're destined for the same fate as the men in the lodge." He seemed on the verge of panic.

"Nonsense!" snapped Andi, although she wasn't entirely convinced. "It's a person, simple as that."

None replied. All were focused.

Baillion!

The voice was closer now. Moving around them. Wailing.

Then the figure emerged from the gloom: a pea-green silhouette. Tall and rangy, gaunt and angular, the figure shuffled and stumbled over tree roots and through undergrowth, cupping long-fingered hands to its face and bellowing, "Baillion!"

A memory of fairytales involving banshees and wraiths flittered through Andi's mind, awakening a long-forgotten fear. But as the man moved closer, those concerns abated. For he *was* just a man, and an old one at that. The most terrifying aspect of the man was how exhausted and sick with fatigue he appeared.

Eidos stepped forward from the tree behind which he had hidden. He put a hand out to beckon the man forward. "Old man, you're exhausted. Take rest."

The man jumped, spying Eidos ahead of him. His glassy eyes rolled to take in Andi, Eidos and Manic; thankfully, Finhead kept a discreet distance. The last thing they needed was for the reptilian to startle the man.

Dressed in a simple wool tunic and pantaloons, a long overcoat of waxed canvas across his shoulders, he resembled any peasant they might meet in Shenmadock. He avoided contact with Eidos's proffered hand. "Who are you people? Have you seen my Baillion? *Baillion!*"

Despite the distance between themselves and the enemy, Andi was nervous about the noise the man was making. Once the mist cleared, he would be audible across the whole forest.

"Quiet, man! Settle a moment and tell us: who is this Baillion you seek?"

"My son," the man sobbed. "He's here in the forest. He

must be! I must find him." With another determined sob he
went to move away, toward the hunting lodge.

The lodge, thought Andi. *The bodies!*

Immediately she realised the bodies were easily old
enough for one of them to be this man's son. She halted
him as he passed, placing a hand on his shoulder. He
flinched from her touch, but stopped nonetheless. She felt
bone beneath the coat.

"How do you know Baillion is in these woods?" she
asked him.

"He hunts up here. This is where he would come to hide
when he was a boy. He knows these woods like the back of
his foot."

Andi ignored the error. "Are you saying he's hiding up
here?"

"No!" the haggard man snapped. "He's a strong man.
A family man." Then the sobs returned, all indignant pride
forgotten. "Our home has changed. The land is ravaged.
Strangers are abroad."

All four travellers exchanged glances. Did this man mean
more slavers?

"What do you speak of, old man?" Eidos asked, trying
to sound officious.

"They came in the night and took them," he sobbed.
"Two that first night, then three more the next. We total a
dozen missing from the last four days!"

"Who came?" Eidos pressed. "Slavers? Men with
weapons and carts?"

"No...no weapons." His voice was low and troubled.
He looked distrustful for a moment, and then seemed
resigned to taking a gamble. "They carried no weapons.
They came in the dead of night, silent as ghosts. Tall men
in black cloaks, their hoods so deep you couldn't see their
faces. I saw them the second night, passing through the
village. I should have done something, but I was paralysed

with fear. I could do nothing! They came three nights in a row, always taking men from the village. This morning my son was nowhere to be seen!"

"What of your local magistrate? Has he done anything?" Eidos bristled. "This is an issue for the court of Hightower to deal with. They must be informed."

"We told Magistrate Jakrat!" The old man spat on the ground. "But the weasel does nothing! Just lounges in his manor house and lives the life of Riley!"

"Jakrat," Eidos muttered to himself with disgust.

"The bastard who tried to hang us," Andi said disdainfully. "You're not a fan, Eidos?"

Andi's mind tumbled back to the first hearing at Hightower, when she and Manic were dragged before the duke. The duke's cousin had been present, full of surly grins and distracted indifference, except for when they emerged from the dungeon with the *Baerv* in their possession. If this young, untrustworthy fool was magistrate to these villagers then they stood no chance. She voiced her concerns to Eidos.

"I fear it might be worse than mere ineptitude," he agreed. "I distrust the duke's cousin. Jakrat might appear incompetent and blasé, but he's far from it. The brat has myriad ambitions but no patience. I guarantee he is not just putting his feet up in that manor house of his; he is more underhandedly proactive than that. Only Duke Reinhart's own vigilance has kept his cousin's ambition in check over the years."

"This does not bode well," said Manic.

"Can you help?" asked the old man, his features drawn and sallow.

"We'll do what we can," Eidos told him. Before Andi could either argue or agree, Eidos cut her off with a stern glance. "We will travel west from these woods and meet with Magistrate Jakrat before turning south for Hightower. It is on our way." He turned his stare back on the old man. "We will press your concerns. We will do what we can. Now, let us escort you from these woods. You should wait at home for your son."

The old man allowed them to shepherd him away from the gruesome reality of the hunting lodge before he stumbled across the remains. They had no real reason to assume the two incidents were connected, or to assume one of the bodies was that of this man's son, but why risk it? The forest was no place for the lonely man to be wandering in delirium.

Soon after starting their descent the group passed out of the mists and made quick time through the trees along deer-paths and wider thoroughfares, pausing once to share more food and water with the old man. At midday they emerged from the wooded hills and found the planes at their feet. They bade good fortune to the old man and wished for the safe return of his son, though they held little hope for him. The man ambled southwest toward his village, leaving Andi, Manic, Eidos and Finhead to march toward Jakrat's manor house across the grazed flats.

The pleasant meadow lasted only an hour, the autumnal sun descending beyond the treeline that the group had vacated that morning. The skies beyond, to the distant eastern lands of Ipsica, were dark and foreboding. Clearly storms were abroad—and not just the metaphorical kind.

A chill was on the air, but thankfully there was no threat of rain. But as the day rolled on and the four travelled in relative silence, the chill grew.

The free-ranging meadow gave way to rolling arable land, divided by low hedgerows and field gates. The ground was soft underfoot and they did their best to avoid trampling crops, but the long walk was doing their limbs no good at all.

A little after the sun had disappeared beyond the clouds

at their backs and the first hours of twilight painted the world that shade of slate-grey that made vision so difficult, they spied the manor house at the crest of a far hill. They would reach Jakrat's home soon after.

Ahead of them was another gate with a stile leading to a gully running across their path. At the bank of the gully was an ageing man wrapped in a traveller's cloak, washing some simple pots in the running stream. A small pack of belongings and a long walking stick lay nearby. He glanced up at their approach, then returned his attention to shaking the excess water from his pots.

As they met the bank of the gully, the four companions stopped to wash in the river and take stock before making the last few hundred yards to the manor house. Manic dropped his pack and began polishing his sword carefully, paying attention to the blade edge. Eidos filled his water skin from the stream. Finhead kept a discreet distance from the group, obviously still not entirely comfortable around strangers in the open and not wishing to startle the man.

"Well met," the man greeted them, placing his pots in a felt bag and pulling the drawstring shut. The bag was then stuffed in the top of his travel pack. He stood to stretch his limbs, before bowing. "My lady!" he added politely.

"Good evening, sir," Eidos replied amiably. "How fares thee?"

Andi had never been one for the traveller-speak that Eidos obviously found so comfortable. It seemed odd to slope into a different dialect, just because you met someone on a road instead of in a tavern. Traveller-speak was steeped in ancient linguistic influences, full of "thees" and "thous". At the level of greetings it was perfectly understandable, but once two fluent speakers got talking about the lay of the land or whatever, it was almost impossible to follow. Andi never saw the point. There was nothing wrong with the common tongue for such exchanges.

However, the stranger's deviation from the traveller-speak to greet her in the fashion he did made Andi wary of him. Once more she was suddenly checking how accessible the hilt of her sword was.

"Well enough, well enough," replied the ageing man. As he settled back against a fallen tree, he took a pipe from his cloak, crammed the bowl with dried brown weeds and lit it with sparks struck from a complex flint device. "How does your party fare, Eidos?" he replied.

The Hightower advisor paused in filling his water-skin and then decided it was full enough. "Do we know each other, sir?"

The man's eyes were kind and his skin well-weathered, grey stubble adorning his jaw. "We've never met, but I have seen you about the duchy from time to time. You spent some time with the merchant navy, correct? Learning the navigator's art?"

"True enough, but you have me at a disadvantage, sir. Your name?"

"I'll get to that in time," the man said, quickly dismissive. "You have more pressing matters to attend to. You need be aware of the nature of the ground onto which you now tread." He tilted his head backward once indicating Jakrat's manor whilst using a tamper to press the glowing tobacco in the bowl of his pipe as he puffed on the stem. He seemed to savour the flavour, humming once in appreciation. "Jakrat is a poor man, and by that I mean morally. He is rich in wealth but lacking in scruples, and has unfortunately aligned himself with some overly nefarious characters. If you stride into his manor this night, without due care, you will not survive to see the dawn. You must conduct yourselves with more care."

"Who *are* you?" Manic pressed.

"Is that important?" the man snapped, an angry billow of smoke rushing from his outburst. All the while, his eyes remained strangely kind and Andi thought he actually seemed mildly amused by the entire exchange.

All in all, she was pretty sure she didn't trust him. She remained silent.

"My name is Barabel. Pleased to make your acquaintance, Eidos of Hightower."

Following rhetoric as wilfully as a donkey follows a carrot, Eidos inclined his head. "These are my companions."

"I'm Manic," grumbled the dwarf, impatient with the ramblings. "This is Finhead. We can't pronounce his real name, but Finhead seems to suit him just fine."

Manic turned to Andi to introduce her too, but her glare halted his words before they could be formed. The dwarf stammered to silence. Andi turned her eyes back to Barabel. He was looking on, patiently.

When it was clear that Barabel would not continue his diatribe until the introductions were complete, Andi pushed things on a little. "Barabel, what interest is it to you if we enter this house or not?"

Barabel nodded his head in acceptance of her decision not to introduce herself. "My lady," he said with a bow of his head. Manic snorted. "I know that your party must enter that manor house," Barabel continued. "This land is set to be ravaged by a pestilence, and you need to see what it is that awaits you in that building before you can accomplish that which needs to be achieved. Without it you will not have adequate belief."

"You speak in riddles, my friend," Eidos replied, "and I want no part of your ramblings." But he remained by the brook, awaiting Barabel's advice.

"You will understand what I mean when you break into this building. Do it undiscovered, for to be met in that building would be to meet with your maker. You will have a greater understanding of what I speak when you return to this river, the devil at your back."

It was an old saying, *the devil at your back*, but somehow it meant something more, coming from this stranger. He added too much weight to the words.

Barabel took another puff on his pipe. "I will not be here for your return, but I can tell you what you need to know before I leave. When you return home, young Eidos, you will find your duchy inhabited by strangers. Darkness now resides in the heart of Hightower, and it will spread before it is foiled. It will grow to cover these lands and more beyond our borders, if you don't take a stand."

"I'm sorry," Manic said, perplexed. "Did you say, *us*? Or just *him*?" He pointed at Eidos, obviously keen to avoid the responsibility.

"It is no coincidence that we have met here, at this juncture in time. I have long known that those people I seek shall meet me here, this autumn, this year. I have waited patiently, watching as the presence of evil in our land grows by the season. I have but one hope. As it turns out, I have but four hopes." He swept a hand, indicating the four assembled travellers.

"What the hell are you talking about?" Andi asked.

"Allow me to clarify, my lady. The darkness that approaches shall herald a time of war. The Land of the Lords will be ravaged and sundered by conflict, and the souls of the living shall hang in the balance, held forfeit to a madman's greed and lust for power. Ancient writings predict an army of death, marching with pestilence and disease at the heart, when all shall fall at their feet. There is but one hope..."

"Isn't it always the way?" Manic muttered. Eidos shushed him. "I'm only saying!" the dwarf continued. "If you know something bad is going to happen, and you're in the business of creating contingency plans, why not make half a dozen? Why is it always 'just one hope'? Wouldn't it be more comforting to be able to tell people 'there's a whole raft of things we can do to avoid calamity'?"

"The belt-and-braces approach?" Andi agreed.

"Exactly!"

"Would you pair shut up and let the man finish?"

Andi cracked a grin and dropped her gaze to a sod of dirt at her feet, distractedly kicking it into the stream. She no longer viewed this man in a serious light.

Barabel coughed once, used his tamper again on the bowl of his pipe, and continued. "All prophecies of this event speak of two ultimate weapons residing in this world: one in the hands of the holy and the other encircled by darkness. One capable of releasing the world from torment and defeating the powers bent on our destruction; the other existing only to murder and destroy all living beings it encounters.

"You must leave this land and journey south. Passage on a merchant vessel from Hightower Port can be readily hired. Seek out the halls of the legendary Aquilla San, at the heart of a sunken city, rumoured to be deep within the risen barbarian deserts of Peena, beyond Boyareen. There you will find the only weapon capable of combating this evil and ending the war—a staff, only two feet in length, constructed of solid gold. At the head sits a perfectly spherical crystal globe, encasing an equally perfect rose. Find this relic and bring it back to these lands and use it to strike at the heart of the enemy."

All were silent for a moment, the sky darkening as twilight gave way to night.

Finally Andi spoke, as much to stop herself from laughing as to actually contribute anything. "It seems doable."

"What?" Manic blurted.

"Well, it is, if you consider that the risen desert of Peena is reputed to be entirely inaccessible, and the *legendary* Aquilla San is precisely that—only a *legend*. If we were to achieve the impossible and enter this risen desert and somehow find some hidden—sorry, *sunken*—city, we're supposed to steal a gold stick, come back to Shenmadock and just smack this nameless evil with it? I mean, if you're going to leave a weapon somewhere that is apparently *this* important, wouldn't you leave it somewhere easily accessible—perhaps even somewhere that *actually exists*? And then, wouldn't you make it something a little more…weapon-like? Perhaps a sword, or a crossbow, or a trebuchet? Even a plank with a rusty nail in it radiates more menace than a golden tube. I mean, gold *is* a soft metal?"

Andi easily stepped across the river and walked up the far bank, leaving Barabel with the others, who quickly gathered their belongings and made to follow. "I'm sorry to sound dismissive, Barabel," she said, without looking back, "but like 'a bucket of shit from Boyareen', it sounds farfetched."

"I understand, Andi," Barabel replied, no anger in his voice.

Manic jumped across the stream after her. "Andi, wait for us!"

Suddenly angry, she turned on Barabel, her humour and sarcasm having fled. "If a war is coming to these lands, I'll fight, most probably for money. Nothing more. I'll certainly not run. An enemy will fall to a swipe of my blade as effectively as a thump from any ancient relic candlestick." She shook her head, calming a little. "We're not your people," she told him simply. "We're mercenaries, not heroes."

The others followed her, Eidos apologising profusely to Barabel for the rudeness of his counterpart. She didn't care.

"The greatest weight of knowledge concerning Aquilla San lies in the heart of the dead twin of Boyareen," Barabel called after them, watching them walk away. She'd never heard of anyone called "the dead twin of Boyareen". Andi spared a single glance over her shoulder in the dwindling light, but did not slow her departure. The others followed.

"What a strange man!" Finhead commented, as they crouched low behind a dividing wall a dozen yards from Jakrat's manor house.

"I want nothing said about him," Andi spat. "I've had enough in my life of listening to bardic yarns, told to frighten young children witless. His tale was fanciful and made no sense; it has no bearing on things. The only words of sense he spoke were when he told us we had more pressing matters to attend to. And he's right."

She finished applying dirt to the black blade of her short sword and silently replaced it in her scabbard. She then jammed her travelling pack against the foot of the wall and took her bow and quiver.

"Take only what we need to defend ourselves. And Eidos, cover up your shining armour, for goodness' sake."

Eidos wrapped a weather-cloak across his shoulders. The material was thin, but covered him well, concealing the gleaming metal. He dropped his gear next to Manic's and removed a shorter blade that Andi hadn't seen him wield as of yet. Manic and Finhead were already prepared, their gear stowed safely.

"Why are we hiding?" Manic asked. "I thought you didn't believe what the old man said."

"I don't, but I trust Jakrat just as much. That means to say, not at all. So we're going to broach the subject nice and quietly. I want to take a look around undisturbed.

"Stay here. I'll break in a window and let you three in on the ground floor—through that kitchen door, I should think. There doesn't seem to be much in the way of light coming from any of these windows or doors. All the activity is round the front, and there's not much of that. I'll not be long."

Manic nodded and moved up against the wall as Andi shouldered her quiver and bow and vaulted the low wall. It was a quick dash across the croft garden up to the kitchen door. Above the door was a shuttered window, the shutters hanging open and the window pane hinged outward.

Although the wall was fairly smooth, it posed no problem for the experienced thief, and she ascended it silently, hooking her fingers onto the ledge and climbing quietly into the room beyond.

The chamber was silent and dark. A single cot bed was set against the left wall and a simple garderobe arrangement dominated the right-hand wall, behind a drape. The chamber was empty, and if the degree of dust was anything to judge by, it was evidently rarely used.

Listening carefully, she could detect no loud noises from nearby rooms. The air in the chamber was a little dry. Somewhere in the building, a fire would be lit. Only faint orange light showed through the foot of the chamber door and she moved quickly towards it. With both hands, she disengaged the latch and pulled the door ajar.

A landing stretched away ahead of her, a wall running from the left and a drop over the banisters to the hallway below on the right. The stairs were to the right also. Two torches were evenly spaced on the landing, burning in ornate sconces.

The landing was deserted, as was the hallway below.

Moving onto the landing, Andi kept low and moved to her right, toward the top of the stairs. Facing the top of the flight was a small doorway, which stood open. A second, steeper stairway descended to where Andi assumed the kitchen to be.

Creeping down, she found that the stairwell indeed opened out onto the kitchen, filled with cured meats and various bunched vegetables. A chopping-board on the central island was filled with gathered herbs. An array of dangerous-looking knives adorned the far wall. The stove heater was not lit and the room was unpopulated.

Two adjacent doors were firmly closed. The door to Andi's left was obviously the external one, and was bolted shut from the inside. The door in the far-right wall was unlocked, and judging by its position Andi deduced it opened onto the hallway she had seen from the landing. One last doorway stood in the middle of the wall across from the stairs, and it stood open. The room beyond was dark also.

She turned to the outer door and disengaged the locks quietly, sliding back the bolts on well-oiled runners. The door stuck a little in the jamb, then it gave with a vibrating thrum.

She waved once, hoping her dark form was visible to her companions. Andi flinched as she heard her three friends traverse the low wall and run toward the open door. She had made such a small amount of noise since entering the house that these three sounded like a musical parade.

She retreated from the outer door, keeping a watchful eye on the other two doorways, expecting to be discovered at any moment. She could imagine the exchange somewhere in the house: "Sire, it sounds like a small battalion is approaching from the west, banging pots and pans together."

Eidos entered first, moving into the kitchen, trying to keep low. At well over six feet tall, it was difficult for him. He entered the kitchen, making room for Manic and then Finhead. Andi carefully closed the door behind them, replacing the bolts as she had found them.

"I've found nothing of interest so far," she whispered. "The room above is a guest room, and is empty. There's a hallway out of that door, and probably a dining room through that one." She indicated the two kitchen doors. "I think maybe Finhead should come with me and you two should stay on these stairs until we reach you."

Manic and Eidos moved onto the thin stairwell Andi had come down, not looking too happy about it but knowing better than to argue with her.

"Come on!" Andi led Finhead to the far dining room door and pressed her ear to it. No sound came from within.

She looked back to the other two. "We won't be long—then you can help search the top floor. OK?" Manic nodded from the distant gloom.

Andi pressed the door open and stepped through into the dining room beyond.

The central table had been cleared of dining paraphernalia and was instead strewn with books and scrolls, unlit candles and lumps of chalk. The centre portion was marked with a scrawl that sent shivers up her spine.

In chalk, a pentacle had been carefully drawn, adorned with candles. At the heart of the pagan symbol was a tacky-looking patch on the table's surface. Instinctively Andi knew it was blood.

"Demon worship!" Finhead hissed.

"You have experience of this?" Andi asked. "Firsthand?"

"I've seen such symbols put to sacrificial use before, mainly with dumb animals. From what little I know, this arrangement is for the purpose of celestial transmortification."

Andi looked at the alien dumbly. "What?"

"I don't know," Finhead said, showing his wicked teeth in an expression that Andi now knew was a smile. "It says so on the spine of that book there." He pointed at a bound volume on top of the table, near one of the unlit candles.

"Right," Andi replied pointedly. Another, double doorway led off the dining room to the right. She deduced it must lead to another room that ran alongside the central hallway. It was their only option.

No sound or light was discernible beyond this doorway either, so she pushed the left-hand door open and stepped into a small drawing room. Two comfortable chairs rested near an empty fireplace and a tall round table stood between them. A single door stood in the far wall and another in the right wall. A quick deduction told Andi this right-hand door led back to the hallway. A sliver of orange light was visible beneath the far door.

Silently she indicated for Finhead to move to the hallway door while she skirted the round table and approached the far door. Stepping lightly, she pressed an ear to it. She could hear the intermittent snap and pop of a wood fire beyond.

Dropping softly to her side, she tried to scan the room underneath the door, but all she could spy was the far fireplace and a pair of crossed feet. Apparently someone was reclining before a roaring fire. She had to envy them.

Using her agility to stand silently once more, Andi moved over to Finhead. He waited patiently while she pushed open the hallway door and stepped through.

The central hall smelled of jasmine and another scent she could not quite place. The door to the kitchen stood to their right and a door to the left obviously led to the room in which their unwitting host reclined before his fire. The hallway turned beneath the stairs to an ornate vestibule and outer door, obviously the main entrance.

The staircase led from left to right.

The wooden floor protested quietly at Finhead's step and they moved very slowly to the stairs, expecting the door to the occupied room to open any second.

Andi's heart thundered in her chest. She struggled to keep her breathing even, feeling the familiar exhilaration of home invasion—something she had known well as a youngster. Her senses were attuned and refined by adrenaline.

They ascended the stairs, Andi keeping her steps to the wide extremities of each tread, to reduce the risk of a board creaking. Finhead followed her example.

The landing was clear, as it had been before, and the torches still burned lightly in their sconces. The doorway at the top, leading to the flight of stairs to the kitchen, still stood ajar. Andi could see Manic peering from the dark space.

She beckoned for them to follow her as she rounded the L-shaped landing and headed for one of the two unexplored rooms. The nearest door was halfway along the landing.

She stopped beside it and pressed an ear to the wood. No sounds came from within.

She disengaged the latch with a startling clunk that made her flinch, then pushed the door in and followed.

The room had once been yet another guestroom, but now it had been pressed into a different use. A *darker* use. All furnishings had been removed save for a single, tall sleeping cot and a set of drawers in the far corner.

There were two additional doors, one in the left wall and one in the right. The far wall seemed to be the southernmost exterior. The room was not lighted.

Andi ushered the other three into the room and pushed the door almost closed, worrying about the noisy latch. Only Eidos's human eyes would be struggling to see, despite the small amount of light offered by the crack in the door.

Andi examined the sleeping cot, which stood in the centre of the room. A waxed canvas sheet covered the palliasse and it was stained with lots of blood. Atop the set of drawers was a series of small pots and ceramic bowls. All were empty and clean. Arrayed beside the pots and bowls were a number of severe-looking blades and probes. One had a small lump of meat trapped in the shears, but most were clean and shiny.

Finhead and Manic examined the western room, which Andi figured must stand above the kitchen below. A washroom was found beyond the door, apparently frequently used. A small pile of clothes sat in the corner, badly bloodstained.

Andi had a terrible feeling. This grisly discovery coupled with the sacrilegious material on the floor below made for worrying conclusions. Something sinister was being conducted in this house.

"This isn't good," she whispered to the others as they gathered near the bloody bed. "I think I've seen enough."

"But what the hell is all this?" Manic hissed.

"Unholy!" Eidos supplied simply, his voice a little too loud for Andi's liking.

"We're leaving," she told them.

"But what about that last room?" Eidos indicated the unexplored chamber.

"To hell with it!" Andi replied, glancing at the collection of surgical equipment and the bloodstains. "Literally."

A door opened in a room nearby. Footfalls on the landing caused all four of them to freeze. Their sounds of breathing seemed like a cacophony.

Finhead had his back to the landing door whilst Eidos stood at his side, near the narrow opening.

Why didn't we close it?

Manic and Andi were near the bed. She slowly, silently, let the bow slide down her arm into her waiting hand. Her fingertips found the nock of an arrow in her quiver, but she did not draw it. She waited.

The footsteps passed their door from left to right. The person was traversing the landing, heading for the stairs.

To Andi's alarm, Eidos reached for the door. At this distance she could make no sound to stop him without alerting whoever was outside.

It occurred to her that she could shoot him. One in the throat would kill him silently.

After a beat she decided against it. The falling body would just make more noise.

Eidos's hand touched the door and he put his eye to the crack. The door didn't move. He just watched, angling his head to get a better view. Andi let out a breath she hadn't realised she had been holding.

Abruptly Eidos snatched his hand away from the door and clapped it over his mouth, his eyes frantic. The door had made a very quiet bump, but the footsteps remained unfaltering as they descended the stairs.

Andi moved quietly to the big cleric's side, bow still in

hand. She stared questioningly into his face.

"I know that man!" he whispered earnestly, his hand stroking his neat beard. "But it can't be him. He died this summer."

"Are you sure?"

"Of course I'm sure!" His voice raised slightly above a whisper.

Andi shushed him. "That makes no sense."

"Devil worship!" murmured Finhead. "Revivification!"

"What the hell does that mean?" Manic asked.

"Reincarnation," Andi answered, looking around at her three companions. "Unnatural reincarnation. We're leaving." She pulled the door in quietly, bow still ready, and stepped onto the landing. The door to the left stood open, firelight coming from within. The man that Eidos had recognised had reached the hall below, and the stairs were deserted. She moved silently along the landing toward the first guest room door. They would have to leave by the kitchen.

Suddenly a figure emerged from the kitchen stairs, carrying a tray laden with more surgical tools. It was clad in a dark robe, the hood dropped to the shoulders to reveal a face that was pallid and waxy; a long scar ran from brow to jaw, dissecting the left eye. Andi stopped still. The stranger's eyes alighted on her and those following her.

He dropped the tray, snatching a long blade from the assortment that clattered noisily to the floor. He opened his mouth to call out. Andi's arrow thumped into him, turning his shoulders and cutting his call off almost instantly.

But not quickly enough. He had raised the alarm.

Another robed figure emerged from the candlelit room across the landing. This stranger hefted a fearsome-looking longsword as he rushed towards Eidos. He brought his short sword up to deflect the attacker's blow and pitched the figure over the balcony. A terrible scream bellowed from the man as his spine struck the stairwell banister below. There was a popping and cracking sound. The scream was cut off.

Andi went to run for the kitchen stairs, but another figure filled the doorway, investigating the calls. She drew another arrow as sounds came from down the stairs and yet another figure emerged from the room at the end of the landing.

They were quickly becoming surrounded.

"Burn it!" Andi called out as she loosed her second shaft, the arrow punching into the eye of the man from the kitchen and dropping him.

Finhead snatched the torch from near him and turned to throw it into the room they had left. The waxed canvas cover caught almost immediately, with a satisfying whoosh.

Eidos grabbed the second torch and headed for the far room, the second figure rushing him. With two quick deflections from his sword he jammed the torch into the dark hood. The robe caught fire immediately and soon the figure was fully aflame, arms flailing wildly. But it didn't scream. It made no sound even as it pivoted over the balcony to the hall below.

The stairs started to burn. People could be heard rushing for the stairwell, and Andi saw robed figures trying to get past the flames.

"Manic: your kerosene lamp!"

Manic understood her intentions immediately, and fished in his tool-belt. The little miner always carried a small kerosene torch with him, with a little strand of rope acting as a wick. He ran back into the room they had left and then re-emerged swathed in smoke and carrying the lit lamp.

A quick flick of his wrist sent it tumbling over the landing balcony and down the stairs, where it smashed onto the next man's head. Flaming kerosene splashed all around, igniting the walls and floor. The man burned brightly, screaming loudly.

Very quickly the hall was an inferno. The heat was intense.

Andi knew the best course of action.

She kicked open the door into the last guestroom and ran

inside, throwing open the windows within. She beckoned for the others to follow.

Manic was first, struggling to crest the sill, but then climbing down fast enough on the other side. Finhead stopped by the door and waited for Eidos. The human's form lumbered toward them through the growing smoke, his short sword slashing about him.

When he was through, Finhead slammed the door and barricaded it with a chair beneath the handle. Eidos reached Andi and looked uncertainly at the drop outside.

"You must!" she implored. Delicately, he traversed the sill and began a steady descent, Manic watching from below. Finhead reached the sill and nimbly exited, hurrying Eidos along as the first blow struck the door. Another slammed into it, but still the chair held. Smoke was pouring beneath the door as Andi escaped the window, pushing it closed behind her.

She looked below to see that Eidos had landed heavily in the croft garden and Finhead was nearby. Andi jumped the remaining distance, landing with agility from a height that would have broken a grown man's ankles.

All four were then up and running for the cover of the low wall to retrieve their gear. Finhead nocked an arrow and took a bead on their window of escape while Andi and Manic ran to cover the main entrance.

Within a minute the manor house was fully ablaze, fire reaching to the heavens and illuminating the night sky. Any figures that attempted to exit the building were shot down by the group and allowed to burn. None escaped; none survived.

Jakrat was not among their number.

Chapter Fourteen
Growing Resolve

Brooss's armoured carriage had driven them from the Tower of Light quickly, thundering over cobbles and through narrow streets, the hammering rain making a tattling timpani of the roof.

Following the dramatic and dangerous escape from Lesjac's clutches, the group knew they needed to reach a point of safety to take stock, and then find a way to flee the city.

They had returned to the basement that they had used previously, leaving the armoured cart a discreet distance away. Under cover of darkness, in a city slowly dying of plague, the friends gathered in the basement and dried themselves in silence. Some had slept fitfully and various had had wounds tended to. But in the main they had rested in silence, fearing a search was being conducted for them as they hid. The entire group showed concern for their fallen captain, Stefon.

Morning had passed uneventfully into day, which in turn had passed slowly into night. At length Stefon had awoken from his stupor, an hour after sundown. They ate a light, cold meal in sullen silence, most eyes turned warily on Stefon. It was Rish who finally broke the silence. "What's happening to you?"

Their leader was silent for a long moment. "I don't know," he replied quietly.

"I mean, that Lesjac guy said some pretty unbelievable things. I figured he was mental. But he's right: you're changing. Some of the things you're able to do! The other day you virtually ran up a wall to get to Brooss when she was hurt, and tonight that stunt with the rope!" Rish shook his head and chewed a dry side of beef. "I thought I was worm food for sure. I should have been."

"I know. Me too."

Jewl thumped his plate down, empty. His lips were greasy from the food, as were his fingers. "How did you do that with the rope? You were nowhere near it, and it just jumped into your hand." He wasn't angry, but his question was nonetheless abrupt; more evidence of his ever-changing moods.

"I…" Stefon struggled for the correct term, "called it to me. It wasn't a conscious thing. It's more…instinct. It was our only chance." Stefon looked from face to face, and Rish could sense a conflict within him. All of this was obviously difficult for him to come to terms with. "When it becomes that simple, something happens to me. When we jumped over the railing and started to fall, it all seemed so confused and complex. Then when I saw Rish was falling and couldn't reach the rope, it suddenly became very simple. If I didn't do something, then Rish would die. So everything just seemed to snap into a different kind of focus. All that mattered was that Rish was going to die and I was the only person that had a chance of stopping that. And so I tried to get to him."

"I remember that," Jewl said. "You put your arms to your sides and arrowed down. I wondered what you were doing. It seemed like suicide."

"When I reached Rish, I put my arm out and grabbed him. Then it was just as simple. Our only chance was the rope. So I reached for that too. I can't explain it any better than that."

"Well that hand should take some time to heal, if it ever will, and yet already it shows signs of recovery. New skin grows!" Brooss commented, trying to remove some of the weight from the conversation. Rish avoided watching her too closely as she spoke. He was still wrestling with his feelings with regard to the little engineer. She brushed a strand of hair from her face and continued. "Strictly speaking, you should have no flesh left on your hand, but you got off lightly."

Stefon shrugged and fingered the poultice Brooss had made for his wounded hand. A combination of fruits, pulses and herbs had gone to making the concoction she had placed against his burns. He had tolerated the pain without much complaint.

"This isn't getting us anywhere," Rish said. "I don't know what's going on with you, but I trust you to keep it under control. Can you?"

"Of course," Stefon replied. "It's been a gradual thing. I've only really noticed it once or twice."

Something in Stefon's demeanour smacked of guilt as he spoke, but Rish let it pass. "Good. We need to decide what we're doing next."

"Lord, I almost forgot!" Jewl blurted out. "I found something outside the Tower of Light in the refuse pile, while I was doing my rounds. Just before I saved everyone's lives." It wasn't the first time Jewl had mentioned that, and it appeared he wasn't going to let it go easily. He would expect to be well stocked with ale for the coming months by way of thanks. "I found a body!" the dwarf stated dramatically.

"Not much of a surprise," Pryn muttered. "This city has a plethora."

"This one *was* a surprise. Governor Meena Saqir is now *ex*-governor."

The weight of the information took a moment to settle on the group.

"So," Stefon began. "The Light arrange a quarantine and bribe the government to allow it. Then the plague hits with full force. During this time, someone escapes the city and is shot. Simeon's scavenger team is commissioned to retrieve only the bodies, and then Governor Meena Saqir makes sure they go missing too. Meanwhile, there are no bodies making it from the morgue to the incinerators, but no one knows *where* the bodies are going.

"The Light are hunting me all over the place just for being different. Then when Simeon finally turns up, Meena Saqir's shadowy group kills him too. Since then they've left *us* alone.

"And now the corrupt governor is found dead on the same night a trap is set for us." The group sat in stunned silence.

"It doesn't look good, does it?" Brooss said.

"No, it doesn't." Stefon took a moment to think, before coming to a positive decision. "We leave tonight. Rish. Make quiet arrangements with Anya: I want to be down through their basement shortly after midnight. No price she names will be too high, although she's already been paid handsomely. Pryn and Jewl, gather what weapons we have left and prepare them for transit. Brooss, you and I will prepare the rations and steal some camping equipment from somewhere."

"No problem!" nodded Brooss, brushing the same errant strand of hair from her eyes again. Perhaps it was her businesslike efficiency that marked her as different from other girls. She was unlike any female Rish had found interesting, and that made him nervous. He continued to avert his gaze. He felt incredibly self-conscious.

"If you have any business left to conduct in this city, I suggest you leave it unfinished. There's a fair chance there will be a trap waiting for us at every juncture. This city is dead to us now."

Some of the others didn't seem particularly amused by this, but Rish agreed with his friend. He had lived his entire life in such a manner that he could walk away without a second thought. The place had been Rish's home for all his life, but Wahib City would be no great loss to him.

One thing rankled him, though. "What about our money? From Ratna?"

"Gone," Stefon stated simply. "I don't like it any more than you do, but we've got to face facts. Even if we took this information to Ratna, he won't pay for information we can't prove. Especially since it would put Ratna's organisation at loggerheads with The Light, and that's the last thing he wants to happen. If we took this to Ratna, then we'd probably be putting him at direct risk, and he'd probably hand us over for a reward anyway.

"The darkest thought I've had about that suggests that Ratna only ever offered us a king's ransom because he knew he would never have to pay up. That further suggests that he was setting us up. He knew we'd end up in this mess, and he's probably ended up getting something out of the deal, now that we've hit this hornet's nest with a catapult.

"No, we leave empty-handed. If you need to go anywhere, then we'll rendezvous back here an hour before midnight. Rish, we'll see you at Anya's shortly before midnight. Don't become dead before then."

In Shen Utah, dusk had crept over the docklands slowly, spreading fingers of darkness across the harbour and the vessels at anchor or moored at the harbour side. Darkness was a thief's friend, but dusk was his eternal ally. The inconstant colour and light of dusk was so strange to the human eye that many guards struggled to see the flittering movement of a skilled thief, and that was also the case at this late hour as Acaelian dropped from the window of the captain's quarters in the aft section of the impressive three-mast ship.

His barely glimpsed form plunged through the night silently, and then snagged a hand around a mooring rope. With effortless ease the thief climbed his way up the rope and slunk over the harbour wall into the shadow of the crates left at the quayside.

Moving with patient grace, Acaelian made his way over to the closed quayside storage shelter and climbed onto the roof, sidling over next to Click, who waited for him on the corrugated roofing.

"That was amazing," Click said. "I even knew to watch for you and could hardly see you, even when you moved across the open ground."

"Thanks," said Acaelian without conceit.

"Is it a worthy score?"

"You bet!" confirmed the thief. "And there are an impressive number of guards on that ship too. Lucky for me, they're less than vigilant at this time of the evening. Still, it took a while to navigate the passages to get a good look at the haul. Lots of gems, lots of gold! Probably more than I can carry on my shoulders." Acaelian lay motionless for a moment, thinking. "The only way to take it all would be to use an accomplice. Someone in a boat on the water side of the vessel to lower the goodies to, and then they and I can both flee."

"Sounds risky," said Click.

"Sounds impossible, actually," confirmed Acaelian. "I'm struggling with how to pull this off. I got the impression that this job needs to be all the goodies or nothing at all. Impossible!" he mused. "And there was something else in one of the other holds that made interesting viewing."

"Look!" Click hissed, interrupting Acaelian as he sank even lower to the corrugated roofing at his side.

Acaelian scanned the entire harbour and quayside, but struggled to fix his vision on what it was that Click had seen. Then suddenly his gaze alighted on a furtive movement in the shadows of a crate near the target vessel. He didn't need to see the face to know who skulked in the shadows.

As they watched on, the hidden form of Grimlaw moved from cover and scuttled against the side of the ship, glancing in through a porthole. At the second porthole, he chose his entry point and dropped into the ship without discovery.

"That's pretty good too," commented Click reluctantly.

Acaelian grunted. "That hold is the one with the score in. He'll discover just as much about the booty as me."

Suddenly a shout went up from the aft portion of the vessel as Acaelian saw his window of escape being angrily pulled shut. A search of the entire vessel would be ordered, and soon the ship would be a swarm of searching guardsmen. It was standard operation, really, and Grimlaw knew it too. They watched him crawl out of the hold porthole before he was discovered.

After a short rest in the shadow of the crates, he scuttled like an insect across the harbour and out of sight.

"Now what the hell do you think he was doing here?" asked Click.

"Casing the ship," replied Acaelian plainly.

"Obviously, but how could he possibly know this is a target? How does he keep doing this? He can't have been following you, or he'd know where you are now."

Acaelian smiled grimly. "I don't usually bother casing jobs anymore," he admitted. "Grimlaw would know this. He's here to scope the job out for himself because he's been tipped the wink. I think Guild Master Faragwin has betrayed me."

"Perhaps he's always been betraying you," offered Click. "That's why Grimlaw is forever stealing your scores."

"Possibly," agreed Acaelian. "We have to work with what we *do* know, though. The sum of that is the fact that Faragwin has betrayed me to Grimlaw, and we can assume Grimlaw is going to try and take this steal. He can't do it tonight, now that the false alarm of the window has gone up; the guards will be on their toes tonight. At best I've bought a day to pull this off."

It felt better to be doing something. At least, that's what Stefon kept telling himself. The only poor action had to be inaction. If they wasted any more time, they were surely done for. It was only a matter of time before the information filtered through to The Light about the exit in the basement of Anya's. It was a sure thing they knew an exit existed, and that many basements in the city might lead to it, but considering Simeon's flight and subsequent death it was unlikely they would be yet aware there was an entrance to the tunnels in Anya's place. She was good like that.

Nonetheless, their luck would only last so long. Then they were worm food.

And yet, here Stefon was, in poortown two miles from Anya's, preparing to do something pretty stupid. He hunkered deep in a tight, ancient alley. Rainwater puddled around his feet, but he was sheltered from the light drizzle by the tall walls on either side. The darkness of night also helped conceal his presence as the odd person passed by on the street ahead. At this late hour only a few people ventured out, most heading for Bunnelshut's Inn.

Stefon could see the door to the establishment across the street. Two doormen were working, both human and very imposing. He hadn't seen a familiar face yet, and was also confident that he had avoided being followed.

It was a fool's errand. If he should have attempted anything, then surely it should have been to try and get the money he was owed from Ratna. In fact, he didn't really know why he was doing this. He only knew it felt like the right thing to do. He was going to warn Quinly Bunnelshut to get out of the city. Quinly was the closest thing to a friend he had outside his close-knit group. And for a man entirely devoid of family, that made for a fairly important person.

Pulling the hood close about his face against the elements, Stefon took a deep breath and stepped out into the drizzle. The smell of decay and faeces was rank on the street and rotten waste could be seen bubbling from drains down the thoroughfare. Wahib City was festering.

One of the doormen put a hand out to halt him mid-stride and Stefon stopped accordingly. Recognising one of the huge men, Stefon revealed his face and smiled a greeting. After a beat, the man recognised him and bade him enter.

Quinly's place was busy, shrill with arguing gamblers and drunken patrons. Two dwarves were attempting to fight in the corner, but were too drunk to land a punch. Their friends wagered on the bout regardless.

Stefon put his hood back up, despite the sweaty humidity of the place. Moving between tables, he made for the back portions, hoping to find Quinly where he had last seen him, at one of the rear tables. But he was out of luck.

That left only the upstairs, trusting that Quinly was here at all.

Stefon made for the bar and enquired of the head barman where his boss was. After giving his name, Stefon was permitted up the central staircase as usual and reached the strange-smelling rooms he had been in earlier that week. This time nobody lounged on the furniture and it was easy to locate Quinly.

Stefon's friend sat alone, puffing on a pipe and reclining languidly. His garish, fancy hat rested on the seat next to him. There was no sign of his elven friend this time. Stefon took the seat across from him and waited for Quinly to register his presence.

"Well, holy hell!" Quinly muttered, putting down the pipe and puffing a couple of smoke rings. Squinting through the smoke, he grew a lopsided smile. "How are you still alive?"

"'Tis good to see you too, old friend."

"There's a price on your head that's got every surviving scoundrel in the city searching for their bear-trap. You're a wanted man."

"So what's new?" Stefon quipped.

"Too true. Only this time it's big shakers looking for your

demise, not busty maidens looking for your coinage. You've messed up."

"It's not my fault," Stefon complained half-heartedly. "Lady Fortune moves against me this time, Quinly. She had to, sooner or later."

"She's a fickle bitch, that's for sure." Quinly sat forward, his eyes focusing. "Why are you here?"

Straight to business, just as always!

"You're probably going to be in just as much trouble. Everyone in this city is going to die, and I mean *everyone*—you included. This is no plague; it's a form of genocide."

"That's a little dramatic," said Quinly flippantly.

"You must listen to me, Quinly. I've come here because you're my friend, and you've helped me. So many times I've relied on your help…"

"And paid well for it," Quinly interrupted.

"…and just this week I fear I may have placed you in great danger asking for your help once more. It is only a matter of time before you are tied into all this. And then they'll come for you. And they won't stop."

"What do you expect me to do about that, Stefon? All I own in the world is here. All I've ever known about is behind these city walls. I served abroad when younger, but Wahib was always my home. I can't run." He sounded exhausted. Beaten.

Stefon wanted to argue and fight. He wanted to slap Quinly in the face to wake him up to the reality of the peril they faced. But that would serve nothing. "I've done what I can," Stefon conceded. "The rest is up to you."

He stood and slowly offered his hand. Quinly looked at it quizzically. "Good luck, my old friend," Stefon said.

Quinly chuckled once and then took the offered hand. "You're a strange one, Stefon, I'll give you that. But this isn't goodbye." Quinly's glib manner rankled Stefon, but he hid it.

He gave the proffered hand a firm and friendly shake, then turned to leave.

As he descended the stairs, Stefon's stomach sank. Suddenly he felt within the confines of a trap. Quinly's unwillingness to run, his knowledge of the quarantine, his laughing bravado in the face of The Light, and his final statement—*this isn't goodbye*—could only mean one thing.

What a fool he had been!

Before reaching the bottom of the stairs, Stefon drew his strange blade and carried it unthreateningly at his side, ready to defend himself. He would not overreact. He still owed Quinly the benefit of the doubt.

No one stopped to intercept him at the foot of the stairs.

Carefully he emerged behind the bar, nodding once to the barman.

Stepping into the throng of people waiting to be served, Stefon cut a path directly for the door, careful not to let his sword show.

People bumped into him on either side.

Any moment he expected to feel the puncture of a stiletto blade in his ribs.

His heart thundered in his chest. His vision swam with the tension.

Reaching the door, he stepped out confidently, his sword rising slightly in the motion. The doormen ignored him.

Rushing across the street, he drove for the alley, desperate for cover. For those few seconds he was an easy target for a sniper's arrow.

He stumbled under cover and didn't stop running. From being an orphan growing up on the streets, he knew the ancient thoroughfares and back alleys of Wahib better than most. He never broke stride, forcing himself onwards between buildings, across streets, past roaming groups of disgruntled Wahibans. His muscles were afire with the strain; his brow bursting with sweat; the sword pumping at his side as he ran.

He arrived at the safehouse basement inside twenty minutes, thundering down the stairs, desperate to be away from this city that had become so alien to him. Pryn and Jewl sprang to their feet. Packages and rolled bags lay around them. They were ready to go.

"What is it?" Jewl yelled, producing his mighty axe. "How many?"

"None, yet. But I'm pretty sure I might have triggered another trap."

"Oh for crying out loud!" whined Pryn. He grabbed up the bags around him. "We were only waiting for *you*. Brooss said to meet her at Anya's."

"Then we're away." Stefon held out a hand for his designated baggage and was handed a heavy shoulder bag. He hefted it and turned again for the stairs.

All three emerged from the rubble of the dilapidated building, the rain starting to abate slightly. The night sky was still overcast. No one lay in wait for them.

Stefon set a heavy pace, guiding them through the narrow routes to Anya's place. He still felt pursued. He still felt on edge.

The other two did well to keep up, although Jewl had replaced his axe in order to carry his gear. The route took them extra time, especially with the additional weight and the lack of a wagon. Just before midnight they returned to the yard across from Anya's, stepping between broken slats in a rear fence. It was a struggle to press the bags through, but they managed it.

Pryn was the first to spot Brooss, hiding near the abandoned cart she had previously lain in. Through the adrenaline dump in his system, Stefon felt the world had taken on a strange aspect of déjà vu. It all seemed horridly familiar. Except this time they were running for their lives.

Brooss carried two bags herself, both canvas and both obviously fairly heavy. Hopefully she had the shelter equipment he had requested. Brooss was resourceful; she could be trusted to be sensible.

"We can't all just go bundling in with these bags, can we?" Pryn asked. "I mean, you see some customers going in with bags and stuff. Mainly the kinky customers! But we'd look pretty perverted stomping in with these."

Something was stippling the back of Stefon's neck. He was concerned. Something was still wrong. He had a bad feeling.

The door to Anya's opened and the now familiar half-orc strong-arm emerged. He glanced up and down the street, avoiding looking in their direction, and then retreated inside, apparently satisfied. However, the door was only closed-to. Neither lock nor latch had been engaged.

That had to be their signal.

"OK, we do this together. Single-file and steady pace. No running. We're just trying to get in out of the rain."

"It's not raining, for once," Pryn told him.

"Tell me about it!" Stefon responded. "I just can't catch a break." He cracked a rueful grin, even though he didn't feel much like smiling. "Brooss, you first. Then Pryn and Jewl. I'll follow last. Easy does it! Head straight for the bar on the left—the room with the fire. Rish will meet us there." He left unspoken his concern that Rish had yet to be seen. Despite the fact that it made perfect sense for Rish to keep out of sight, this still made him nervous.

Another trap could await them inside Anya's.

But he had to take a chance. He had to gamble. You got nothing of worth if you didn't risk a little first.

"Go!" Brooss stood and virtually race-walked across the cobbles, her bags, heavy on her side, making her walk at an angle. It looked suspect. Pryn was close behind her, his impressive fighting gauntlets gleaming in the murk of night. Jewl stood and Stefon followed quickly behind him. It was as Brooss stepped in through the door to Anya's, and as Pryn's massive frame filled the golden shape of the brothel within, that Stefon heard the word that pierced the deepest layer of his soul.

"*Seer!*"

Stepping from the shadows of an old abandoned warehouse to their left, a cleric emerged, followed by a second. They clutched their cloaks about them like pious abbots, hiding their identities; the hoods still deep and mysterious.

They had been waiting for them. And Stefon had walked right into the trap.

But there were only two, stepping out alone. They had only shown themselves when he had appeared from the shadows. So this wasn't a trap; it was a gamble on Lesjac's part. These two were here "just in case". Pairs of clerics would be all across the city "just in case".

He had only one chance. They *all* had only one chance. He skidded to a halt.

The two clerics threw off their cloaks, revealing their own strange swords. Neither wore armour and neither carried a shield.

Stefon pitched his bag underarm toward Jewl's back, hearing it thump onto the ground. "Go!" he called. "I'll catch up!"

He knew it was a lie. This was where he would die. There was no catching up.

He had no chance, but the others did. If he held these two back, or took them with him, then his friends would make it.

He'd had enough of running for one day.

Wearily Stefon raised his stolen weapon and challenged the clerics. He expected howls of derision. He even half-expected a bolt of lightning to sizzle from these strange foes.

But instead, they hesitated: a slight falter in their step as they approached.

And it gave Stefon belief. As the first few drops of a new rainfall pattered on the cobbles, Stefon took a step forward. These men were clerics, yes. These men were dangerous fanatics and religious zealots, yes. But they were still men. And if Lesjac was correct, Stefon was a little more than just a man now.

Stefon took a deep breath, trying to focus. The first cleric calmly stepped forward, sword high. The blade flashed down at him with great power and Stefon's arm seared with pain as he deflected the blow with his own. Sparks hissed on the wet cobbles as he took a backward step.

Blade high once more, the cleric stepped in with two quick strikes at Stefon's head and shoulder. He deflected both attacks and stepped under the cleric's arm, running the edge of his blade along the rib cage. The cleric grunted and turned, startled pain etched on his face.

Seeing this, the second cleric also stepped forward, his blade held low.

They had Stefon flanked. His heart thundered.

Time cascaded around him, the rain tumbling slowly to the cobbles. Each raindrop was a crystal falling. The world slowed and Stefon's vision sharpened. With each step that the clerics took, the small splash of rainwater unfurled gracefully. Time was impossibly retarded. The sounds around him became thick and guttural, drawn out.

Each cleric attacked simultaneously, their strikes high and low. Though moving slowly, Stefon didn't feel sluggish. He felt power surge through his limbs. He blocked high left and low right. A quick turn of his wrist blocked a midriff strike.

He caught both blades on his own and turned full circle, his sword arm overhead. Both clerics' blades were parried away by the turn.

And though moving inexplicably slowly, Stefon knew he moved faster than these men ever could. Each strike should have killed him. But he dodged; he evaded.

Holding his sword in a single-handed grip, Stefon stepped between the clerics, lashing out either side of him, parrying and riposting with each movement. Often on one foot, sometimes jumping clean over low strikes, Stefon fought on.

The clerics retreated as signs of their defeat grew. First a nick on the cheek for one; then a slice to the leg for another.

The first lost a finger; the second lost two. He even pierced a standing foot with one clean jab.

The clerics were tired and weary, but Stefon's vision was blurring. This unreal time was taking its toll. His limbs grew heavy. The sound of rushing in his ears was more urgent; almost deafening. The resonant pounding of his heart filled the world.

He drove at the leftmost cleric, only parrying to the right. Stefon slashed at his foe's face and hands, deflecting his blade up and away repeatedly.

And the man tripped. He stumbled. Holding his blade defensively, he staggered backwards.

Stefon's sword took him low in the chest, beneath the block.

In agonising clarity, Stefon saw the man's face empty of feeling. The cleric was dead before he hit the ground.

The world rushed in around Stefon, raindrops hammering down. Time returned to normal—rain falling, feet splashing.

Stefon whirled to defend his back as the other cleric attacked. He was exhausted. His limbs were drained. The sword suddenly felt so heavy. There was a clattering in his ears.

Despite his block, an overhand attack drove Stefon to his knees, defeated.

This was it. This was where...

The cleric was struck from the side. A galloping horse ploughed clean through him, throwing him to the ground. As Stefon watched, the wheel of a wagon clattered over the body, crushing the head like a watermelon.

"Get going!" a voice called. "I'll lead any more away!" Stefon looked across to see Quinly Bunnelshut driving the wagon on, his dandy hat being twirled in the air above his head. "You owe me one!" he shouted.

Gauntleted hands grabbed Stefon beneath the armpits and lifted him to his feet. Pryn's broad face smiled at him. "Come on, hero!" he grunted. Stefon was dragged inside Anya's Brothel semi-delirious, and the door slammed shut behind them.

Chapter Fifteen
A Sweet Darkness

Firstday morning, another week begun, and Acaelian sat in the company of friends around an outdoor table outside a small alehouse on the corner of a quiet street. Despite the relatively early hour, and the tiredness they surely all felt, the mood was a happy one.

Martin Galvan was recounting the tale of a brawl that had broken out at the hostelry in which he had been playing the night before. He had been forced to smash his lute over the head of a drunkard who insisted on grabbing the arses of all the serving staff. He had been invited back as a guest of the hostelry any time he liked for the protection he had afforded the serving girls, who happened to be the owner's daughters. In addition, he was told his music would always be welcome. Martin regarded this as folly, considering he would now have to find a way to replace his finest instrument, since the smashed lute was presently nothing more than firewood on the hostelry floor.

Martin, and his ever-present friend Delgado, were travellers from Briadranon who had journeyed to Shen Utah many years ago and found themselves immediately at home in the busy city. Each man was in his thirties, worldly-wise and witty at the same time, and Acaelian enjoyed their company immensely.

Martin Galvan always had a tale. Ostensibly a musical performer, Acaelian knew Martin was more of a storyteller than anything else. It was simply easier to get work as a musician, and he used the stage to tell his stories anyway.

Click and Claudia were both at the table too, sitting on the far side, enraptured by Martin's story. In the cold light of morning, Claudia's features were pinched and chilled, but she kept a shawl around her shoulders and sipped at her warmed wine. Every so often she would look Acaelian's way and roll her eyes or pull a face at some element of Martin's diatribe, but mostly she was quiet and still. Acaelian, as always, could hardly keep his eyes from her.

But there was plenty more he should be mulling over. The Guild Master of the Glimmers had betrayed him, and given his closest rival the job at the docks. Unless Acaelian wanted to risk certain death by attempting the daylight robbery of a dockside vessel, he had tonight to arrange to empty the ship of all the gold and gems he could. The only sensible and effective way he could see of doing so involved an accomplice.

And yet despite Jon the Black Cat's advice to forget his feelings for Claudia, he found it impossible to do so. He knew the old man was right, and that especially now he ought to be focusing purely on his real problems, but his mind always turned to Claudia.

"The trouble last night exploded from nothing, really," said Delgado. "I can't help but feel that people are more high-strung than normal. Tempers are more easily frayed than usual these days; I'm sure of it." The massive companion to Martin Galvan was a bear of a man. Standing easily over six feet three, Delgado had lived as a slave fighter in the Free Cities of Briadranon. He had killed his first opponent with his bare hands at the age of twelve. By eighteen he was the champion of his whole region and his owner struggled to find others who would risk presenting their slaves for Delgado to fight, for no opponent who would stand across the dust of the slave arena from him would survive the ordeal. Despite his success, he had lost his ability to make money, and Delgado's owner had sold him to a mercenary group. That didn't last long before his owner's mercenary clan was smashed to pieces in its very next encounter. Acaelian had only heard Delgado speak of it once. He had not refused to fight, as his friend Martin Galvan would have people believe, but had simply not understood his role. The enemy had struck and Delgado had simply turned and walked away. It was not his fight. He had no desire to seek out destruction.

Since that day Delgado had not turned his hand to combat of any type. He had met Martin Galvan soon after and immediately fallen in with the troubadour: the minstrel provided Delgado with the friendship that he had never known. In return, travelling with the huge Delgado dissuaded bandits from attacking; this could be a constant threat to travelling minstrels.

Sitting at the table, Delgado shook his head ruefully.

Martin agreed with his friend: "It seems clear that there is tension in Shen Utah, and especially The Lows."

Acaelian glanced meaningfully at Claudia, as though Martin's opinion might somehow make more of an impression on the Wheel, but she was watching him and Delgado as they spoke. Acaelian tried to dismiss the thought that she might be deliberately avoiding his gaze.

"This Shredder business is ruining the city," mused Martin. "I wonder how close they are to finding him?"

Acaelian remained silent, careful to keep his expression neutral, even though he could sense Click glance his way. Acaelian had told no one that he had been to see the city watch, not even Click.

"I hear the Bishop of the One God Temple gave a sermon yesterday that caused quite a stir," said Click. "He renounced the private debauchery of those living within Temple Link. Called them hypocrites and ungodly, worshipping gods of money by day and darkening their souls in the arms of devil-driven whores by night."

"Hey!" complained Claudia.

"Not my words," confessed Click.

Martin took a big gulp of his drink and wiped his lip with the back of his hand. "I think it's interesting how people like that just lash out. I doubt the Shredder gives a toss where he kills his victims, and he's sure as hell not a weapon of the devil. The Temple is turning the events to their own ends; to stab at the hearts of the aristocracy that dominate the Temples' higher echelons."

Click nodded. "Gareth has some interesting thoughts about it," he said, referring to Gareth the nightwatchman of the Glimmer Guild. Gareth was Faragwin's equivalent in the hours after sunset, but his antithesis in every way. Whilst one could never trust Faragwin, one could trust Faragwin to *be* Faragwin. The Glimmer Master could be anticipated for his untrustworthiness, and that made him workable. Gareth was simply trustworthy: a rare quality indeed for a second-in-command of the Guild of Thieves. "He says it's entirely possible that the Temple Shredder is a member of one of the five Guilds."

"Really?" asked Acaelian, acting surprised by the idea.

"Yep. He thinks that the best time to have caught the Shredder was when he first started his killing. Back then his behaviour pattern would have had a clear change, and he'd have been easy to spot. Gareth believes that if this had occurred outside the Guilds it would have been identified by people close to the murderer, and he'd have been caught.

"But the Guilds protect their own, and without question. If the Temple Shredder is a Guild member, his Guild would have made nothing of his change in behaviour, and the blanket of protection afforded to all members would have provided his perfect cover. The more you think about it, the more it makes sense."

"That's bloody worrying, though," admitted Martin. "I think it's obviously unlikely that he's a Wheel, but whether he be a Black Cat, Glimmer, Pillar or Whisper, what if his Guild Master *knows* that he's the Shredder, and is still protecting him?"

A silence dropped over the table like a cloth.

As Click and Martin had discussed their suspicions, Acaelian's mind had been working on what they said. The killer clearly used an accomplice. The killer could indeed be a Guild member. A Guild Master could be covering it up, knowingly or not.

Grimlaw, Acaelian's loathed enemy, was a member of the Guild of Whispers, and had shown more than a dark streak of hatred and cruelty. Grimlaw's brother, Toothless Bill, was also a Guild member—a Pillar—and he had shown unflinching loyalty to Grimlaw. And Glimmer Guild Master Faragwin had already made it clear that he favoured young Grimlaw.

This past weekend, Grimlaw had been awfully busy casing Acaelian's harbour job...too busy to get around to killing?

Martin Galvan pushed his drink away with a rueful laugh, bringing Acaelian from his reverie. "There's nothing we can do, so as I've got to buy a new lute, I'd better be about it."

As the group finished their beverages, they departed the table one by one. Each sought the daytime rest that was a feature of their work. Martin Galvan and Delgado stood away from the table and bade their goodbyes in their thick, eastern accents. Soon after, Click left too, leaving Claudia and Acaelian alone.

There were literally a hundred issues the young elf wanted to address with her, but something in the air between them halted his words. There was a loaded moment, a pause of portent, as though the city itself were holding its breath. "I'll see you tomorrow," Claudia said quietly, sitting forward.

"God willing," Acaelian said. It was a standard reply, but he felt some greater meaning in the words.

Claudia stood and regarded Acaelian for a moment. She looked tired, brushing a strand of hair behind her ear with a sigh. "You worry too much," she told him. "Always pondering, always thinking."

He simply shrugged. "Of all the things to be accused of, I would settle for that."

With a soft laugh, she once again graced him with a friendly kiss, that familiar scent of jasmine and green tea wafting across him, and then she turned and left.

Acaelian rested his head back onto the chair and closed his eyes. His neck popped and cracked, relieving some tension therein. He lost track of time as his mind whirled with possibilities. Yet as tired as he was, and despite being lost in his own worrying thoughts, Acaelian still heard the approach of a stranger. The man, a heavy-set individual by the sounds of his footsteps, came to stand by the table without a word.

Putting two and two together, Acaelian guessed the man's identity without opening his eyes. "Feel free to take a seat, Constable Foord."

The fat man laughed and Acaelian lifted his head again, his vision swimming a little as he opened his eyes. Acaelian had no idea how much time had passed since his friends had departed, but he figured the constable wouldn't have approached him if he thought his friends were still about.

The city watch officer took a seat across from the thief and placed both hands, folded, on the table. "Hello, boy."

"How are you faring, Constable?"

"Well, little thief, I'm faring well." The overweight face of Constable Foord took on a knowing look. "I can understand your concern now, little Guild rat. She's certainly a looker. Nothing of the princess about her. Nothing traditionally beautiful, but she's got some figure. Just like your typical Wheel: built for f…"

"Is there something I can help you with, Foord," Acaelian interrupted, "or are you just wanting to pick a fight? Either

way, I've little time for this; and I know there's something you
should be doing."

"Touché, boy. Well, enough said, but harken unto me
and mark me well, thief. The Shredder didn't strike last
night. This is the first time he's missed a weekend. That
makes me twitchy. If I were of the ilk to be distrustful of
people, I might assume that someone had tipped the killer
off. Maybe warned him to lay low. I'd hate to think that
was the case."

"What would I gain from that, you simpleton?" Acaelian
snapped.

"Easy, rat!" Foord warned him. "Now that I've stumbled
upon your little morning session here, I can see your
motivation, and I understand it. She's got an appeal. In
fact, she's just the Shredder's type: buxom, comely, young,
brunette, and with just the right hint of sleaze about her."

"I do wish you'd stop talking about her that way."

Foord leant forward and jabbed a finger at Acaelian.
"You need to brighten up, Guild rat! I hate to tell you,
but she's just his type, and the Shredder has never missed
a weekend. If he's not been tipped off then we've every
reason to believe he'll deliver this night. Watch over your
friend; sit your vigil over her; do whatever it is you urchins
do for each other. I figure you'd feel her loss."

The news sank a needle of sorrow into Acaelian's heart.
His world had just been thrown into stark relief. He had
tonight to complete his job and get the money he needed to
make his tithe. In order to do the job properly he would need
Click's help, and it would take them many hours.

And now he had learned that tonight the Shredder was
bound to strike, and Claudia was in danger. Fate had dealt a
loaded hand, for the one night he wished more than any to
be able to sit vigil over Claudia was the one night he could ill
afford to do so. His mind crashed with indecision. "You're
a shit, Foord."

"I don't care what you think of me. The fact is, you're right: I've a job to do, and I don't want another victim falling beneath this lunatic's axe if I can help it. I don't care what you do; I'm just here to tell you that you were probably right about the wagon, and to give you that chance to circle your own wagons. Now we're even."

"Big of you."

"I'm a regular hero."

The darkness of the night seeped through the streets of Shen Utah like a blade between the ribs. Insipid, rebarbative, nauseating; the life of the city bled from its gutters and the stench of corruption clogged his nostrils like a clot. He hated the city.

Blacker than the night, blacker than the grime underfoot, blacker than the churning bile of the fetid scum who lived in The Lows; his black, black heart thundered in his chest. His palm was slick with sweat, eager to grip the handle of the axe that remained hidden in his tunic.

Eyes like jets scowled from within the shadows of a narrow lane, through which even the slenderest feline might struggle to pass. A cruel grin crept across his face as the thrill of the hunt rippled through his body.

There she was, laughing with her other whore friends, her dark hair about her shoulders, deep cleavage shining in the lamplight. Her nose wrinkled as she laughed.

She disgusted him and attracted him. His body responded, but he willed patience. He had waited all weekend, hidden in the shadows of the city that once he had loved but now loathed so much, stalking his prey. Patience had ever been his friend. Patience delivered the prey to the predator. Patience gave the prey room to make mistakes. Patience gave him time to anticipate the kill, the rape and the slaughter. Patience painted his life a blacker veil of longing.

Grimlaw chuckled softly to himself. He was almost disappointed with the legendary elf thief, as he watched Acaelian's shadowy form skirt the periphery of the harbour and approach the ship, whose aft port cargo hold was loaded with gold and gems.

From his vantage point hidden within the shadows of the gangway, Grimlaw flexed and relaxed his straining muscles. He had been in his hiding place since shortly after noon, and he was aching all over as a result. However, getting the drop on Acaelian once more was worth it.

The hours had lengthened past sunset and now it neared midnight. Grimlaw had to admit to being surprised, for he had expected Acaelian to be all over this job as early as possible. Yet here the elf was, arriving near midnight, and doing it rather shabbily.

Grimlaw knew that Acaelian had a lot on his mind. Perhaps he couldn't handle the competition. In all fairness, he had been making it hard for the elf, but that was the life for a Glimmer in Shen Utah. Nothing was easy. Nothing was ever really free, even to a thief.

He watched as Acaelian climbed down a mooring rope and up the hull to reach a porthole. Working nimbly, the elf—nothing more than a silhouette upon a dark canvas—angled himself impossibly in through the window, and then Grimlaw caught the slightest hand signal.

So that was it. That was how he was extricating the haul from the hold of the vessel: by line dropping it to a confederate who would, no doubt, be in a dinghy fast approaching. Well, it was more imaginative than his own plan.

He crawled out from beneath the gangway and sidled along to the harbour wall. Dropping down to the wall-ladder, he prepared himself, took a deep breath and then jumped away from the wall. He turned in the space hanging above the sloshing water below. His jump was perfectly timed and his palm snagged the edge of the porthole amidships. He used the clamp he had secured in the hull the day before to swing along to the next porthole. Silently he crawled through the hole and dropped to the floor of the cargo hold.

The ceiling was low, the lighting lower still, and the air smelled musty and damp. All was precisely as it had been yesterday. Somewhere in the cargo hold, Grimlaw could hear movement, soft and subtle. He drew his stiletto blade and moved over to the middle portion of the wall wherefrom he would have the best view of the entire hold.

White tunnels of light from the arrangement of portholes in the right-hand wall punched across the hold, highlighting dust-motes in the air. The sounds originated from halfway along the hold, precisely where the concentration of gold was—easily the heaviest haul to shift. Grimlaw smiled softly, adjusting his grip on the dagger.

He moved forward, keeping in the shadows.

He reached the corner of the crate and stole a glance around it. The shadowed form of Acaelian hunkered over a crate at the far wall, still nothing more than a silhouette illuminated by the pale light of the porthole.

He was tired of the elf. Grimlaw was the best Glimmer in Shen Utah, and that was how it would remain!

He moved forward, ready to drive the blade into Acaelian's heart.

He stepped quickly and silently on his toes. Suddenly he realised too late that something wasn't right. The shadow was just that: only a shadow.

He whirled around. There, on the sill of the porthole, a figurine sat suspended on a spring fixed to the hull. It cast the shadow on the wall.

Trap!

Too late, he tried to react. A snapping sound echoed around the room. From the ceiling, a heavy net whistled down with alarming speed. The corners were pinned and the net crushed Grimlaw to the ground, forcing his knee into his chest and doubling him over. He let out an agonised cry as his blade skipped away, out of reach.

For a long moment his eyes scanned the darkness, looking for Acaelian. He feared the gloating eyes, but none emerged. He remained crushed to the floor of the hold, a fortune in gold and gems no more than a dozen yards from him. His breaths came in shallow gasps and his muscles cramped. The discs of his spine stretching agonisingly as the ropes of the net dug deep.

Consigned to his fate, Grimlaw's only thought as he lay ensnared was that Acaelian the Glimmer certainly was a legend.

Outside on the harbour, a lone figure strode calmly from the vessel in which Grimlaw had just become trapped. He allowed a sly grin to cross his face at the thought of that fool struggling against his bonds within the port-side hold. He grinned more generously when he heard the burning fuse take light inside the starboard cargo hold.

The figure stopped and watched the ship. The trap had been genius, and Grimlaw had stumbled right into it. A small distraction in the hold had acted as bait; a long fuse ran down the starboard hull, unseen from shore. But the cherry on the icing was the "poison" used to ignite the trap.

The other cargo hold had made interesting viewing, Acaelian had told Click.

With a whoosh and an almighty boom, the highly illegal naphtha containers caught the flame of the fuses dotted around the hold, and the night sky was suddenly brightly lit by a series of explosions like golden oak trees. The hull of the ship was immediately rent and began taking on water.

The sailors and deckhands still aboard the stricken vessel scrambled to leap to the dock wall as the gangway collapsed. The ship began to list and sink, the flames coursing through the rigging with deadly speed.

Walking away from the mess in the harbour, the dark figure removed his hood and stowed it in his tunic before ruffling his blond hair. It was a habit he had. Click smiled at the thought of that wealth of gold and gems sinking to the bottom of the harbour. The idea of his best friend's nemesis, Grimlaw, following it to the depths caused him no small delight either.

Acaelian crouched in the familiar shadows of the dormer gable and watched his beloved Claudia as she chatted away the night with her friends. Several times throughout the evening he had seen her move from one position to another in the square, in groups of no less than three. Only a few times had she crossed the square on her own to join another group as the Firstday night business picked up; it was surprisingly busy on the streets for the season. The weather was inclement, and at times Claudia had stamped her feet against the cold. This had caused her cleavage to jiggle a little, her hands buried deep within a knitted roll for warmth. Even at this distance the sight had seized Acaelian's attention, ensnaring him between fascination and self-loathing.

Abruptly the sky to the north bloomed with golden colour. Reflected in Acaelian's eyes as he sat transfixed for a moment, the crests of folding flame from the erupting ship curled into the night sky, and then the thunder of the explosion rippled across the darkness.

Many in the city cried out in fear. Shrill whistles could be heard on the night air, coming from the docklands. Right now port security would be scrambling to rescue the stricken ship, but Acaelian's trap had been planned well enough. He hadn't expected the explosion to be quite that big, but the ship would sink to the depths of the harbour before the flames were even dampened by the waters.

He turned his gaze back to the square, where many patrons had stepped from the inns, brothels and gambling holes to see the spectacle, although no good view would be afforded from street-level.

At first Acaelian couldn't locate Claudia, for many had moved about excitedly during the explosion. His eyes searched with growing agitation. He crawled forward from the darkness, his anxiety increasing.

She had gone. Had she gone back inside? It seemed unlikely, with all the people stepping from inside to out.

He had only looked away for a moment.

He cast about, seeking some sign of her. He spied her friends, but there was no glimpse of Claudia.

His stomach turned.

There, stamped into the puddle at the corner of the square, leading to a darkened lane, was Claudia's knitted roll. It lay unnoticed in the filth of the street.

With scant self-regard Acaelian dropped from the roof and used the extremes of his agility and strength to traverse the building front, windowsill to windowsill. He dropped the last few yards to the street, took the impact through his knees and rolled to his feet. Without hesitation, he rushed for the lane that stood black and foreboding in the corner of the square.

He skidded to a halt by the corner and snatched up the knitted roll. It was filthy and soaking, but it was definitely Claudia's. Drawing his short knife, it suddenly felt like the smallest weapon ever. Regardless, he proceeded into the darkness.

The lane was high on one side, with the windowless wall of the brothel climbing into the night. To the right was a tall wall, perhaps ten feet high. Over that, Acaelian knew there were allotments and sheds. None of the light from the lamps in the square behind him penetrated the shadows of the lane.

The darkness was deep and solid. Acaelian's elven eyes began to adjust, melting to greyscale. The walls of the lane and the stones of the floor sang to him with sorrow. The city spoke to him:

He is here.

Moving low and silent, Acaelian spied movement ahead. A hunched figure struggled with something on the floor. He moved closer. The figure, on one knee, uttered a grunt and heaved at something at his feet.

Acaelian heard the ripping of fabric and then a sickly, satisfied sigh. The black figure—blacker than death—slowly lifted a gleaming hand-axe as if to strike at the floor.

Acaelian hurled his knife overhand. It flashed through the dark lane and punched into the murderer's hand, slicing three fingers clean off. The man let out a squeal and the axe fell from his grip. Reflexively the figure clutched his hand and turned his blackened, featureless face to scowl at his assailant.

The elf thief had already made his move. His slender shoulder slammed into the killer, propelling both of them across the floor of the lane. Acaelian was quick, but the killer was quicker still. An elbow crashed down on his shoulder and then the dark figure bucked out from under his light weight.

Before the killer could escape, the elf jumped at him again. He was enraged, his normal elven composure gone entirely. He screamed as he crashed into the killer, slamming him against the wall. The Shredder kneed him twice in the ribs, dizzying him. With a snap of movement, Acaelian pulled his head up sharply, hearing a satisfying crack of bone from above as his hard skull slammed into the softer face.

Suddenly the two broke their grapple and stood to regard each other.

Acaelian recognised him! The Temple Shredder was a

Guild member; a Black Cat; an ageing assassin. *Jon!*

Acaelian's one-time mentor's hair, greased black for the night, was grey underneath. His face was withered and grey, too. Blood gushed from his broken nose.

Jon snarled, "Acaelian, you fool, you'll regret this! I told you to leave those whores well alone! I warned you!"

As Acaelian rushed forward once more, the old man threw something at his feet. Before the smoke bomb went off, the old assassin flicked his wrist and Acaelian felt a sting in his ribs. He clutched them as Jon made to flee. His hand came up caked in blood.

A glance to the floor on Acaelian's right revealed the still form of Claudia, her bodice ripped open to the night. He saw no sign of an axe attack, but a small pool of blood could be seen seeping from a head wound. She rested on a large leather sheet, stitched to cover a broad area.

Stomach turning, Acaelian gripped the sharp edge of a metal star that jutted from his side, and pulled. The metal made a scraping sound against his ribs and blood jetted across the floor. He dropped the weapon and, ignoring the agony of even breathing, took to his heels after the Black Cat Jon.

The smoke bomb made it impossible to see down the lane, but the elf figured he knew which way he had gone. The city sang to him:

Kill him!

Scrambling up the ten-foot wall, Acaelian scuttled along the top like a cat in the night. At the end of the lane was a carriage. Rushing toward it was the killer.

As blood seeped from his side, Acaelian pressed on. His face awash with sweat, he gritted his teeth, his skin pale.

Five yards short of the carriage, he leaped from the wall and slammed into the assassin, dropping him to the floor. Once again, Acaelian heard the nauseating crack of a broken bone. The assassin cried out.

The elf rolled to his feet as the murderer rose once more,

his left leg limp beneath him. Acaelian rushed at Jon as he
saw the carriage making good its escape, abandoning the
murderer. He glanced Jon's young apprentice at the reins.

Acaelian threw a punch at the killer's broken nose, but
Jon was still quick for his age, and Acaelian was no fighter.
He found his wrist caught in a vice like grip, and suddenly
the Black Cat rolled onto his good leg. Using Acaelian's
weight against him, he threw the young elf over his hip
and crashed him to the floor, blasting the wind from his
damaged lung.

Jon twisted his wrist and pain coursed through his arm. He
let out a scream of agony. Looking up into the face of death,
Acaelian felt fear for the first time. The assassin produced
a punching dagger, pulled Acaelian's hand down behind his
own head and went to plunge the short blade into his heart.

The blow never came. Instead the murderer's grey face
snapped sideways, an arrow lodged in his temple, protruding
from the left side of his head. The force of the blow dropped
the killer away to the side, releasing his painful grip on
Acaelian's wrist.

Clutching his bleeding flank, the elf thief rolled to his side
on the cold stone floor. A pair of boots suddenly filled his
vision. He let out a groan, any fight left in him having fled. A
pair of burly hands lifted him to his seat and then up to his
feet. Before him stood Constable Foord, a sly grin on his face.

"Good work, lad! I think you might have even saved her.
Now get out of here before I have you clapped in irons, you
Guild rat!" The words were mean, but they were spoken with
a strange affection.

Acaelian trudged down the narrow lane, back toward the
still form of Claudia. The smoke of the assassin's bomb had
blown away on the chill night breeze. Only one other man
stood in the lane with them: a tall, human ranger wearing
a captain's insignia. He held an impressive longbow at his
side and regarded Acaelian closely as they passed. The young

elf touched his forelock and the captain afforded him a wry smile of appreciation.

By the time Acaelian had reached Claudia's side, a small crowd had gathered at the entrance to the lane, though none dared to enter the darkness. Acaelian knelt next to her. The bodice of her Wheel's garb still lay open, the chill night air goosing her naked skin. Taking no pleasure in her semi-naked form, Acaelian quickly covered her up, closing the bodice as best he could. He was careful not to touch her intimately.

He lifted her wounded head, ripped a section of cloth from her torn dress and placed it behind her. The bleeding had slowed. He placed another arm beneath her knees. Being sure to move her carefully, the elf ignored his own lancing pain and lifted his friend from the coldness of the stone lane.

Bearing her weight without complaint, Acaelian was surprised at how slender she felt through the dress. She felt *fragile*.

He stepped slowly and carefully from the lane, the grimness of his expression causing the onlookers to make a space for him to pass. Some of her Guild friends saw the victim, and a couple cried out in grief. "She lives!" he told them. Without needing instruction, they led him to the entrance to Grig's Wheelhouse and opened the door for him to carry Claudia into the warmth.

The darkness of that darkest of nights gave way slowly to a beautiful morning. The seabirds cawed, circling in the sky to the north without care. All across Shen Utah the sounds of the waking city chattered at Acaelian's restless form as it sat dejectedly atop the tallest church in Temple Link. An excited energy resonated not only through the populace, but throughout the fabric of the city too. The metropolis had been freed of an evil that had stalked its streets for months, and Acaelian had been paramount in his capture. It had been Captain Carpion of the city watch, leader of the Shen Utah wayfarers and cousin to the nation's Knight-Marshall, who had slain the killer with his arrow; but in The Lows it was the name of Acaelian the Legend that was on the lips of every soul.

Still, the elf felt bereft.

Climbing up beside him, his friend Click settled on the edge of the massively high house of worship, looking down on the grand square. Before them rose the Shen Utah Royal Palace, resplendent in the early morning light, her fingers reaching for the heavens.

"I told you: you're a legend," Click told him. It felt like an accusation.

Acaelian's silence was the only reply Click needed.

"It was an impossible choice." Click tried to comfort him. "I'm sure the Guild will understand."

"The Guild will understand nothing," the elf said. "I owed a tithe payment to the Glimmers by this morning and I've no money. I'll be a freebooter now, cut from the Guild for good. It's as good as a death sentence, and I'm not even sure I care all that much."

"Surely there's something that can be done... you're a hero!"

"I'm a thief, nothing more. But I can't help but feel that was never enough. I think I always wanted more. Perhaps this is a blessing."

In the square below, Acaelian caught sight of a familiar figure. Striding slowly though the square, making a show of nonchalance, Captain Carpion made his way from the Shen Utah Palace toward the far-right corner of the square. As Acaelian watched, the tall ranger looked up at him and then inclined his head subtly. It was an invitation.

"Maybe I should consider a career change," Acaelian said with a dark, humourless smile. With that he began the perilous descent from the church roof.

In less than five minutes, Acaelian walked to where

Carpion waited and stepped into stride with the captain as he led them over to a beautiful café overlooking the river that ran through the city to meet the River Shen. Carpion took a seat and indicated another nearby. With only the merest hesitation, Acaelian took the proffered seat.

He waited for Carpion to speak, but he did not. Instead a voice came from beside him and Acaelian turned to see an old acolyte sitting on the far side of the table, hidden in shadows. "Always the Glimmer, I see," the old man commented on his initial reluctance to sit.

"Hardly," replied Acaelian.

"You sound so sure." The elf looked closely at the bespectacled priest, dressed in crimson robes and wearing one of those silly high hats. He wore a grey beard and a kind smile. A glance around the posh café terrace revealed that they were alone. No serving staff could even be seen.

"Do we know each other?" Acaelian asked.

"No one knows me," the acolyte replied enigmatically. Only then did Acaelian see through the disguise, effective as it was. So good was the disguise, indeed, that the elf almost blurted his name: Swindle! The Sinecure Head, leader of the Shen Utah underworld, here masquerading as a simple temple acolyte, smiled happily at the reaction. "I am happy to see you fit and well. How is the injury?"

"I heal quickly," Acaelian replied, refusing to admit weakness. In truth the burning pain of the chest wound was constant, and would be for weeks to come. "Why the disguise? I'm sure no one here would recognise you."

Swindle smiled behind the beard. "No one would recognise me as Swindle, for sure. But I'm not worried about being recognised as Swindle; I have many pseudonyms. This disguise is as much for your protection as mine." He smiled enigmatically again, and Acaelian knew not to press the matter. "You acted bravely last night. You have my compliments."

The thief tried to wave the comment away. "I found myself in a bind and tried to fight my way out. It wasn't bravery; it was foolishness. I rushed in without thought, and almost got myself killed. If the ranger here hadn't been so quick with his bow, I would be rat food by now."

"That's the truth of it," agreed the false acolyte. "But that is not of what I speak, Acaelian. You had a clear choice to make last night. I know you had no chance to pull the ship job on your own and still protect your girl. That was precisely why I asked Faragwin to give you that job."

Acaelian glanced worriedly at Carpion, but the captain seemed unconcerned.

"Not to worry," Swindle told him. "Carpion and I have an understanding. We keep the lines of communication open, for the good of Shen Utah. We would make very poor enemies, but admirable allies.

"Now then, I commend your bravery for making the decision you did. You found yourself in a position in which one hopes never to be. In one hand you held the life of the one you clearly love; and in your other hand you held your own life, for to ignore your tithe is to renounce your Guild membership—tantamount to a death warrant. Such a bind, such a position; it defines a person. The choice one makes in such a quandary reveals one's deepest nature."

Swindle held up his hands in illustration. His right hand: "Make the job, steal the gold and gems; you make your tithe payment and save your skin, but risk the life of your beloved." Left: "You turn your back on the job, renouncing your Glimmer membership, and try—against all odds—to protect your girl."

"She's not my girl," Acaelian replied, without really knowing why.

"Regardless, you showed startling ingenuity and no small amount of intelligence. I told you the details of the job were that the gems and gold in the ship must never reach their destination. The job assigned to you had nothing to do with theft, unless you count the fact that you had a tithe to make.

"So you arranged for the explosion to take the fortune to the bottom of the harbour, where they will just as likely never be seen again, and you ensured your greatest rival went with it."

Acaelian shifted uncomfortably.

"Relax: I know everything. I wouldn't very well be who I am if I didn't. I know Grimlaw was being helped by his father."

With only a missed beat, Acaelian said: "Faragwin?"

"Of course. He's been favouring the boy for years, but never with such obviousness as last night. As such, Faragwin is no more. He has been Bled."

Acaelian's body shuddered at the thought. To be Bled was as serious a punishment as a Guild member could face. It involved each limb being systematically sliced apart: from finger to shoulder; toe to hip. Then your guts and genitals were burned before your eyes; your head was severed from your body; and your remains were pushed down the sewers to the river. It was a notorious death, and one without honour.

Suddenly Acaelian felt trapped in the grounds of the café.

"This leaves you and I with a dilemma," Swindle told him. "You still need to make that tithe payment, and you can't afford it, I assume?"

The elf shook his head.

"And I have a Guild without a leader. So who would you take your tithe to, even if you had it? Don't answer; I'm being rhetorical." Abruptly Swindle seemed to change tack. "Did you know the killer?"

"Yes. He was a Black Cat. Years ago, when he was still active, he had mentored me for a period. Ironically, I think his instruction might have saved my life last night. I knew a few tricks."

"Indeed. Jon had lost his mind. Normally a Black Cat

doesn't live that long. It's a dangerous career," Swindle explained to Carpion as an aside. The captain rolled his eyes and took a hearty bite of a green apple. "Anyway…" he returned his attention to Acaelian. "He clearly lost his mind. Jon carried on killing, even though he wasn't getting jobs any more. In fact, there tend to be fewer Black Cat jobs these days in general. Personally, I prefer Guilds to work… differently. Assassination is a last resort. Unfortunately, sometimes it is necessary, so I cannot do away with the Black Cats altogether."

"Who was Jon's accomplice?" Acaelian asked, out of turn. Swindle seemed not to care overly about the interruption.

"Turns out it was his apprentice, who also happened to be his son. Tragic tale, really. The boy now resides at the bottom of the harbour, not a hundred yards from your fortune in gold and gems, eternally chained to a rock for his poor judgement."

"Ah."

"Well said," commented Captain Carpion sardonically.

Swindle adjusted his redundant spectacles and then tapped his chin thoughtfully. "So what to do with all this change? Change…change…*change*. Change isn't a bad thing, you know. For example, historically it has not been uncommon for assassins to fall foul of each other in the city. It is Black Cat law that should an assassin fall to a fellow Black Cat, his belongings and estates are split in twain. Half goes to the Guild, and the remainder goes to the Black Cat's slayer.

"The Temple Shredder happened to be a particularly successful assassin in his time, as it transpires. Indeed, Jon was quite wealthy, and had a delightful converted manse in the East End. The Black Cat Guild will do quite nicely out of this, as will the Shredder's killer."

Acaelian looked at Carpion, who shrugged. "I'm no Guild member," he said in his rich voice. "I have no need or desire for that blood money, boy. It was you who killed the Shredder by delaying him long enough for my arrow to do its work.

The money and the manse are yours. More than enough to make your tithe to whosoever will be the next Glimmer Master, I suspect."

The elf looked back at Swindle, his mind awhirl.

"If you'll accept it?" Swindle asked softly. Acaelian nodded enthusiastically, which made him laugh. "Good. Then our friend Carpion brings me to the last issue I have to straighten out. I need a Glimmer Master to replace Faragwin. I'd offer it to you, Acaelian the Legend, but I suspect I know enough about you to be certain you'll decline?"

"People might think me a legend now, sir, but that won't last. I'm not your Glimmer Master. I'm sorry."

"Don't be," Swindle said. "You're destined for greater things, I warrant. So, your recommendations then?"

Acaelian was surprised at the question, but didn't hesitate. "Gareth, the nightwatchman. He's always been a fair man, and his judgement of things is usually sound. He'd command respect, but wouldn't exploit it, I feel."

Swindle narrowed his eyes thoughtfully at Acaelian, appraising him as the elf might regard a rare jewel. "Hmm..." murmured Swindle. "Great things indeed!" he mused. "Yes indeed."

Long after noon had passed, the throng of people congratulating Claudia had melted away to consist of just her closest friends. Her head still pounded insufferably, but she was alive—and that was miracle enough. She had survived an attack by the Temple Shredder, who now lay dead in an unmarked grave near the docks. And her saviour, from all accounts, had been Acaelian. Sweet Acaelian!

The young elf had been the only one of her friends yet to come and see her at Grig's, and suddenly she missed him. She wanted to thank him personally, yes; but that was

not why she wanted so desperately to see him. She just *did*.
She longed for his quiet company and warming smile. He
seemed so dark and brooding to others, but he always had a
smile for her. It made her feel special.

A soft knock came at the door of the chamber reserved
for her rest, and Click popped his head round. Claudia
ushered the others out of the room and bade Click to enter.
She sat up more in the bed and fought down the nausea that
the movement caused.

"Well met, lady," Click said.

"Don't be silly, Click. Just tell me where our friend is."

"I don't know," the apprentice spy replied. "Gareth the
nightwatchman has been made Glimmer Guild Master,
now that Faragwin has gone. He told me Acaelian had paid
his tithe and left the Glimmer Guild, with the blessing of
Swindle himself."

"What?" Claudia was inexplicably alarmed at the news.

"He came to me before he went to see Gareth. He gave
me something for you."

For no real reason, Claudia began to cry. Perhaps sensing
the same thing, Click handed over the envelope without
another word. He then sat in a chair nearby, eyes downcast.

The envelope was heavy. Claudia peeled back the flap and
tipped the contents out into her hand. A set of keys dropped
onto her lap and a flap of parchment tumbled into her palm.
She fingered the keys as tears ran unbidden down her face.

She unfolded the parchment to read the neat handwriting.
"It's a steal," she read aloud. "Don't forget to look in the
cellar...it's the closest thing to buried treasure I could find.
Leave The Lows; live your dreams. All my love, Acaelian."

Claudia clutched the letter to her chest and cried. She
believed, in her heart, that she would never see her friend again.

Chapter Sixteen
Cuckoos in the Nest

Five exhausted figures stirred in the undergrowth near a sewage entrance at the foot of the Great Northern Wall of Wahib City. Drenched in mire and filth, the figures were completely camouflaged from any searching eyes that might be atop the city wall. Physically drained from travelling throughout the night along conduits and slurry pipes, the group had discovered long-lost subterranean streets and lanes, built upon so many times that they had become forgotten. Traversing these forgotten portions of the city for a full day, they had found the outer sewage ducts and a route to freedom.

It was the first piece of luck Stefon considered he had had for more than a week.

"I'm bloody stinking!" complained Jewl, not for the first time.

"Quiet, dwarf! You have your life, don't you?" Rish told him. "Be thankful for that small mercy."

"We're not home and hosed yet," Stefon warned.

The nearest bank of trees was more than two hundred yards from the wall. The grass plains to the immediate north of Wahib were fabled killing grounds. No army had ever successfully laid siege to the city from any direction in all of history. Unfortunately that also made it equally difficult to escape the city.

Glancing to the west, Stefon judged it was almost the time to move. He motioned for the rest to be ready, massaging tired, numb limbs in preparation for movement.

The northern wall was designed and adjusted over centuries of warfare to be the perfect defensive structure. Thankfully, Brooss's knowledge of modern battlefield tactics gave Stefon's group the edge.

In order to repel and deflect siege engines from attacking the walls, various anomalies had been cultivated in the topography of the land to the north. The curtain wall slanted to the grasslands abutting it. Periodically the height of the batter at the foot of the wall fluctuated, making it nigh-on-impossible to run a siege tower straight for the battlements without it toppling. A few dozen yards from the wall, trenches had been furrowed, to be filled with naphtha in times of war. Beyond that, the slope of the land dropped to the treeline, called a glacis, making rams and ladder-bearers slow on their approach and therefore susceptible to arrow-fire from towers and battlements alike.

Stefon used this unnatural topography to crawl through more filth and muck. Even on such a murky morning, they used the rising light of dawn to help mask their passing, for vision was most difficult at this peculiar time of day, and the sentries at their most fatigued. Using the undulations of the land for cover, they crawled on their bellies to the trenches, then used the rain-filled ducts to move unseen to the outer fields. That left them a twenty-five-yard crawl in the open, but with the morning mists approaching they were afforded more good fortune.

By the time the full light of day was trying to pierce the rainclouds over Wahib, the five fugitives were away and free, jogging wearily between tall trees and through damp undergrowth.

Despite the fatigue, the wounds and the filth, the five were steadily swept up in elation. Betraying abject relief at surviving the rigours of the quarantine and the traps that had befallen them, each face was adorned with a gleeful smile. Inexplicably and without any reason, Jewl laughed to himself: the belly laugh of a dwarf.

And the sound was music to Stefon's ears.

Dark forms were abroad in the town of Hightower. Robed figures like that they had seen in Jakrat's company days before moved freely amongst the populace—strangers to this land. Andi's group had stolen horses from stables south of Jakrat's manor, and worked them into a sweat. Two had died within a mile of Hightower, and so they had left the others and approached the capital of Unedar Duchy on foot. The sun had set on the second day's ride from the burned shell that was Jakrat's manor, and now they skulked in the shadows of a disused barn on the westernmost outskirts of the foulberg around Hightower.

Eidos was clearly discomfited by the appearance of these strangers in his hometown, especially following the mysterious things they had witnessed in the past week. The fact that these strangers were present in larger numbers was obviously of concern, but the appearance that they seemed to command some level of authority over the local soldiery was more worrying.

Even more discomfiting was that this development only served to lend weight to Barabel's claims.

Several times the group had seen a robed figure issuing orders or passing instructions to groups of guards on duty within the foulberg. And it was clear that a dragnet had been established in the villages around Hightower to dredge up someone in particular.

"I think it safe to assume they're looking for me," Eidos mumbled from close by in the dusty confines of a barn.

"That's the only explanation. I'm the only senior member who was scheduled to be absent from Hightower Court this week."

"You're being pretty paranoid, Eidos," Manic told him.

"I don't agree," said Andi. "It seems clear that these figures are operating with official consent. It's also clear that they're searching for someone. If some elements have managed to subvert Reinhart's authority then it would make absolute sense for them to make their move this week, especially considering the things his cousin Jakrat appears to have been involved in. If the Duke's fool cousin has allowed nefarious elements into his duchy then there is no telling how far their influence now reaches. I think it's entirely possible that this dragnet is for you, Eidos."

"And I'm only one man," Eidos said weakly, the impact of the possibility that his town had fallen to enemy elements finally settling on him.

"That's not the point," Andi continued. In the dark she pointed a finger Eidos' way. "Where you're wrong is that you weren't scheduled to go anywhere this week. You were instructed on Reinhart's personal orders to lead us north on a reconnaissance mission that was due to take no more than two or three days at the most. He would not have scheduled such an absence because it was arranged on the spur of the moment. These enemy forces were expecting all members of the court to be here when they usurped Reinhart's authority, including you. This week was their best chance of ensnaring the whole court."

Eidos swore.

Manic thumped his hand down in the straw in frustration, eliciting a cloud of brittle dust. "It's simply too convenient. It's too much of a coincidence for there to be a coup at Reinhart's court at exactly the same time that a staging area is being prepared on just the other side of the border."

Eidos took up his train of thought. "We're in the very

depths of autumn. Very soon it will be winter; it may be even a matter of weeks or days before the cold snap seals the mountainous border. That staging area in Ipsica is awaiting some kind of army. This side of the border, agents who are working in collaboration with Ipsica may be subverting the nearest ruling duchy; a duchy that has been responsible for defending this border for centuries. It is too late in the year now to survive the march across that range, but by the time spring is upon us there may be an Ipsican army marching from the wooded hills unopposed. They could use Hightower and the surrounding area to launch a major offensive on Shenmadock without warning.

"For decades Hightower and the surrounding ducal lands of Unedar have acted as the buffer for the border with Ipsica. The garrison at Hightower and Hightower Point along the coast have acted as an able deterrent to war. Reinhart's court and agents have long held the responsibility for warning the rest of the nation of any attack upon Shenmadock by Ipsica. It is the reason for the size of the garrison here and the training facility at Hightower Point. With the loss of such a strategic stronghold, there would be little to stand in the way of a rolling army. Shenmadock would be powerless. The entire nation could fall by the following winter!"

"Right, so the situation is pretty dire, we get that. What are we going to do about it?" Manic asked.

Eidos said, "We must journey west as fast as possible and reach the Capital of Shenmadock, Shen Utah. Their armies are vigilant and have the best chance of mobilising in time to meet these potential invaders on the planes of Unedar, before they have advanced during the summer. The best chance is to hold the line at the ducal border of Shen Utah and Unedar. It is too late to attempt to hold the border with Ipsica, I fear."

Finhead huffed a sibilant breath. "Why Shen Utah? What in the capital can help us? Is that not just giving up most of Shenmadock to the invaders? Are there not strong garrisons guarding the southern border with Boyareen? Or perhaps we could start a resistance now? As a small band, it may be possible to begin an uprising here and now; crush these cowled figures and drive them from Hightower altogether? Then we can free Reinhart and the others and send word to Shen Utah, while we mobilise what is left of the garrison here."

"We must carry word of this possible dissension to Lord Handee," Eidos explained. "He will know what to do."

Manic said, "Wasn't he the weird-looking beast that rode in to Hightower as we were leaving?"

Eidos's mouth dropped open. "By Gods! What perfect timing! What if they've captured Handee too? He was visiting this very week! Shenmadock will be without a ruler!"

"I thought Shenmadock, the fabled Land of the Lords, was a republic?" argued Andi, with more than a little derision, for she had no trust of politics. "One thing Shen Utah has plenty of is ambitious politicians. Just because the most senior lord might be captured doesn't end our resistance. It's not chess."

"But that would be catastrophic. We would be at the mercy of the invaders."

"This is all assuming that we're right," Andi said, playing devil's advocate. "Not so long ago you were reticent to believe Ipsica even meant to invade. Now you're sure they mean to? Why the change of heart?"

"You know why, Andi. What we saw in Jakrat's manor was unholy. For a long time the duke's cousin has plotted to further his own gains without wanting to expend much effort. I fear he may have sold his cousin's duchy into slavery, and his soul to the devil. We did well to rid him from this world, but these cowled figures suggest we're too late, and the foes Jakrat served are too far advanced in their planning for his death to hinder them."

"You paint a bleak picture, Eidos," hissed Finhead. "To suspect a cousin would plot to have his own kin slain for personal gain would suggest much politicking in the Land of the Lords."

"Like I said: politicians," Andi spat. "But we're acting on information made up of too much conjecture. Here's what we need to know: is Reinhart alive or is he a captive, and if the latter, can he be rescued? What has become of Lord Handee: did he leave Hightower safely? And finally, precisely how are these cowled people linked to Jakrat or the necromancy we saw in his manor house?"

"Just where do you plan to find the answers to these questions?" Finhead asked.

Andi pointed squarely at the fortified walls of Hightower in the early evening twilight and muttered, "In there." Then she looked at Eidos, "And you're coming with me."

Eidos moved quietly ahead of Andi and settled against the low wall of a lean-to on the western wall of Hightower Keep. He had doffed his gleaming armour and left it in the care of Manic before doing as Andi instructed and applying liberal amounts of mud and oil to his face and hands.

His simple clerical garb beneath his armour and tabard was drab and dark—perfect for moving unseen when required. Without the weapons, he actually moved about as quietly as an untrained thief might. It would have to do.

Andi moved across to Eidos's side and chanced a glance round the corner of the small lean-to. A single guard moved slowly along the alure, next to the battlements, on sentry duty. At face value he seemed almost bored, and not much seemed to have changed since their absence. However, on closer scrutiny—even from this distance—Andi was able to discern the guard's stern facial expression. He seemed alert and wary, despite his seemingly nonchalant gait. Something had him keyed, on edge.

Once he had reached the far Curtain Wall Tower, the guard disappeared from sight. Andi made sharply for the foot of the wall, preparing her climbing gear quickly. Eidos followed her and waited as she ascended the first portion.

They would have to be fast.

Andi scampered up the rough stonework, applying clamps and metal footholds where she could to help the inexperienced Eidos. The noise it made to hammer them home was worrying, but she'd decided it was preferable to Eidos falling to his death. To his credit he made decent time, and managed to reach the top of the wall without tumbling into the night.

As fast as she could, Andi helped her tall companion over the wall and they hunkered out of sight behind an extinguished brazier, catching their breath.

Beneath them the inner bailey grounds were poorly illuminated. While various torches burned brightly in the growing darkness of night, they did nothing to push back the shadows that dominated the majority of the grounds. Andi could see what she assumed was the buttery door off to the side of the central keep, a room used for storing and dispensing wine. Not far from this was the grating down which she and Manic had begun this entire escapade more than a week ago. Off the edge of the alure directly in front of them there was a series of stables with slanting, thatched roofing.

Moving swiftly, Andi rolled across the walkway and dropped nimbly to it, making little noise. She stayed hunkered low to the wall and tested the strength of the roof. It seemed sturdy enough near the joists and she blew softly through pursed lips for Eidos to follow her.

As she heard guards talking quietly in the distance she eased herself over the edge of the slanted roof and dropped to the inner portion of the stable, moving to give Eidos room to drop.

A single horse was stabled here, but the mare paid them no heed.

Eidos dropped heavily into the stable following Andi, loose straw falling around him. He was quiet, but less than dainty.

"The buttery?" Andi enquired in a whisper, as he gathered himself behind the stable wall.

"Yes, in the near wall. A single door then leads to the kitchen proper. From there we can gain the stairs and ascend to the upper levels. These should be unpopulated at this late hour."

"Perfect!" Andi said. "Follow me."

Waiting for the sounds of guards nearby to dissipate, they then vaulted the stable wall and made quickly for the keep wall less than twenty yards away. At any moment they could be discovered. But fortune smiled on them as they thumped to the keep wall undetected.

The buttery door was unlocked and they entered silently.

Inside they passed unopened casks on the floor and innumerable bottles on various racks. The room smelled of lavender and stale, spilt wine. It was dark, aside from the illumination from the door to the kitchen.

They moved from room to room swiftly, ascending the stairs beyond the abandoned kitchen quickly and without challenge.

Reaching the top landing, they came to an enclosed corridor that ran the length of the keep. The floor was covered in a thick pile carpet and the walls were finished in plaster. Various doors adorned the left wall and a single door stood at the far end.

Of main concern was the guard who stood languidly, reading a small book in the light from a sconce-held torch halfway along the corridor. The soldier hummed to himself absently, his back to them, right shoulder to the wall. He had not seen either intruder yet.

Andi signalled for Eidos to remain where he was as she moved forward on her belly. Her hood was pulled up to cover her face and her torso and limbs were protected by a tight-fitting suit tailored of a strange material, which had been made especially for her many years ago. It made her nigh-on-impossible to see, even if one looked directly at her.

Pressing herself to the floor, she made painstaking progress along the corridor. Halfway to her prey, the guard stopped humming and glanced over his shoulder. He seemed more concerned with being discovered reading on duty than with any possibility of detecting an intruder. Despite looking directly at Andi lying flat on the black floor, he paid her no attention and returned to his book. It took all of five minutes to cover the full twenty yards to his back.

Carefully, Andi brought her knees up beneath her and slowly rose to a crouch. Unfurling like a coiled cobra, she drew her wicked punching dagger from the secreted sheath behind her belt buckle and took diligent aim at the guard's neck. Very slowly, she fully exhaled before taking a final, soft step and delivering two quick blows. The first drove the short blade deep into his spinal column. The second tore through his windpipe, silencing any call of alarm.

Her empty hand caught the body beneath the chin and quietly guided his paralysed, dying form to the floor. She positioned him against the wall and placed the book on his knees, as though he was sitting, reading.

She glanced at the book cover, recognising the translated work of a Boyareen poet. The guard had had good taste. Even as her victim sat slumped against the wall slowly dying, she felt no guilt at all. It was a necessary death: better him than her.

Turning to motion for Eidos, she saw he was already making to follow her.

In the confines of the corridor he knew not to speak, but his face was red with fury. Apparently he had expected her to knock the guard out.

Well, if that was the case, Eidos was naïve and would have to learn fast if he wanted to survive. He probably wants to cut the man's throat to end his suffering, she thought. Well tough, that would leave a big puddle of blood, and that they could ill afford. The trauma to his neck had already pulled her victim into the warm embrace of shock, and death would bring him home soon enough.

They moved unopposed down the corridor and crept to the simple wooden door at the end, extinguishing the nearest torch as they passed by.

Remaining close to the floor, they pulled the door open and crawled out onto the unmanned balcony.

They were overlooking Reinhart's main audience chamber, in which the Duke had originally heard the charges brought against Andi and Manic. Now, however, the room had been changed considerably.

The fireplace was fully banked and burning brightly. The heat in the large room was intense. Lined up before the fire was half a dozen of the cowled figures identical to those they had seen in the village. This time their robes were thrown back and they could see they were merely men. Each one tall beyond six feet, they wore fine-mesh chainmail shirts tied adroitly at the waist by a thick leather belt, from which hung a longsword. So, they were warriors then.

Sitting slumped in his throne, Reinhart leaned heavily on one side, his head resting against the knuckles of his fist. His face was drawn and pallid, the eyes wild and crazed. Most concerning of all was the condition of Lord Handee. The Senior Lord of the land was chained to a device close to where Andi had stood previously. His limbs were riveted to wooden pillars. Open, fresh wounds were visible across his torso. He was close to death.

Andi could hardly believe her eyes.

As they looked on, Reinhart bellowed, "Again!" His

voice was noticeably altered: his previously rich tones were replaced by guttural, tortured strains. He was not himself. He was utterly changed from the serious but charismatic man who had placed Andi and Manic in his employ.

At his command two of the robed warriors continued to administer punishment upon Lord Handee using barbed lashes, eliciting howls of delerious agony from the prisoner, who seemed beyond questioning or rescue. They were just torturing him for the glee of it, which was written across Reinhart's maddened features.

"It's your own fault, you alien!" snarled Reinhart. "If you will not submit, you will suffer and die for it!"

Andi glanced at Eidos, thinking it was time they made themselves scarce; she'd seen enough to answer all the important questions. But the man's face was set in a firm expression of anguish and fury in equal measure. Andi heaved a heavy sigh and then turned to look once again into the throne room, seeking to assess their options for intervention. That was when Eidos stood up. Andi tried to reach out to stop him, but he ignored her scrabbling fingers.

"Reinhart!" he boomed. His voice, usually quiet and unsure, suddenly filled the high-ceilinged chamber. Andi noticed he'd dropped the duke's title.

Only Reinhart turned to look up at them, his wandering eyes finally fixing upon Eidos, high on the balcony.

"My Cleric Eidos, welcome home."

"What is going on?" Eidos demanded while Andi cursed herself for having left her bow behind.

"Cleric cleric cleric," rattled the duke quite insanely. "I have lots of clerics now, Eidos. Look." He indicated the six warriors before the fire and the two before the tortured form of Senior Lord Handee. Neither the torturors nor their victim had acknowledged their arrival. The barbed whips continued to take their toll. "These are my faithful servants, Eidos. They will herald a new age, a new beginning for Unedar and

Shenmadock. Their arrival heralds a new epoch."

"You've lost your mind," said Eidos. It wasn't a question.

Reinhart stood, anger now flaring in his face. "No, idiot, it is you who is lost! All will submit to us." He pointed at the dying form of Handee, suspended on the torture apparatus. "They will submit or they will die a most painful death!"

"Jakrat's dead," Eidos said, breaking Reinhart's crazed flow. "We found his manor house, and the evidence of devil worship within. We burned it to the ground. Your experiments, and those of your cousin, are at an end."

For a moment there might have been the merest flicker of regret on the Duke's face, but then it was gone, and he was laughing maniacally. "That matters not, my cousin's work was long ago complete, that house means nothing…and neither does Jakrat's death. Our preparations are complete."

"You fool! While you conduct your sick experiments and make your play for power, seeking to usurp your friend Handee, an army readies to invade from the east! You'll never rule as Senior Lord, for you're ill prepared to defend such an attack! We must prepare while there is still time!"

Andi was impressed by Eidos's bluff, and Reinhart took the bait without a flinch.

"More idiocy! I know of those preparations. My master grows more powerful by each passing night, and soon he will march across this land. The Harbinger rises in the east, and will sweep all before him, and I will stand upon his right hand."

"Despots don't share power, Reinhart. This master of yours will smite you just as surely, and all your evil deeds will be for naught."

This is taking too long, Andi thought, glancing back down the corridor at their back. It was still empty, save for the now-dead guard.

"I think not," Reinhart grinned. "The Harbinger needs faithful servants, and rewards them all the more. I shall be at the front of his host, for I serve him the best." With that he produced from his tunic the gem Andi and Manic had retrieved from the caverns below Hightower: the *Baerv*. It caught the firelight and a diffused spectrum of colour shone around the walls.

"With this in our possession the Harbinger can never be stopped. His enemies are powerless to resist, and it is I that has delivered this most precious gift to him. Me! I will not be forgotten!"

Andi, still secreted behind the balustrade, began crawling for the corridor, hoping Eidos would sense her movement. It wouldn't have surprised her had the cleric jumped down to the throne room to take Reinhart on single-handedly, such was his fury.

"I'll certainly not forget you, Reinhart. I'll end this!" Edios barked as he retreated from the balcony. Wasting no time now, they made for the kitchen, still trying to remain silent but being driven by rising panic. Reinhart would have set those six ferocious looking clerics on their trail, and they would do well now to flee safely.

Once in the buttery, they hurled the outer door open and burst into the grounds of the inner bailey, which appeared equally as poorly manned as it had been on entering the keep.

They ran low to the ground in the shade of night and hid in the shadows of the stable once more. Voices could be heard shouting from the main keep. Figures began pouring out into the inner bailey. Making a cradle of her fingers, she hoisted Eidos to the thatched roof and then followed him herself, making for the alure and the battlements themselves before the guards could react.

Once upon the low wall, Andi guided Eidos to the portion of the battlement where her clamps would be. Suddenly the guards were upon them, seeming to come from nowhere. Reacting swiftly, Eidos took the first attack high, forming a cross of his forearms to block the overhand attack. He then kicked at the guard's foot, unbalancing him and pitched the man over the edge to the bailey floor below.

Andi ducked an attack from the second guard, lunging forward to drive her shoulder into his stomach. His wind blasted from him as he doubled over, dropping his sword. She stood up sharply, whipping the back of her skull into his face. He fell backwards, bleeding from a broken nose.

Before more guards could react, she climbed over to show Eidos the way. She crossed the nearest merlon and dropped her legs into the empty space behind her and started scrambling down the wall, trying to recall where the clamps had been set.

She could see Eidos's form hulking above her. Having crossed the wall, he was now coming down too fast. One slip and they were both dead.

A dozen feet from the ground, Andi leaped away from the wall and turned in midair. She landed on her feet, dropped to her knees and rolled forward away from the walls. More shouts on the battlements could be heard above.

Eidos was still coming too quickly.

Suddenly, halfway down, a clamp gave way, spinning out into the night with a twang. And Eidos fell.

But it was an odd fall. In his panic, he kicked at another clamp. As a result his body was hurled away from the stone. For a strange moment, Andi crouched in the short grass near the curtain wall and Eidos span through the night sky above her, surely tumbling to his death.

He made no sound until he smashed onto the roof of a lean-to. The little building exploded in splintered planks and shredded hay. Dust erupted into the air, and even a chicken took to startled flight.

The cacophony alerted the guards to where the intruders had gone, and soon arrows began to rain down.

Andi lunged frantically into the thick of the devastation that Eidos's fall had created from the barn. She tugged at his gambeson jersey, trying to pull him from the debris as the arrows thumped down nearby.

He seemed to be alive!

She forced Eidos to his feet using all the remaining power in her arms and legs. Inhuman strength levered him to a standing position, as he seemed to come round.

"Run!" she urged through his grogginess.

And they took to their heels.

Incredibly, Eidos wasn't badly hurt by his fall from the wall. The lean-to had apparently broken his drop sufficiently to negate any injury more serious than a few cuts and abrasions. His brow had bled for a while from a welt above his eye, but that had required only light bandaging and a single stitch. Andi had applied the suture herself. He would no doubt scar, but it was likely as not merely the first of many wounds the whole group would receive before this mess was over.

The four companions stood at the back of a large wooden canopy that was part of a complex pulley system on the face of the cliff to the south of Hightower Keep. Using tidal power from a long row of waterwheels at the base of the contraption, a tangled web of ropes and cables passed through pulleys to connect to the top of the wooden platform. At the foot of the cliff was a small shed containing gears used to transfer the tidal power to the cables at the pull of a lever. This in turn made the platform raise or lower on demand.

It didn't seem the safest of machines to Andi, but it was quicker and safer than climbing down the huge cliff, and far less conspicuous. This way, after paying the meagre toll to use the platform, they were able to descend to the port at the foot of Hightower Cliff without being challenged. The strange guards and clerics from the keep hadn't succeeded in ensnaring them thus far.

Eidos had, of course, changed his attire to disguise himself, donning his plain monk's robe and hood. His arms and armour had been stowed in a canvas tent-bag, which he carried on his back.

The view from the descending platform was indeed impressive, even at the late hour. The moon cast an awesome vista across the rolling seas to the South, and the lights of Hightower Port burned brightly below them.

Hightower Port itself was just as complex as the platform contraption that led to it. The entire southern coast of the Land of the Lords was dominated by high bluffs and cliffs.

As the only point of contact to the southern coast from Shenmadock, Hightower Port benefited greatly from the commercial advances made once trade treaties had been established with many of the southern lands, which had previously been considered barbaric.

Having started life as a series of temporary pontoons and larger jetties, the port now spanned four miles across the base of the cliff, and a mile and a half out to sea, in the form of floating docks, marinas and wide flotillas. The result was the largest centralised commercial port in the known lands. Any depth of keel was serviceable at any one of the hundreds of docking points throughout the facility, allowing for rapid loading and unloading of cargo and markedly shorter mooring times. Dozens of trading houses, naval administration buildings, guilds, wholesalers, brothels and inns had found a home in the floating port and contributed to its cosmopolitan nature. In short, it was hugely unique and the perfect place to disappear from sight.

Without issue, the group passed into the midnight throng of hawkers, merchants, gofers, traders and sailors moving throughout the concourses and alleys, heading for one of the outermost quarters, little known to Andi. They were following Eidos's lead.

After no small amount of walking, sometimes in circles, they rounded a corner onto a long, floating wharf with

several medium-keel vessels at berth on the southern edge
and a series of taverns and trading houses to the north. Some
of the vessels on the left were discharging cargo, but most
were offloading or boarding late-night passengers.

For a moment Andi's heart plunged as she thought he meant
to stow away, but then the tall cleric turned into a doorway of
an inn and threw back his hood. The others quickly followed
him into the tavern.

Despite the late hour, Andi had expected the watering-
house to be packed with stereotypical drunken sailors, but only
a dozen patrons were sipping ales or wines, and none paid
them any heed. The atmosphere wasn't silent, but it was also
far from raucous.

Eidos ordered four lightly brewed honey ales and moved
over to a wide table in the corner. The others followed as
though simply members of his entourage. He sat with his
back to the other customers, allowing the hawk-eyed Andi
and the weary Finhead to take the seats with the best views
of the room.

The table was cleanly swept and the floor was neither
badly stained nor awash with spilled ale. The place seemed
quite civilised.

"Where are we?" Andi asked quietly. "I know it's deep into
the autumn season, but surely this place should be busier at
this hour?"

"This is The Constant Keel. It's a navigator's establishment.
Sailors don't find the studious navigators particularly good
company, and so traditionally they tend to avoid it. The owner
does quite well on higher-value ales, seeing as navigators tend
to be well paid officers." He took a sip of his ale. "We'll not be
disturbed. I've not been here since I was a young apprentice in
the fleet auxiliary."

The place was fairly low-lit and cosy, and they relaxed a little,
taking stock. Andi ensured she remained vigilant, but it was
evident after half an hour that they had not been followed.

"So what the hell are we going to do now?" Manic finally asked. The question was weighted with importance, and no one jumped to answer.

Eidos put his tankard down, his expression ominous. "The whole nation is in danger. We have to assume that the threat we perceived across the border in Ipsica is not only a threat posed to the Duchy of Unedar. In fact, we must assume that Unedar has essentially fallen already, with the subversion of the local government.

"With the capture and imminent death of Lord Handee, I'm afraid that the neighbouring duchy of Shen Utah may be under threat if we can't get word to them in time, in order that they prepare to receive and repel this Harbinger's invading army when it marches at spring thaw. If Shen Utah is not ready, then the whole of Shenmadock may fall into Ipsican hands, and under the dark influence of these necromancers.

"I wonder at the significance of that gem," muttered Eidos. "For years growing up it had been a meaningless and baseless legend, saved for mid-summer fetes and drunk adventurers lusting for riches. There was no reason to believe the *Baerv* actually existed."

"The fact that Reinhart seems to think it significant should probably mean we should be worried about it, but I can't think of a reason to be concerned about a little gem," said Finhead. Andi and Manic exchanged a silent look, both no doubt thinking about the other jewel they had stolen. Andi wondered, not for the first time, if the jewel Reinhart had in his possession was the the true *Baerv*.

She tapped her chin thoughtfully before changing the subject back to matters of more immediate concern. "Can we risk heading west? And if we go west, what proof do we have that we will cause them to rally in time? They must have crazy people coming to them all the time, spouting this nonsense. All that our report will do is to draw Shen Utah into sending their own scouts to investigate. Perhaps the fortress at Shen Utah will be protected, but then they're under siege. They will fall, come what may. And the surrounding farmlands will be pillaged."

"It's a desperate situation," Manic mused. "It's probably worse than we think, though."

The others stared back blankly.

The dwarf went on. "Whoever this Harbinger is, it took them less than a week to spring their trap and capture Hightower."

Andi nodded. "Reinhart was unrecognisable from the man we dealt with just a short time ago."

"I don't know why Reinhart would turn so quickly," Manic agreed. "Maybe they possessed him." Eidos made to argue, but he continued. "Brainwashing, possession—whatever you want to call it. His mind is obviously not his own. Our enemy has powers at hand that we cannot fully fathom.

"Now, these agents were in place long before the trap was sprung, and I have no doubt it was designed to coincide with Lord Handee's visit. Reinhart's own gloating testimony only proves that these agents have been in place for quite some time."

The rest nodded agreement. "So what would be served by our heading west, if it's possible that a similar trap has been prepared in Shen Utah…or perhaps everywhere?"

The idea rocked Andi. Could the highest echelons of rule in the land be so easily subverted? The idea seemed preposterous. But so many things that had occurred recently would seem preposterous in a sane world. Dead men walking around seemingly revived, for example. Demonology. Witchcraft. All of it now seemed possible. At least, possible enough to be deemed a threat.

"We certainly can't trust anyone in Hightower to transmit word to Shen Utah," Eidos said. "Staying here to try and raise a resistance seems folly too. What else can we do but go west? We're the only ones who can do anything now."

An absurd idea had long since crossed Andi's mind. She chose this moment to voice it. "We could go south."

"Run away?" Eidos almost raised his voice. "You scoundrel! You might not have an affiliation with this land, girl, but this is my home!"

"I'm no scoundrel," Andi countered quietly, adding *anymore* in her head. "And don't raise your damned voice!" She quickly glanced around the room, but only the barkeep seemed to have noticed the elevated tones, and appeared more interested in ensuring his tankards weren't in danger. With a barman's professionalism, he was ignoring the argument. Still, careless voices made Andi nervous. They had to be more surreptitious.

"I'm suggesting something far more foolish than simply running away and saving our own hides." They stared back at her blankly. "Dead people walking around nice and healthy; people being possessed; demonic torture; a wealth of arms on the border awaiting an army that isn't in sight: all of this is pretty beyond-the-pale. What if…" She hesitated, as if completing the thought might confirm her own insanity. No one at the table seemed ready to press her to finish, either. Perhaps they knew what she meant to propose. "What if that crazy old man Barabel knew more than we gave him credit for?"

Manic laughed and Eidos simply said, "That's absurd." And he was right.

As for Finhead, he merely sat and regarded Andi closely. "You're not entirely what you seem, Andi," he hissed. Although his sibilant tones would always seem threatening, this time he merely appeared inquisitive. "I've never seen a human traverse a forest so easily and at such a pace as you. And in the treetops, too. It's what we call at home *brachiation*: the ability to travel through tree canopies as easily as walking. Your talent is raw, but it exists in you nonetheless. This is not a human trait. And I've never seen such strength and power in someone so slender. Your ability to see at night is no mean feat either." He counted off the points on his green, talon-tipped fingers.

The others now regarded her with scepticism. Perhaps even suspicion. Andi had been in this type of position before.

"And that old man knew there was something about you, didn't he? He focused on you when we were all speaking, even though you were the only one not to introduce yourself." Finhead leaned forward, pressing his case as the pieces fell together. "What are you?"

Andi slumped in her seat. Eidos had a hand on the hilt of his short sword in warning. It was not lost on her. "I'm…different," she admitted. "You're right; I can do all those things. And my art with a bow is well practised over many years."

"Only years?" Finhead queried.

"Well, I'm a little older than I seem, too. I was born to a noble family more than five decades ago."

Manic looked shocked. Eidos said, "But surely you're early twenties at the very most? I would mark you as no more than eighteen."

"I'm fifty-four," she confessed, a feminine spark of defiance igniting in her.

"She is in her teens," Finhead said, "for a half-elf. She will still be in early adulthood when you and I depart this world…" That revelation left the rest aghast.

The progeny of the union between human and elf was almost unheard of. Mostly existing in romantic legend, the union traditionally took place between a male human and a female elf, due to the unique elvish female anatomy, and because elven males were often arrogant and almost racist in contemplation of human females.

Because of this, half-elves were almost always born into and kept within the elven community, fathered by human travellers and brought up by their elven mothers. It was, however, beyond doubt that Andi was born of her mother, and her mother was certainly human. Andi was the very picture of her, in fact. The suggestion that she was half-elven seemed absurd at best, not to mention insulting to the elves.

Besides, Andi knew that both her parents were human. She was born to the Marquis de Krasital and his wife, and that was documented fact.

"I can't fully explain why I'm different. My parents were both human," she said, still plagued by that defiance and not willing to voice the rumours that surrounded her parents...not yet.

"What does it matter?" Manic asked, seeming to come to Andi's defence. "If she proved to be an orc, it doesn't change the fact that she's clearly on our side. She's my friend, I trust her."

Andi glanced around the table. She usually considered herself to be on only one person's side, and that was her own. She wasn't sure how comfortable she was with Manic's friendship.

"Andi's race does matter, but not for that reason," Finhead said, clarifying his accusation. "I didn't mean to cast suspicion on you, Andi. I mentioned it for one reason: the strange old man knew who you were, and that there was something unique about you."

"What makes you think this Barabel knew Andi?" Manic asked.

It dawned on Andi first. "He called me by my name," she said. "I didn't tell him my name—I was the only one not to introduce myself, but he called me out anyway, as we were leaving."

"So if he knew your name, then it seems a little strange that he should have been waiting there for us," Finhead said, his golden eyes widening in wonder. "He said he was waiting for a traveller, and was pleasantly surprised to meet four. I don't think he was waiting for us at all…he was waiting for you."

"He called me 'lady'," Andi said softly to herself.

"Barabel was polite, that's for sure," Manic said.

"You don't understand. That's how I can prove my parents were both human." She took a deep breath and looked at each of her companions. This was the first time in a very long while that she had spoken of such things. "I was once Lady Andrijanna de Krasital, of the Free Cities of Briadranon. My father was the Marquis de Krasital."

The rest sat in silence for a while before Eidos said quietly, "You don't mean the disgraced Marquis Edwin de Krasital?" He obviously seemed reticent to mention it to save her feelings.

"The same," she confirmed.

The story of her father's fall from grace was one long told in the decades since his death. Inglorious and rife with intrigue, the circumstances surrounding his passing, and that of his wife, had been the subject of speculation ever since, especially regarding a motive. Even Andi herself knew only half the truth. She knew enough to know the advantage of disowning the name de Krasital.

"So you see, I have no way to explain why I'm different." She looked challengingly at Finhead. "I'm no half-elf. I'm human."

He held up a hand, placating her sudden fury, and inclined his head. He did not appear convinced. "There are humans of legend who were known as the Long-Lived. There may be many explanations for your youthful appearance. My point is that this mysterious man Barabel knew more than was obvious; perhaps things you have told no living soul. And if he knew more than almost anyone alive does about who you are, then perhaps he knows a little about this mysterious threat that faces us; Reinhart's Harbinger.

"I'm not suggesting that we are going to find some all-conquering weapon. But I am stating my agreement that it might not hurt to look into this Aquilla San individual. And in order to do so, it would make sense to go south."

Eidos nodded in reluctant agreement. "Yes, from what I've heard Aquilla San was a general of some repute. His exploits may well be comprehensively documented in that area. To some, he is still a hero figure."

Manic picked up the thread of thought. "Barabel mentioned a famous dead twin. Perhaps we might find references to a famous pair of twins?" The others shook their heads thoughtfully. None had heard of such a story.

"The only thing I've noticed the south being famous for is wine and spices," Andi confessed. "There is nothing in my memory about famous twins."

"Twins?" came a voice from over Eidos's shoulder. The cleric visibly jumped at the unexpected interruption. The figure of the barkeep rose from behind him. The burly man replaced a pewter cup he had retrieved from the floor nearby on the bar and took the empty ale jug from their table. "You mean the Twins of Boyareen?"

The group sat in silence, some glancing uncomfortably at each other; a couple of them seemed to wonder whether to cut the stranger down without question.

The portly barkeep seemed to notice their discomfort. "Er...more ale?"

Eidos nodded for more beverages and then asked, "What do you know of these Boyareen Twins?" He tried to sound nonchalant, but it still sounded direct, interrogatory. "Do they have a surname by which we might find them?"

"Oh no, they've no family. The Twins of Boyareen, Mrnak and Jrnak, are siblings in situation only. If you're talking about the Twins of Boyareen then you probably speak of the cities Mrnak and Jrnak." The table stared back blankly. The barkeep smiled again, obviously pleased to be able to show he knew something that others did not. "Nak means twin in the Boyareen language. They are twin cities, at the western end of the Inlet of Theed. Passage can be bought almost daily to Jrnak from the new shallow-keel vessels that have started mooring here. I know Captain Bophamel sails to Jrnak during his charter."

Andi tilted her head questioningly. "No sailings to Mrnak?"

"Oh no, there are no sailings to the port of Mrnak anymore, miss."

"Why is that?" Manic asked.

"Mrnak's the Dead Twin of Boyareen, good sir. She's a dead city. If you go visiting Mrnak, there's a more-than-even chance that you won't be coming back."

The group exchanged glances. The Dead Twin.

The barkeep broke into a gap-toothed grin. "Or so the legend says. Now then, I'll fetch your ale."

Chapter Seventeen
Seeking Siblings

*D*espite the inherent fatigue they all felt, Andi and the rest of the group found it impossible to sleep during the window of three hours afforded them by the rental of lodgings above The Constant Keel. They had taken a single room for three nights, despite intending to leave these shores before the sun lost touch with the eastern horizon on the very next morn.

Eidos had spent two of his three hours forging a letter of passage, to be stamped with his courtly seal. The counterfeit document was to gain them clearance of passage without customs intrusion. The whole group agreed that dealing with customs was the most likely way to get caught. Now, with departure seemingly so close, they were all growing visibly nervous.

The cleric made an admirable job of the forgery, including Reinhart's own signature. A small amount of creative doctoring of Eidos's seal ring brought about just the right amount of smudging to adequately mask the actual identity of the seal. But it was still clear that this was a court stamp; a seal not to be ignored or questioned. The letter of passage seemed pretty authentic to Andi's untrained eye.

Even while Eidos toiled silently on his forgery, it was impossible to sleep. Thoughts of Andi's past, awoken by

Finhead's inquisition earlier, plagued her tired mind. She had managed to avoid thinking that far back for a long time. She had led a childhood of relative privilege in the regal citadel of Krasital, and had subsequently been robbed of that life by the tragedy that befell her family.

Turning her mind from that depressing time, Andi thought of the challenges that awaited them. They had passed word by messenger—dock urchins known as Quay-Runners—to Captain Bophamel, the trader who frequented the southern coast of Boyareen. The message simply stated that they desired emissary passage to Jrnak at the earliest opportunity. The barkeep of The Constant Keel had revealed that Bophamel was in port now, and they wished to waste no time.

The Quay-Runner returned an hour before dawn. Captain Bophamel's vessel *The Moistened Barnacle* was due to depart at dawn. A rudimentary passage booking had been drawn up on the back of a piece of packing parchment, stipulating that passage was subsequent to receipt of suitable documentation; precisely the kind of documentation that Eidos had just finished forging.

The Runner also spoke of shadowy figures stalking the pontoons of the port, searching. This would not be easy.

They departed their lodgings almost immediately, paying enough to retain the room for the next two days. The barkeep knew they would not return, but also knew well enough not to question why they wished to retain his premises. He bade them farewell with another toothy smile. Andi only hoped that the man could be trusted to hold his tongue, should Reinhart's people come with probing questions. More importantly, with the dark arts employed against them, it was entirely possible that any human not blessed with mighty powers may be unable to resist.

Perhaps that was how the wemik Handee had resisted them, she thought. Well, he'd died for his strength.

Either way, they had to be well under way from these

shores before their trail was picked up by those clerics. She was not arrogant enough to believe they hadn't been tracked. Their enemy could be certain that they had not passed through the foulberg landward of the keep. That only left the docks. A search would be underway for the thief and the hulking cleric of the court seen jumping from the keep walls the previous night. And that search would surely be focused on the expansive port.

"False dawn breaks," Manic murmured in wonder as the eerie predawn light danced across the high cloud banks of the morning sky to the east. Honey and citrus colours rippled in reflection of the coming dawn, not quite illuminating the deep shadows of the docks of Hightower Port.

The group moved quickly down a southern quay, making for Captain Bophamel's *Moistened Barnacle*. The tall clipper came into sight through the thinning morning mists that were retreating to the southern seas. Burly seamen were transiting the last of the light cargo from the quayside up wide gangways. A couple noted the group's approach, but not a word was said to them.

Upon the aftercastle, overseeing the final loading, an impressive figure stood with fists on hips. Over six feet tall, Captain Bophamel was amphibian in appearance. Andi didn't know the name for his species, but she had seen his kind before. Resembling toads or frogs, the green-skinned beings walked on two sturdy legs and boasted a powerful chest, which expanded impressively with each breath.

Their facial features also resembled a frog, if somewhat humanised. The mouth was still wide, and the nasal passages were broad and shallow. Large eyes rolled beneath a slanted forehead. There wasn't a single hair on the face, head or body. One might mistake such a being for a disfigured orc or large goblin, were it the case that these creatures were ever seen away from water.

As it was, they were almost always found amongst the

sailing fraternity; further testimony to their amphibian roots.

"Our emissaries, I presume," Captain Bophamel called down. "Do I enjoy the pleasure of the Lady Andrijanna?" His speech was guttural and moist.

"You do, Captain," Eidos replied, holding out the papers he had prepared.

Andi shifted slightly within the unfamiliar confines of her gown. She often kept a posh frock to hand in her kit, and she had unfurled it while Eidos had continued his midnight forgery. The disguise was easily packed and concealed; one she had used many times before, although not recently. She'd just never used it to escape, only ever to infiltrate some lordly manor without invitation. But it was suited to their purpose nonetheless.

She feigned an aloof smile before turning her gaze away from the ship and scanning the headland to the north in a display of indifference. The rest of the group were a shambling attempt at an entourage: Manic trying to appear as a personal servant and Finhead doing his best to behave like a mischievous pet. Their weapons and equipment were stowed in a luggage chest they had purchased from the barman, which Manic and Finhead carried between them for their lady.

The captain didn't seem particularly convinced by their retinue. Something in his demeanor betrayed his suspicions; and yet he still seemed willing to allow them to board. That was when his attention seemed drawn away from the new arrivals, focussing instead down the quayside from whence they had just come. "Your security detail, my lady?"

She and Eidos both turned to look back down the quayside, Andi's stomach plummeting as she spied the fearsome warriors from Reinhart's throne room approaching at a steady march, their hoods thrown back and robes billowing behind them on the morning breeze.

Falling in to his training, Eidos immediately turned to

face the enemy, shouting out into the morning air, "To arms!" Finhead and Manic both dropped the case they were carrying and wrenched it open, revealing their weapons at easy reach.

"Not friends of yours then!" shouted Bophamel. "Well, I'll be flayed alive before *The Moistened Barnacle* is boarded! Men, prepare to repel boarders! All hands on deck, that means you lot too!" He pointed at those still upon the quayside. Andi decided she'd take that as an invitation.

Finhead snatched up his bow and quiver before taking cover behind a crate and drawing down on the nearest target. By the time he'd loosed his first arrow at the approaching enemy, Manic already had his impressive broadsword in hand and Eidos likewise had retrieved his axe, the metal gleaming in the morning sun.

"Belay the order to repel, Mr Quayle; let's just get underway!"

Another voice was heard calling for the dockhands to cast off all lines and to run out all sheets. Two keen cargo hands slammed the lid of their case shut before she could retrieve her bow, and then they proceeded to run to the ship with it. She decided to follow them. Trapped within the confines of her gown, she knew there was little she could do. Moving as fast as she could she rushed for the gangway as Finhead fired a second and third arrow.

Further down the quayside, she could see a large group of city guards rushing to intervene, most armed with bows. In their number she thought she spied the towering figure of Reinhart, but couldn't be sure. The clerics, now within twenty yards of Finhead, Manic and Eidos, drew their longswords, and Andi gawped in astonishment. The blades seemed to glow a furious orange, despite the brightness of the morning. One cleric even used his blade to cut one of Finhead's arrows from the air as it flew toward him.

Andi knew that was impossible, but she saw it all the

same. "Eidos, get the hell off that dock!" she yelled, running up the gangway behind their case. He signalled agreement and he and the dwarf began to retreat toward the ship.

That was when she felt the scorching pain of an arrow bite into her shoulder, the glancing blow unbalancing her. As she reached the prow of the ship she lost her footing, pitched off the end of the gangway, and slammed bodily into the hull of the ship.

Then she was falling.

Dazed from her thunderous impact, only the shocking cold of the frigid autumn sea water revived her enough to start pulling for the surface.

And yet she couldn't. The seaweed and reeds around the underside of the pontoon snagged her feet as she kicked; her ridiculous dress entwined with the same, all conspiring to pull her further down.

Her lungs swelled with the effort.

Above her the plank of the gangway splashed into the water, forming a silhouette. For a terrible moment she pictured herself at the bottom of an impossibly bright grave, a distant oblong of night sky spinning towards her.

No!

She ripped at the shoulders of the gown, tearing the material from her torso and freeing herself from its confines. As her lungs screamed from her held breath, she kicked free of the dress and reached for the surface. Above her she could see the hull of her only escape moving away from the quayside steadily. Arrows dropped into the water all around her. Reaching up, she clawed for the open air, her hand finally snagging onto something slippery and elusive: a rope!

She grasped onto the mooring rope and allowed it to pull her to the surface near the rear hull of the ship as it moved off. She sucked in great gulps of blessed air, and then started pulling at the rope.

Without the dress to hold her back, and shocked into

action by the chill of the water, she surged up the rope and emerged from the water. Ascending hand over hand, she ensnared the loose rope below with her feet, quickly climbed to the gunwale, and then flopped over the edge onto the quarterdeck, exhausted.

Immediately Eidos was at her side, his expression a mix of relief to see her and shock at her lack of attire. She was hardly naked, still wearing a corset and her underwear, but it still must have been a shock for him.

"There you are! Thank—"

"Where's my bow?" she snapped, jumping to exhausted feet.

He needn't have replied: she spied their case near the foot of the stairs to the aftercastle. She ran for it and threw the lid open, snatching out her bow and just a single arrow.

"But they're still firing!" Eidos shouted. Indeed, sailors not required to drive the ship on were hunkering down for cover as arrows fell indiscriminately around the ship.

She took the slippery stairs to the aftercastle two at a time and ran to the rear railing of the ship, ignoring the appraising eyes of the cowering sailors all about. The helmsman, desperately trying to remain out of the firing line, fought to keep the ship on line between other moored vessels as they made good their escape from the port. Only the captain stood, seemingly unafraid.

Sliding to a halt at the rear railing, she took her single arrow and nocked it, drawing the string back to full tension, the graze in her right shoulder burning. She let her breath out; focusing, willing herself to concentration.

And fired.

The arrow soared into the dawn sky as those from their attackers fell uselessly into the harbour.

As she and the captain watched, the tiny sliver of her arrow dropped from the sky, unseen by those on the jetties. Down it fell, punching in through the crown of Duke Reinhart's skull and into his brain, dropping him to the quayside, instantly dead.

Andi allowed the bow to hang at her side tiredly as the sense of vengeful satisfaction washed over her. As she leaned on the gunwale and watched the port retreat behind them, she was sure she saw the nearest cleric staring at Reinhart's motionless body before he stooped to retrieve something from the dead duke.

In the clear morning light she saw him lift the *Baerv* from her victim and place it carefully in his own tunic protectively, before walking away...the Harbinger's faithful servant utterly forgotten.

Epilogue

Acaelian the Legend sat upon the mat within the silent temple, his mind at rest. He had been accepted into the temple without question. In fact, if anything, they had seemed to expect his arrival. They cared not for his background or reasons for being drawn there, deep within a hidden location at the heart of Shen Utah. They didn't ask him to believe or try to indoctrinate him. Instead his training had started in earnest. His work, they said, was vital. He hadn't known what they had meant, but had given himself to his studies and training entirely, sensing a rightness in them.

Deep in his heart, Acaelian would always remember the beauty he had known when living in the Guilds: his loyalties, his achievements, his friends…Claudia. She in particular was a deep rent in his soul, for he already missed her greatly. But now his consciousness was being trained to transcend such things. He was searching for peace. His mind soared through unseen clouds; calm and serene.

From the corners of the training room a group of instructors stepped forward, their robes tied and wrapped carefully to afford ease of movement. They moved toward Acaelian as he breathed deeply, eyes closed. Once they were within a dozen yards of the meditating elf, his eyes flashed open; pupils like shining jets. A wry smile crept across his face and without preamble he jumped to his feet, ready for his next test.

Stefon sat upon a moss-covered rock in the morning light, an oatcake in his hand. A drop of honey tempered the dryness of the cake, but it was not enough to make the breakfast palatable. But that was the least of Stefon's worries.

Nearby the trader caravan watered their horses at a shallow pond while the rest took refreshment of their own. Stefon and his crew had managed to gain employment as escorts for the trading caravan, bound for the city of Choat, across the border in Shenmadock.

All his life he had endeavoured to avoid responsibility. He had sought only his own success. He had focused only on fostering his own reputation (or disreputation). He saw no advantage in having others rely upon him. This was not the result of greed; he was happy to share his wealth with those who aided in acquiring it.

The fact was that Stefon didn't want people relying on him because he didn't actually think of himself as being particularly reliable. But looking around his gathered band of renegades, Stefon realised his discomfort was something more than simply dwelling on his own unreliability.

They had become the hunted. Ipsican renegades. Fugitives in their own land. The wanted. And that man Lesjac didn't seem the kind of person to simply let Stefon leave. It was this that concerned him, more than being unreliable.

He didn't want these lives in his hands. He had managed to live his adolescence without forming attachments. But now…he cared. Brooss, Pryn and Jewl had become his comrades. Through the last few days they had survived many perils, and had saved each other's lives more than once— sometimes in spectacular fashion.

And then there was Rish. In Stefon's life there had been colleagues and business partners, acquaintances and such. But Rish was a friend. Friendship: it made you weak and vulnerable. Stefon found something alien in such a relationship.

Finishing his oatcake he took a draw from his water-flask. "We need to keep moving," he told the others. "If we travel throughout the day and early night, we should make it across the northeastern border into Choat by week's end."

They reluctantly gathered their belongings and made to vacate the glade, heading for a path alongside a nearby river.

"What happens when we reach Choat?" Rish asked, falling into step beside Stefon.

"I don't know," he replied honestly.

Stefon was scared.

The spectacular happenings in the Tower of Light, and the revelations of Lesjac were weighing heavily on him. His fear was palpable. He was changing, and into what he had no real clue.

The fact was, having lived his life in total independence, Stefon didn't want to face what lay ahead on his own. That loss of independence terrified him.

Ultimately, perhaps he feared less being relied upon than he did relying on others.

Andi turned to look over her shoulder at the receding headland of Shenmadock as *The Moistened Barnacle* raced south. The graze on her shoulder gave her a pinch of pain. The saltwater spray would play hell with her skin, and they had given little thought to preparing for a sea voyage, such had been their desperation to get away, but get away they had, and by the skin of their teeth.

Or the skin of my shoulder, she thought.

Manic was currently vomiting over the side of the vessel as the morning swell cradled the ship. Eidos stood near him, holding onto his cuirass tightly to ensure he didn't fall into the surf. Intermittently the dwarf would apologise for his fuss, but the tall cleric dismissed it each time. "This morning the seas are choppy, Master Dwarf. But be thankful for small mercies. The waters are made choppy by the changing tides and the northerly winds. We will make good time this morning."

The dwarf's only reply was to retch, ejecting more bile.

In the back of her mind, Andi thought about the strange gem that Jakrat had sent them to retrieve. Undoubtedly it had been one of those cowled clerics that had been whispering in his ear on the day Manic and she almost went to the gallows. She pictured, not for the first time, the distant cleric holding the gem in the morning sky before depositing it protectively in his tunic. Then her mind turned to that other strange gem that Manic still kept about his person. The significance of either had her mind spinning when Finhead came to stand beside her, watching the southern seas.

"I wouldn't worry about your past, Andi," he told her, mistaking the path of her thoughts. She allowed him his misconception, choosing to keep the knowledge of their gem between herself and Manic for the moment. "Nothing is ever as it seems. I'm sure your parents were good people. One day you will surely know the truth of it."

Surprisingly, her usual angry reaction failed to flourish. Instead she found herself introspective. "If we ever meet that old lunatic Barabel, maybe I'll be able to wring it from his neck." After a quiet moment, she laughed to herself.

"What?" asked the green being.

"I'm just amused by the entire episode with the old man. I think if anything is 'not what it seems,' it must be that old codger. And now look at us all! We're sailing south to lands we've never visited, to try and accomplish something that a week ago would have seen us locked up for brain-fever. And yet here we are: believing we can make a difference by achieving the seemingly ridiculous. Something changed when we witnessed the horrors in that manor house. Maybe instinctive fears, long buried inside, were awoken by witnessing the evil of those ancient arts."

There was a pregnant pause between them.

"He said that," nodded Finhead. "'Without it, you will not have adequate belief', he told us. That manor house was an eye-opener, and no mistake. We've left a land in turmoil there."

"Indeed," Andi muttered. "But what kind of perils are we hurrying toward? And will Reinhart's strange Harbinger send anyone after us?"

The two stared south in silence, the sea breeze cutting against their faces.

Acknowledgements

This project was originally begun in 2005 and would never have been completed but for the encouragement and support of Bryony Harrison. However, the world of Peternu Lorzi itself, and many of the primary characters, too, were the beloved inspiration of a large group of people. To name the main protagonists: Steven Cubbon, Mark Jewell, Jip, Erik Lunt, Jessica Lunt, Phaser, and Stephen Wood. Stephen is mentioned last for the sake of the alphabet, but his input and work in the creation of the world and the sowing of the seeds that have grown this trilogy were nothing less than vital, and my thanks go to him. I may have brought this baby up, but it was through Stephen that it was born.

Happy days, Biscuit Boys!

About the Author

Simon Barron is a freelance magazine editor, writer and business consultant based on the Isle of Man.

An English literature and psychology graduate, Simon has been writing magazine articles since 2011, when he was editor of Gallery Magazine IOM. Having written fiction since his teenage years, he is an avid fantasy and science fiction reader, as well as being a faithful Liverpool FC and *Star Wars* fanatic. Being heavily influenced by fiction fortissimos like Raymond E. Feist, the late-great David Gemmell, Richard Laymon, and Carlos Ruiz Zafon, amongst many; Simon is a self-confessed geek, smart-arse and linguistic pedant who one day hopes to graduate to full-blown 'grumpy old man'.

Lightning Source UK Ltd.
Milton Keynes UK
UKOW04f1806280415

250483UK00004B/281/P